THE FATAL FLYING AFFAIR

A Lady Hardcastle Mystery

T E KINSEY

THOMAS & MERCER

Text copyright © 2020 by T E Kinsey
All rights reserved.

Published by Thomas & Mercer, Seattle

www.apub.com

Amazon, the Amazon logo, and Thomas & Mercer are trademarks of Amazon.com, Inc., or its affiliates.

ISBN-13: 9781542020909
ISBN-10: 1542020905

Cover design by Tom Sanderson

Cover illustration by Jelly London

Printed in the United States of America

The Fatal Flying Affair

Chapter One

Lady Hardcastle was in the garden offering the new gardener a scone. This was our fourth summer in Littleton Cotterell and we had finally engaged the services of Jed Halfpenny to tend the overgrown wilderness behind the house. We'd made a stab at it ourselves, of course, and the housemaid's husband, Dan, had kept the worst of it under control, but it needed the tender ministrations of someone who properly knew what he was doing. And that someone, as I'd been saying for quite some time, was Jedediah Halfpenny.

We'd met him soon after we moved to the village and he'd supplied vital information to help us catch the killer of a farmer who'd died in his beef and mushroom pie on market day. He made his home in a caravan in the woods and lived for the most part on foraged food and occasional poaching. He had always seemed to me to be the ideal chap to fettle the garden.

As I approached, he was leaning on a spade, and listening patiently to Lady Hardcastle as she extolled the virtues of the scones.

'They really are delicious,' she said. 'I know a scone's not much of a culinary marvel in itself, but Miss Jones works wonders with them. Do try one.'

'Thank you, ma'am,' said Jed. 'Don't mind if I do.'

'Flo agrees, don't you, dear?'

'Agrees with what, my lady?' I said.

'That Miss Jones's scones are second to none.'

'They're certainly up there among the better examples of the scone-maker's art,' I said.

'I was just asking Mr Halfpenny—'

'Jed, ma'am. I keep tellin' thee I'd be much more comfortable if tha just called me Jed. Everyone does.' Years of military service abroad and a long life in the West Country hadn't softened his broad Yorkshire accent.

'I was just asking Jed if it would be possible to cultivate an air of artful wilderness out here.'

'As opposed to the actual wilderness we currently have,' I said.

'Well, quite,' she said. 'I've never been much of a one for formal gardens – neat borders and regimented plants afraid to step out of line. I wondered if we might have something a little more . . . well, natural, I suppose.'

'And what do you think, Jed?' I asked.

'Sounds like a grand idea to me,' he said. 'You could have wild herbs and flowers along this side. I could build you a little wall or sommat there for climbers.'

'We seem to be of one mind,' said Lady Hardcastle. 'I'd like plants and flowers that attract bees and butterflies. I want undergrowth for mice. A pond, perhaps, for frogs. Oh, and newts. I want to wake up in the morning and find that moles and badgers have dug up the grass and not care about it because it's not a croquet lawn. I want somewhere I can sit with a cup of tea and be at one with nature.'

He chuckled. 'I can give you all that,' he said, 'but this table and chairs is goin' to need some work. You've left 'em out 'ere on't grass and they've rotted right through.'

'Can you do anything with them, do you think?' she said.

'There's some useful wood up top,' he said. 'But the legs is gone.'

'We could get some new ones, of course, but it's a shame to throw these out. Would they be of any use to you? Could you turn them into something else?'

'I dare say I could,' he said. 'What about bird boxes? They'd be nice. But if you replace t'chairs and table you're goin' t'ave same problem wi' next lot. Sittin' on't grass is goin' to do for 'em just the same.'

'Oh, bird boxes would be delightful,' she said. 'And whatever's left over is yours.' She looked once more at the table and chairs under the shade of the apple tree. 'What about some sort of paved area here, then?' she said. 'Nothing too formal, just a few rough flags.'

'Aye, that'd do it,' he said with a smile. 'I reckon I know where I can get sommat just right.'

'Wonderful.' She turned to me. 'And what of you, dear? Did you want me?'

'Harry's here, my lady,' I said.

'Harry? My brother Harry?'

'In the flesh,' I said.

'What on earth is he doing all the way out here? What does he want?'

'He wants to talk to us.'

'Does he, by jingo? We'd better indulge him, then. You'll have to excuse us, Jed. Duty calls and all that. I'll get Edna to bring you out some tea.'

'Thank you, ma'am. I'll crack on here. You see to your brother.'

We returned to the house.

◆ ◆ ◆

Although it was difficult to imagine anyone having any sort of control over Lady Hardcastle, her brother, Harry, was notionally her boss. And mine. He worked for the new Secret Service Bureau in a basement somewhere in Whitehall, and had asked us to return to government service the year before, after our 'holiday' in Weston-super-Mare. We had refused, of course – we had retired to Gloucestershire to get away from all that nonsense, after all – but Harry was as stubborn as his sister and refused to accept our refusal. Eventually, we caved in to his repeated entreaties and had resumed our employment as agents of the Crown. Our duties had been light so far, and apart from a little casual surveillance at the docks at Cardiff, we had had little to do.

We had seen plenty of Harry and his wife, Lady Lavinia, though, but only socially. Their daughter had been born on the fifteenth of January and Aunt Emily had been her first visitor. And the second. She adored little Addie – the infant Featherstonhaugh had been named after her grandmother, Ariadne, who had been known all her life as Addie – and we had been down to London at least once a month ever since.

'What ho, sis,' said Harry as we entered the drawing room. He peered over the newspaper he'd been reading.

'Hello, Harry, dear,' said Lady Hardcastle. 'It's all right – don't get up.'

Harry grinned. 'It's only you, sis, why would I stand when you enter a room? I might stand for your delightful lady's maid, but she doesn't like it, do you, Strongarm?'

It had become our habit for me to mispronounce Featherstonhaugh as Feather-stone-huff instead of Fanshaw, and for him to call me Strongarm instead of Armstrong. It had long since ceased to be properly amusing, but there was a comfortable familiarity in it.

I smiled.

'Have you been offered tea, dear?' said Lady Hardcastle. 'Or scones?'

4

'Edna's already on the job,' I said.

'Splendid, splendid. So, then, my darling brother, what brings you to our humble abode? Are there dark dealings afoot in the Woolly West?'

He folded the newspaper where he had been reading – page three of Monday's copy of the *Bristol News* – and handed it to her, tapping a story in the middle of the page.

'Take a look at that, old girl,' he said. 'Ah, here comes the tea. Thank you, Edna.'

Edna, the housemaid, had come in with a heavily laden tray.

'Will there be anything else, m'lady?' she said. 'I've sent a mug out for Old Jed. He must be parched workin' out there in this heat.'

'Oh, thank you,' said Lady Hardcastle. 'I was going to ask if you would. I say, do we have any of Mrs Bland's jam left?' She turned to Harry. 'The vicar's wife makes the most delicious strawberry jam – it would go wonderfully with these scones.'

'I think there's a jar in the pantry,' said Edna. 'If Miss Jones a'n't used it for somethin'.'

'Would you mind having a look?'

'I'll be back in two shakes,' said Edna, and bustled off.

'Are you staying to dinner?' asked Lady Hardcastle.

'No can do, sis, sorry,' said Harry. 'Got to get the train back to the Smoke at the earliest opportunity. Already been away for three days.'

'You've been here for three days and this is the first we've seen of you?' said Lady Hardcastle.

'I've been away from home,' he said. 'But not all the way out here. Bureau business in town.'

'That's all right, then. You can always stay here if you need to, you know. We've plenty of room.' She was patting the pockets of her light summer jacket.

'Thank you,' he said.

'Think nothing of it, dear. Now where have I left my spectacles?' She sat upright in the armchair and began to scan the room. 'This is most frustrating,' she said. 'I bet you know where they are, don't you, Flo?'

'I do,' I said. 'They're—'

'No, don't tell me – you'll be insufferably smug about it. "If only you'd tidy up after yourself," you'll say. "I always know where things are because I always put them back in the same place," you'll say. I shall find them on my own.'

'Sis, they're—' began Harry.

'And don't you start, either,' she said. 'It's bad enough with her goading me in my hour of need, without you joining in.'

'But—' he began again.

'But nothing,' she said. 'I'll find the blessed things if it kills me.'

She stood up and began to hunt around the room.

Edna returned with a pot of jam and a spoon. She gave Lady Hardcastle a slightly puzzled look. 'I wouldn't leave your glasses up in your hair like that, m'lady,' she said. 'They'll fall out and get broken.'

She put the jam on the tray and left again.

Lady Hardcastle retrieved her reading glasses from atop her head and settled back down to read the newspaper article.

'Oh, we talked about this yesterday,' she said. 'It's about that poor chap who died at the aeroplane factory, Flo.'

'Ah, yes,' I said. 'There wasn't much to the story, though, was there? Tragic accident . . . engineer killed. Awful news, but light on detail.'

'The lightness of detail is rather down to us,' said Harry. 'You know what a parachute is, I presume?'

'Of course,' said Lady Hardcastle. 'I'm reasonably sure we saw a chap use one to jump out of a hot air balloon near Paris one time. Or was it Berlin?'

'Paris,' I said. 'It was very impressive, if a bit cumbersome.'

'Cumbersome, yes,' said Harry. 'That's always been the prob. But we've got some chaps at Bristol Aviation working on a new design. Carrying it and deploying it are the issues, you see. People have tried wearable ones, but they had trouble getting them to open up. There's one you sort of hold in your arms, ready to go, but it's a blessed nuisance to have to carry it around.'

'If it's not a stupid question,' I said, 'what do they want them for?'

'Aeroplanes,' he said. 'We're rather of the opinion that aeroplanes are going to be uncommonly useful in any future conflict – artillery spotting and whatnot, general surveillance, that sort of thing. So we need a way to make sure our spotters can get back to terra firma safely when it all goes awry. And that seems to happen alarmingly often where aeroplanes are concerned.'

'I'd love to have a go in one, even so,' said Lady Hardcastle.

'Cling steadfastly to that thought, old girl. So our chaps at Bristol have come up with a parachute that can be packed into a sort of knapsack affair. Still as heavy and cumbersome as you like, but you can wear it in your flying machine and it opens up all by itself when you need it most. It was all going frightfully well until last Friday. They'd done multiple tests with dummies and it really looked like they'd cracked it. They were just doing one last test before showing it off to the army bigwigs in a few weeks' time. Sent a young lad up in a tethered gas balloon wearing one of the new designs. He jumped. It opened perfectly – billowed out, they say, like some giant flower. Arrested his fall and he started to float down. But then it failed. Ripped apart, by all accounts. And young Dickie Dupree fell two hundred feet to his death.'

'Good heavens,' said Lady Hardcastle. 'How awful.'

'Well, quite. But, of course, we've had to hush it up. Aeroplanes manned by pilots with effective parachutes could give our chaps a bit of an advantage if things cut up rough on the Continent, and we don't want anyone else getting wind of what we're up to. Hence the paucity of detail in the news story.'

'And how does it involve us?' said Lady Hardcastle.

'Well, the death itself is being sold to the public as nothing more or less than a tragic accident. It's a dangerous business, flying, and with new equipment there are bound to be heartbreaking tragedies. But we've got a sniff of some leakage from the factory. This weekend, one of the foreign agents-for-hire we keep tabs on was found in possession of detailed information about the failed parachute test. We intercepted him before he could pass anything on, but it's very troubling. Someone there is blabbing.'

'Intercepted?' I asked.

'Fatally.'

'It never occurred to you to question the fellow before you did him in, I don't suppose?' said Lady Hardcastle.

'It all got a bit messy, I'm afraid. We tried to nab him but things cut up rough. One thing led to another and before you could say, "Where did you get those plans?" we'd had to shoot him through the heart.'

'I see. Subtle as ever, then.'

'Needs must when the devil has a gun pointed at you, and all that.'

'Who was he working for?' I asked.

'We didn't find that out, either, I'm afraid. He was a freelance, a hugger-mugger mercenary, if you will, who worked for whichever nation was prepared to pay him. Could have been any of a number of countries, to be honest.'

'Not a rival company, then?'

'No, that much we *are* pretty sure of. He was definitely in the international espionage market. But that's by the by. What concerns us now is that if there's someone on the inside up to no good, we can't rule out deliberate *damage* as well as espionage.'

'But how does that involve us?' persisted Lady Hardcastle.

'Ah, well now,' he said. 'It rather has to do with your good friends the Farley-Strouds.'

◆ ◆ ◆

Sir Hector and Lady Farley-Stroud had known Lady Hardcastle's parents when they were all in India together and had befriended Lady Hardcastle within days of our moving to the village. They were an endearingly dotty couple of indeterminate age – though I placed them in their mid-sixties – who lived in the local manor house, The Grange.

Lady Farley-Stroud – Gertie to her friends – ruled the roost, while Sir Hector trailed cheerfully in her wake, playing the amiable lord of the manor and generally doing as he was told. They had one child, a daughter named Clarissa. I had always thought her quite young, but that was an impression gained more from her giggling inanity than her looks. I had been surprised to learn that she was, in fact, around thirty years old, and her success as a writer for a popular London magazine had made me reappraise her vacuity, too. There was clearly more to the woman than met the eye.

Her new career had begun shortly after she had moved to London, following a failed engagement to a local businessman's son. There she had met and quickly married a young aeroplane engineer by the name of Adam Whitman. She had believed herself to be with child shortly thereafter and had told her parents that they were to be grandparents in early 1910, but she had been mistaken about the dates – calendars can be confusing. Diaries were checked and physicians consulted, and the next announcement proved to be correct, and baby Louisa had been born in France in July that year.

Louisa had been brought to England to celebrate her first birthday with all four of her doting grandparents, and although Adam's parents had returned to Suffolk, the younger Whitmans were still at The Grange.

'What you need to do, sis—' said Harry between mouthfuls of scone. 'I say, these scones are a revelation. I was always told they're the simplest of all the cakes, but these are magnificent. Your cook is a marvel.'

'I was saying much the same thing myself to our new gardener when you arrived, but you seem to have become somewhat side-tracked,' said Lady Hardcastle. 'What is it that I need to do?'

'What? Ah, yes, what you need to do is to contact your dear old pal Gertie Farley-Stroud and ask if you can drop in for tea or whatever it is you country folk do. Once there, you should engage young Adam Whitman in conversation about aeroplanes, and oh-so-casually ask if he might be able to arrange a trip to Bristol Aviation. For a look round. Because you're so fascinated by aeroplanes.'

'I *am* fascinated by aeroplanes,' she said.

'No dissembling required, then, old thing. Piece of cake.'

'But Mr Whitman works for Louis Blériot in France,' I said. 'Not Bristol Aviation.'

'Actually, he's a materials engineer for Aéroplanes Vannier, but you're right that the firm is in France – just outside Bordeaux, as a matter of fact – and Blériot has indeed done some work for them.'

'Hector told us it was Blériot's company,' said Lady Hardcastle. 'He can be such a buffle sometimes.'

'I wouldn't know about that,' said Harry. 'But I do know that Adam Whitman has been visiting Bristol Aviation as a guest while he's been in England. A touch of the old *entente cordiale* and what have you. They like to share their knowledge, these engineering types. I do wish they wouldn't.'

'You've been keeping tabs on him?' said Lady Hardcastle.

'I told you – aeroplanes are going to be important, and the men who design and build them even more so. We're keeping tabs on the whole lot of them, especially the foreign ones, and specially especially the English ones working for the foreign ones, even if they are our allies. I'm well aware of Mr Whitman's comings and goings.'

'I see,' she said. 'So Flo and I go on a little tour of the factory, ooh and ahh over the flying machines and . . . and what, exactly?'

'I leave that to your discretion, darling sis. You're the expert when it comes to the hugger-mugger stuff. I'm more of an admin and management sort of a chap.'

'We're not going to be able to spot a spy while we're on a factory tour, dear. They don't wear badges.'

'Then you'll have to find some excuse to hang about the place, won't you?'

'Oh,' I said, somewhat more excitedly than I had intended, 'do you think they might let me fly an aeroplane? We could go back there so I could have lessons.'

Harry laughed. 'No offence, Strongarm, but why would they let a lady's maid have a go in one of their precious flying machines?'

'If I were thinking of buying one, they might,' said Lady Hardcastle. 'I've yet to meet anyone who hasn't suddenly put their objections to us aside once I started waving money under their noses. If I want to buy an aeroplane and I want my maid to pilot it for me they'd be foolish to say no.'

Harry laughed again. 'I shall leave the finer details to you,' he said. 'But Whitman is your key to the door. And if you could also keep an eye on him for me while you're at it, you'd be doing me a great favour – resources are a bit stretched and I could really do with having my men working on other things.'

'Well, it all sounds like a lark to me,' said Lady Hardcastle. 'Are you game, Flo?'

'Just try and stop me,' I said. 'Flying lessons and snooping? I couldn't ask for a better summer.'

'We're in, then,' she said. 'Will you stay for lunch, at least, Harry dear? Then I'll telephone Gertie later this afternoon and make arrangements to call on them tomorrow.'

'Oh, all right, then,' he said with mock weariness. 'If I must. I'll get a later train and still be home to see Addie before bedtime.'

'I'll alert Miss Jones,' I said, and went off to the kitchen.

◆ ◆ ◆

Harry left straight after lunch. Lady Hardcastle offered to drive him to the station at Chipping Bevington but he insisted on walking the quarter of a mile or so into the village, where he fully expected the driver of the dog cart that had brought him to be still supping at the Dog and Duck.

'If he's not there, I'll give you a shout,' he said as he walked off down the garden path.

'He'll have to shout jolly loudly,' said Lady Hardcastle as I shut the door. 'The only telephone is in the police station.'

She picked up our own telephone and asked the operator to connect her to The Grange.

'Hello, Gertie, dear,' she said after a few moments' wait. 'It's Emily . . . Emily, dear . . . Quite well, thank you. And you? . . . I'm glad to hear it. And little Louisa? . . . She's a delight, isn't she? It's such a treat to have them to stay . . . Indeed, yes. When are they going? We were hoping to see you all again before they left for Bordeaux . . . Oh, they're staying for a few more weeks? Plenty of time, then . . . Tomorrow? Oh, that would be lovely, thank you . . . Afternoon tea? Delightful. Always a treat at The Grange, dear. Mrs Brown might be something of a termagant but she puts on a lovely spread at teatime . . . A termagant . . . No, dear, not a ptarmigan, a— Oh, never mind . . . Yes, we'll see you at four . . . Love to Hector and Clarissa . . . Goodbye, dear.' She replaced the earpiece on its hook.

'Her hearing's no better, then?' I said.

'She does her best,' she said. 'The receiver is as loud as it will go but she still can't tell a termagant from a ptarmigan.'

'Well, they're both . . . "grouses".' I was quite pleased with that one.

'You make an excellent point, dear,' she said, absently. Her mind was already elsewhere.

'Does Jed know what's expected of him?' I asked. 'Do I need to pop out there?'

'It's all in hand,' she said. 'He has to leave at three. I'm not sure what appointments a chap who lives in the woods has to keep, but if he has to go, he has to go.' We were walking in the direction of her study. 'I have a few items of correspondence to sort out. Shall we take dinner early and then walk it off with a stroll? It's such a glorious day.'

'Evening stroll it is,' I said. 'We'll have dinner ready for six. Yell if you need anything.'

We took dinner early in the garden, on the rotting furniture beneath the apple tree. It was another glorious summer's evening and it was a pleasure to be outside. Even the wasps were good-natured.

Miss Jones and Edna still only worked half-days, so I tidied up while Lady Hardcastle prowled around the garden making notes for Jed. I remained steadfastly unable to tell a lupin from a locomotive, but she had become enthused by the garden project and was determined to create a bucolic paradise.

By seven o'clock we were in boots and hats and ready for a stroll into the village.

'I thought a turn around the green and perhaps a little something damp at the Dog and Duck,' said Lady Hardcastle as we set off down the lane.

'I like the way you think,' I said. 'Although it's a shame to be stuck indoors on a night like this.'

'It is,' she mused. 'I've often wondered if we might persuade Old Joe to put a few tables outside in the summer – Continental style.'

'A Parisian pavement café in Littleton Cotterell?'

'Or a Bavarian *Biergarten* – he could colonize a little bit of the edge of the green. We could watch the world go by over a glass of cider.'

'For the two weeks a year when the weather is nice enough,' I said.

'Pish and fiddlesticks – there are plenty of days when sitting outdoors would be a pleasure. And we'd be able to see the cricket, too, if they were playing. I wonder if we shall see a game this evening. I do enjoy watching a game of cricket.'

'I know,' I said. 'I still don't understand it, but I'll grant you it's an oddly relaxing way to pass the time. Shall we?'

We continued down the lane.

There was, to Lady Hardcastle's delight, a game of cricket in progress. We skirted round the edge of the green, saying hello to the wives and sweethearts of the players as we went.

'Your Davey needs to get his weight further forward on his front foot when he's playing a cover drive like that,' said Lady Hardcastle as we passed a cluster of young ladies.

'He does,' said one of them. 'Arthur says it to him all the time. But I i'n't gonna be the one to tell him again. I told him a million times he has to listen to the captain, but he just gets the hump with me.'

'Davey Bishop!' yelled Lady Hardcastle. 'Put your weight forward if you're going to try a cover drive like that. Lean your head and shoulder towards the ball.'

Davey scanned the boundary to see who was giving him the unsolicited advice.

Arthur Tressle, the club captain, was at the non-striker's end. Before Davey could respond, he said loudly, 'She i'n't wrong, Davey, she i'n't wrong.'

The opposition laughed. Davey Bishop scowled. The bowler took a long run-up and delivered the ball at extraordinary pace. Davey played the same stroke again and the ball shot towards us.

'Like that?' he called as the umpire signalled four runs.

'Exactly like that, dear,' called Lady Hardcastle. 'Well played.'

I retrieved the ball from the road and threw it back towards the wicket, where it was scooped up by the chagrined bowler.

We walked on.

As we neared the village hall we could hear the sound of a piano coming from within.

'That doesn't sound like the Tuesday night embroidery club,' said Lady Hardcastle. 'Unless they need musical accompaniment for their split stitches and French knots.'

'They've had to stop all the club and society meetings for the time being so the hall can be used for rehearsals for the village show,' I said. 'That'll be someone trying out their act.'

'I hope their act isn't "Playing the Piano",' she said. 'They're bally awful.'

'And that's why they haven't invited you to be a judge in the contest. It's supposed to be a bit of fun. Everyone's going to do their best, and we're all going to cheer and applaud as though we're watching the finest show in the West End. Then we'll award a prize to the best act and retire to the pub for a well-earned drink.'

'Oh, I'd be kind in person, you know I would. In private, though, I'm more than comfortable pointing out that they're bally awful.'

'Well, yes,' I said. 'You're not wrong. Have you given any more thought to performing?'

'I still can't decide,' she said as strolled towards the pub. 'I don't really have any unique talents. Every man and his dog will be playing the piano.'

'I'd pay extra to see a dog playing the piano.'

'If we can find one, he could accompany me as I demonstrate my new loom, perhaps. Weaving to music.'

'You'd win easily. But I'm in an even worse position. I don't have any talents at all.'

'You play the banjo beautifully.'

'What is it Harry says? "A gentleman is someone who knows how to play the banjo, but doesn't."'

'Pish and fiddlesticks,' she said. 'I love your banjo-playing. And you're not a gentleman anyway. Oh, I know – you could do your knife-throwing act.'

I laughed. 'With you as my glamorous assistant, standing in front of the target in a sequinned leotard?'

'Oh, I like the idea of that. The death-defying knife skills of the Great Coltellina and her fearless assistant . . . What would my name be?'

'Oh, I never name my assistants,' I said. 'Dangerous job, knife-thrower's assistant. I get through so many – it doesn't do to get too attached to them.'

'Very wise, very wise.'

'I'll give it some thought, though.'

'Oh, do. I'm rather taken with the notion of wearing a sequinned leotard.'

We had, by now, arrived at the Dog and Duck, where a number of drinkers were standing outside on the pavement, drinks in hand, watching the cricket.

'You see?' said Lady Hardcastle. 'A few tables and chairs out here would be perfect.'

'You're right, as always,' I said. 'Brandy?'

'No, I think the weather calls for a small glass of cider. No, make it a pint – no point in trudging back and forth to the bar.'

I raised my eyebrows.

'Oh, no one will mind,' she said. 'Don't be such a dodo. It's the twentieth century.'

I went to the bar and tried to attract the attention of the barmaid, my good friend Daisy Spratt.

'All right, Flo?' she said with a grin when I finally caught her eye. 'Out on your own?'

'No,' I said. 'Herself is outside watching the cricket.'

'We gets a lot of that in the summer. I keeps tellin' Joe he needs to put a couple of tables out there. People'd love it.'

I smiled. 'I know at least one person who agrees with you – she's been harping on about it all the way here.'

'So you're out for an evenin' constitutional, then? Been anywhere nice?'

'Once around the green,' I said. 'A quick listen to whoever's rehearsing in the village hall and then straight here for a drink.'

'Sounds nice enough to me. Two brandies?'

'Not tonight, no,' I said. 'Apparently it's cider weather.'

'It certainly is. Two small ones?'

'One half, one pint,' I said. 'No, make it two pints. She's right – it'll save me trudging back and forth to the bar.'

Daisy laughed. 'I reckon Old Joe would love it if all the women round here started drinkin' by the pint.'

'She's always been one for flouting convention.'

Daisy drew two pints from the cider barrel.

'You doin' anythin' for the show?' she said.

'We were just talking about that. I don't think I've got any talents worth sharing. We thought about banjo-playing or knife-throwing, but I'm not really keen. Other than that, though, I've drawn a complete blank, so it might come down to one of those.'

'Or both together.'

I laughed. 'That's not a bad idea. What are you going to do?'

'I don't know,' she said. 'Our dad's gonna get his violin out. And our ma'll be doin' a song with Edna Gibson. But I don't know what to do.'

'Can you sing?'

'Not a note. Tone deaf, me.'

'Dance?'

'Two left feet.'

'Tell jokes?'

'Can't remember the endin's.'

'You're scuppered, then,' I said. 'You'd better just man the bar.'

'I knows my place. 'Ere, what about animal noises and birdsong?'

'Can you do that?'

'No, you idiot, you. You loves makin' noises.'

'Not sure I can make an act out of it, though – I'm hopeless at remembering animal names. "And now the haunting call of the Scandinavian elk."' I squeezed my lips together and blew, making a trumpeting sound. '"No, I'm sorry, that's an elephant. Which one's the elk again?" I'd need Lady Hardcastle in the wings reminding me what all the animals were.'

She seemed oddly enthused. 'No, it'd be me. We could do it as a comic turn.'

'I'm not sure,' I said. 'Maybe . . .'

'I'll work on some ideas. It'll be hilarious.'

I paid for the cider and left her pondering her – our – new act.

'You took your time,' said Lady Hardcastle as I handed her a glass. 'Davey Bishop just made his half-century.'

'Well done, Davey Bishop,' I said. 'I was talking to Daisy. Apparently we're doing a comic animal impressions act in the show.'

She pouted. 'Looks like I'll have to play the piano after all. But I'm still wearing the leotard.'

We watched the cricket and chatted until the light faded, then made our way home. Littleton Cotterell might have won, but it's always hard to tell with cricket.

Chapter Two

On Wednesday morning I was sitting in the kitchen doing a little mending. I was with Miss Jones, Lady Hardcastle's cook, and Edna, the housemaid-cum-housekeeper. The coffee was brewing, there were eggs and bacon sizzling in the pan, and there were four rounds of toast browning nicely on the grill.

'I wish we had electricity,' said Miss Jones as she checked for the twentieth time that the toast wasn't burning. 'I saw one o' they electric toasters when I took our ma into town on the bus, t'other week. Change my life, that would.'

'Electric lights would be enough for me,' I said. 'Oh, or an electric iron. They've got them up at The Grange.'

'They gots their own generator though, a'n't they?' said Edna sagely. 'It's as modern as you like up there. In some ways, anyway.'

'Well, I shan't be disappointed when the electric comes to Littleton Cotterell,' said Miss Jones. 'They wants to get on with it. It's like we're the poor relations out here in the countryside. The telephone lines only made it out here just before you and Lady Hardcastle moved in. And even then it only reached the police station. You had to have poles and that put up to get it out to the house. Remember?'

'I remember it well,' I said. 'I'd still not swap country living for a return to the city. We've only been here three years but this feels more like home than anywhere else we've been.'

'Three years,' said Edna. 'Is it really? Well I never.' She laughed. 'So it's only taken three years to get the garden sorted out? Our Dan does his best but he i'n't no gardener.'

'It's not for want of nagging,' I said. 'I suggested Jed as gardener soon after we met him, but we just didn't get round to it.'

'He's a nice old chap when you gets to know him,' said Miss Jones. 'Our ma heard stories from her pals in the village. She was on about not trustin' a bloke like that what lives in a hut in the woods. But he's as nice as can be.'

'It's a caravan,' I said. 'And he is nice. He's an old soldier, I think.'

'He knows his way round a garden,' said Edna. 'I got chattin' to him yesterday. I asked if we can 'ave some 'erbs by the back door. He said sommat about the sun and the drainage but then he said Lady Hardcastle wanted wild 'erbs anyway so he'd see if she wouldn't mind puttin' a little 'erb garden over by the back wall.'

'I'd like that,' said Miss Jones. 'I've been bringin' 'erbs from our ma's garden when I needs 'em. It'd be nice to have a selection here.'

'I'll give her a nudge to make sure it doesn't get forgotten,' I said.

When the breakfast was ready, I loaded up a couple of trays and Edna helped me carry everything through to the morning room. Of Lady Hardcastle there was no sign.

'Shall I nip up and give her a knock?' said Edna. 'I gots to start on the upstairs rooms this mornin' anyway.'

'Only if you're actually planning to head up there right away,' I said. 'I have an alternative plan if you need to gather your accoutrements.'

'Well, I does need me duster and some polish,' she said. 'And a bucket. And a brush. And—'

'Leave it to me,' I said.

I went into the hall, where I put two fingers in my mouth and whistled shrilly.

'That'll do it,' said Edna with a chuckle, and went off to the kitchen to fetch the tools of her trade.

I returned to the morning room and was joined a few minutes later by a bleary-eyed Lady Hardcastle.

'You whistled, m'lady?' she said as she sat down.

'Breakfast's ready,' I said.

'So I gather. And a lovely spread it is, too. Thank you, dear.'

'Miss Jones did all the hard work. I was mending that floral dress you ripped.'

'Well, thank you for that, then.'

'I thought you might like to wear it this afternoon.'

'Ah, yes, tiffin at The Grange. One needs a nice frock for the social whatnots, even when it's with pals.'

'Especially when one is taking advantage of one's pals' connections to an aeroplane factory so one can snoop for one's brother.'

'Snoop for King and Country, dear. I love Harry, but I'd not put us to this much trouble just to indulge one of his whims. We've both got better things to do than traipse off on factory tours just for his amusement. But I've taken him at his word. He says aeroplanes are the coming thing – vital to the national doo-dah in times of thingummy – and this new parachute will change something or other for the better.'

'Even if you are light on the detail.'

'Oh, you know what I mean. He does lay it on a bit thick, but I entirely see his point. So if there's a leak and it's within our gift to plug it, we should.'

'And we might get a go in an aeroplane.'

'That would be rather fun, wouldn't it?' she said.

'It would. How will we know what we're looking at? What we're looking for?'

Before Lady Hardcastle could answer, the doorbell rang, followed by the clatter of a dropped box of cleaning tools and the clang of a bucket. And swearing. Lots of swearing.

'I'd better get the door,' I said. 'Sounds like Edna's having trouble.'

I stood and went out into the hall where Edna was mopping up a large puddle of soapy water.

'Are you all right there?' I said.

'I'll be fine, my lover,' she said. 'Doorbell startled me is all. I tried to rush to get it and fell over me own feet.'

'I'll get the door,' I said. 'Then I'll help you mop up.'

'Oh, don't you worry about that. You just leave I to it. T'i'n't nothin' but a bit of water. So long as I gets it up quick it won't do no harm.'

It was the postman bearing a large package wrapped in brown paper. I thanked him and took it back through the hall. Edna had already mopped up most of the mess and was busy picking up the contents of her, now broken, toolbox.

'Jed will be able to mend that for you,' I said as I passed.

'Oh, I reckon he will, at that,' she said. 'I was goin' to ask my Dan, but he'll take weeks. Jed'll do it quick as a wink.'

'There's a couple of bottles of beer in the pantry,' I said. 'I'm sure he'd do it for nothing, but offer him a drink anyway.'

She smiled and started carrying things back through to the kitchen. I returned to the morning room.

'Anything for me?' said Lady Hardcastle.

'It's always for you,' I said, handing her the package.

'You get letters. You're always telling me the latest news from your sister, or from young Eleanora Wilson.'

We had met Ellie Wilson and her aunt the previous summer at Weston-super-Mare. They were visiting from America and hadn't had quite the stay they were hoping for. After all the excitement was over and the two had returned to Annapolis, Ellie and I had struck up a correspondence. She had also, to my amusement, kept in touch with our musician friend, 'Skins' Maloney.

'Well, that's not from Ellie,' I said. 'It's postmarked London W. Have you bought anything exciting?'

'Not lately. Consider me intrigued.'

She opened the package and was somewhat disappointed to discover two large files and a note from Harry.

'What ho, sis,' she read. 'Herewith some background bumf on aeroplanes, parachutes, and Bristol Aviation. Usual rules – keep it mum. Love, Harry.'

'He's sent you some homework,' I said. 'How thoughtful.'

'He's a kind and generous boy, my brother. Still, at least I don't have to make any decisions about what to do today before tea. Did you have any plans?'

'Nothing I can't put off,' I said.

'Then we shall find a quiet spot and do our prep together. But not until after breakfast.'

I'd been working for Lady Hardcastle since 1894. Seventeen years. Half my life. I'd officially served as her 'lady's maid' for those seventeen years, but my role for most of that time had been more that of an aide-de-camp and general right-hand woman who also did a bit of mending.

Even now that Harry had persuaded us to return to government service as part of the Secret Service Bureau, it suited us to maintain society's approved roles for a working-class girl from the Valleys and a titled lady from London. I was readily accepted as a maid, whereas had I tried to pass as Lady Hardcastle's equal, I'd have been laughed out of most of the places we needed to work.

As I've said often before, being naught but a humble lady's maid gave me the opportunity to pass unnoticed in parts of society, both high and low, where a jumped-up circus girl would stand out like a . . . I'm trying not to say 'sore thumb' – I'd never thought of myself as a sore thumb – but I only got as far as 'some sort of flower in a field of some other sort of very different flower' and there my humiliating ignorance of the wonders of nature brought me to a shuddering halt. You get the picture, though. No one notices a lady's maid in a country house drawing room, nor in a country house servants' hall. She remains virtually invisible in a swanky dress shop as much as in a backstreet boozer. When your best friend and close colleague is a loud and outgoing maelstrom of social exuberance, it pays to be the unseen one, quietly getting things done in the background.

To Lady Hardcastle's credit, it had long troubled her that the world saw me as 'merely' a maid. Not that she thought there was anything 'mere' about the work servants do, but it irked her to know how little many of her peers thought of me. She offered many times to 'promote' me to companion, but this would have brought its own set of problems. Companions were usually drawn from the upper classes, so my background would have raised eyebrows. And as a companion, many of the doors I've already mentioned would be suddenly closed to me. My access to the world of everyday folk would be severely restricted.

And so we had decided that my official title would remain 'lady's maid'. It was professionally expedient, it raised fewer objections and, if I'm honest, it suited me. I actually liked looking after her. I could have found a thousand ways to fill my days, but I took genuine pleasure in mending her dresses, arranging her hair and nagging her to tidy her studio in the orangery. Edna and Miss Jones had been with us for three years, and even working half-days they took care of the house with practised ease. It wasn't at all onerous to be Lady Hardcastle's lady's maid.

In some situations, though, it all became a little fuzzy. Lady Hardcastle had met Sir Hector and Lady Farley-Stroud within days of our arrival in Littleton Cotterell. They had become firm friends at once, and I had been introduced soon after. It took Lady Farley-Stroud a little while to get used to the way Lady Hardcastle treated me, but after a short spell of having her objections completely ignored, she began to accept my presence as an unavoidable consequence of her friendship with Lady Hardcastle. Sir Hector, I should point out, took people as he found them and treated everyone with the same affable courtesy.

All of which was very splendid and lovely, but it did mean I never knew quite how to dress when we went to The Grange. At home I wore my uniform dress when I expected to get dirty, and when we were 'working' I always packed it as my cloak of invisibility, but increasingly I dressed in mufti. But what should I do at The Grange? They knew I was less maid than assistant, but I never wanted to make them uncomfortable. But what might make them uncomfortable? Did they feel worse when a friend were dressed as a servant, or when a servant dressed as a friend? It was always a minefield and I was never sure I got it right.

As usual, I approached Lady Hardcastle for advice. She was in her study.

'You seem discomfited,' she said, looking up from her letter-writing. 'What troubles you, old pal?'

'The usual,' I said. 'How should I dress for tea?'

She laughed. 'Some sort of frock would be in order, I think – the denizens of The Grange are not noted nudists. At least, I don't think so. They certainly keep it quiet if they are. Although one can never tell. I think they were quite the social rebels in their youth.'

'You're a tremendous help, as always. Come on, you know how I fret about this.'

'I do. Something summery and light. And a big hat – I rather think they might seat us outdoors on a lovely day like today.'

'So, not my uniform, then?'

'Do you anticipate doing any maiding?'

'My life is maiding from morn till night, but no, I was hoping to scoff sandwiches and cake while playing with baby Louisa.'

'Then unless you fear the sticky hands of the infant Whitman might ruin your outfit, I suggest the white dress with the lace bodice. And the white boots.'

'Was that so hard?' I said.

'Teasing you is never hard, dear. Who's driving?'

'I thought we could walk,' I said. 'Sir Hector is never parsimonious with his booze.'

'Then hasten ye to your wardrobe, tiny servant. Get changed at once and we shall have plenty of time to stroll up the hill.'

The Grange began life in 1561 as a weekend retreat for a wealthy Bristol merchant. It had changed hands many times in the intervening three hundred and fifty years, and every owner had sought to alter it to their own taste. As each new architectural fashion was indulged, though, very little of the existing building was

27

demolished, so that by the time the Farley-Strouds had taken possession it was quite the mishmash. The Tudor hall formed the core, but the façade and the rooms at the 'new' front of the house were in the Georgian Palladian style, while the most recently added wing was Victorian neo-Gothic.

The house sat atop the hill that climbed from Littleton Cotterell. This left it slightly exposed to the infrequent winter storms, but afforded splendid views back down towards the village in one direction, and out across the valley of the River Severn in the other.

The house was approached through a large pair of stone gateposts (the traditional adjective is 'imposing'). The gate itself was never closed, though it was unknown by this point whether it still could be – the iron-bound oak gate was folded back against the stone boundary wall and was overgrown with climbing plants. Visitors then proceeded down a long drive ('sweeping') to the enormous front door ('impressive'), which had recently been painted navy blue ('tasteful').

Our boots scrunched on the gravel of the drive as birds of unknown designation and vintage chirruped, twittered and otherwise called all around us. Crows, I could recognize. Jackdaws, too – I had used a jackdaw call as our secret signal many times. The terrifying banshee screech of the swift was easy enough to spot, as was the chattering 'Look at me – I'm actually blimmin' well flying' of a passing blackbird. But everything else remained a high-pitched mystery to me.

'Did you know that swifts only land to breed?' said Lady Hardcastle as she watched them swoop above us. She told me this every time we saw them.

'No,' I said. 'That's remarkable.'

'Isn't it just? I should love to be able to fly.'

'Get on the right side of Adam Whitman and you might have a chance.'

'I'm already on the right side of Adam Whitman, dear,' she said. 'He finds me delightful.'

'Does he?'

'He does.'

'How can you tell?'

'Everyone finds me delightful. The trick is going to be to get him to invite us on a tour of the Bristol Aviation and Aeronautics Company.'

'That's a tiresome tautology,' I said.

'Tedious. If you're going to merge the Bristol Aviation Company and the Bristol Aeronautics Corporation, you have an opportunity to come up with a new and exciting name, wouldn't you think? "Onward to Glory". "Up and Away". "Flights of Fancy". "St Joseph's Flying Miracles".'

'I hesitate to ask.'

'Joseph of Cupertino is the patron saint of flying, dear. Everyone knows that. Just as everyone but the board of directors can see the silliness of the "Bristol Aviation and Aeronautics Company" and just calls it Bristol Aviation.'

She pressed the doorbell.

The door was opened almost immediately by Jenkins, the Farley-Strouds' butler.

'Good afternoon, my lady,' he said. 'And Miss Armstrong.'

'Good afternoon, Jenkins,' said Lady Hardcastle. 'Two more for tea?'

'Of course, my lady. Sir Hector said – now let me get this absolutely correct – he said, "When Lady Hardcastle and Miss Armstrong arrive, tell 'em to come straight round the back. We'll be takin' tea on the terrace, d'you see? Don't make the poor blighters traipse all through the house, there's a good chap." Of course

I'd be more than happy to accompany you through the house, but I feel duty bound to convey that message to you.'

His impersonation of Sir Hector was uncannily accurate and we both smiled.

'Don't worry, Jenkins, we'd best do as the lord of the manor says,' said Lady Hardcastle. 'We know the way. Consider your duties and obligations discharged.'

'You're very kind, my lady. Tea will be served shortly.'

We picked our way round the outside of the house, past the stables, and through an arched opening in the wall of the kitchen garden. We were suddenly on the terrace at the rear of the house.

'Emily!' said Lady Farley-Stroud warmly when she saw us. 'How lovely of you to come. And Florence. Don't you look lovely.'

'Always happy to join you for some of Mrs Brown's famous cakes,' said Lady Hardcastle.

'She's on fine form at the moment, m'dear,' said Sir Hector. 'I'm havin' to be careful of the old waistline, what?'

'He's careful of nothing of the sort,' said Lady Farley-Stroud. 'I'm the one on restricted rations and he's supposed to be joining me out of spousal solidarity. But he just stuffs his face.'

'Be rude not to,' said Sir Hector with a grin. 'Mrs B wouldn't take too kindly to us both not eating her fare. Skilled woman, that. And slightly terrifyin'.'

Lady Farley-Stroud tutted. 'Clarissa?' she said. 'Emily's here, darling.'

A young woman stood up from the grass, picking up a baby who had been playing happily on a rug.

'I say, hello, Emily,' she said. 'Say hello, Lou-Lou.'

Baby Louisa waved a pudgy hand.

'Hello, Lou-Lou,' said Lady Hardcastle. 'Will you walk for Emily?'

The small girl wriggled in her mother's arms and Clarissa set her on her feet. Lady Hardcastle crouched down and Louisa waddled unsteadily towards her, waving her arms for balance.

'You're getting rather good at that, old thing,' said Lady Hardcastle. 'We'll have you out to work in no time.' She swept her up and stood. 'Not bad for a one-year-old. Have you developed any new skills since we saw you last week? Are you writing yet, like Mama? Or will you follow Papa into engineering?'

Louisa smiled beatifically and tried to pull at Lady Hardcastle's hat.

'Ah, you fancy a career as a milliner? A fine choice. Ladies will always want hats.'

Louisa wriggled again and Lady Hardcastle put her down to allow her to return to her mother. She completely ignored Clarissa and headed instead for Sir Hector's three springer spaniels, who were snoozing contentedly in a patch of sunshine on the flag-stoned terrace.

'Come and sit down, m'dears,' said Sir Hector. 'Made a jug of rum punch. Just right for this sort of weather.'

We settled into comfortable wickerwork chairs and accepted our drinks while the dogs patiently endured Louisa's tender ministrations.

'Never known the gels be so easy-goin',' he said. 'That sort of attention would usually send 'em into a boisterous frenzy. They'd be bouncin' about expectin' fun and games. Must be the old maternal instinct, what?'

'It must be,' said Lady Hardcastle.

A tall, gangly man in shirtsleeves emerged from the French window that led to the ballroom. It was Adam, Clarissa's husband. He looked faintly harassed.

'Hello, Emily,' he said. 'Hello, Flo. Hector, are you sure those dogs are all right with her poking them about like that? Do stop her if she's a nuisance.'

'They'll soon let her know,' said Sir Hector. 'Best leave 'em to find their own equilibrium, what?'

'If you say so,' said Adam. He sat down with us. 'Is that rum punch? I could do with one.'

'Oh, dear,' said Lady Hardcastle. 'That doesn't sound good.'

'Oh, it's nothing to worry about,' he said. 'Just had to finish off a report for the chaps back in Bordeaux. Sent me some specs for a new wing design and wanted me to do some stress calculations for them. We're nowhere near even starting to think about considering the possibility of one day contemplating building a test piece, so I've no idea why it can't wait till we get back. But there you are, that's businessmen for you. Everything in a hurry.'

'I thought the French took a more relaxed attitude to life.'

'It's an image they like to cultivate, but they're just as nervous and jittery as the rest of us. They wear me out sometimes, they really do.'

'Well, get yourself on the outside of a couple of glasses of this and it'll all cease to matter,' said Sir Hector. 'Patent remedy for frets, fuss, and fatigue.'

Adam accepted the drink. 'Getting sloshed is your patent remedy for everything,' he said.

'And look how well I am on it,' said Sir Hector. 'Bottoms up, old chap.'

They clinked glasses.

'Easy on the rum, Hector,' called Lady Farley-Stroud. 'We don't want a repeat of Sunday.'

'Right you are, my little plum duff,' said Sir Hector. 'Takin' it easy.'

'What happened on Sunday?' said Lady Hardcastle.

'Bit of an incident in the library,' said Sir Hector with a wink. 'Minor breakages. No injuries.'

Adam smiled ruefully.

'And don't you sit there grinning like you weren't involved, Adam Whitman,' said Clarissa.

We were prevented from finding out further details by the arrival of Jenkins and Dewi Rees, the footman, bearing heavily laden trays.

Afternoon tea was served.

◆ ◆ ◆

Tea, as anticipated, was utterly splendid and the lower part of my skirt, as Lady Hardcastle had predicted, was entirely covered in jammy hand prints. Although it was not exclusively jam. There was some butter there, too, and a small quantity of piccalilli that had been angrily flung when Louisa discovered that she did not, after all, like piccalilli.

'My compliments to Mrs Brown, as always,' said Lady Hardcastle as Jenkins and Dewi cleared away the trays. 'Quite the most splendid tea I've had since the last time we were here. Wouldn't you say, Flo?'

'Absolutely,' I said. 'Although household loyalty compels me to point out that Miss Jones can put on a splendid tea of her own when you ask her.'

'She can indeed. Between us we seem to have the best cooks in the area.'

'I shall pass on your kind words, my lady,' said Jenkins. 'Thank you.'

'Now, then, young Adam,' said Lady Hardcastle. 'I have a favour to ask of you. I had fully intended to tiptoe around the subject and drop subtle hints that you might absorb subliminally.

You would then, I hoped, hit upon the idea as though it had come to you spontaneously, and jolliness would ensue.'

'Ask away,' said Adam. 'I'm not sure subtle hints are quite my forte, to be honest, so it's probably better to be direct.'

'Much better,' said Clarissa. 'I've never met a man so incapable of reading between the lines. I've long since learned that if I want a particular gift for Christmas or a birthday I need to ask for it. Dropping hints has never done me the slightest bit of good.'

'There you are, you see?' he said. 'Not at all one for obliquity, I. Ask and ye shall receive and all that. Beat about the bush and all you'll get is a nervous bush. Shrubs are wary of being beaten.'

'Very well, then,' said Lady Hardcastle. 'Are you planning to go back to Bristol Aviation before you return home? And if so, can we come?'

He laughed. 'Of course you can. You're interested in aeroplanes?'

'Rather,' she said. 'We've been wondering about buying one.'

'Gracious!' said Lady Farley-Stroud. 'Whatever for?'

'For flying. Don't tell me you've never wanted to fly.'

'If the good Lord had meant us to fly He'd have made falling to the ground a great deal less deadly, dear.'

'Well, I've dreamed of it since forever.'

'What about you, Florence?' said Lady Farley-Stroud. 'Don't tell me you're as mad as her.'

'I'm afraid so,' I said. 'I can't think of very many things I'd like to do more.'

'I can,' she said. 'I'd like to live a long and happy life and not fall to my death from a flying machine.'

'Oh, Gertie,' said Adam. 'Don't be such a pessimist. It's perfectly safe.'

'What about that fella who died the other day?' she said. 'He wasn't perfectly safe.'

'He wasn't in an aeroplane. He . . .'

'He what, dear?' said Lady Farley-Stroud.

'Never mind,' he said. 'But Bristol Aviation's aircraft are top-notch. Not as good as the ones we make at Vannier's, but safe as houses.'

Lady Farley-Stroud turned back to Lady Hardcastle. 'Do promise me you'll be careful, dear,' she said. 'I don't wish to be referred to in the newspapers as "friend of the late aviatrix Emily Hardcastle".'

'Oh, Mama,' said Clarissa. 'You do talk rot. I think it's a wonderful idea. If I didn't have Madam here to worry about, I'd be up there, too.'

'You're all barmy. Tell them they're barmy, Hector.'

'No can do, *mon petit chou-fleur*,' said Sir Hector. 'I'd be up there with 'em meself if it wasn't for . . . Actually, I'll be blowed if I can think of a reason not to. Big, are they, these aeroplanes? Room for an old fella?'

'I forbid it,' said Lady Farley-Stroud. 'You silly old fool.'

Sir Hector grinned like a naughty schoolboy.

'I'm going down there tomorrow,' said Adam. 'Bert will be driving me if you want to join us. It'll be first thing, though – they like to make an early start.'

'I think we'd better come down under our own steam,' said Lady Hardcastle. 'That way you won't have to worry about us if you need to stay on. Nothing worse than having to worry about taking guests home when one has work to do.'

'Right you are, then. I'll prepare the ground, as it were. I'm sure we can give you a tour. I don't think it will be hard work to persuade them to show you every hospitality if you're serious about buying one, but I'll make sure you see the bits the other customers don't see.'

'That's very kind, dear. Thank you.'

Lady Farley-Stroud harrumphed. 'What are you doing for the village show, Emily, dear?'

'Well done,' said Sir Hector. 'I don't think any of them noticed you changing the subject there, m'dear. Seamless.'

She harrumphed again.

'I haven't quite decided,' said Lady Hardcastle. 'I offered to be Flo's assistant in her knife-throwing act, but she's set on doing a comic turn with Daisy Spratt.'

'A comic turn?'

'Something like that,' I said. 'Daisy wants me to do animal impressions while she gives a humorous commentary.'

'Oh, I say, how precious,' said Clarissa. 'I didn't know you could do animal impressions.'

'I can't,' I said. 'Not really. I think that's where the humour comes in. I may yet end up throwing knives at Lady Hardcastle, if it goes as badly as I'm expecting. Or at Daisy. That's more likely.'

'What about you two?' said Lady Hardcastle. 'What's your party piece?'

'I shall be singing, of course. I haven't decided on a song yet, mind you.'

'How lovely. And you, Hector?'

'I shall be doin' a dramatic recitation, m'dear. "The boy stood on the burning deck / Stout-hearted, full of pluck. He only had but one regret—"'

'Hector!' said Lady Farley-Stroud. 'That's quite enough of that, thank you. Why don't you pour everyone another glass of rum punch?'

Hector grinned again. 'And then can I tell 'em what happened to the poor lad's pet duck?' he said.

'Just pour the punch, you silly old fool,' said Lady Farley-Stroud.

Sir Hector obliged. Our pleasant afternoon was turning into a fun evening.

◆ ◆ ◆

'Cocoa?' I said as Lady Hardcastle finished one of her favourite Chopin nocturnes.

'I think that would be most welcome after all that rum punch this afternoon,' she said. 'Before you go, though . . .' She played a note on the piano. 'Do you think that's out of tune? Ever so slightly?'

'It does sound a bit "back-street boozer",' I said. 'I'll call the tuner in the morning.'

'Would you? That would be lovely. Is there any shortbread? Or any sort of biscuit? I fancy something to go with the cocoa.'

'I'll see what I can find.'

While the milk was coming to the boil I rummaged through Miss Jones's assorted biscuit tins and managed to find some short-bread, as requested. There were some lemon-flavoured something-or-others, too, so I added them to the plate.

I returned to find Lady Hardcastle standing strangely in the middle of the drawing room.

'I know I'll regret asking,' I said, 'but what . . . ?'

'I'm practising my glamorous assistant poses,' she said. 'What do you think?'

'Most . . . alluring,' I said.

'I thought so. Where do you imagine one might acquire a sequinned leotard? A sporting goods emporium?'

'They'd certainly have leotards, but not sparkly ones. You need a theatrical costumiers. Preferably one specializing in circus wear.'

'Do such places exist?'

'I'm sure we can find something if you're determined.' I looked her up and down. 'You'll have to have a bespoke fitting,' I said. 'With a reinforced top half – you'll have someone's eye out otherwise.'

'Cheeky wench. I'm a fine figure of a woman.'

'You're a danger to shipping. I brought biscuits.'

'You're a poppet. Is your banjo freshly strung?'

'It's strung, at least. I can't remember how fresh they are.'

'Then let's see if we can play something jolly. I've not ruled out the idea of us doing a musical act, you know.'

I retrieved the banjo from its case.

Chapter Three

'How do you want me dressed today?' I said as Lady Hardcastle and I ate breakfast in the morning room the next day. 'Humble maid or girl about town?'

'I think if we're going to play the "dizzy widow buying an aeroplane for her maid to pilot for her" card, you'll need to be recognizably maidly, dear. Sorry.'

'No, it's fine. We're working, so whatever best suits the job. Do you want me to drive, too?'

'That would help to reinforce our little story, wouldn't it? Dear Adam did rather seem to accept my rambling explanation for the visit at face value so I'm sure he'll set things up nicely, but a little extra set-dressing can't hurt, can it? We shall arrive in chauffeuse-driven splendour.'

'I'll get my cap.'

'Don't overdo it, dear. Is the Rolls fully fuelled?'

'And finely fettled,' I said. 'It's ready to go as soon as we are.'

'Then let us gird our loins and dress for action.'

By nine o'clock we were washed, dressed and ready to go. I put in a last-minute request to Miss Jones for a ham pie for dinner, and went out to join Lady Hardcastle in the Rolls.

The Rolls-Royce Silver Ghost Roadster was a recent acquisition. For a short while during the year before we had been the proud test drivers of a prototype vehicle designed by Lady Hardcastle's friend Lord 'Fishy' Riddlethorpe. It was a magnificently futuristic machine that Lady Hardcastle had named Phyllis. It was inspired by Lord Riddlethorpe's celebrated racing cars and boasted some of the most advanced engineering ideas of the day, including an electric starter motor of his own design. In November, though, it had, sadly and rather suddenly, blown up. Quite literally. We had been bowling merrily along the Gloucester Road on our way into Bristol and before either of us could say, 'What's that peculiar grinding noise?' there had been a loud bang. Phyllis was blasted sideways into the hedge and the road was showered with bits of bonnet and shattered engine pieces. The sturdy bulkhead had protected us from harm, but the Riddlethorpe Shinatobe was no more.

Lord Riddlethorpe himself had come down from Rutland to supervise its retrieval, but there was nothing to be done to revive the poor motor car. He had returned to the factory promising an improved version 'within a year', but in the meantime we were vehicle-less. Lady Hardcastle had immediately contacted the local representative of the Rolls-Royce company to enquire about purchasing a new Silver Ghost. She liked the vehicle, she told him, but thought it a little frumpy and wondered if it might be possible to remove the rear seats and reshape the bodywork a little to turn it into a natty roadster. Like most salesmen, he had been reluctant to take her seriously at first, and suggested that while bespoke coachwork was certainly an option, ladies usually preferred to leave the Silver Ghost as it had been originally designed. She smiled sweetly and presented him with a set of sketches detailing the proposed alterations. He had been sufficiently impressed that his condescension turned to admiration, and he promised to oversee the alterations himself.

The work had taken several months, during which time Lady Hardcastle had rented an Austin from a garage in Clifton, but by

June we were in possession of a new motor car named Marley. It wasn't anywhere near as thrilling as Lord Riddlethorpe's race-inspired vehicle, but we judged it a good deal less likely to explode on the Gloucester Road.

The interior was comfortable and the controls well laid out. Lord Riddlethorpe had kindly sent one of his eggheads to install an electric starter to save me from the tyranny of the crank handle, so within moments of taking our seats, we were off.

The Rolls attracted much less attention than Phyllis, not least because whereas the latter had bellowed and roared her way down the road, Marley purred calmly.

We arrived at the headquarters of the Bristol Aviation and Aeronautics Company before ten and found a convenient place to park outside a two-storey office building.

◆ ◆ ◆

The solid outer doors opened on to a small vestibule with another pair of altogether less sturdy doors leading into the main reception area. We pushed open a door each and entered together.

The reception was painted a drab and functional greenish-grey, with framed photographs of aeroplanes the only real decoration. There was a plain desk in the corner, behind which sat a pretty young woman in her twenties wearing a tweed suit and a white blouse with a black-trimmed collar and golden buttons. She already looked uncomfortably hot, but her blue eyes caught the electric light on her desk and appeared to sparkle as she smiled warmly in greeting.

'Lady Hardcastle, is it?' she said.

'It is, yes. You're expecting us, I take it.'

'We are, my lady,' said the woman. 'Mr Whitman from Vannier's said you'd be popping in for a look round. Mr Sandling, our managing director, would be pleased to see you in his office, if you have the time.'

'We have time aplenty, dear,' said Lady Hardcastle. 'We should be delighted.'

The woman picked up the earpiece from a large wooden telephone on her desk, pressed one of the Bakelite buttons and leaned forward to the mouthpiece.

'Lady Hardcastle is here, sir,' she said, enunciating each word clearly, her faint Bristol accent all but disappearing as she spoke. 'Yes, sir. Right away.'

She replaced the earpiece and stood up.

'He's looking forward to seeing you,' she said. 'Follow me and I'll show you the way. I'll bring some coffee shortly. Oh, if you want it, that is. Will you take coffee?'

'We'd love some. Thank you. That's a lovely blouse.'

'Thank you very much,' said the woman, going slightly pink. 'Actually, I made it myself. No one here ever notices.'

She led us through a door and up a flight of echoey concrete stairs. Another door at the top gave on to a linoleum-floored corridor with windows on one side looking out on to the courtyard where we'd parked, and half-glazed office doors on the other. Mr Sandling's office was at the far end.

The woman raised her hand to knock, but before she could make contact, the door opened from the inside to reveal a short, plump man in shirtsleeves. His own smile of welcome was as warmly genuine as the woman's had been.

'Lady Hardcastle,' he said. 'How wonderful to meet you. Walter Sandling.' He held out a pudgy hand, which Lady Hardcastle shook enthusiastically.

'How do you do?' she said. 'This is Armstrong.'

'How do you do, Miss Armstrong?' he said, grasping my hand and shaking it.

'Do you need anything apart from the coffee, sir?' said the woman.

'No, thank you, Miss Matthews,' he said. 'That will be splendid. Unless there are any biscuits. I could kill for a biscuit.'

'I'll see what I can find,' said Miss Matthews. 'The boys in the drawing office usually have some in their tin.'

'Thank you,' he said with another smile. 'That would be grand.'

I couldn't precisely place his accent, but I was prepared to guess somewhere north of Birmingham and south of Manchester. Stoke, perhaps.

'Come in,' he said. 'Come in. Make yourselves comfortable. We don't get many visits from the general public, I'm afraid – mostly government types and engineers round here – so we're a bit rough and ready. Miss Matthews makes a cracking cup of coffee, though, so as long as you don't mind sitting round my little meeting table, there'll be a decent drink in it for you, at least.'

He indicated a circular table just inside the door, around which four chairs were arranged as though for dinner. He pulled out one of the chairs for Lady Hardcastle and I seated myself.

The rest of the spacious office was as utilitarian as the reception and the corridor. Mr Sandling's desk was large and cluttered, and he had a drawing table by the window upon which lay a complex technical drawing of what looked like an engine of some sort. There were filing cabinets against one wall, while the other was decorated with more framed photographs of aeroplanes.

'Now then,' he said. 'How exactly can we help you? I understand you're a friend of young Whitman's mother-in-law. He speaks very highly of you, I must say.'

'That's very kind of him,' said Lady Hardcastle. 'It's all a bit of a cheek, really. It's just that aeroplanes absolutely fascinate me, you see – actually I have a bit of a thing for all things mechanical. So when I heard that Adam was going to be spending part of his time with you while he was back in England – he and darling Clarissa are over from France showing off little Louisa to her doting grandparents – well, I couldn't stop myself from asking him if he'd give me an introduction and perhaps show me round your enchanting facility.'

The friendly smile returned. 'I'm sure we could arrange that,' he said. 'He also suggested . . . well, he seemed to be of the opinion that you might be interested in purchasing one of our machines.'

Lady Hardcastle laughed. 'I confess I did say something to that effect. It would be a glorious lark, wouldn't it? Up above the trees, keeping company with the birds. No need to follow roads – just straight to one's destination. As the crow flies there fly I, as it were.'

'You'd need a pilot. Perhaps your chauffeur could be trained.'

'I'm sure she could,' she said. 'Armstrong takes care of the driving.'

He frowned. 'Does she? Does she, indeed? Well, I never. I'm not sure I've ever . . . I mean . . . a woman? I'm not sure we've ever trained a woman pilot. There are a few famous lady pilots, of course, but you'd be the first one in Bristol.'

'Oh, how wonderful,' said Lady Hardcastle enthusiastically. 'Won't that be fun, Armstrong?'

'Tremendous fun,' I said. 'I always like to be a pioneer.'

After a few moments' thought, Mr Sandling's smile returned. 'Why not? Why not, indeed? We're in the business of breaking boundaries, after all. They said man would never fly and yet here we are. It would be rather churlish of us to turn round and say that man can fly but woman can't, eh?'

'That's the spirit,' said Lady Hardcastle.

The door opened and Miss Matthews came in with coffee and biscuits on a tray.

'Lady Hardcastle here is thinking of buying one of our aeroplanes,' said Mr Sandling. 'And she wants Miss Armstrong to pilot it. What do you think of that?'

It was Miss Matthews's turn to frown. 'Well . . . I . . . are you sure, miss? It's . . . well, it's . . .' Her voice had choked and she seemed on the edge of tears.

'I'm so sorry, my dear,' said Mr Sandling. 'I wasn't thinking at all. I'm so sorry. I really am.'

'There's no need, sir,' she said. 'It just gives me a turn sometimes, is all. I'll be fine. Will there be anything else?'

'No, no, we have everything we need. If you see Mr Whitman, though, could you tell him we'll be down presently?'

'Of course, sir.'

She left.

'Poor lass,' he said, once she was safely on her way down the corridor. 'I don't know if you were aware, but we had a tragic accident on the airfield last week. One of our young engineers lost his life. Terrible business. It hit us all pretty hard, but young Miss Matthews harder than most – she and Dickie Dupree were engaged to be married.'

'Oh, I say,' said Lady Hardcastle. 'How awful. No wonder she's upset. Was he flying one of your aeroplanes?'

Mr Sandling frowned again. 'No. No, he . . . Well, let's not dwell on it. Suffice to say she's still trying to make sense of it.' He gave a sad shrug. 'But our planes are perfectly safe, if that's what you were worried about,' he added quickly.

'I'm sure they are, Mr Sandling.' She turned to me. 'I say, dear, would you . . .' She indicated the coffee pot.

I poured three cups, and we drank together while Mr Sandling and Lady Hardcastle talked earnestly about the latest developments in aeroplane technology and I daydreamed about putting on a flying display as part of the village show, possibly with Lady

Hardcastle dangling underneath the aeroplane from a trapeze and wearing her spangly leotard.

Further ruminations were curtailed by the return of Miss Matthews to tell us that Adam Whitman had been found and was waiting for us in the drawing office. It was time for our tour.

◆　◆　◆

Adam was leaning against a drawing desk talking to one of the engineers when we found him.

'Emily,' he said warmly. 'Flo. You made it all right?'

'It was a lovely drive, dear, thank you.'

'She drives a Silver Ghost,' he said to the man he'd been talking to. 'Got them to take the back seats out and reshape the body. Beautiful motor car.'

'Sounds it,' said the man as he stood. 'Adam isn't terribly good at the social niceties, I'm afraid. I'm Godfrey Parfitt. Call me Goff.'

He shook our hands.

'Emily Hardcastle and Florence Armstrong,' said Lady Hardcastle.

'Lady Hardcastle is after a tour,' said Mr Sandling, who had just caught us up.

'Are you now?' said Mr Parfitt. 'I can spare young Paul Curtis if you need a guide.'

'I think I know my way round,' said Adam. 'If it's all right with you, Walt?'

'Fine by me,' said Mr Sandling.

Lady Hardcastle affected a puzzled frown.

'First names only round here,' said Mr Sandling. 'Formality's all well and good if you're running a firm of accountants, but I like my engineers to get along. It's all about the team in our business – if we let old-fashioned hierarchy get in the way, people are afraid to speak up. A good idea is a good idea whether it comes from a junior or a greybeard. So they call me Walt – only my mother called me Walter. Goff here is our senior engineer and the lead on . . . on a number of current projects. Paul Curtis is one of our junior engineers and Goff's right-hand man on . . . well, on those projects. More importantly, though, they're the ones to talk to about the Dunnock. Beautiful little plane. Just right for the amateur enthusiast.'

I wondered how many professional aviators there might be – it seemed to me that everyone would be an amateur – but said nothing.

'Happy to show you round one if you have time,' said Goff.

'That would be marvellous,' said Lady Hardcastle. 'Perhaps after your tour, Adam, dear?'

'I'd like a good look at one myself, so yes, please,' said Adam.

'We'll see you later, then . . . Goff,' she said.

With that, Lady Hardcastle took Adam's arm and allowed him to pretend he was leading her out of the drawing office. I offered an apologetic smile to the managing director and senior engineer and hurried after them.

It was a short walk along a broad paved roadway to the first factory hangar. Whereas the office block had been disappointingly mundane, the two hangars were magnificent cathedrals to modern technology. As we approached, I noticed that we'd been spotted by two guards who were patrolling the area.

'Security seems to be quite good,' I said.

'What?' said Adam. 'Oh, the guards, you mean? I suppose so. I've never really noticed, to tell the truth.'

We arrived at the side door of the building whose painted sign proclaimed it to be 'Hangar A'. It was a double door, slightly taller than average, but it looked like a mouse hole compared with the giant wall it was set into.

Adam noticed my widened eyes. 'Impressive, isn't it?' he said. 'They like to tell people you could fit two football pitches inside, but I'm not sure why you'd want to. Bristol Aeronautics built it for airships but after the merger the new company switched entirely to aeroplanes, so now they have these two massive edifices with tiny, tiny planes inside. Come on in.'

I was trying to imagine how big two football pitches might be. It was a struggle to imagine one outside the context of a football ground, but two . . . what was I supposed to do with that information? But people always seem to say it. That and, 'It's bigger than a double-decker omnibus,' or, 'It's taller than three elephants standing on top of one another.' Is it? Is it really? I grew up in a circus so I've seen elephants and I'm confident I know what they look like. But I also know that I can't accurately imagine how tall they are when stacked.

As we stepped through the double doors, though, I could see that the hangar definitely needed some sort of imaginative hyperbole to express its sheer vastness. There were acres of concrete-floored space – almost three acres, if my mental arithmetic and assumptions about the size of football pitches were correct. And the height of the ceiling was difficult to take in. It must have been the equivalent of almost twelve elephants stacked on top of each other. It could easily accommodate Bristol Cathedral with room to spare, although the towers would probably poke out through the roof (they're thirteen and three-quarter elephants high). The colossal sliding doors on one of the short sides of the building were open to allow a cooling breeze to blow in. Even only partly opened it would have been possible for three Clydesdale horses and a Friesian cow to pass through in line abreast, and still leave room on either side for a policeman on a bicycle and two men pushing a grand piano.

There were four islands of activity in this sea of empty floor, each centred around a tiny, partially completed aeroplane.

Obviously they were full-sized aeroplanes, but in the hangar, even two elephants stacked on top of one another driving a double-decker omnibus would have looked tiny.

'The parts are made and stored in Hangar B,' said Adam as we set off on our trek towards the first plane. 'And then brought in here as they're needed. This is the exciting room, definitely. The other one is just lathes and bandsaws and shelves full of widgets. This is where the magic happens.'

Eventually we reached a fully built aircraft. Its body resembled one of Lord Riddlethorpe's racing cars, with room for a pilot and a passenger in their own separate cockpits fore and aft. A large engine protruded from the cowling in front of the pilot, driving a huge propeller that must have been a good three-quarters of an elephant long. The canvas-covered wings were supported by an intricate lattice of wooden struts and steel wires, including a wooden A-frame rising from the body and holding up the wings like the tower of a suspension bridge. A long tail stretched out behind the body, fanning out like the tail of a bird. It all rested on what looked like two bicycle wheels.

The plane was surrounded by earnest men in overalls. Two were fussing with the supporting wires. Another had removed the engine cowling and was finely adjusting something with a small spanner. Yet another was applying a coat of some sort of lacquer or resin to the tautly stretched canvas of the wing.

The last man in the group was wearing slightly more rakish overalls, unfastened at the collar, and brown military-style laced riding boots. He was standing with his hands on his hips, an unlit pipe clamped between his teeth, surveying the plane with a proprietorial air.

He caught sight of us and gave a cheery wave. 'What ho, Adam,' he said. 'Roughing it with the real workers today, eh? I say, visitors. How do you do, ladies?'

49

'Lady Hardcastle,' said Adam, 'allow me to introduce Rupert Herbert, Bristol Aviation's chief test pilot. Rupert, this is Lady Hardcastle and her lady's maid, Miss Armstrong.'

'Delighted, I'm sure,' said Rupert with a bow.

'Don't lend him any money,' said Adam. 'And if you shake his hand make sure you count your rings afterwards.'

Rupert Herbert just grinned.

'We're taking a tour,' continued Adam, 'but Goff has promised us a proper look at this Dunnock later if you want to chuck in your two penn'orth.'

'I'll be here or here abouts,' said Rupert. 'Just waiting for them to put the final touches on the old girl, then I'll be taking her up for a spin.'

'We'll see you later, then,' said Adam, and he led us off across the vast open plains of the plane factory to a small door on the far side.

Hangar B wasn't nearly so disappointing as Adam had suggested. For reasons I never understood, I found the work of engineers and craftsmen utterly fascinating. The lathes and bandsaws Adam had dismissed as unexciting were, to me at least, magically intricate machines of infinite wonder. In this massive hall, metal and wood were turned into engines, control rods, spars and struts, all by the ingenuity and skill of men in overalls. Assembling an aeroplane was impressive enough, but crafting the individual components from lumps of metal and slabs of tree – that was magic.

'Told you it wasn't much fun in here,' said Adam. 'It looks a tiny bit more impressive if you go up to the office, though.'

He pointed to a small room that appeared to have been bolted to the wall and that was reached by a long flight of rickety iron steps. There'd been a similar office in Hangar A, but there the aeroplanes had held Adam's attention and he hadn't mentioned it.

We mounted the steps, and from the platform outside the office we were able to survey the whole of the hangar. A decent pair of field glasses would have been necessary for us to see into the furthest corners, but it was a good view nonetheless. We could see the toolmakers and woodworkers crafting components. Sailmakers were cutting and stitching the canvas for the wings. Warehousemen were shifting and sorting parts to put on to the 'shelves of widgets'.

'Surely you find this fascinating, really,' I said. 'You're an engineer. This is your life.'

'Oh, I love it,' said Adam. 'It's just defensiveness, I suppose. I've seen so many eyes glaze over when I start talking about it that I just sort of pre-empt them. Lissa's the worst. She actually yawned once while I was telling her about a new strut design for a Vannier wing. If I'm the one who's already said it's boring, I'm immune to the yawning.'

'Well, I think it's utterly enthralling,' I said.

'Me, too,' said Lady Hardcastle. 'What's going on over there?' She pointed towards the front of the hangar.

'They're finishing the parts from the foundry,' said Adam. 'Some of the engine components are cast at a foundry in the Midlands and shipped down here by rail. They arrive comparatively neat and tidy, but they need to be properly finished to quite tight tolerances – precision machines, aeroplane engines.'

'No, beyond them, in that area behind the screens.'

Adam squinted – his eyesight wasn't all it should be. 'Oh, that's the project Walt kept almost talking about,' he said. 'Top secret.'

'Ah,' she said, tapping the side of her nose. 'Mum's the word, eh?'

He laughed. "Fraid so. Sorry.'

'Fairy snuff. It's a splendid operation, though, isn't it?'

'It is indeed. I like to imagine we've got the edge on them at Vannier's, but this lot certainly know their onions. And that Dunnock is really quite something. If it flies half as well as it looks, we've got some work to do to catch up.'

'Speaking of which, do you imagine their man Geoffrey Prefect—'

'Godfrey Parfitt,' I said before I could stop myself. She got me every time.

She grinned. 'Of course, dear. So sorry. Anyway, do you think "Goff" might be free to give us the lowdown by now?'

'It's worth a try,' he said. 'I'm dying to see it myself.'

With everything on such a huge scale, the comparatively short distance back to the other side of Hangar A felt like miles and seemed to take an absolute age to traverse.

'Perhaps you might suggest they supply visitors with bicycles,' I said as we trudged across the hangar floor to the almost-ready Dunnock.

'Oh,' said Adam. 'Really? Would that have been all right? They have them for the engineers to get about but I didn't think you'd be . . . well, I've never thought it especially . . .'

'Ladylike?' said Lady Hardcastle. 'You are a silly old thing.'

'Sorry,' he said.

We arrived back at the Dunnock just as Godfrey Parfitt entered the hangar. He waved and we waited beside the aeroplane for a few minutes until he caught us up.

'Sorry to keep you,' he said. 'Just having a natter with Walt about one or two things. Have you been waiting long?'

'We've only just this minute returned from Hangar C,' said Lady Hardcastle.

'B,' I said. She'd got me again.

'Good-o,' he said. 'So, what do you think of our baby?'

'She looks magnificent,' said Lady Hardcastle. 'Before we got here I was expecting something altogether flimsier and with at least one extra wing. She looks terribly sleek and modern.'

'We experimented with biplanes,' he said. 'We've had some success with the Goldfinch – she's a lovely little plane – but this monoplane design generates just as much lift with less weight and much better visibility for the pilot and passenger.'

'Is she quick?'

'About fifty miles an hour in the prototype. We're hoping for something similar from this one. We changed the wing design a little for more lift, which might slow her down, but we managed to squeeze a little more power from the engine so we're hoping that might compensate.'

'Can I have a look in the . . . what do you call it? Cockpit?'

'Of course you may. And yes, that's exactly what we call it.'

'Just like one of Fishy's racing cars, dear,' she said to me.

'Fishy as in Fishy Riddlethorpe of Riddlethorpe Racing?' said Mr Parfitt.

'The very same,' she said.

'You know Fishy Riddlethorpe? Good Lord.'

'He's a good friend,' she replied as she clambered up the step-ladder recently abandoned by one of the engineers and peered into the pilot's compartment. 'I used to have one of his prototype road cars but it . . . well, it sort of blew up.'

'That was you?' he said with a laugh. 'On the Gloucester Road? We saw it in the *Bristol News*. Well I never. How marvellous.'

'You enjoy motor racing?'

'Rather. We're building a racing machine as a little side project in one of the smaller sheds. We've won a couple of races with it, actually. Nothing to match Lord Riddlethorpe, but it's tremendous fun.'

'You know him too, I take it.'

'Sadly not. He's something of a legend in our world, though, so I'd love to chat to him. Tap him for some of the secrets of his success.'

'I'll introduce you – you'd get along famously.'

'That would be wonderful,' he said. 'Thank you.'

We looked around the aeroplane for a while longer, with Mr Parfitt explaining various design features while referring to coefficients of lift and drag, power to weight ratios, and the relative merits of tails versus canards. Lady Hardcastle nodded earnestly and asked perspicacious questions while I tried to work out how we could get a look at the screened-off area in Hangar B. It was obviously the home of the parachute project and was very definitely worth investigating if we were to get anywhere with our enquiries for Harry.

'. . . of course we'd like to experiment with separate control surfaces on the trailing edge instead of having to warp the whole wing, but our current designs are just too heavy,' Mr Parfitt was saying.

The engine-fitter returned with some new tools.

'Jack?' said Mr Parfitt. 'Have you seen Rupert?'

'He was here a little while ago,' said the fitter. 'Said he was going to be here to show off for the visitors, but he wandered off and we a'n't seen him since. We're due to have this'n ready for two, mind, so he'll be back afore then.'

'Ah, well,' said Mr Parfitt. 'Is there anything else you'd like to see?'

'No, I think we've taken up plenty of your time for now, but I'd like to come back. Often. This is a fascinating place and I need to learn a great deal more about aeroplanes if I'm going to buy one.'

'Right you are,' he said. 'Shall we walk back to the office, then? I think we have a sales brochure somewhere, and I can take a look at the diary, see if we can't get you booked in for a flight.'

'That would be delightful, thank you.'

'We've a canteen if you'd care to stay for lunch. It's not Escoffier but it's good hearty scran.'

'That's very kind,' said Lady Hardcastle, 'but I have a luncheon appointment with a friend. Another time, perhaps.'

We set off on the long journey back to the office block.

Chapter Four

After dinner that evening we sat in the garden in the fading light, enjoying the summer warmth.

'We ought to get Hector down to make some of that rum punch of his,' said Lady Hardcastle as she sipped her gin and tonic. 'That's what one needs on a tropical night like this.'

'I can knock you up a jug of rum punch if you want one,' I said. 'One of sour, two of sweet, three of strong and four of weak. It's not alchemy, it's just lime juice, sugar, rum and water.'

'Where on earth do you learn these things?'

'Do you remember that chap from the pub on the London job in '06?'

'Oh, the Barbadian fellow? John Something?'

'Clarke. He taught me. He taught *us*, actually, but you weren't listening.'

'I was watching the door – there were people after us.'

'There are always people after us. Sometimes it's more important to listen to West Indian rum punch recipes.'

'I listened to him when he was talking about the case, but I've always been a duffer when it comes to food and drink. One has staff for that.' She grinned at me and I poked my tongue out.

'Speaking of staff,' she said, 'would you be an absolute poppet and nip up to the attic for the crime board? I need to be able to see all the runners and riders if we're going to make a decent fist of finding Harry's spy. The light's all but gone here so we'd better decamp to the drawing room.'

'Of course. And do you want some rum punch? Miss Jones has limes.'

'No, let's stick to the gin. And perhaps some coffee. No, forget the gin, let's have some brandy with the coffee. Is there one of those chocolate bars? Bournville, is it called? Oh, or Fry's Chocolate Cream? I loved those as a child. Miss Jones has a sweet tooth – she's bound to have some stashed somewhere.'

I laughed. 'I'll see what I can do,' I said.

'I knew I could count on you. Off you pop, then, tiny servant. I'll get into the drawing room and start sketching.'

I put the kettle on for coffee and then set about heaving the blackboard and easel down to the drawing room where she was, as promised, sketching.

'Oh, I say,' she said as I struggled the recalcitrant thing into place, 'that does look heavy.'

'You're welcome to help,' I said. 'Any time. Just jump up, hop over here and lend a hand. There's nothing stopping you but you.'

'You're very kind, dear, but I'm rather enjoying my sketching. What do you think? I've rather captured his likeness, even if I do say so myself.'

It was a pleasingly accurate representation of Bristol Aviation's managing director, Walter Sandling.

'Nice work. We could open a little gallery featuring all the scallywags and ne'er-do-wells we've investigated over the years.'

'Now there's a thought,' she said.

'I'll leave you to plan that while I finish the coffee. There's Bournville, by the way, but I think it's Miss Jones's private stock so you'll have to replace it.'

'We can do that. I'm sure she won't mind. I have a craving.'

I returned a few moments later with the coffee tray and a bar of Cadbury's Bournville chocolate. Lady Hardcastle had discovered its delights on a trip to London – it had only been around for a few years – and hadn't mentioned a burning desire to eat it again, so I hadn't asked Miss Jones to add it to the grocery list. I made a note to mention it in the morning.

In the short time I'd been away, she had begun work on another sketch, this time of Miss Matthews, the receptionist.

'We should start at the top, I think,' she said as she added a little more shading to Miss Matthews's hair. 'So, we have Mr Walter Sandling.'

She passed me the sketch, which I dutifully pinned up. The blackboard was beginning to look a bit the worse for wear. It had come from the London music shop where Lady Hardcastle had bought her piano, and rather than the usual slate, it was made of the new Scandinavian 'plywood' coated with a matt black paint so that it could be written on almost exactly like a blackboard. Lady Hardcastle had initially been tempted by the portability of this cheaper alternative, but it had other advantages, too: it was less likely to crack if dropped and, more importantly for us, would take a pin – very useful for displaying sketches and notes. Sadly, after three years of murders, mysteries and the musings thereon, it was starting to look a trifle shabby.

'Walter Sandling,' I said as I wrote his name in chalk beneath the sketch. 'Managing director. Seems easy-going. Rather good with people.'

'What did you think of, "Everyone calls me Walt"? Does that work? Or does chumminess get in the way? One needs respect for leaders, wouldn't you say?'

'Does one?' I said. 'He can earn his respect by being a good leader, surely. Calling him "Mr Sandling" isn't going to make him a better manager.'

'You're right, of course. I do think it smacks too much of a desperation to be liked, though.'

'Perhaps,' I said. 'But his argument rang true – deference is no use in his line of work if it stifles good ideas.'

'Again, you're right. Over-chumminess notwithstanding, though, I'm not keen on him for the leak. He might sell his company's ideas, but for commercial reasons, not ideological. And I can't see him as someone to be tempted to sacrifice a commercial advantage even if he were the type to betray his country.'

'Blackmail?' I said.

'Always a possibility,' she said. She picked up her pen to make a note in her notebook. 'I'll tell Harry to do some digging. They must vet these people if they're working on projects vital to the national interest. He'll know if there's anything in Just-Call-Me-Walt's personal life that might make him a blackmail target.'

'You'll "tell" Harry?'

'I'll tell him, dear. There's less room for misunderstanding that way. Asking lacks urgency and gives the mistaken impression that compliance with the request might be optional.'

'Fair enough,' I said. 'What about Miss Matthews?'

'Polite, friendly, and engaged to be married to the engineer who died. She might bear a grudge.'

'Enough of a grudge to betray her employer to a foreign power?'

'Her employer was responsible for the death of her betrothed. And there might have been resentment brewing for years – she's not allowed to call him Walt, after all.'

'Good point. We never heard her first name.'

'I'm betting on Mildred. Or Mabel. She looks like an alliterative sort of girl.'

'I'll leave it for now,' I said. 'Who's next?'

'Godfrey "Goff" Parfitt,' she said, handing me the next sketch.

I pinned him up and wrote his name under the picture. 'Senior engineer and motor-racing enthusiast,' I said.

'With a silly name. "Goff"? Who calls themselves "Goff"? Makes it sound like he's off to play nineteen holes at Royal St George's.'

'We met a Geoffrey who went by "Goff" at Goodwood racecourse.'

'The bookie? I remember.'

'No, he was an owner. Fitzroy's Fandango. You lost a fiver betting against her in favour of Emily's Jollity in the third race.'

'Oh. But you can see why I would. And it was a poor choice of hypocorism then, too, if you ask me. Geoffreys are Geoff, not Goff. My objection to its silliness stands.'

'Duly noted,' I said. 'He seemed down to earth.'

'To the point of dullness. Again, not someone I'd suspect of ideological betrayal, and far too mundane a fellow ever to have done anything scandalous.'

'It might just be boring old money,' I said. 'I bet you could make a packet selling secrets to foreign powers if you were on your uppers.'

'You could. It depends on the power, though. Some of them can be quite parsimonious when attempting to purchase information.'

'True. They tend to be the ones who go in for blackmail and thuggery, though. It's a pity we don't know who the agent Harry's men intercepted was working for.'

'It is. Ah, well. I'm sure they'll let us know if they find anything. These engineers and whatnot might have connections to other countries. Here,' she said, handing me a picture of the test pilot. 'This is the last one.'

'Rupert Herbert,' I said.

'Parents can be so cruel.'

'Perhaps that's why he turned out to be—'

'Such an oily tick?'

'Well, yes. There was something about him—'

'That made you want to slap his face?'

'You weren't keen, I take it,' I said.

'Not really, no. From his leering "I say. Visitors" to the way he said "taking her up for a spin", everything about him gave me the creeps.'

'Spy?'

'It would be wonderful, but his sort are always rampant jingoists.'

I wrote 'Lecherous – probably a jingoist' beneath his name.

'We're assuming it's not Adam?' I said.

'I do hope it isn't – I'd hate to be responsible for ruining two marriages for poor Clarissa. He strikes me as being a bit naive so he might have said something by accident if he'd known what was going on, but he's not one of nature's dissemblers and he was adamant he didn't even know what the project was.' She chuckled. 'Adamant. How could he be anything else? I'm happy to ignore him as a suspect.'

'There are dozens more working there,' I said. 'This could take months.'

'Start at the middle and work outwards.'

'You said we should start at the top.'

'I did, didn't I? But in this case I mean start closest to the parachute project. When we've eliminated all of them we can move outwards to fitters and toolmakers and Uncle Tom Cobley and all.'

'Then we need to meet the junior engineer,' I said. 'Paul Curtis.'

'We do. Perhaps you could seek him out while I'm on my test flight tomorrow.'

It had been a source of some disappointment to find that Lady Hardcastle was to be the first of us to get a ride in an aeroplane after having decided our ruse would involve me training as a pilot, but I didn't make a fuss. My time would come.

'I meant to ask you,' I said. 'Have you any idea where they got the name "Dunnock"? I racked my brains trying to remember if there'd been a famous Mr Dunnock in the files – someone associated with the development of flying machines, perhaps. But I came up blank.'

'It's another name for the hedge sparrow,' she said. 'Dumpy little brown bird with a pointy beak.'

'Oh. That's rather unglamorous. I'd have gone for "Osprey" or "Peregrine". Even "Starling" has a bit more about it than Dunnock.'

'I'm sure they have their reasons. Will you be bringing the field glasses so you can watch us as we swoop Dunnock-like about the sky?'

'Actually,' I said, 'I was planning to slip away unnoticed and have a poke round behind the screens at the secret parachute project. We'll be there at lunchtime – it should be deserted.'

'I say, that's a good idea,' she said. 'Well done, you. In that case you do that and I'll try not to be too nauseated by Rupert Herbert.'

'If you are, you can blame it on the flight. He's not to know you're never affected by travel sickness.'

'*Mal de l'air*, one might say.'

'The spirit of Oscar Wilde lives on.'

She bowed.

'We have a plan of sorts, then,' she said. 'Cards or books before bed?'

'I've got a book I'm enjoying if you don't want to lose any more money at cards.'

'Books and brandy, then. My fortune is safe for another night.'

◆　◆　◆

Lady Hardcastle's 'trial flight' had been booked for noon, but we decided to get there early in case it was decided that her old driving clothes weren't going to be adequate for keeping her comfortable aloft. It was another wonderfully warm summer's day, but our experience with hot air balloons had taught us that the air at altitude was much cooler. And she'd be moving at fifty miles an hour, which was sure to add a certain chilliness to the proceedings. If her heavy coat and gauntlets weren't going to be up to the job, she'd need time to change into whatever ill-fitting garb they supplied instead.

I packed my own driving togs as well, in case by some miracle I got a chance to fly. My hopes weren't high but it would be horrible to have even those small hopes dashed for want of a decent overcoat and a pair of boots.

Despite our best intentions, we didn't manage to get away at quite the time we'd intended. We were almost out the door when the telephone rang.

'Chipping-Bevington two-three,' I said. 'Hello.'

'What ho, Strongarm, it's me. How the devil are you?' said Harry's distorted voice.

'Muddling along,' I said. 'You know how it is.'

'Only too well, old thing. How did the visit go yesterday?'

'We've made our presence felt, at least. We had a quick tour of the factory and met a few of the top-billed cast.'

'How's it looking down there?'

Lady Hardcastle was hovering nearby. 'Is that Harry?' she whispered.

'Tell her it is,' said Harry. 'She's got the loudest whisper of any living person.'

She shrugged and whispered, 'Well?'

'It is,' I said. 'And he says your whispering needs work.'

'Tell him to—'

'You tell him,' I said, handing her the telephone earpiece.

She took it.

'Hello, brother dear,' she said. 'How stands the empire? . . . Seems like a well-run establishment so far. Managing director's a bit chummy but there were no obvious candidates . . . Well, quite. I can't remember – is it purely technical stuff that's seeping out to foreign powers? Or a mix? . . . I see. We'll have to pay more attention to the engineers, then . . . That's what we were thinking. Can you look into the financial affairs of the senior engineer, please, dear? . . . His name?'

She clicked her fingers at me. I scowled.

'His name is . . .' she said, and clicked her fingers again.

'Godfrey Parfitt,' I said brusquely, still scowling.

'Did you get that, dear?' she said. 'No, she's fine. She's sulking because I clicked my fingers at her . . . Oh, very well. My apologies, Flo . . . Yes, so would you use the mighty apparatus of the state to find out if there's anything lurking in Parfitt's private life that might make him receptive to a bribe, please? . . . The same for Sandling. And take a look in your vetting files to see if either of them might be blackmailable . . . Well, it's a word now – I just made it up . . . Shakespeare made up words all the time . . . Yes, we're off there now. They're taking me up in a Dunnock and Flo is going snooping in Hangar C.'

She grinned at me but I just shook my head.

'Sorry, dear, I meant Hangar B,' she continued. 'Yes, where the parachute team is working . . . We'll be careful, dear, yes . . . Right you are. We'll be in touch. Toodle-oo.'

She replaced the earpiece on its cradle.

'That saved us a call,' she said. 'Right, are we ready now?'

'We are,' I said, picking up the bag containing our driving togs and Lady Hardcastle's new folding camera.

I had my hand on the front door handle when Edna came scurrying through from the kitchen.

'Beggin' your pardon, m'lady,' she said, 'but Old Jed has arrived with some 'erbs and whatnot in his barrow. He says would you mind 'avin' a look afore he plants 'em out.'

'Of course,' said Lady Hardcastle. 'Sorry about this, Flo. I'll only be a moment.'

She followed Edna out towards the garden and I carried the bag out to the motor car.

◆ ◆ ◆

We parked the Rolls in the same spot as before and strolled in through the main doors. We passed once more through the interior doors and were greeted immediately by Miss Matthews, who stopped what she was doing and came out from behind her desk.

'Hello, my lady,' she said warmly. 'I'm so glad you came back. You're here for a test flight with Rupert, aren't you?'

'I am, dear, yes,' said Lady Hardcastle. 'But why the enthusiasm? Don't your potential customers usually come back?'

Miss Matthews laughed. 'Oh, all the time. But they're stuffy military men or toffs who fancy "a bit of jolly old flyin', what?". We don't get any ladies. And not ladies like you. I kept the newspaper clippings about what you did for that suffragette last year. I didn't realize it was you when you came in yesterday. It's an honour to have you here.'

'Thank you. Our fame precedes us, Armstrong. You're a suffragist, Miss Matthews?'

'Suffragette and proud of it,' she said, and flipped the lapel of her jacket to reveal a WSPU badge pinned on the reverse. 'Mr Sandling won't let me wear it openly, but I keep it hidden and he never notices.'

Lady Hardcastle laughed. 'Good for you, dear. We're still in touch with the Bristol branch.' She turned to me. 'We really should invite Lady Bickle for lunch – we haven't seen her since Easter.'

'I'll remind you later, my lady,' I said.

'Thank you. So, then. Where's this Rupert Herbert fellow?'

'He should be here soon,' said Miss Matthews. 'He's a bit of a law unto himself, but he's usually roughly on time.'

'He deserves a bit of leeway,' said Lady Hardcastle. 'Being saddled with a moniker like Rupert Herbert can't have made the poor chap's life easy.'

'Oh, you don't know the half of it. I see all their personnel files – it's part of my job to keep the records up to date, you see? His full name is Rupert Gilbert Hubert Herbert.'

'Oh, my word,' said Lady Hardcastle. 'The poor chap.'

The front door opened and Mr Herbert swaggered in.

'And here he comes now,' said Lady Hardcastle. 'The man of the hour.'

'Lady Hardcastle,' he said with a bow. 'I'm so sorry to have kept you waiting. I just wanted to make sure everything was in order with the Dunnock before we took you up.'

'Please don't worry,' she said. 'I'd much rather the aeroplane was safe. And actually, we've only just arrived.'

'Thank you. Now, it's going to be a bit nippy up there so we'll need to get you into some warmer togs. We've some spare jackets and whatnot that should fit you.'

'I come prepared,' she said. 'I have a heavy driving coat in the Rolls. Boots, gauntlets, and goggles, too.'

'I say. That's a first. Well done. Chaps usually turn up in a country suit and brogues like they're out for a summer's walk on the moors and look surprised when I tell them they'll freeze to death.'

'We usually wore big bonnets in the old Rover. I assume that'll be no use in an aeroplane.'

'Might not be too comfortable. If you can fit it over your hair, we've a leather cap that'll keep your ears warm, too.'

'I'm sure we can do something with the old barnet, eh, Armstrong?'

'You'll have no problems with a cap if you let it down, my lady,' I said. 'I can put it back up once you're on terra firma and no one will ever have witnessed your chevelural shame.'

'Splendid. Be a poppet and fetch the bag, would you? Then we can get me togged up and airborne.'

I helped Lady Hardcastle change for her adventure in a small side room, then walked across with her and Mr Herbert towards the waiting Dunnock. Engineers and fitters from both hangars were streaming towards us on their way towards the office block which, I presumed from the cooking smells, also housed the canteen. If not deserted, the hangars would certainly be a good deal less busy.

The Dunnock had been brought outdoors and sat on one side of a large, reasonably flat, field. The aeroplane looked much bigger and more substantial out here in the open. There were two men in overalls standing beside it, waiting patiently for us to arrive.

I was once again unbecomingly jealous that Lady Hardcastle was going to get to fly while I loitered on the ground. She, meanwhile, all but bounced her way to the aeroplane, such was her excitement. She hadn't even complained about being hot in her flying clothes and boots.

'I can't tell you how much I'm looking forward to this, Mr Herbert,' she said with a level of glee that bordered alarmingly on 'girlish'. If she had giggled at that moment I shouldn't have been surprised. Dismayed, certainly, but not surprised.

'Then I hope it doesn't disappoint,' he said with what I'm sure he imagined was a winning smile.

The safety briefing took an absolute age, but offered an excellent opportunity for me to photograph Lady Hardcastle beside the aeroplane. My duties as chronicler discharged for the moment, I allowed my mind to drift to matters more germane to my own plans. We were a mere twenty yards from the giant hangars, the doors of both of which were open to roughly the same extent as they had been the day before.

My research had told me that aeroplanes needed to face into the wind for take-off and landing, which seemed somewhat contrary to intuition. Surely, I had reasoned, they needed to be travelling quickly in order to get airborne, and battling against the wind would slow them down. Lady Hardcastle had come to my rescue and explained that it wasn't the aeroplane's speed on the ground that caused it to leap majestically into the skies, but the speed of the air over its wings. Running into the wind was, she said, 'a jolly sensible idea'.

The wind – what little there was of it – was blowing more or less directly towards the hangars, so the Dunnock was facing away from them. This, I thought, was going to be to my advantage. Mr Herbert would be facing away from the hangars and concentrating on not killing Lady Hardcastle by smashing her into the ground in a tangle of wood and canvas. Any guards who happened to be present, human nature being what it is, would be watching the aeroplane. So no one outside the hangars would be looking at them. It being lunchtime, there would be few men left inside, and any who remained would be unlikely to be watching the big doors. All of which, when added together, might very well give me the opportunity to slip in and have a good old nose about.

Finally, they were ready. By climbing a stepladder and edging along a reinforced section of the wing, they clambered into their individual cockpits – Mr Herbert sitting in the front seat with Lady Hardcastle behind him. One of the technicians removed the stepladder and I managed to get another photograph, this time of a grinning Lady Hardcastle in her goggles and leather flying cap, ready for the off.

The other technician reached up to grab the enormous propeller, and on a signal from Mr Herbert gave it an almighty yank to start the engine. With a cough and a splutter, it rattled to life, and I could feel the draught from the propellers on my face as the Dunnock slowly began to roll away. The two technicians had taken position at the wingtips and now began to run alongside the aeroplane as it gathered speed, making sure it didn't topple over. When it was moving too fast for them to keep up, they let go and turned to walk back to the canteen. They'd seen aeroplanes flying before and lunch was far more interesting.

I, on the other hand, was fascinated. I watched eagerly as the flimsy little Dunnock bounced and trundled away from me. Vehicles should be rugged. Carts, wagons, carriages, motor cars, sailing ships, steamships . . . all sturdy things capable of withstanding the capricious whims of nature and fate to protect the precious human cargo within, should anything go awry. This aeroplane was fragile and insubstantial. Made of sticks held together with wire and covered with cloth, it didn't even look as sturdy as the dumpy little hedge sparrow after which it was named.

It suddenly occurred to me that I ought to take another photograph, and I just managed to get the camera to my eye as the bicycle wheels left the ground and the Dunnock struggled into the air. I had imagined something a little more majestic as the aeroplane freed itself from gravity's shackles and leapt exultantly towards the heavens. The reality was less dramatic. It looked as though the aeroplane had been intending to trundle around the field for a bit but had suddenly found itself accidentally airborne and had decided to try to make the best of it.

They climbed slowly away and I turned towards Hangar B and my own little mission.

The patrolling guards had resumed their slow plod round the airfield perimeter and were oblivious to my own more purposeful march towards the open hangar doors. I kept my eyes open for returning engineers as I approached so as to avoid having to look around suspiciously as I entered. Nothing draws unwanted attention quicker than someone endlessly checking that they're unobserved.

My way was clear, and I slipped unobtrusively through the opening, close to the edge of one of the giant doors. Even with the light from the many electric lamps at the work stations, the hangar seemed dark compared with the bright summer's day on the airfield. It took a few moments for my eyes to become accustomed to the gloom, and I was momentarily disorientated as I tried to locate the screened area that housed the parachute project.

There was some sort of electric machinery at work somewhere towards the far distant corner of the hangar, but no other signs of life. I spotted the screens off to my right and was surprised by how tall they were. From the gantry, and in the oddly distorting context of the hangar, they had seemed inadequate to the task of shielding the project from the rest of the room, but actually they were at least an elephant, if not an elephant and a half, tall. I walked quietly but casually towards them, still mindful of the need not to draw attention to myself by behaving like I was trying not to draw attention to myself.

I reached the partition screens and found no way in. From the gantry it had been obvious that there was no ceiling, but I had entirely failed to notice that there were no gaps in the walls. It took me another minute of walking around to find the door. It was locked.

One of my favourite birthday presents from Lady Hardcastle was an ornate silver brooch in the 'Modern Style', depicting swirlingly intertwined roses. I wore it always, partly because it was beautiful, partly because it was a gift from a dear friend, and partly because that dear friend knew me well enough to have specified when commissioning the brooch that it should conceal a pair of picklocks. The door was open in moments.

I'm not sure what I expected to find, but I was definitely disappointed. There were two extremely large tables, each with a sewing machine mounted at one end. The operator could sit on a stool and work the treadle fitted underneath. I presumed the tables were big so that they might hold the silk panels I could see hanging on a rack against the wall. They'd need that space both for cutting the panels and stitching them together.

There were cupboards and cabinets against another wall. A swift search confirmed that they contained tools, supplies and a few files. There were two drawing boards surrounded by all the usual paraphernalia of the draftsman, each holding annotated diagrams of the sort of device we'd seen in Paris and which I knew to be a parachute.

Propped up in the corner of the room was a heavy-looking mannequin. On the floor were three oversized knapsacks with an elaborate arrangement of straps, clasps and buckles. There was a fourth, but whereas the others appeared to be packed and ready for use, this one sat on a jumble of white silk and sturdy-looking cords. There was a note pinned to it that said, 'Failed. Do not use.'

I had found the parachute that had killed the engineer Dickie Dupree. I had found the room where the plans for the parachute were most likely to be stored. And . . . what? Well done, Flo, I thought to myself, you've found the room where they design and make the parachutes and learned that it contains parachutes and designs. Good work.

I was trying to fathom out what to do next when I heard distant voices and the clatter of boots. Lunchtime was over and I had to skedaddle.

I let myself out and headed quickly towards the shadows by the far wall of the hangar. The men were still some way off and it wasn't obvious they were coming my way, but I still needed very much to be elsewhere. Staying in the shadows as much I as could, I made my way to the open doorway and out into the near-blinding sunshine. I blinked to try to clear my vision and checked that the guards were nowhere near, then set off back towards the field.

I was just in time. Barely clearing the roof of the hangars, heading into the wind, was the Dunnock. It descended swiftly, but landed reasonably smoothly, bumping quite some way off across the field before turning and trundling back towards me.

I got another photograph and waited for the excited account of Lady Hardcastle's flying adventure.

Chapter Five

'We flew towards the city,' she said exuberantly. 'Right down over Redland, then Clifton and then . . . then . . .' I thought she might burst. '. . . then we actually went under the Clifton Suspension Bridge. Under it. Carts and bicycles and pedestrians all stopping to look over the railings as we swept up the Avon Gorge beneath them. I've managed to persuade Mr Herbert to take you up. You absolutely have to try it, Flo, dear, you really do.'

'Thank you,' I said with a grin. 'Thank you very much.'

We had left Mr Herbert to talk to the technicians who had arrived shortly after we landed, and had set off back towards the office block.

'How was your own little expedition?' she said.

I quickly explained what I'd seen and done, including my conclusion that it wasn't an especially productive trip.

'No,' she agreed. 'But it's nice to have some context for Harry's shenanigans. If a spy is stealing the secrets of this parachute contraption, it's a good idea to know what's going on with the project itself, don't you think?'

'I suppose so,' I said. 'And now we know that the designs and files aren't locked away. They're in a locked room but a child could break in and take them.'

'A particularly talented and devilish child, perhaps, but I take your point. If nothing else comes of all this we can at least tell Harry they need to step up their security.'

'It might be worth another look – I was interrupted, after all. And if you ever want some silk for an evening gown, I certainly know where I can nick some. It might be worth going back just for that.'

'I'll bear it in mind. What colour is it?'

'White.'

'Oh, that's a shame. I thought we'd agreed I look dreadful in white.'

'You look shocking,' I said. 'But we could have it dyed.'

'It's still probably not quite the done thing to be stealing silk while we're engaged in the service of HM the K. Doesn't look good.'

'I thought you and the king were pals. He invited you to his coronation in June.'

'True, true. I was at his father's coronation as well. And his father's funeral. I say, I do get about, don't I?'

'But you're right – he probably wouldn't take too kindly to you nicking a few yards of silk while on active duty.'

'I thought you were the one doing the nicking?'

'I'm your employee, my lady – I only ever act on your instructions. I'm just an 'umble servant girl doin' as she's told.'

'Hmm,' she said. 'I'm not sure even the most dimwitted and credulous judge would believe that one.'

'Where are we going, by the way?'

'Back to the office. I desperately need to get out of these hot togs, but then I thought we might have a word with Miss Matthews. We can natter under the pretence of being so excited about the aeroplane that I simply have to explore the process of buying one.'

'There won't have to be a great deal of pretending.'

'Oh dear,' she said. 'I thought I'd done such a clever job of hiding my excitement. Does it show?'

'You are, shall we say, a trifle giddy. But don't worry, it's only obvious when you speak. Or hop excitedly from one foot to the other. I'm sure no one would notice.'

She harrumphed.

We entered the office block.

◆ ◆ ◆

'Hello again, Miss Matthews,' said Lady Hardcastle.

'Welcome back, my lady,' said Miss Matthews. 'Please call me Myrtle.'

'Of course, dear. It's all first names round here, isn't it?'

'Not for me. They all call each other by their first names, but I'm always "Miss Matthews".'

'It's probably out of respect,' I said. 'I imagine you and the secretaries are the only women here – there can't be many female aircraft engineers.'

'We've never had any,' she said. 'I don't imagine there are any anywhere. And I'm the only woman here at all. I'm Mr Sandling's secretary, but I work the front desk because the two clerks are . . . well, I mean you wouldn't want to . . . '

'Not the sort of chaps you'd want as the first person clients and customers meet when they walk in the door?' suggested Lady Hardcastle.

Miss Matthews grinned. 'Something like that, yes. How can I help you, though?'

'Actually, we just came in for a sit-down. Mr Herbert will be taking Flo out later and we rather needed somewhere comfortable to put our feet up for a bit. And I very much need to take some of this heavy clobber off – I'm absolutely boiling.'

'You're welcome to wait here,' said Miss Matthews, indicating a few almost comfortable chairs on the other side of the room. 'Can I get you some tea? Oh, no, you're coffee ladies, aren't you?'

'A cup of coffee would be most welcome,' said Lady Hardcastle. 'If it's not too much trouble.'

'It's no trouble at all. I could do with one myself.'

Miss Matthews set off through one of several doors that opened off the reception, while Lady Hardcastle shrugged out of her driving coat and kicked off her heavy boots. We settled ourselves as best we could in a couple of the almost-comfortable chairs.

'Is there anything I need to be aware of before my flight?' I asked.

'No, dear, just relax and enjoy it.'

'Did you get a chance to control the plane?'

'He offered – there are controls in both whatnots . . . cockpits . . . but I declined. I wanted you to have the first go at that.'

I grinned. 'Thank you. How did you manage to talk to each other? Isn't it awfully noisy up there with the engine and the wind?'

'There's a speaking tube like they have in some big houses for yelling at the servants.'

'For making polite requests of the servants,' I said.

'Or for that, yes. Anyway, it makes it easy to talk. You couldn't conduct any sort of complex philosophical discussion, but simple back-and-forth is more than possible.'

'Do you think it's possible to take photographs from up there?'

'It's a bit shaky and wobbly, but it's worth a try.'

I grinned again.

Miss Matthews returned with a tray and set it down on the little coffee table in front of us.

'Would you care to join us?' said Lady Hardcastle. 'It seems a shame for you to have to sit on your own all the way over there when there's company over here.'

'I'm not really supposed to,' she said. 'I should be at my desk to see to visitors.'

'Nonsense, dear. We're visitors – potential customers at that – and you'd be doing the firm an enormous service by acting as our host and promoting your products over a cup of coffee. You must be due a break.'

Miss Matthews looked doubtful, but didn't move away.

'And if anyone says anything,' continued Lady Hardcastle, 'they'll jolly well have me to answer to.'

Miss Matthews smiled and gave in. I didn't blame her. It's always best to give in to Lady Hardcastle – it saves an awful lot of unpleasantness in the long run. I poured three cups of coffee.

'That's the spirit,' said Lady Hardcastle. 'Now, dear, at the risk of weakening my own negotiating position, I have to tell you that I absolutely adored flying around in the Dunnock and I really am terribly keen on the idea of buying one.'

'I can understand that,' said Miss Matthews. 'It's very exciting.'

'Do they let you fly?'

'Yes, Dickie took me up a couple of times. It was wonderful. He was wonderful . . .' Her eyes were glistening.

'I'm so sorry, dear. We heard about your fiancé's accident. A terrible, terrible thing. I didn't mean to—'

'No, no, it's all right,' said Miss Matthews with a sniff. 'It just creeps up on me sometimes. I'll be going about my business and I'll suddenly think of him and then that's me gone – "blubbin' like a babber", as they say.'

'It still catches me from time to time, and I lost my husband thirteen years ago.'

Miss Matthews sniffed. 'I could probably have coped if he'd been ill – if it were expected. But it was all so sudden. He wasn't even supposed to be up in the . . . in the air. They were supposed to be testing the . . . doing the test with a dummy. But they changed their plans at the last minute. He wasn't even supposed to be up there.' She began crying in earnest. 'I'm so sorry.'

I reached across and put my hand on hers. 'Don't worry,' I said. 'We understand. It's a credit to you that you're coping so well. I'm not sure I'd have made it back to work after something like that. Especially not if . . . well, if that was where . . .'

She put her other hand on top of mine and gave me a reassuring squeeze. 'Don't you worry, either,' she said. 'No one knows the right thing to say. I just appreciate having the chance to let it out.'

Lady Hardcastle offered her a handkerchief and she dabbed her eyes. She moved as if to return the handkerchief, but paused for a moment.

With a smile, Lady Hardcastle said, 'It's all right dear, you have a good blow. You can keep the handkerchief – I have plenty.'

Gratefully, Miss Matthews blew her nose and pocketed the hanky.

'This can't be doing much to sell you one of our aeroplanes,' she said with a little smile.

'People are more important than aeroplanes,' said Lady Hardcastle. 'I'd rather take care of a grieving young woman than buy an aeroplane.'

'You're very kind. Thank you.'

'What's it like to work here?' I said.

'It has its moments,' she said with a shrug. 'You know how it is with any job.'

'I'm afraid not,' I said. 'I've been in service since I was thirteen. I've never had a proper job.'

'Good heavens,' she said. 'Then I'd say you've had to work a damn sight harder than I have. But it's fine here, really. The engineers are all very pleasant. Mr Sandling can be a bit demanding, but he's not so bad. Mr Herbert gives me the creeps – I feel like I need a bath after I've spent any time with him. But the rest are all right. Oh, except for—' She looked around to make sure we were still unobserved. 'If you go ahead with the purchase you'll end up needing to speak to Mr Milhouse, our accountant. Watch yourselves there. He's a bit of a goat as well. Fancies himself as a ladies' man, and he's not even as charming as Hubert Herbert Heebert Hawbert.'

We both laughed.

'Other than lecherous accountants and oily pilots, though, you'd say it was a respectable enough firm?' I said.

'Best I've ever worked for,' she confirmed.

'That's good,' said Lady Hardcastle. 'I sometimes wonder—'

We never found out what she wondered. At that moment, the double doors burst open and Rupert Herbert strode into the room.

'Everything's been checked over on the old Dunnock,' he said, 'and we're ready to fly again. Where's my next victim?'

Back in the little side room, we set about restoring Lady Hardcastle's hair to its customary splendour, and then dressing me warmly in my own heavy coat and boots. It took a while, and by the time we re-emerged, Mr Herbert was nowhere to be seen.

'Rupert's gone on ahead,' said Miss Matthews. 'He said you know where the aeroplane is and waltzed off. I told him he was an arrogant, ill-mannered oaf, but not out loud so I don't expect he heard me.'

'We know where we're going,' I said. 'We'll see you later.'

We set off once more towards the field and the waiting Dunnock.

'I have to commend you on your forbearance,' I said, as a bead of perspiration trickled down my forehead and into my eye. 'This really isn't the day to be wearing all this heavy gear, and you barely complained.'

'I know,' she said chirpily. 'That's not like me at all, is it?'

'It really isn't. I'll be glad when I'm up in the cooler air.'

'It does come as something of a relief, yes. Oh, I completely forgot to check – have you got the camera?'

I held it up.

'Good girl,' she said. 'I can't wait to see the photos.'

By the time we reached the Dunnock I had gone beyond a little gentle perspiration and was sweating freely and profusely. Mr Herbert was chatting to the technicians.

'Welcome back, ladies,' he said. 'All set for another jaunt into town and back?'

'Yes, please,' I said.

'Marvellous. You've already heard the safety briefing, haven't you?'

'Oh, yes,' I lied. I hadn't paid even a moment's attention.

'Good-o. Any questions?'

'None,' I said.

'Right, then, let's get you settled aboard and we can see what this old girl can do.'

I mounted the stepladder and clambered into the narrow cockpit where I found myself standing on a canvas seat stretched on a wooden frame. I stepped down and lowered myself into the seat with my legs either side of some sort of control lever. With her being so much taller than I, Lady Hardcastle's shoulders and arms had been well clear of the lip of the cockpit, but I was sitting quite a bit lower. I realized it was going to be difficult to get my arms up to take photos. But that was only part of the problem – I'd also completely forgotten that I'd not be able to look directly downwards because the wing was in the way. Never mind – something would occur to me once we were flying.

The ladder was removed and the technicians took up their places. The mighty engine spluttered to life and I felt the rush of air from the propeller. From the side it had been a strong draught, but here in its direct path, it was a decent blast of wind.

We began to roll. It was bumpy.

We slowly gathered speed and I saw the wings flex as the mysterious controls in front of me moved, apparently of their own volition. I quickly worked out that they were duplicates of the controls Mr Herbert was working in the front of the aeroplane.

We were moving at a fair clip now and I was a little nervous as I anticipated the stomach-dropping lurch of take-off. At least, that's what I imagined it would be like. I had strong memories of playing on swings at the circus and I reasoned that the feelings would probably be the same.

Any second now.

Just a little faster.

Just a tiny bit—

There was a bang from the engine followed by a great plume of black smoke. The engine coughed.

Spluttered.

And died.

We began a wide, slow turn back towards the hangars.

A voice came from the speaking tube in front of me.

'Sorry, miss,' said Mr Herbert's oddly ringing voice. 'Looks like the old girl's had enough for the day. I'll try to roll her back as far as I can, but I'm afraid we'll probably have quite a walk.'

We trundled a small part of the way back, but the Dunnock wasn't designed for freewheeling and we soon slowed to a frustrating stop.

Mr Herbert climbed on to the step on the wing and let himself gingerly down to the ground. I followed. When I reached the edge of the wing he held up his hand to help me down.

'Take my hand, miss, and we'll get you down nice and safe.'

'Thank you,' I said, 'but there's no need. I think it would be less awkward if I did it myself.'

He frowned, but when I still declined to take his hand he stepped reluctantly aside. He couldn't resist a smug grin as I readied myself – watching this idiot woman fall flat on her face would be a great story to tell the lads in the pub. He probably thought me one of those 'insufferable suffragettes'.

I crouched slightly to get clear of the supporting wires and leaped forward on to the grass. I landed cleanly, brushed some loose grass from my skirt and turned to face him.

'Shall we go?' I said.

As we walked back towards the hangars, I took off my heavy coat. It was little cooler carrying it than wearing it, and I soon gave in and just held it by the collar, dragging it along on the dry grass behind me. It would get a little dusty, but that would brush out.

Lady Hardcastle had started towards us when she heard the bang, but once she had seen us safely leaving the aeroplane she had slowed to a dawdle and waited for us to reach her.

'Are you two all right?' she called, once we were within hailing distance.

'I've been happier,' I called back. 'But we're all in one piece.'

We caught up with her and she turned and fell into step with us.

'Here,' she said, 'let me drag that for you.'

She took my coat and we continued our long trudge back to the hangars.

'I think it's back to the drawing board for the engine-wallahs,' said Mr Herbert.

'I'm glad you feel able to be so blasé about it,' said Lady Hardcastle. 'What if you'd been in the air when that had happened?'

He laughed annoyingly. 'Nothing to worry about. Well-designed plane, the Dunnock. Fantastic glide ratio. We'd have sailed gently groundwards and landed in a convenient field. Or a park if we were in town. Perhaps the Downs. I do love to land there – the gels all swarm round like bees to a flower.'

Lady Hardcastle and I exchanged looks of disgust, but said nothing about it being more like flies and what they might be attracted to.

'Well I, for one, am relieved it happened on the ground,' she said. 'I shall be thinking long and hard about whether to proceed with the purchase now.'

'Oh,' he said disappointedly, seemingly aware for the first time that there might be commercial consequences to this little engineering mishap. 'Don't let a little thing like that put you off. These engines have been terribly reliable until now. It's an aberration. An anomaly.'

'We shall see,' said Lady Hardcastle.

He looked as though he might speak but opted – sensibly, I thought – to remain silent.

A little further along, Lady Hardcastle said, 'Thank you for today, Mr Herbert. We shall leave you here and make our way back to the office. I'm sure you and the engineers have much to say to each other.'

'It was my pleasure, my lady,' he said. 'And I'm sorry again that things didn't work out so well for us, Miss Armstrong.'

I nodded my acknowledgement and followed Lady Hardcastle, who had already turned away.

'I can't believe he was so casual about it,' she fumed.

'It was only a bang and a bit of acrid smoke,' I said. 'I'd be quite casual about it. I *am* quite casual about it.'

'But you could have been killed.' She was really rather agitated.

'He's an oily tick, but he'd have got us down safely. You heard what he said about the aeroplane.'

'I did. "Fantastic glide ratio", my eye! I'll give him a fantastic glide ratio.'

I laughed. 'What are we going to do now?'

'After we've killed Rupert Herbert and left his body in a ditch?'

'No, instead of killing Mr Herbert. It's not his fault and we've got work to do.'

She harrumphed. 'Very well,' she said. 'But he's on notice. If he endangers my tiny servant again he'll wake up on a mortuary slab with important bits missing. And if he's glib about it as well . . . I mean, really. "Sailed gently down". The man's an absolute excrescence.'

'He is, but we have other fish to fry. What say we exploit this little mishap to press Mr Sandling on the safety features of his aeroplanes? He might use it as an opportunity to flog us some of his new parachutes. And then we can ask him about what happened to Dickie Dupree.'

'That's thinking like a member of the SSB,' she said. 'You see now why I couldn't do without you?'

'There are so many reasons why you couldn't do without me. Let's try to make ourselves look presentable and see if we can sweet-talk Myrtle Matthews into getting us some time with Mr Sandling.'

'Good idea,' she said. 'Follow my lead.'

'Oh,' said Miss Matthews as we entered reception for the third time that day. 'You're back early. Is everything all right?'

'I should jolly well say it isn't,' said Lady Hardcastle. 'Just as they—'

'There was a little engine trouble,' I interrupted. 'Nothing too serious, I don't suppose, but it meant that we couldn't get airborne.'

'That's a terrible shame. But no one was hurt?'

'More by good fortune than good judgement—' began Lady Hardcastle.

I interrupted again. 'No, we're both fine,' I said. 'We left Mr Herbert to discuss it with the technicians. It is slightly concerning, though. We were wondering if we might speak to Mr Sandling. He might be able to allay Lady Hardcastle's fears.'

'I'm sure he'd be very keen to do that. He has someone with him at the moment but I'll see what I can arrange.'

'Thank you,' I said. 'Do you mind if I use that little side room again? I need to get out of these boots and into something a little more dainty.'

Lady Hardcastle snorted.

'Oh, "pish and fiddlesticks",' I said. 'I can be dainty.'

I left Miss Matthews to her work, and Lady Hardcastle to her exaggeratedly affected harrumphing while I disappeared back into the makeshift changing room.

I re-emerged a few minutes later, reshod and with everything brushed and straightened. Lady Hardcastle was sitting in one of the almost-comfortable chairs reading the *Bristol News* and Miss Matthews was busy typing in the corner of the room behind her reception desk.

Lady Hardcastle looked up from her newspaper.

'Well,' she said, 'don't you look dainty? Come and join me – there's a copy of the *Western Daily Press* and *The Times* here if you want them. I'm afraid I declined the offer of more coffee, but I'm sure Myrtle would be only too happy to oblige if you want one.'

'I think I've had enough for a while,' I said. 'I'm hungry more than thirsty, to be honest.'

'Me, too. We should have brought sandwiches.'

'We should. Or I should have come down to the canteen for pie and mash instead of . . . instead of waiting for you.'

Obviously we could be overheard.

'I can have them send some sandwiches through if you'd like,' said Miss Matthews from the other side of the room. 'It's no trouble.'

'Thank you, dear,' said Lady Hardcastle, 'but knowing our luck Mr Sandling will be free the moment we tuck into our butties.'

'Your what?'

'Butties. Sandwiches. Northern word. I rather like it.'

'I've never heard that before. But the offer's open if you change your minds.'

'Thank you.'

The telephone on her other desk jingled shrilly.

'Hello, Mr Sandling,' she said. 'Yes, they're here with me now . . . Of course, sir.'

She replaced the earpiece. 'Mr Sandling is free now if you want to go up,' she said. 'Do you remember the way or would you like me to come with you?'

'I think we can find it,' said Lady Hardcastle. 'Thank you very much for looking after us.'

We set off for the stairs and the managing director's office.

'Lady Hardcastle,' said Mr Sandling as we entered. 'I'm so sorry things haven't worked out well for you this afternoon.'

'Thank you, Mr Sandling,' she said, 'but I think you ought to be apologizing to Miss Armstrong. She was the one whose flight was curtailed. She was the one who could have been killed.'

'Well, now. Really. I think—'

'What would have happened if the engine had exploded while she was in the air?'

'It hardly exploded, my lady.'

'You might recall that we have some experience of exploding engines, Mr Sandling. I know an exploding engine when I can hear one from three hundred yards away.'

'A slight technical malfunction, I can assure you. Please, do sit down, both of you. Miss Armstrong, you have my sincerest apologies for any distress we might have caused you.'

We sat.

'Let's have a cup of coffee and see if I can't address your concerns,' he said. He picked up his telephone earpiece and asked Miss Matthews for a pot of coffee.

'I think I made it clear, Mr Sandling, that I'm very seriously thinking about buying an aeroplane. I've dreamt of flight since . . . well, for as long as I can remember. And this has come as a bit of a blow, I must say. I expected some degree of risk, but I really hadn't anticipated the possibility of such . . . such catastrophic failure. I should have, of course, given our own recent experiences with engines, but this has brought home the very real dangers involved.'

'I understand,' he said, nodding sympathetically. 'But I can assure you—'

'Can you, Mr Sandling?' she interrupted. 'Can you really assure me? Of what, precisely? I don't mean to labour the point, but you *can't* assure me it won't happen again. What happens when such a failure occurs hundreds of feet in the air?'

'Well,' he began, 'the Dunnock has an excellent glide ratio. It's—'

'So Mr Herbert tried to explain. But it's not going to stay in the air indefinitely without locomotive power, now, is it? What can you tell me to set my mind at ease?'

Mr Sandling paused for a moment in thought. He was about to speak when there was a knock at the door and Miss Matthews came in with the coffee tray.

'Here's the coffee, sir,' she said. 'The ladies missed their lunch, so I had the canteen send over some sandwiches. They're only ham and tomato, I'm afraid. It's all they had.'

'Oh, that's lovely of you, dear,' said Lady Hardcastle. 'Thank you.'

'Yes, thank you,' I said.

'I brought enough for you, Mr Sandling,' said Miss Matthews. 'There's no need to look so sad.'

She bustled about with the tray for a little while, making sure we all had everything we needed. Mr Sandling waited until she had gone before he spoke again.

'There is something,' he said at last. 'We're working on . . . well, I'm not really supposed to say, but . . . I can rely on your discretion?'

'Of course,' said Lady Hardcastle. 'Discretion would be my middle name were not the space between my Christian name and surname already so cluttered.'

He smiled. 'Of course,' he said. 'Of course. Have you ever heard the word "parachute"?'

'I have,' she said with a smile of her own. 'We saw one demonstrated a number of years ago in . . . Paris, wasn't it, Armstrong?'

It was my turn to smile as she acknowledged that it had been me who had corrected her before.

'Paris, my lady,' I said. 'A gentleman jumped from a hot air balloon and landed safely.'

'Quite, quite,' said Mr Sandling. 'We've been developing something a little more usable. We have a design that an aeroplane pilot can wear in a knapsack so that if he – or she – should get into difficulties he can leap from the stricken aircraft and float safely to the ground.'

'Good heavens,' said Lady Hardcastle. 'How remarkable. Isn't that remarkable, Armstrong?'

'Quite remarkable, yes,' I said.

'The thing is, though, we've hit something of a snag. The reason I didn't want to say anything while Miss Matthews was in the room was that it was a failed parachute that killed poor Dickie Dupree. Split right open. We really haven't fathomed why.'

'What's it made from, this parachute?' said Lady Hardcastle. 'Sailcloth?'

'Good heavens, no – canvas is far too heavy. Good and strong, of course, but a canopy large enough to arrest the descent of a fully grown man would weigh more than the man. No, we use silk.'

'Silk is very strong, too, as I recall. Did it rip?'

'No. Unaccountably, one of the seams failed. We've never known anything like it. We stitch the gores together—'

'I'm so sorry,' interrupted Lady Hardcastle. 'The what?'

'The gores. The panels of the parachute.'

'Ah, of course. My apologies. Do continue.'

'It's my fault – one gets so used to the jargon of one's own specialism that one forgets others might not be so familiar with it. It's a dressmaking term, I believe?'

I nodded. 'The triangular panels of skirts are called gores,' I said.

'Is that so? Well, I've learned something new today, too. We stitch the gores – the panels – with a top-stitched felled seam. Are you familiar . . . ?'

'I'm sure Armstrong can explain later,' said Lady Hardcastle. 'It's a good strong join, though, I presume.'

'Extremely reliable. Usually. But this one failed in the middle somehow, and the whole thing unravelled. We're not sure if it was weak thread, or a mistake in the stitching process. Everything was thoroughly checked once it had been made, though, so we're all somewhat baffled. But when we've completed our investigations, we're confident that the parachute will be a viable safety device for use by aeroplane pilots.'

'I see. Well, that does put a slightly different complexion on things. But only slight. So far we have a failing engine and a failing parachute. All we need is for there to be something wrong with the aeroplane itself and we'll have the complete set.'

'I can assure you, my lady, that—'

'Of course you can,' she said. 'I should expect nothing less than earnest assurances from anyone keen to relieve me of my money in return for their wares. But the truth is I shall need more than that. It's Friday today so I shall take the weekend to think it over. Perhaps we can arrange to meet again next week? I should like a chance to talk to your accountant about the financial side of things. And perhaps your engineers might be able to shed a little light on matters technical by then. Shall we say Wednesday at eleven?'

Mr Sandling reached for a pen and made a note on a pad at the side of his desk. 'I shall ask Miss Matthews to put it into the diary for Wednesday, my lady,' he said. 'I'm sure we'll be able to work something out.'

'I'm sure we shall,' she said. 'And if you can . . . assure us of her safety, I should very much like it if Miss Armstrong were able to gain some experience aloft. If I'm going to buy one of these things, I'll need my pilot to be comfortable.'

'Of course. We can make the arrangements when everything has been checked.'

'Thank you, Mr Sandling. You've almost set my mind at rest. We shall leave you to your work.'

'Think nothing of it, my lady. And thank you for your patience. I can assu— I'm certain all will be well.'

We all stood, and they shook hands.

'Oh,' he said. 'You didn't get a chance to eat your sandwiches. Would you like me to ask Miss Matthews to get some greaseproof paper from the canteen and wrap them for you?'

'You're very kind,' she said. 'But we'll not be able to eat them on the road. We'll have to have an extra-large dinner to make up for it. Good day, Mr Sandling. Have a pleasant weekend and we'll see you again on Wednesday.'

We said our goodbyes to Miss Matthews in reception and settled ourselves in the Rolls for the journey home.

Chapter Six

'You were laying it on a bit thick back there,' I said as we purred up the Gloucester Road towards home.

'Laying what on, dear?' said Lady Hardcastle.

'The anger and indignation.'

'I wasn't putting it on. They endangered your life. I was furious. I still am.'

'Oh,' I said. 'That's very sweet but I was still worried you might have overdone it a bit. You went from charmingly eccentric prospective customer to fierce harridan in the blink of an eye. The poor chap didn't know what had hit him.'

She laughed. 'True,' she said. 'But he did give up the goods about the parachute project.'

'I'll grant you that, but he didn't tell us anything we didn't already know.'

'Did he not? We know now that the company is struggling financially. Why else would he have put up with all my nonsense? I'd have sent me out with a flea in my ear if I were he.'

'I thought he was going to,' I said. 'It was hard to keep a straight face while you were rattling on about catastrophic failures and exploding engines.'

'We also,' she ploughed on, 'learned that it was a failed seam on the parachute that did for poor Mr Dupree.'

'Did we not know that already?'

'It wasn't in the official report, nor in any of the confidential supplementary bumf Harry sent over. All anyone's been told so far is that the parachute tore open. But a failed seam gives a stronger hint at it being deliberate.'

'Which is what Harry said they were concerned about.'

'Just so. It's hardly proof, but it certainly doesn't rule it out.'

'Then I take it back,' I said. 'Your "Angry Toff" routine worked wonders. Well done, you.'

'I keep telling you, dear: it wasn't an act. I was livid. Taking you out in an unsafe aeroplane with an exploding engine. Even though they failed in their obvious attempt to kill you, they still spoiled your afternoon. I so wanted you to see the city from the air. It's quite beautiful.'

I laughed. 'It was hardly an attempt to—'

'It was shambolic negligence of the first water. They might as well have taken pot shots at you with an army .303.'

I was still laughing. 'You can be an old ninny sometimes,' I said. 'Changing the subject, though: what happens to the aeroplane?'

'When?' she asked.

'After the pilot has jumped out with her parachute. What happens to the aeroplane?'

'I rather suppose it crashes.'

'I see,' I said.

'Better to lose an aeroplane than a pilot.'

'Unless it crashes into someone.'

'Unless that happens, yes. Or it smashes into a building, causing hundreds of pounds' worth of damage.'

'Risky proposition all round, then,' I said. 'Not something to be entered into lightly.'

'We probably ought to take out some sort of insurance.'

'We probably ought. Do we have any plans for the weekend other than our trip to The Grange tomorrow?'

'I'm not at all sure we'll have time for anything else. I was hoping to get a chance to pop into town to look for some new garden furniture, but that shall probably have to wait. I need to find a spangly leotard, too.'

'A reinforced spangly leotard.'

'I'm beginning to think I'd have been less bothered by your demise than I previously imagined.'

'In a tangle of snapped wires, broken spars and torn canvas,' I said.

'Exactly like that. I might nobble the aeroplane the next time you go up.'

'It's one way of getting rid of me. Probably the only way.'

We turned off the main road and wound our way through the lanes towards the village. The sun was shining, unidentified birds were singing. And there was chaos on the village green.

There were cows. On the village green. This, as has been well documented already, is one of my worst nightmares. I have no idea where my distrust of our bovine friends came from, but they give me the willies. And they were on the green. Loose.

'There are cows on the green,' I said.

'More amusing than that, dear, there are men chasing them.'

'I saw that. But the men don't bother me nearly so much as the stupid cows.'

'I wonder what happened,' she mused.

'I'd offer to stop and find out, but I'm really not fantastically keen on the idea of sitting in a stationary motor car while there are killer cattle on the loose.'

She laughed. 'Killer cattle,' she said. 'You are funny. Look, there's Daisy. Pull over and let's ask her what's going on.'

Reluctantly, I did as I was bidden.

'Hello, Lady Hardcastle,' said Daisy, as we drew to a halt. She grinned. 'All right, Flo? How's it goin'? There's cows on the green, look.'

'So I see,' I said. 'What happened?'

'Old Toby Thompson was drivin' some new cows back up from Chippin' – market day yesterday, see? – and they come over all excited when they saw the fresh grass.'

'A veritable feast,' I said.

'Too right. They been on the road since mornin' – must have been starvin', poor things. So, anyway, they trampled over there. Then Arthur Tressle comes out of the pub and sees 'em. And he goes mad, shoutin' and wavin' his arms tryin' to get 'em off the wicket. But o' course, that just makes 'em trample about more. Then Jag Bland is walkin' by with her stupid big old dog and 'e thinks it's a great game and goes chasin' after Arthur and the cows. The vicar tries to help his wife control the dog, but neither of 'em can get near 'im on account of how 'e don't want to stop the game and anyway there's always cows in the way. Toby, meanwhile, just give up and come in the Dog and Duck for a swift one.'

I could see Arthur Tressle, bent double and trying to catch his breath. Hamlet, the vicar's wife's irrepressible Great Dane, was still bounding gleefully about, exhorting the cows to join in the game with his huge bellowing bark. The cows were ignoring them both and had resumed their purposeful consumption of the outfield.

Arthur was striding angrily towards the pub.

'Here comes trouble,' said Daisy. 'Old Toby's gonna get an earful now.'

Before the cricket captain was halfway across the green, though, Toby Thompson emerged from the Dog and Duck, wiping his lips with the back of his hand. He gave a shrill whistle and the cows looked up from their meal. One, clearly the leader of this sinister cadre of cattle, took a step towards him. She lowed commandingly and the others fell into step behind her.

They were on the move, and they were coming our way.

'Well, then,' I said breezily. 'We'd better be off.'

I reached for the brake but Lady Hardcastle stayed my hand. 'Not just yet, dear,' she said. 'Don't you want to see what happens?'

'Not enough to sit here and be trampled to death by killer kine,' I said. 'No.'

'Oh, who's being a ninny now? They won't come near us.'

To my intense relief she was right; they didn't. Toby began to drive them off in the direction of the lane that led, eventually, to his farm.

'There,' said Lady Hardcastle. 'Perfectly safe, and now you have an entertaining tale of English country life to share with our American friends.'

'I'm sure Eleanora will be thrilled,' I said. 'Can we go now?'

'Of course, dear. Cheerio, Daisy. We might pop in later for a swift one ourselves.'

'I look forward to it, m'lady,' said Daisy.

I drove off.

As we rounded the green, though, it appeared that all was not proceeding entirely according to Toby Thompson's plan. Arthur Tressle, in the company of Hamlet the Great Dane, with the Reverend Bland and his wife still some way behind, had caught up with Toby and was remonstrating with him about the damage done to the hallowed cricket pitch so close to such an important match against local rivals from the village of Woodworthy.

The lead cow, sensing that her overseer was otherwise engaged, decided to test her autonomy by leading the small herd towards our own lane.

'Oh,' said Lady Hardcastle, 'that's not good. If they start wandering up there we'll never get home. Speed up and cut them off.'

'I beg your pardon?' I said. 'Put ourselves deliberately in harm's way?'

'They'll be frightened of the motor car – they won't come near us. And we'll be doing Toby a favour. Come on now, quick sticks.'

Once more I reluctantly did as I had been asked and hastened the tiny, fragile motor car into the path of the oncoming wall of beefy death.

The lead cow looked us calmly up and down and altered her course to lead her henchwomen off towards the lane that led to the Thompson farm. I could see the evil in her big brown eyes but held my nerve and waited with the engine running and my foot hovering above the accelerator until the last of her followers had passed.

'There,' said Lady Hardcastle. 'That's our good deed for the day. And you have an even better tale to tell Ellie – we were like Wild West cowgirls, but in a Silver Ghost instead of on horseback. Come on, let's get back and find something to eat – I'm famished.'

Still shaking slightly, I drove up the lane and parked the Rolls in front of our little garage.

◆　◆　◆

While I pottered about in the kitchen assembling an early dinner of salad, cold meats, and a couple of slices of my own famous ham pie, Lady Hardcastle busied herself with the crime board. Everything was almost ready when she arrived at the kitchen door.

'Any chance of a hard-boiled egg?' she said. 'And perhaps some boiled new potatoes? And could you whip up some mayonnaise? I have a hankering for mayonnaise.'

I indicated two pans on the stove. 'Eggs and spuds,' I said. 'And there's some fresh mayonnaise in that bowl there.'

'You're an absolute marvel. What are you?'

'I'm an absolute blimmin' marvel,' I said. 'If you can lend a hand carrying things out, we can eat in the garden again. Make sure we get some use out of the old furniture before it gets turned into bird boxes and magazine racks or whatever it is Jed has in mind.'

'What? Fetching and carrying in my own home? Whatever will my friends say?'

'They'll say what a kind, helpful, thoughtful woman you are. And then bar you from polite society. But give me a hand anyway – it'll be quicker. I've only got little legs.'

We carried the plates and bowls to the garden table and I returned for the potatoes and boiled eggs. Lady Hardcastle, meanwhile, retrieved a bottle of the Chablis her vintner had insisted she try, and uncorked it.

'What did your musings amount to this evening?' I asked as we helped ourselves to food.

'I revised Myrtle Matthews's entry on the board. She's very upset about the death of her poor fiancé and we've seen that sort of grief turn to spiteful revenge more than once. If she holds her employers responsible for his death, she might want to ruin them by selling their secrets. She might balk at being a traitor, but if they made out she was aiding a competitor, she might very well take the offer.'

'Sounds reasonable. And if your observations about the company's financial difficulties turn out to be true, perhaps they're having trouble paying her. She might just need the money.'

'Also reasonable,' she said. 'It's another thing Harry can check for us.'

'It's odd that a company like that should be struggling. They're making something novel and exciting, and the government is interested in their products. I'd have thought they'd be rolling in cash.'

'Hmm. Me, too, when you put it like that.'

'I'd like to take a good look at that parachute,' I said. 'That failed seam sounds extremely odd.'

'A topside fouled—'

'Top-stitched felled seam,' I said with a sigh.

She grinned.

I held up both hands with my fingers curled towards the palms, then hooked them together.

'Like that,' I said. 'Then two rows of stitching lock the whole lot together and the cut edges are tucked away inside the seam. It's neat, and very strong.'

'Unusual for such a seam to spontaneously spill open, would you say?'

'Most unusual. As Mr Sandling said, it would have to be down to weak thread or a mistake in the stitching.'

'The silk could tear on either side of the seam.'

'It could, but he was very specific about it being the seam itself that came apart. He might not be terribly familiar with the seamstress's arcane arts, but I'd wager he knows the difference between a rip and a burst seam.'

'He knew enough to know it was a terpsichorean foetid—'

'You're just being silly now,' I said.

'It's part of my charm. But he knew the name of the process, so you're right – he almost certainly understood the nature of its failure.'

'But if the company does turn out to have financial troubles, does that make it more or less likely that Mr Sandling is selling its secrets?'

She thought for a moment. 'Actually, I don't know,' she said at length. 'On the one hand, an injection of cash might keep the wolf from the door. On the other, selling a potential golden-egg-laying goose for less than the full market value isn't the shrewdest of moves.'

'Unless he knew the project was doomed. Better to get a few quid for a duff idea than keep throwing good money after bad trying to get it to work.'

She paused again and I wondered if she might be composing a profound observation. Instead, she said, 'Is that the telephone?'

I listened. It was.

'Who can be calling at' – she looked at her watch – 'half past six on a Friday evening?'

'Only one way to find out,' I said, standing up. 'You coming? It's almost certainly for you.'

◆ ◆ ◆

It was for both of us, as it turned out.

'What ho, Strongarm,' said Harry's familiarly distorted voice. 'It's only me.'

'Who is it?' whispered Lady Hardcastle.

I took the earpiece away from my ear and held it so that we could both hear Harry laughing.

'Whispering skills not improved since this morning, then,' he said.

Lady Hardcastle harrumphed. 'Hello, dear,' she said. 'How lovely of you to call.'

'Just checking up on my two favourite field officers,' he said. 'How did today go?'

Between us, we quickly recounted the events of the day, including our speculation that Bristol Aviation might not be in robust financial health.

'I say, good work. Shame about missing your flight, though, Flo.'

'It always works out that way for me,' I said. 'I've given up being bothered by it.'

'Oh, that's right. You missed out on your drive at Fishy's place, too. I remember now.'

'We both did,' said Lady Hardcastle.

'Ah, yes, of course. The ladies' race was scrubbed, wasn't it? Dashed bad luck.'

'Ah, well,' I said. 'Such is the lot of an 'umble servant girl.'

'Quite, quite,' he said. 'You're a poor, hard-done-by old thing. But I have news that might cheer you. Or temporarily distract you from your crushing disappointment, at least. I've had some of the chaps here looking into the financial affairs of the senior chaps at Bristol Aviation. It seems your man Godfrey Parfitt, the engineer, was quite impressively overdrawn at the bank until recently, but then his debt disappeared in one fell swoop when he paid the whole lot off. In cash. He's definitely one to watch.'

'It could be anything,' said Lady Hardcastle. 'But a pay-off from a foreign agent would certainly fit the bill. We'll do a little digging of our own.'

'Thank you. Now, it happens that your instincts about the company itself were dead right. We'd already started looking into them and despite what they've been telling the War Office, all is not entirely well. Their accounts show a healthy turnover but when we put some pressure on their bankers we learned that their cash reserves are low. They're living pretty much from hand to mouth, as far as we can make out. The order books are less full than one might hope, too. I imagine a couple of recent setbacks – including the parachute disaster – haven't helped on either score.'

'Well, that opens up a dismaying cornucopia of possibilities,' she said. 'Senior men could be taking bribes to plough the money into the company to try to save it. They could be lining their own pockets before the whole thing goes under. Junior men could be doing the same. Competitors or foreign powers could be undermining the projects to hasten the company's demise.'

'All of that and more, sis. All of that and more. Did you say you were going to speak to the company accountant next week?'

'We are, yes. Wednesday. I say, no one has told us his name.'

'Miss Matthews mentioned him,' I said. 'Mr Milhouse. She told us to watch out for him.'

'You're right, dear. Of course she did. My mistake.'

'You're to watch out for him?' said Harry.

'A bit of an old goat, apparently,' I said. 'Fancies himself as God's gift to the fairer sex, or so Myrtle Matthews told us.'

Harry laughed. 'I wouldn't back him in a fist fight if he should chance to offend either of you two,' he said.

'Do you still have your Special Branch bully-boys on the payroll for removing dead bodies?' asked Lady Hardcastle. 'We might need them.'

'Do try not to kill anyone, sis. Unless you absolutely have to. But the reason I asked was that our finance-wallahs are a little confused by the company accounts. There appear to be some . . . I want to say holes, but it's not quite as straightforward as that. In fact, there's nothing straightforward about the bookkeeping at all. The brains here tried to explain it all to me, but I got the sneaking suspicion that they didn't understand it, either. Anyway, the gist is that there's something fishy about the accounts and they would dearly like to know more.'

'And if your highly trained accountants can't fathom it out,' said Lady Hardcastle, 'how do you imagine we'll be able to make sense of it?'

'I don't know . . . Maybe there's another set of books or something. Just do your best.'

'Do our best, indeed,' she said, shaking her head. 'Are you listening to this, Flo?'

'We'll see what we can see,' I said. 'Don't worry, Mr Feather-stone-huff.'

'Good show. Knew I could count on you. Got anything else for me?'

'No, dear,' said Lady Hardcastle. 'I think that's everything. Are you still at the office?'

'Just packing up to leave now,' he said. 'It's been one of those weeks.'

'We shall leave you to hasten home to your family, then. Give our love to Lavinia and Addie.'

'Will do,' he said. 'Have a splendid weekend.'

We hung up and returned to the garden where we finished our meal.

'I think it's time for a cider at the pub,' said Lady Hardcastle as she polished off the last hard-boiled egg.

'I'll get this lot tidied away and we can stroll into the village,' I said.

'I'll help. Many hands spoil the gift horse's broth, as they say.'

'Do they? Do they really say that? Oh, don't just chuck your eggshell on the grass.'

She grinned as she picked it up. 'You can't take me anywhere.'

'Just put it on this plate here. You can bring the glasses and the wine.'

In no time at all, we were ready to amble back down the lane to the village.

◆ ◆ ◆

By the time we got to the pub, cricket captain Arthur Tressle had rounded up as many members of the team as he could find and they were doing their best to repair the bovine damage to their beloved pitch. The rest of the village, backed up by local farmers and their labourers, were standing outside the pub with their drinks, watching.

'Come on, lads,' shouted one young farmhand. 'Put your backs into it.'

'Yeah, get a moo-ve on,' shouted his friend.

A few choice replies drifted back from the pitch, but the team laboured slowly on regardless. Divots were replaced and smoothed while the many, many cowpats were shovelled up as best as could be managed and dolloped into a wheelbarrow. Two men were slowly hauling a massive roller up and down the wicket under Arthur's agitated direction.

'It's almost as entertaining as a match,' said Lady Hardcastle. 'I wonder if we could introduce "competitive gardening" as a sport at the Olympic Games next year.'

'Groundskeeping, surely,' I said. 'These are manly men maintaining a sporting arena, not tending their delicate begonias.'

'You're quite right,' she said.

'Davey Bishop can maintain my sportin' arena any time,' said a nearby young lady.

'It needs a lot of maintainin', from what I've heard,' said her friend. 'Gets a lot of visitors, don't it?'

'Ladies, please!' said a plump farmer's wife.

I suppressed a chuckle and nodded towards the pub door. 'Pint of cider?' I said.

'Rather,' said Lady Hardcastle.

'Well, really!' said the older lady as she bustled off. 'No wonder the young 'uns is so ill-behaved if that's the example you're settin'.'

I found Daisy deep in conversation with her mother at the bar.

'Evening, Mrs Spratt,' I said. 'Daisy.'

'Hello, dear,' said Daisy's mother. 'Daisy was just tellin' me about your cattle-drovin' expertise. You could rent yourself and that motor car of yours to some of the blokes round here – keep them herds in order, you would.'

'I'd rather face a gang of armed men than a herd of cows, Mrs S,' I said. 'Terrifying creatures.'

She laughed. 'I'd best get out to Fred afore 'e says sommat as 'e shouldn't,' she said. 'Last I saw he was bein' taken to task by old Maggie Newton about some scrag end 'e sent her for the doctor's dinner. He's a lovely bloke but 'e don't take too kindly to criticism of 'is scrag end.'

'No man would,' I said.

She laughed again. 'You're a caution, you are,' she said. She picked up two drinks from the bar. 'Put these on the slate, Daisy love. We'll see Old Joe right at the end of the week.'

'It's the end of the week now, Ma,' said Daisy. 'I can't keep—'

'Thanks, love,' said Mrs Spratt over her shoulder as she headed for the door.

'She'll be the death of me,' said Daisy, exasperatedly.

'Is the butcher's shop struggling?' I asked.

'Is it, heck?' she said. 'They're rakin' it in. She just likes hangin' on to her money. She'll settle up eventually, but she'll leave it as long as she can.'

'Can't say I blame her,' I said. 'And it's not like Joe's business is in the doldrums. Look at the place.'

'I know. I've been rushed off me feet.'

'Get us a couple of pints of cider and take a break,' I said. 'Tell you what, get yourself one while you're at it and come outside with us. You can have a chat with me and herself. She's dying to tell someone about her adventures – you're just the audience she needs.'

'Can't she tell you?'

'Oh, she has,' I said. 'She definitely has.'

She laughed.

'Joe?' she called to the toothless landlord. 'I'm nippin' outside with Flo for a breather.'

'Right you are,' he said. 'And tell your ma to settle 'er slate while you's out there.'

Daisy poured three drinks from one of the huge barrels behind the bar and we took them outside.

We found Lady Hardcastle sitting on the grass with the vicar and his wife.

'Come and join us,' she said. 'We were just discussing the forthcoming village show.'

Daisy and I put the drinks on the ground and sat down.

'Are you sure I can't tempt you to another?' said Lady Hardcastle. 'My treat.'

'Oh, but the ladies have only just sat down,' said Mrs Bland. 'James – you go. I'll have a . . . Actually, I'll have what they're having.'

'Ciders all round, then,' said the vicar as he struggled to his feet.

'Emily tells us you don't know what to do for the show,' Mrs Bland said, turning to me.

'Well, I—'

'I thought we was doin' a comic turn with animal noises,' said Daisy, sounding slightly disappointed.

'Well, I—'

'Oh, you should,' said Mrs Bland. 'That would be most amusing, I'm sure.'

'What will you be doing?' I asked, keen to shift the conversation in any direction other than me and my animal impressions.

'I'm afraid the only skill I possess is playing the piano. And everyone will be doing that. I should have loved to play the sitar, but my father wouldn't allow his daughters to learn.'

'What's one o' they?' said Daisy.

'It is a stringed instrument,' said Mrs Bland. 'It has a beautiful and haunting sound if played well.'

'Imagine an Indian banjo, Daisy,' I said. 'Only much, much more impressive, and unbelievably difficult to play.'

'You have heard the sitar?' said Mrs Bland.

'Oh, yes. And the little hand drums?'

'Tabla.'

'Thank you. We spent some time in Calcutta and we attended a couple of recitals.'

'Oh, how wonderful. When were you there?'

'We arrived . . . must be ten years ago, now. We were there a couple of years.'

'Is it really?' said Lady Hardcastle. 'Ten years? Well I never. Doesn't time fly?'

'Talking of which,' I said.

'Of what, dear?'

'Of flying,' I said. 'You're dying to tell them.'

She grinned. 'Let's wait for the vicar to return,' she said. 'Then I shall regale you all with tales of my daring aerial adventures.'

'You've been flyin'?' said Daisy. 'Really?'

'I have, dear.'

'I'd give anythin' to fly. You been up as well, Flo?'

'No,' I said. 'Not I. But it'll sound much more impressive if we let Lady Hardcastle tell you about me not flying.'

Daisy frowned but knew better than to press for an explanation.

Reverend Bland arrived with two ciders.

'Here you are, dear,' he said.

'Why did you get such small glasses?' said Mrs Bland. 'Look what the other ladies have.'

'I just thought—'

Mrs Bland harrumphed and took a good swig of her drink. 'It'll just mean you have to get up and fetch me another in a minute,' she said.

'I shall time my story with a break for more cider,' said Lady Hardcastle with a chuckle.

'Oh, splendid,' said the vicar. 'I do love a story.'

And that was all the encouragement she needed.

Chapter Seven

On Saturday morning I was seized by an uncharacteristic urge to take my morning coffee into the garden. I usually preferred to sit in the kitchen with Edna and Miss Jones, but the delights of the summer were calling me. The sights, the sounds, the smells – there's little in the world to beat the pleasure of an English summer's morning.

'Would you ladies care to join me in the garden for a cuppa?' I said. 'Take the air before the labours of the day begin?'

'That sounds like a lovely idea, miss,' said Edna, 'but I gots loads to do. I'd like to get on if that's all right. I was wonderin' if I might get away a bit early today, with it bein' Saturday, an' all.'

'Of course,' I said. 'Are you and Dan planning something nice?'

She laughed. 'I don't know about "nice",' she said. 'Dan's taken it into 'is 'ead to get 'isself a bicycle and we's goin' over to Chippin' to see a bloke there.'

'That sounds fun,' I said. 'I didn't know there was a bicycle shop in Chipping.'

'There i'n't. It's some bloke Dan knows – 'e's sellin' 'is bike. Dan says it'll 'elp 'im get about for work, like.'

'It still sounds fun, though. I sometimes wonder about getting a bicycle. What about you, Miss Jones?'

'No, I never liked 'em,' she said.

I smiled. 'I meant, would you like to join me for coffee outside. But why don't you like bicycles?'

'Oh, sorry. No, I'd like to crack on same as Edna if it's all the same. And as for bicycles . . . I tried when I was little but I couldn't get the 'ang of it. Kept fallin' off. And they saddles? Not built for comfort, are they?'

'They do rather dig in,' I agreed.

'Where no one ought to be diggin',' said Edna with a chuckle.

'Well, if you promise not to think badly of me,' I said, 'I still think I'll take this outside. I can admire Jed's handiwork and listen to the birds.'

'You go out and enjoy yourself,' said Edna.

'You're out for lunch today,' said Miss Jones. 'Is that right?'

'Yes,' I said. 'Up at The Grange for lunch, and possibly tea if I know the Farley-Strouds. Then home for supper, but I can't imagine us needing much to eat. We should be in all day tomorrow.'

'I'll make sure there's something for you,' she said. 'Is there anything you fancy?'

'No,' I said. 'Don't got to too much trouble. Do we have any chops?'

'I'll see what Spratt's has got in. I'll see you right, don't worry.'

'Thank you.' I stood to leave. 'You know where I am if you need me.'

I went out through the boot room and into the garden. Unidentified birds were singing, unidentified plants were blooming, the sun – I could identify the sun – was shining. There wasn't a cloud in the sky and all was right with the world. Well, mostly. We were no nearer catching the leaker and Dickie Dupree's death may yet prove not to have been a tragic accident, but we'd clear it all up eventually – we always did. I may yet get to fly in an aeroplane, but I was less confident of that.

I finished my coffee and was just thinking of going back indoors to find a book to read when I was hailed from the back door.

'Ah, there you are,' said Lady Hardcastle with a morning croak in her voice. 'I wondered where you'd got to.'

'Just enjoying the morning sunshine,' I said. 'I told the others where I was.'

'Miss Jones was on the telephone talking to the butcher, and of Edna there was no sign. I was left to find you unaided.'

'You poor old thing. But you prevailed, despite the loneliness of your task. Here I am.'

'There, indeed, you are. I think you've hit upon exactly the right idea. Shall we breakfast out here?'

'Why not?' I said. 'I'll ask Miss Jones to bring it out.'

We ate our breakfast together in the garden while Lady Hardcastle patiently identified all the birds and plants for me. I listened assiduously and forgot all their names at once.

The Farley-Strouds had also spent the morning in the garden and there was a game of croquet in progress by the time we arrived.

Lady Farley-Stroud welcomed us warmly and offered to forgo her turn.

'You'd be doing me a great service if you were to take the mallet,' she said. 'Hector's cheating quite appallingly and I'm suppressing the urge to tell him off.'

It wasn't like her to suppress that particular urge – having baby Louisa about the place seemed to have warmed her a little.

'Cheating?' said Lady Hardcastle. 'How?'

'Just watch, m'dear. Just watch.'

Sir Hector played a slightly weak shot.

'Go on, girl,' he said.

I thought he was giving encouragement to the ball, but at his command, one of his spaniels bounded into action. She loped over to the ball and used her snout to push it through the hoop.

'That's it, girl,' said Sir Hector. 'There. Leave it there. Good girl.'

'Oh, Papa,' said Clarissa. 'You can't keep using the dogs. It's not fair.'

'You could use 'em too, if you had the knack,' he said. 'It's all in the rules. Just usin' the features of the landscape.'

'They're not part of the landscape,' she said. 'You're cheating.'

He gave a chuckle, but didn't relent.

'D'you see?' said Lady Farley-Stroud. 'It's maddening. He thinks he's found the cleverest loophole.'

'It is rather ingenious,' said Lady Hardcastle.

'Well, it's driving me batty. Are you sure you won't . . .' She held up her mallet.

'Not for me, thank you. Flo? Fancy showing them how it's done?'

'Would you, m'dear?' said Lady Farley-Stroud. 'I could do with a sit-down, if I'm honest.'

'Happy to help,' I said, and took the proffered mallet.

'They're in trouble now,' said Lady Hardcastle. 'She's a dab hand at anything that involves aiming at things.'

'You give 'em what for, Florence, m'girl.'

Lady Farley-Stroud had lately taken to calling me Florence. I took this to be a sign of acceptance, at last.

I gave them what for.

It was a tight game and Adam fought bravely, but I was first to peg out. I returned to the table where the two ladies were sitting with baby Louisa and handed the mallet back to Lady Farley-Stroud.

'You won,' I said. 'Congratulations.'

'That's m'girl,' she said. 'We need you here more often. We need her here more often, don't we, Lou-Lou?'

The baby earnestly nodded her approval and wiped a sticky, pudgy hand on Lady Farley-Stroud's dress.

The others finished the game and came to join us.

'Tell Jenkins we're ready for lunch, Hector,' said Lady Farley-Stroud.

'Right you are, my little plum duff,' he said, and disappeared through the French windows to summon the butler.

'I heard about your little misadventure the other day, Flo,' said Adam. 'Dashed bad luck.'

'Misadventure?' said Lady Farley-Stroud. 'Another accident? Are you hurt? What happened? I would never have asked you to play if I'd known you were injured.'

'I'm fine, honestly,' I said. 'The aeroplane's engine blew up, that's all.'

'Blew up?' she exclaimed. 'Blew up? In the sky? Were you flying? Oh, my word.'

'We were on the ground,' I said. 'Just a loud noise and some black smoke. Nothing bad.'

'She missed her chance to fly, though,' said Adam.

'Good!' said Lady Farley-Stroud. 'I forbid you both to have anything more to do with those dreadful machines. I forbid it.'

Sir Hector had returned from his mission. 'Not entirely certain you've any authority there, m'dear,' he said. 'Free to do as they please, those two.'

'I still forbid it. I'll not have friends of mine putting their lives at risk like that. Lord knows I've precious few friends as it is, without them trying to kill themselves in those wretched aeroplanes.'

'You never say anything like that to me,' said Adam.

'But don't think I don't think it,' she said. 'I have palpitations every time Clarissa tells me you've been out flying.'

'It never occurred to me that you'd fly,' said Lady Hardcastle. 'I don't know why. I just assumed you were one of the chaps on the ground with the slide rules and the serious expressions.'

'Oh, I am that, too,' he said. 'But I like to get airborne as often as I can. It's good for business if the engineers have enough faith in the aeroplanes to get up in them.'

Lady Farley-Stroud harrumphed.

'How go the preparations for the show?' said Lady Hardcastle.

'You're as transparent in your attempts to change the subject as I am, m'dear,' said Lady Farley-Stroud. 'And it'll backfire on you. I have plenty to say on the subject of the blessed show, too.'

'Oh, dear. Has something happened?'

'It would be quicker to list the things that haven't happened. One member of the committee – do you know Higgins? Local farmer.'

'I can't say I do.'

'Well, he's as obstreperous as you like. Won't agree to anything. So committee meetings are fraught. Mrs Newton—'

'Dr Fitzsimmons's housekeeper?' interrupted Lady Hardcastle.

'That's her. She's supposed to be performing a duet with Mrs Grove—'

'The vicar's housekeeper.'

'That's right. But Newton has had a falling out with Mrs Spratt—'

'Over the scrag end?' I asked.

'Scrag end, if you please,' said Lady Farley-Stroud. 'How did you . . . ?'

'I keep my ear to the ground,' I said with a wink.

'Well, Mrs Spratt and your Mrs Gibson are also doing a duet. In cases where two acts are proposing to perform the same song, we've encouraged them to try to come to amicable agreements between themselves, but this dispute over a couple of pounds of lamb has made any sort of amity impossible. Meanwhile, I've been cast in the role of Lord Chamberlain and am being required to pass judgement on the suitability of songs, jokes, and comic mono-logues. Most of them are funny, a few of them are hilarious, and all of them are absolutely filthy. What's a woman to do? Ban them like some old-fashioned prude, or allow them and offend the village's new breed of prudes? Damned if I do, damned if I don't. Damned if I've got the strength to carry on, some days.'

'Oh, you poor thing,' said Lady Hardcastle. 'Is there anything I can do to lighten the burden?'

'No, m'dear, you've enough on your plate as it is. I shall soldier on. I don't usually complain. I must be hungry.'

As if they had been waiting for their cue, Jenkins and Dewi arrived at that moment with the luncheon trays.

Mrs Brown had excelled herself again, and lunch was delicious. When the last of the cream-filled gateau had been consumed and the jug of rum punch refilled, Grandma and Grandpa joined Clarissa on the lawn, where they entertained Louisa with a ball under the watchful and protective gaze of the spaniels.

'I swear those dogs have adopted Lou-Lou as part of the pack,' said Adam as he took a sip of his drink. 'She's going to miss them when we go home.'

'When will that be?' asked Lady Hardcastle. 'Do you have long at Bristol Aviation?'

'A couple more weeks, I think. We're working on a new project together and I just have to make sure we're all singing from the same hymn sheet before I leave them to it.'

'You don't go in every day, though, do you? We didn't see you yesterday.'

'Good Lord, no,' he said with a laugh. 'I couldn't face the journey down there every day.'

'It is a bit of a trek,' I said.

'What's it like as a place to work, though?' asked Lady Hardcastle.

'I've known worse,' he said. 'It can get a bit gloomy at times, but they seem like a good bunch.'

'That's understandable,' I said. 'They have just lost one of their own.'

Adam nodded. 'Quite,' he said. 'Obviously young Myrtle Matthews is devastated. She puts a brave face on it, but she'll break down at the drop of a hat. Walt Sandling is a good egg, though. He keeps the place going.'

'Does it need someone to keep it going?' I said. 'Are they in trouble?'

'That's what I would have presumed, but . . .' He looked around to check he couldn't be overheard, though who he imagined might be earwigging was beyond me. 'Well, I gather from Gertie that you two know what's what. It won't surprise you to know that Vannier's has connections with the French government and they . . . they have certain "resources". They've rummaged in Bristol Aviation's official records and they seem as buoyant as anything on the surface, but there's a bit of a shortage of ready cash. And that's borne out at the factory – everyone's terribly jumpy about the order book. I do wonder if that's why they've been so keen to work with us. A joint venture with Vannier's could keep them busy for the next couple of years.'

'Are you able to say what you're working on?' asked Lady Hardcastle.

'In the broadest terms, I suppose I can. It's essentially a new aeroplane design and some safety equipment.'

'Parachutes?' I said.

He frowned. 'As a matter of fact, yes,' he said. 'How did you . . . ?'

'Gertie isn't wrong,' said Lady Hardcastle. 'We do know what's what.'

'You really do seem to. It's supposed to be ever so very thoroughly on the QT.'

'Don't worry,' she said. 'We shan't ask you to betray any confidences. Are there any concerns about security?'

'Concerns?'

'Are your colleagues at Vannier's – or your contacts in the French government – aware of any attempts by foreign powers to obtain information about the parachute?'

'We always have people sniffing about in Bordeaux,' he said. 'From everywhere. Much more so than here, certainly. No man is an island, but Britain certainly is.'

'What sort of people?' I asked. 'Where are they from?'

'From everywhere, like I said. Germans, Austrians, Italians, Hungarians, Bulgarians, Turks, Russians, even a couple of Japanese chaps. It's like some sort of massive international conference there some days.'

'And have any of them given you any cause for concern?' persisted Lady Hardcastle.

'Oh, I see what you mean. Well, we've been told to keep an eye on the Triple Alliance lot, obviously – you know, the Germans, Italians and Austro-Hungarians. But that's just good sense these days.'

'But nothing suspicious has happened?' I asked.

'No, no, I don't think so.' He paused a moment in thought. 'Well, unless you count . . . no, it's stupid, really.'

'Nothing is stupid in our game,' I said. 'You should hear some of the ridiculous things we've been involved in.'

'Well, it wasn't suspicious, as such, just decidedly odd. Files kept going missing. We'd look for a file and it wasn't where it was supposed to be. Then someone else would look for it a little later and it would be there, but slightly out of order.'

'Could it just have been missed the first time?'

'That's what we all thought at first – engineers can sometimes be a bit . . . absent, after all, a bit vague – but it kept happening.'

'A poltergeist?'

He laughed. 'Someone suggested that, too,' he said. 'I think it was more likely some bored junior engineer playing a prank.'

'Did no one own up?' asked Lady Hardcastle. 'Pranksters usually like to take credit for their mischief.'

'Actually, now you come to mention it, no, no one did. That is odd, isn't it?'

'Did it happen at particular times?' I said. 'Perhaps when certain people were in the office?'

He thought for a moment. 'Oh,' he said. 'Yes. The chaps from one of the German universities. Nice bunch. Very interested in what we were doing.'

'I thought the Germans had all their eggs in the dirigible basket,' said Lady Hardcastle. 'They're looking at aeroplanes now?'

'I don't know what their army wants, but their academics are interested in everything, just like academics everywhere. I say, you don't think . . .'

'I don't know what to think yet,' she said. 'But it's not something you should worry about.'

'Leave that sort of thing to you, eh?'

'Something like that, dear, yes. But I'm more interested in matters closer to home. We're going to see the chief accountant on Wednesday.'

'The lecherous Mr Milhouse,' I said.

Adam laughed. 'I've heard that, too. Myrtle Matthews isn't keen, is she?'

'She warned us to be careful,' said Lady Hardcastle.

'So you're talking about the finances, eh? You're serious about this aeroplane business, aren't you? That'll please them.'

'We remain undecided, but I'd like to know more about the costs, certainly. What's the rest of the company like? What about your lot?'

'My lot?' he said with a smile.

'Your lot with the slide rules and the serious expressions.'

'Much as you'd expect for men obsessed with tensile strengths and the Bernoulli effect. You've met Goff, though. He's a nice chap.'

'What about his assistant?' I said. 'Paul Something.'

'Paul Curtis. He's all right. Bit of an odd fish, but see above. We're all odd fish.'

'Are you talking about work again?' said Clarissa. 'Honestly, Emily, you must stop him if he's boring you.'

She had left Louisa with her parents, and the little girl was clapping delightedly along as Lady Farley-Stroud sang to her. We'd been to two of the Christmas gatherings at The Grange, but it was traditionally the villagers who put on a show there and I'd not heard Gertie sing before. She had a rather pleasant voice – she might be quite a hit at the village show.

'Not at all,' said Lady Hardcastle. 'We were just sharing our observations on the staff at the aeroplane factory.'

'If they're anything like the ones at home in France, "odd fish" just about sums them up,' Clarissa said. 'I'm lucky to have married the only normal one in the bunch.'

'Thank you, Mrs Whitman,' said Adam. 'You're too kind.'

'Well, nearly normal, anyway. It's about time for Lou-Lou to have a snooze so I've come to ask you all to join us in a Farley-Stroud archery tournament. Papa is the insufferably unbeaten champion and Mama and I would absolutely love it if someone would knock him off his perch. What do you say?'

'Archery?' said Adam. 'You know I've never arched in my life.'

'There's nothing to it,' she said blithely. 'I'll show you how. But it's these two I'm interested in. Something tells me they could be the ones to give Papa the thrashing he so richly deserves.'

'We can but try,' said Lady Hardcastle. 'What say you, Flo? Shall we show these country bumpkins how it's done?'

'I am, apparently, a dab hand at anything that involves aiming at things,' I said. 'It seems rude not to.'

◆ ◆ ◆

Once Louisa was safely in bed and the dogs had been sent indoors for a nap of their own, Dewi set up the archery target and Clarissa gave Adam some tuition in the taxophilic arts. He was utterly hopeless, and Sir Hector made no attempt to conceal his glee.

'Looks like my crown's in no danger,' he said. 'The Farley-Strouds were archers at Agincourt, y'know?'

'No, they weren't, you silly old fool,' said Lady Farley-Stroud. 'Your ancestors were wool merchants from Painswick.'

'Still doesn't change the form, though,' he said. 'Young Adam's a duffer.'

'You've not seen Emily and Flo yet, Papa,' said Clarissa.

'Hah!' he said. 'Let's see 'em beat this.'

He took an arrow from an upright quiver on the ground. He nocked it with practised ease, drew, and shot it towards the target about thirty-five yards away. It sailed into the bullseye, just off-centre, with a heavy *thonk*.

'Hah!' he said again.

I looked to Lady Hardcastle and gestured that she should take her turn.

She picked up one of the spare bows and made a show of rummaging through the quiver looking for just the right arrow.

'They're all the same, m'dear,' chuckled Sir Hector. 'You'll find no advantage there.'

She eventually found one she liked, and slowly nocked and drew it. She looked clumsy by comparison. She loosed it and it flew gracefully towards the target and landed in the bullseye, less than an inch above Sir Hector's.

'Not so sure of yourself now, Papa, eh?' said Clarissa.

She took her own shot and her arrow cut the line between the seven-point and eight-point circles at about ten o'clock.

Lady Farley-Stroud was next and landed squarely in the eight-point circle at two o'clock.

Adam, as predicted, missed completely, and Sir Hector let out a bark of a laugh. He wasn't quite as gracious in victory as I would have imagined.

Finally it was my turn.

Lady Hardcastle handed me a bow.

With slight hesitation and almost as much apparent clumsiness as Lady Hardcastle, I took my shot. It cut the line between the bullseye and the nine ring.

'Looks like your crown might be in danger after all, Papa,' said Clarissa. 'Well done, ladies.'

'No,' said Sir Hector. 'No danger yet. Ten points each for me and our charming guests. Let's see if they can do it again before we start handin' out medals.'

Clarissa shook her head. 'It's still all to play for,' he said. 'Off you go, Adam. Fetch the arrows for Round Two, there's a good chap.'

After ten rounds, Sir Hector, Lady Hardcastle and I were even on ninety-five points each. Lady Farley-Stroud and Clarissa were trailing us slightly, and Adam was getting bored.

'Come along, Hector,' said Lady Farley-Stroud. 'You've met your match. Time to call it a day. They'll be bringing tea out in a minute.'

'But I haven't beaten 'em yet,' he said. 'Tiebreaker. Seventy yards. Let's see what you can do with that.'

Lady Farley-Stroud sighed. 'All right, dear, but you're going to regret it.'

Adam was dispatched to move the target while Sir Hector paced nervously about.

'This is for all the years of gloating, Papa,' said Clarissa.

'She has a point, dear,' said Lady Farley-Stroud. 'Your hubris was bound to be your downfall in the end. You're a terrible winner.'

'And I shall be again,' he said with a gleeful chuckle. 'M'crown is safe. Mark my words. They can do it at beginners' range, but no one beats the archers of Agincourt.'

'Or the wool merchants of the Cotswolds,' she said.

Lady Hardcastle shot first, scoring a solid eight.

Sir Hector was next. Nine.

'Hah!' he said. 'The crown'll still be mine.'

Lady Hardcastle handed me a bow and leaned in close. 'Don't hold back,' she whispered. 'I know what you're like, but not today. Show him.'

I nodded. 'You're sure about this?' I said. 'The crown's still yours if I don't shoot.'

'You'll never do it,' he said with a grin. 'Many have tried and failed. Do your worst, young Florence.'

'Where would you like me to put it?' I said, nonchalantly.

'Dead centre, m'dear,' he said. 'Where everyone else has been aiming for. Ten points and the crown is yours.'

I'm very much of the opinion that if you're going to show off, you might as well do it properly. Without any of my earlier feigned clumsiness, I nocked, drew and shot in one smooth motion. I turned away from the target to face Sir Hector while the arrow was still in flight.

'Will that do you?' I said, a second before we heard the thunk.

His mouth gaped and the others applauded. Clarissa had been observing the target with a pair of field glasses.

'Hah!' she said. 'Absolute dead centre. I believe that makes Flo Armstrong today's champion.'

'Well, I'll be blowed,' said Sir Hector. 'I never thought I'd see the day. Well done, Florence. Well done indeed.'

I curtseyed. 'Thank you,' I said.

'Were you holdin' back all that time?' he said. 'Is that why we were tied?'

'Only a little,' I said. 'It seemed rude to beat my host at his favourite game in his own home.'

He laughed delightedly. 'Well, you certainly showed me,' he said.

Tea was served almost immediately and the rest of the afternoon passed in a happy haze of convivial company and Clarissa ceaselessly ragging her father for finally losing his crown.

The sun was low in the sky by the time we walked down the hill to the village. As we emerged from the lane and on to the green, Lady Hardcastle gave a delighted clap.

'Look,' she said. 'How utterly wonderful.'

Outside the Dog and Duck were half a dozen trestle tables, each with half a dozen folding wooden chairs. We could hear the cheerful buzz of weekend chatter from the other side of the green.

'Joe finally did it, then,' I said. 'Good for him.'

'It's hardly a Parisian pavement café,' she said, 'but it brings a certain joie de whatnot to our little village, eh?'

'It certainly does.'

'If I weren't already completely stuffed and at least two and a half sheets to the wind, I'd suggest we join them. Another time, perhaps.'

'Another time,' I agreed. I waved the cardboard crown Clarissa had made for me. 'For now, the Archer Queen demands a nice sit-down and a cup of tea.'

'Anything you desire, your majesty,' Lady Hardcastle said with a bow.

We walked home.

Chapter Eight

The bank holiday Monday was spent on correspondence and creativity. Lady Hardcastle was an enthusiastic writer of letters and was engaged in several conversations with people from around the world on subjects as diverse as science, music, politics, gardening, motion pictures, modern art, and – for reasons I could never fathom – clockmaking. We had been busy with other matters of late and so she had a lot to catch up on.

I, meantime, had few correspondents. I wrote semi-regularly to my twin sister Gwenith with news of our lives and adventures. She replied only rarely, so the correspondence was seldom onerous and could be conducted entirely on my own terms.

I wrote with slightly more enthusiasm and frequency to Eleanora Wilson – Ellie – the young American we had met the previous summer. I would give her heavily censored accounts of our work (her aunt was an American spy – no need to reveal sensitive details, even to allies). I also kept her up to date with Lady Hardcastle's moving-picture projects and my own efforts to learn whatever new skill it was she was trying to teach me (it was photography that summer).

In return, Ellie would write long, gushing letters about the wonders of a certain drummer of our mutual acquaintance with whom she was somewhat smitten. We had introduced her to Skins Maloney in Weston-super-Mare and they had struck up an international correspondence of their own. He was, I was told at endearingly great length, quite the most wonderful human being ever to stand upright and she would spend pages enumerating his many admirable qualities. I was, of course, fully aware of Skins's charms, and thought they were a splendid match.

My opinion on that score was reinforced by my latest correspondent: Skins Maloney himself. He had taken to writing to me to ask how he might 'improve' himself so as to appear a better prospect for the young heiress. I was in the fortunate position of being able to reassure him that no improvement was necessary and that she very much seemed to adore him just the way he was.

I was considering setting up a matchmaking agency.

Ellie was owed a letter, so I spent Monday morning describing the offices and factory of Bristol Aviation, with special mention of the Dunnock and my failure to fly therein. I also recounted the terrible tale of the killer cows, which I hoped might amuse her.

The afternoon was spent in Lady Hardcastle's darkroom in the orangery, where I developed the photographs I'd taken on Friday. I made copies of the more interesting ones so that I might send them to Ellie with my letter.

We took a walk into the village in the early evening to see the end of the bank holiday cricket match and to join in the raucous celebration of Littleton Cotterell's victory over Woodworthy.

Tuesday was devoted to household administration and the inevitable pile of mending generated by Lady Hardcastle . . . being Lady Hardcastle. If a dress was worth wearing, it was worth catching on something and ripping a big hole in.

On Wednesday, though, we were back to work. There was to be another trip to Bristol Aviation.

'What's our story today?' I asked as I drove us smoothly down the Gloucester Road.

'The same as before, I think. Against all reason and common sense, I'm still interested in buying one of their unreliable death machines and we shall need to speak to . . . to . . .'

'Mr Milhouse,' I said. 'Company accountant.'

'Even he. We'll speak to him and grill him most intently.'

'On what?'

'What do you mean, dear?'

'What are we asking him, and what do we really want to know?'

'I shall enquire about payment terms in such a way that I sound canny with money rather than impoverished. Meanwhile, we'll subtly hint at having reservations about the whole thing to try to gauge how desperate the man is to make a sale. If Harry's information about the company's financial position is correct, he'll be keen. But let's see how far he's prepared to go.'

'Desperate enough to betray his country?'

'We've seen people do more for less.'

'Ideologists for the most part, though,' I said. 'I doubt we'll expose him as a sympathizer with foreign powers during a quick chat about payment options.'

'We'll see. In the meantime, my mind has wandered. Why is this called the Gloucester Road when it leads to Bristol?'

'It's called the Gloucester Road at this end because it's the road that leaves Bristol and heads towards Gloucester,' I said. 'At the other end it's called the Bristol Road because it leaves Gloucester and heads towards Bristol.'

'I say. Excellent general knowledge, Miss Armstrong.'

'I spent a lot of time travelling England's roads growing up. One learns things.'

'One does seem to. But where does the name change?'

'I beg your pardon?'

'Well, at some point it stops being the Bristol Road and becomes the Gloucester Road. Who decides where that is? Presumably somewhere around Berkeley there's a chap saying, "But this road goes both to Bristol *and* to Gloucester. How on earth shall we name it?" Is he responsible for choosing the name? Does it just depend upon where he wishes to go that day? And what if he wants to travel on the road for just a short way and then turn off to Dursley? Is it the Sort Of On The Way To Dursley Road that day?'

'Yes,' I said. 'Yes, that's what he calls it that day.'

I turned to roll my eyes at her and saw that she was grinning.

'I've packed a small picnic,' I said, keen to change the subject.

'Oh, you are a treasure.'

'I'm not sure where we'll be able to eat it, but I didn't enjoy going hungry on Friday.'

'We shall think of something, even if we have to sit in the Rolls outside the office building.'

'We'll not be leaving?' I asked. 'I thought we'd take our picnic somewhere nice.'

'No, I was hoping to make an appointment to speak to whatshisname in the drawing office again. Engineering Johnny. We can't be trekking down here every day – it will begin to look suspicious. Best catch them all while we can.'

'Godfrey Parfitt,' I said.

'No, not him. Well, yes, it would be useful to speak to him again, but I was thinking of his junior. We've not met him yet.'

'Paul Curtis,' I said.

'How do you remember all these names?'

'I write them on my sleeve,' I said.

'I knew it was something like that. Oh, look.'

I looked and saw a Dunnock struggling into the air ahead of us. We were almost at Bristol Aviation at last.

◆ ◆ ◆

At eleven on the dot, Myrtle Matthews showed us into Mr Milhouse's office. She gave me a little grimace and a wink as she closed the door and left us to our fate.

'Good morning, Lady Hardcastle,' said the handsome middle-aged man in the well-cut suit. 'John Milhouse, at your service.'

He came out from behind his desk and shook both our hands.

'Please,' he said, 'do sit down. I've already asked Miss Matthews to bring us some coffee. I hope that's acceptable. And some McVitie's digestive biscuits. I know some people look down their noses at factory-made biscuits, but one doesn't always have a pastry chef on hand and they're so very moreish.'

'That will be splendid, thank you,' said Lady Hardcastle.

He waited until we were both seated and then returned to his own chair behind the modest desk.

'You must forgive me,' he said. 'Walt told me you were coming, Lady Hardcastle, but he didn't mention your . . . companion.'

'I'm so sorry,' she said. 'This is my lady's maid and right-hand woman, Miss Florence Armstrong.'

'Delighted to meet you, Miss Armstrong.' He looked down at an open file on his desk. 'Ah, so you must be the lady who was denied her flight with Rupert on Friday.'

'I am,' I said. 'There was a problem with the engine.'

He looked down again, then laughed. 'I should say so. Bally thing blew up. Connecting rod shattered, it says here. Seals failed. Oil got in the . . . I can't pretend to understand. I'm sorry you had a disappointing afternoon.'

'I'm sure it was just unfortunate happenchance,' I said quickly, before Lady Hardcastle could get up a head of steam and launch into another rant about safety.

'Certainly never known anything like it before,' he said. 'But they fitted a new engine to the test model yesterday and she's been buzzing about the place all morning.'

'We saw . . . "her" taking off,' I said.

'Did you? Splendid. So you know all is well. We should be able to get you up for your test flight before too very long. Walt says you're still interested in purchasing one of our aircraft, though, Lady Hardcastle. Despite everything.'

'I'm slightly more wary than I might once have been,' she said, 'but I am still open to the idea, yes.'

'Splendid, splendid . . . Splendid.' He was still scanning the documents in front of him. 'So. Well, now. How is it that I can help you? What can I do to get you to sign a purchase order and set you on the path to experiencing the delights of powered flight? I'm sure I can arrange a very attractive payment plan.'

'How attractive?' she said. 'I've always been very keen on the idea of keeping my money in my account for as long as possible. What terms can you offer me?'

He launched into a long and involved description of his preferred credit arrangement to which I barely listened – I had other things on my mind. He was interrupted by the arrival of coffee and biscuits, but only briefly. Scarcely had Miss Matthews put the tray down before he was back into amortized this, deferred that, and favourable something else.

My mind returned to my examination of the contents of the room. I had already spotted the hefty iron safe, equipped with a combination lock, in the corner by the window. It had an aspidistra on top in a glazed and decorated pot.

Along the wall was a set of oak filing cabinets. Odd, I mused, that I had no difficulty identifying trees once they'd been cut down and turned into furniture, but I still couldn't tell a poplar from a plumber's mate in the wild. Although the plumber's mate would probably be wearing a cap. That would definitely be a clue.

I tried to read the labels on the drawers of the filing cabinets without turning round too much and giving myself away. There seemed to be two alphabetical runs, and I presumed one was for incoming and the other outgoing – invoices and bills.

There were hefty ledgers on the shelves above the cabinets, with year ranges embossed in gold on the spines. The last was for 1910–11 and there was a gap large enough for another volume. I made another presumption: the 1911–12 ledger was on his desk somewhere.

I returned my attention to his desk, still trying not to make it too obvious that I was snooping and not paying attention to his fascinating lecture on simplified financial instruments. His desk was the cluttered workspace of a busy man. Pencils, pens, bottles of ink in at least three colours, and mounds of papers. There was a charming photograph in a gilt frame of a young Mr Milhouse in his best suit, standing next to a smiling, round-faced, dark-haired lady in a long dress, holding a small bunch of flowers. A wedding photograph. On the side of the desk nearest the window, under a pile of manila folders, was a fat book of about the same size as the ledgers on the shelves.

So they were the books the tax inspector would see if he called to query the returns for corporation duty. But where would he keep the 'real' books? Anyone who was serious about defrauding His Majesty's Inspector of Taxes would need to keep two sets of books, and keep them in very good order. Good enough to fool the Inland Revenue, at least – if Harry were to be believed, he had accountants on his payroll who had seen discrepancies that HMIT had missed. But where were they?

There was a large portrait behind Mr Milhouse's desk. It was of a stern-faced man in Victorian clothes and was housed in an elaborately ornate frame. Everything else about the company offices was uncluttered and modern. Decoration was elsewhere limited to photographs of aeroplanes and the men who built and flew them. Not even the managing director had something as ostentatious as this absurdly oversized portrait in his office. It was there for another reason, of course. That's where the other safe was.

The only people who thought that hiding a secret safe behind a painting would fool a burglar were people who had never burgled. Which was comforting, in a way. It showed that even liars and cheats had lines they wouldn't cross. They might be defrauding the government, but they'd never stoop to burgling another man's home or office. Obviously anyone who had ever indulged in a little breaking and entering, whether for larcenous or investigatory reasons, knew that absolutely everyone hid their special safe behind a picture and imagined they were the cleverest person in the world for having thought of something so ingenious.

We were going to have to find an opportunity to break into Mr Milhouse's office as well as the parachute project room.

'. . . very helpful, isn't it, Armstrong?'

I had no idea what they'd been talking about, but it was plain I was expected to agree.

'Most illuminating, my lady,' I said. 'Very helpful indeed.'

'If I can do anything else to ease things along, you must let me know at once,' said Mr Milhouse. 'My card.'

He pushed a business card across the desk and Lady Hardcastle swept it up without looking at it.

'Thank you,' she said. 'We shall certainly be in touch.'

We all stood and shook hands once more. Mr Milhouse made as though to show us out.

'Don't worry,' said Lady Hardcastle, 'we've become quite familiar with the layout of the building over the past few days. We can find our own way back to Miss Matthews in reception.'

There followed another round of goodbyes and expressions of hope for further meetings in the near future, and within no more than another five minutes we were on our way along the corridor and back towards the stairs.

◆ ◆ ◆

Miss Matthews told us that all the engineers were at lunch, but promised to let Goff and Paul know that we'd like a word. She offered to take us to the canteen, but we declined, explaining that we'd brought lunch of our own.

'There's enough for three if you'd care to join us,' said Lady Hardcastle.

'Oh, that's very kind of you,' said Miss Matthews, 'but I don't have time for lunch myself today, I'm afraid. There always seems to be more to do than hours to do it in.' She indicated a pile of papers and files on her desk.

'If you change your mind, we'll be out on the grass under that tree by the fence. As long as that's all right.'

'It's fine. I often sit there myself.'

We left her to her paperwork and hauled the picnic basket to the indicated spot under the tree.

'That was an unexpected experience,' I said as I set out the feast on the picnic rug.

'Being asked to lunch in the works canteen?' said Lady Hardcastle. 'Hardly. I get luncheon invitations all the time.'

'You know full well I mean our meeting with Mr Milhouse.'

'The "lecherous" Mr Milhouse.'

'Exactly. I've never known a lecherous goat be more polite and respectful,' I said.

'It's almost a disappointment. Perhaps I'm losing my charms. Am I over the hill, Flo?'

'Of course you are. But I'm not. And even I got no lascivious stares. I usually get at least one lascivious stare.'

'So if our charms are still fully functioning – well, you claim yours are, at least – then why was there not even a hint of oiliness?'

'He was on his best behaviour?' I suggested. 'It's an important sale, after all.'

'That's one possibility. Another is that Miss Myrtle Matthews has been fibbing to us.'

'Or perhaps he's only like that with her. Perhaps he's got a pash on her.'

'Intriguing,' she said. 'But with Dougie Dulay—'

'Dickie Dupree,' I said, wearily.

'With Dickie Dupree in the way,' she continued, with a stupid grin I knew was there without even looking, 'his path to true happiness was blocked.'

'There was a framed wedding photograph on his desk. He's married.'

'Then with Dickie Dupree in the way, his path to extramarital naughtiness with the attractive secretary was blocked.'

'So he nobbled the parachute to facilitate illicit wantonizing?' I said. 'I'm not even slightly convinced. If you want to suggest he did away with Dickie Dupree because Dupree had stumbled on to the accounting fiddle and was threatening to blow the gaff, then I'm happy to listen. But I can't believe even the most libidinous libertine would commit murder for a chance to do rude things with someone he worked with, no matter how attractive she was.'

'He might be infatuated.'

'You might be talking nonsense.'

'That's always a possibility, dear, but let's not start ruling things out just because they sound nonsensical. We'll stick to ruling things out only because they're provably untrue.'

'Lack of lechery notwithstanding,' I said, 'what did you make of his sales pitch? Did you see the desperation you were hoping for?'

'You were there. What did you think?'

'I wasn't listening – I was getting the lie of the land.'

'Of course. Well, no, then, not really. He was eager, and frightfully well prepared – I couldn't quite see our file, but to judge from the things he said it seemed comprehensive – but there was no desperation, as such. Although that's the mark of a good negotiator, isn't it? Doesn't do to reveal too much of one's true disposition. What did you see?'

'Filing cabinets, a set of accounting books, an aspidistra and a hidden safe,' I said.

'Behind that ghastly portrait? Yes, that's what I thought.'

'I need to get in there on my own for an hour.'

'That might be hard to arrange during the daytime. And one assumes they have round-the-clock guards.'

'Nightwatchmen are famously unobservant,' I said. 'They're usually just there for show. They don't really expect to be burgled.'

'Then we'll have to see if we can arrange a trip down here at dead of night. Pass the bread, would you, please, dear?'

We continued our leisurely lunch and relaxed in the shade of the tree until it was time to visit the drawing office.

◆　◆　◆

We returned to reception but there was no one there. We waited for nearly ten minutes but Miss Matthews still hadn't returned. We were still playing the roles of Keen Customer and her Maid, so it wouldn't have been appropriate to make our own way to the drawing office, even though we knew exactly how to get there. Instead, Lady Hardcastle left a note on Miss Matthews's desk and we went for a walk to enjoy the sunshine.

'I think we should take a stroll around the grounds,' she said as we stepped back out into the blazing August sunshine. 'It'll be pleasant exercise and we can see if there are any weaknesses in their defences. There's bound to be a hole in the fence somewhere.'

'Holes in the fence aren't the issue, though, are they?' I said. 'What we need is an entry point that'll allow us to get to the hangar and the office block with the least possible exposure to the gaze of the nightwatchmen.'

'I thought we'd agreed that nightwatchmen are unobservant and idle.'

'We had. But there's a special term for complacent burglars: gaolbirds. Just because we think the guards are probably idiots doesn't mean we have to be idiots, too.'

'I can be as idiotic as I like, dear,' she said. 'I'll be on the main road in the Rolls with the engine running.'

'In charge of the getaway.'

'It's only right and proper. You drive like my grandmother.'

'I'm a steady and sensible driver.'

'There's a term for steady and sensible getaway drivers: gaolbirds.'

I harrumphed.

We crossed in front of the two enormous hangars and headed towards the perimeter fence. Of the guards there was no sign. The land now occupied by Bristol Aviation had once been a dairy farm. Several fields had been merged into one and levelled off to make space for the airships the company had once built. The enlarged field was now ideal for aeroplanes, which needed something of a run-up to get to flying speed.

The boundary, though, was still marked by the same thick hedgerows that marked the boundaries of all the local fields. A few feet inside the hedge was a chain-link fence, supported every few yards by stout wooden posts. The fence was about an elephant high and topped with a line of barbed wire.

'What do you think?' asked Lady Hardcastle.

'It should be easy enough,' I said. 'The hedge gives good shelter so there'll be plenty of time to get through. I'd prefer to leave no trace of our having been here, though, so I'd rather not cut the fence. I might need some assistance from Mother Nature . . .'

'I think I know what you're hinting at. Let's walk out for a bit and see what we can see.'

Thirty yards further along the fence we found what we'd both been hoping for. Badgers. Not actual badgers – not in the middle of the day – but a short stretch of fence where our stripy-headed friends had dug away the ground under the wire to allow themselves to pass unhindered on their nightly patrol route.

Still uncertain whether we were being observed, and still unwilling to check and make ourselves appear suspicious, we continued walking past Badger Gap, but I took the opportunity to have a good look as we went by.

'That should do nicely,' I said. 'Can you see any landmarks to help me find it in the dark?'

'Can't you just wait for Brock and follow him in?'

'This is why I stick with you – you have the very best solutions to all our problems. No. No, I can't wait for a badger. We need to triangulate. Do you have your compass?'

'Now who's being silly?' she said. 'Of course I don't have my compass. We'll have to pace it back to the end of the hangars. That should get you close enough.'

Casually, as though we'd had quite enough exercise for such a hot day, we slowly turned around and walked back towards Hangar B, counting as we went.

'Seventy-three,' I said as we drew level with the corner of the building.

'I made it sixty-five,' said Lady Hardcastle. 'And my stride is exactly one yard.'

'Thank you,' I said. 'So if you can just lend me your legs the night we do this, I'll know exactly how far sixty-five yards is. On the other hand, why don't we call it seventy-three Flosteps? I carry my own legs with me everywhere and removing yours in the dark will be messy and inconvenient.'

'I was just saying. We might want to mark it on a map at some point. The Flostep isn't an internationally recognized unit of measurement.'

I shook my head and we crossed in front of the massive doors. A familiar figure in overalls and cavalry boots strode out of the building and stood basking in the sun for a moment. He caught sight of us walking towards him.

'What ho, ladies,' said Rupert Herbert. 'Lovely day for a walk, what?'

'Glorious,' said Lady Hardcastle. 'How's the Dunnock behaving today?'

'Purring like a kitten,' he said. 'Oh, no, wait a moment. That can't be right. That would lead to all sorts of problems, wouldn't it – putting a kitten-powered engine in an aeroplane named for a garden bird?'

'That would be most inadvisable,' she said.

'I should say so. Anyway, we took a look at the duff engine – seems to be a faulty casting on one of the con rods. We've checked all the other engine parts from the same foundry. Sound as a bell.'

'That's reassuring.'

'I keep saying we should cast our own – take complete control of the whole manufacturing process. But they don't listen to me. They just smile and nod, and pat me on the back. "Just keep flying your planes, old chap," they say. "Just shut up and keep flying."'

'That must be terribly frustrating,' I said.

He nodded. 'I can't say it's not a little galling,' he said. 'I know these machines better than anyone, but I've no letters after my name. "Leave it to the chaps with the degrees," they say.'

'You should set up on your own,' said Lady Hardcastle. 'You could hire your own experts and they'd have to follow your lead.'

He smiled. 'Don't think I haven't thought about it,' he said. 'Just lacking the oof. Pa's loaded, of course, but he refuses to lend it to me. Says I'm wasting my life. Should have gone into the law like he did, and his father before him.'

'Parents can be like that.'

'I have plans, though. I'll get there in the end.'

'Oh?' I said. 'Might we see a Herbert Aeronautics aeroplane in the near future?'

'I say,' he said. 'Wouldn't that be wizard? Not sure about the name, though. Never been overly fond of the family moniker, to tell the truth. Doesn't have quite the grand ring to it for an exciting new venture.'

'Up and Away,' said Lady Hardcastle. 'Onward to Glory. Flights of Fancy. St Joseph's Flying Miracles.'

He grinned. 'After Joseph of Cupertino,' he said. 'Patron saint of flying.'

'I told you everyone knew that, dear,' she said, looking in my direction.

'Everyone except me, it seems,' I said.

'Well, I'll think of a name for it later,' he said. 'For now, I still need to get my hands on the money. But I've got a few irons in the fire – something will turn up. In the meantime, though, my job is to persuade charming ladies like you to part with their fortunes and purchase one of our fine aeroplanes.'

'You're doing a grand job so far, dear,' said Lady Hardcastle. 'Just get the slide-rule-and-spanner brigade to stop the engines exploding and all will be well.'

'I'll hold you to that,' he said. 'Got a bonus resting on the sale.'

She smiled. 'We shall leave you to your labours, Mr Herbert,' she said. 'We need to get ourselves back to the office.'

'Right you are. Pleasure to see you as always, ladies. Good day.'

We set off once more for the office building.

Chapter Nine

Miss Matthews took us through to the drawing office where Godfrey 'Goff' Parfitt was deep in conversation with an awkward-looking young man who I presumed to be his junior engineer, Paul Curtis.

'Sorry to interrupt, Goff,' said Miss Matthews, 'but Lady Hardcastle and Miss Armstrong would like a word.'

'Of course,' said Goff. 'Paul and I were just going over some revised stress calculations for the Dunnock's tail.'

'How fascinating,' said Lady Hardcastle. 'Are you sure you don't mind the interruption?'

'Always happy to talk to prospective customers. We tend to get forgotten out here in the drawing office. It's nice to chat about our work.'

'Thank you. You're jointly responsible for the Dunnock, I gather.'

With a friendly nod and wave to Miss Matthews, who was heading back to reception, he said, 'We are, yes. How can we help you?'

'Oh, just a few minor technical questions. You remember I took a test flight on Friday?'

'It went well, I understand. Rupert's report was very positive. The aeroplane performed slightly beyond expectations and he said you were pleased.'

'I was pleased. Very pleased. My maid's experience wasn't quite so positive, though.'

'Ah, yes,' he said. 'Sorry about that, Miss Armstrong. We've not long since finished the post-mortem on the engine. It could have been foreseen if we'd thought to carry out a full inspection of the con rod before we installed it. The trouble is that it requires some quite sophisticated gubbins and the expertise to use it and . . . well . . . one tends to expect that the foundry would have carried out that level of testing before they crated it up and sent it to us. We know better now, of course, and all the other engines have been inspected.'

'So we heard. And that's reassuring, but it does raise other issues.'

'Oh?' he said with a little frown. 'How so?'

'Well, if your procedures allow for exploding engines to be installed, can I really be certain your wings and bodies will hold together?'

He laughed. 'I'm an engineer, Lady Hardcastle,' he said. 'I can't offer you certainties. We deal in probabilities and margins of error. We can calculate the stress on a spar to the tiniest fraction of a pound-force per square inch in a perfect world, where all materials are uniform and always behave exactly as the simplified equations predict. But that's not how it works in real life, unfortunately. Trees tend not to grow their wood in accordance with strictly controlled manufacturing tolerances. Canvas is a little more reliable, but it's still woven from an organic substance. Our rigging wires are made under tightly controlled conditions, but they're fitted and tightened by hand. The only thing we can predict with one hundred per cent confidence is that the lump of meat in the pilot seat will behave like an idiot at some point. Even then we can't say at exactly what point.'

I looked over and saw the younger engineer stifle a yawn. I smiled at him and rolled my eyes. He smirked. I mimed drinking a cup of tea and he nodded in the direction of a door in the far corner of the room.

Lady Hardcastle had already embarked on her next question, so I touched her elbow to attract her attention and nodded towards the door previously indicated by the young engineer. She nodded her own acknowledgement without breaking her conversational stride and I left her to it.

The door led to a small kitchen with a large metal teapot and an even larger gas-heated urn.

'Paul Curtis,' said the young man. 'They are not terribly good at introductions sometimes.'

'I'm Armstrong,' I said. 'Pleased to meet you.'

He inclined his head in greeting. 'The tea is not up to much, I'm afraid,' he said, 'but it is all we have to offer.'

'I confess I'm not so bothered about the tea,' I said. 'I just wanted to leave Lady Hardcastle to her technical enquiries. She's fascinated by things like that and it can all get a bit intense at times.'

'You are not interested yourself, then?' he said. He was helping himself to a cup of extremely dark tea. 'You're sure I cannot tempt you? It looks stewed, but that's only because it is.'

I smiled. 'No, really,' I said. 'But thank you. You're not a tea connoisseur, then?'

'What is it they say? "I don't mind as long as it's wet and warm." I didn't drink much tea before I came to work here, but I've become a little addicted, I think.'

'British industry is entirely fuelled by tea. It's classed as an essential supply by the government.'

'I can well believe it.'

'As for your question . . . I am interested, just not to the extent that she is. She has a scientific background and she can go from a general outline anyone could follow to the most abstruse technical discussion in the blink of an eye. I prefer an overview.'

'She'll be a hit with Goff, then. He loves nothing more than a good technical conversation.'

'She's a hit with everyone,' I said. 'I've been working for her for seventeen years so she must have something going for her. What's Goff like to work with?'

'He's all right, I suppose. I've nothing to compare him with, though, really. This is my first job since graduating.'

'I say. What a wonderful first job. Where did you study?'

'University of London,' he said.

'A lively city. I bet you had a fine time.'

'I'm afraid I rather love to study so I saw little of the city. Mostly lecture theatres and laboratories.'

'Oh, that's a shame. I love London. Where are you from?'

'Out in the country.'

'I see. So, this Dunnock, then,' I said. 'Is it any good?'

He laughed. 'Straight to the technical questions, eh?' he said. 'Yes, it's a fine aeroplane. I know the fashion is for biplanes, but I really think this is an exciting design.'

'Unique?'

'No, there are similar ideas in Austria and Germany, but I don't think they've made quite the progress we have. Their aviation industry is focused on airships.'

'So I gather. Is there much cooperation in the aeroplane industry? Do you share your ideas?'

'Heavens, no. Well, sometimes. You know Adam Whitman from Vannier's, don't you? We've been working on some ideas with them, but it is a very competitive world. And quite political.

Doesn't do to share too much with Britain's enemies, so if we talk to anyone at all, it tends to be the French and the Americans.'

'Everything is so political these days,' I said. I nodded back towards the drawing office. 'Do you think we've given them enough time to get through the worst of the technical stuff?'

'Goff will only just be hitting his stride,' he said. 'But if we wander back he might realize he's been talking for too long.'

Paul finished his tea and we walked back through the drawing office. There were two other groups of drawing boards, but no one sitting at them.

'Are you the only ones working here?' I asked.

'Not usually. We've two other teams, but they're all off talking to the War Office about designing a spotter plane for the artillery.'

'That sounds dangerous.'

'It's the next step. Artillerymen went from standing on hills or climbing up trees to floating in tethered balloons. And now they want to be able to zip about the sky in a robust but nimble aeroplane.'

We had by now arrived back at the Dunnock team's desks.

'Robust and nimble?' said Goff. 'I'd hardly say the Dunnock was robust and nimble, Paul. Don't go overselling it. I'd stick with elegant and sedate.'

'Don't worry,' said Paul. 'We were talking about something else.'

'Ah. Right you are. Where have you two been? You've missed a most interesting discussion about stall speeds.'

'Just getting a cup of tea,' I said.

Goff looked at our empty hands. 'Didn't bring me one, then?' he said, slightly disconsolately.

'We were going to, but it didn't look very pleasant. It had the colour of a muddy puddle and we didn't think you'd thank us for it.'

'Ah, well. We need to do something about the quality of the tea in this place. British industry runs on tea.'

'But it's not running at all while we're here taking up your valuable time,' said Lady Hardcastle. 'We'd better get away and leave you to your stress calculations.'

'It's been a delight to talk to you,' said Goff, reaching out to shake us both by the hand. 'If you ever need to know anything else about the Dunnock, just ask. You know where to find us now.'

'We do,' she said. 'Thank you so very much for your time.'

We made our own way back to reception.

Miss Matthews was away from her desk again, so Lady Hardcastle left her another note and we set off for home in the Rolls.

I had intended to drive – we were still very much in character as lady and maid – but she had insisted it was her turn and was already in the driver's seat before I could say, 'Whatever happened to keeping up appearances?'

The journey was a little less sedate than our previous trips to and from Bristol Aviation. Carts were overtaken at speed and horses spooked. Fists were shaken and oaths exclaimed. As we turned off the main road towards the village, at least one of the motor car's wheels left the ground.

'I wonder if Fishy's engineers could do something with the suspension,' said Lady Hardcastle as the Rolls returned to upright with a jolting clonk. 'I'm reasonably sure it shouldn't do that.'

'I'm absolutely certain it shouldn't,' I said. 'Although I do wonder if it might have more to do with the overexuberance of the driver than any failings on the part of the designers and engineers.'

'Nonsense, dear,' she said. 'If we'd been going any slower we'd have stopped. Gertie could have run past us. Carrying Hector. And the dogs. It's definitely a fault with the motor car.'

'As you wish. What are we doing this evening?'

'I thought we might go wild and have a spot of supper and a game of cards. Did Miss Jones say anything about this evening's nosh?'

'She said she'd got a couple of nice trout for us. She was going to prepare them so I could "just bung 'em in the oven" for a bit. There'll be new potatoes and some salad, I shouldn't wonder.'

'We've got a smashing Sancerre to go with that. How lovely.'

'I'll start getting things together as soon as we get in, then we can eat in the garden. That'll leave plenty of time for me to take all your money at cards.'

'I'd protest at you casting nasturtiums on my card-playing prowess, but the evidence is against me – I owe you thousands by now, I'm sure.'

'You're good for it,' I said. 'And I know where you live. Slow down a bit.'

'Oh, don't be such a fussy drawers. I'm not going fast at all.'

'No, really. Just slow down a bit. Look at the house.'

We were still a little way from the house, but even from there it was obvious that the front door was wide open.

'Good Lord,' said Lady Hardcastle. 'Were Edna or Miss Jones working late today?'

'Not that they told me. And Jed had business in Chipping so it can't be him. Just drive past and pull over up the lane. We'll walk back and surprise them.'

'Good idea. Unless there's nobody there, in which case it's a lot of traipsing about for nothing.'

'I'll put up with a bit of traipsing if it means we have the drop on a burglar.'

She drew to a halt twenty or so yards past the house and we hopped out. She rummaged in her bag and drew out a tiny Colt Vest Pocket pistol.

'Why on earth are you carrying that about with you?' I asked.

'One never knows when one might need a handgun, dear.'

I tutted, but said nothing.

We walked back along the lane, keeping close to the hedge in case anyone was watching from the front windows. We stopped when the hedge was replaced by the low wall of the front garden, and I scanned the front of the house for observers.

'No one there,' I said quietly. 'We'd better hop over the wall, though. That gate still shrieks.'

'In this skirt?'

'You'll manage. If it comes to it, just lie down on the top and I'll roll you over.'

With only a small amount of undignified faffing, we managed to get her into a crouch on the other side of the wall. I followed nimbly after.

'How do you manage to do everything so elegantly?' she said. 'I always feel like such a lubber next to you.'

'That, my lady, is because you're a clumsy great oaf. Would you and your popgun like to lead the way?'

'I think it's for the best. If they overpower me you can stand ready to give them a punch up the bracket. I know how you enjoy that.'

We made our way stealthily across the newly mown lawn, keeping an eye on the dining room and drawing room windows as we went. There was no one looking out at us.

At the door, I allowed Lady Hardcastle to enter first, and then followed her in.

There was a slight noise from the drawing room, and Lady Hardcastle signalled her intention to investigate.

Holding her tiny pistol in both hands, she crept towards the door. She looked in, but the layout of the room and the position of the door prevented her from seeing anything. She moved in a little further, the gun still levelled.

Suddenly, she relaxed. 'Oh, for heaven's sake,' she said.

'Bloody hell, sis,' said a familiar voice. 'Steady on with that thing. You'll have someone's eye out.'

I followed her in to see Harry sitting in one of the armchairs.

'You left the front door open, you nincompoop,' she said. 'We thought we had burglars.'

'Sorry, old thing,' said Harry. 'I thought I'd latched it behind me. There was no one in so I made myself at home.' He indicated a teapot, cup, saucer, and milk jug on the table.

'So I see.'

'It's fresh, if you want one. Only just made it.'

'We might as well.' She turned to me. 'Could you be a dear and fetch a couple more cups.'

I headed out towards the kitchen.

'And some biscuits, if you have any,' called Harry. 'Or some cake. I could murder a slice of cake.'

I returned moments later with a tray laden with cups, saucers, plates, and a freshly made Battenberg I'd found under a cloche beside the bread bin. I poured the tea and distributed the cake.

'I do love a Battenberg,' said Harry. 'Thank you. I've always wondered about the alchemy of it, though.'

I frowned at him.

'The nine squares,' he continued. 'What sort of culinary witchcraft keeps them so uniform and separate while it's baking? I've seen sponge mixture – it's quite runny. Why doesn't the pink stuff mix into the yellow stuff in the tin?'

I frowned again, but said nothing. I wasn't sure whether he was joking.

'Harry, dear,' said Lady Hardcastle, 'you're an idiot. You bake a thin pink sponge and a thin yellow sponge, then cut them into long strips and glue them together with apricot jam. Mixed together in the same tin, indeed. You really are an absolute wump sometimes.'

He grinned sheepishly. 'How was I supposed to know?' he said.

'If it comes to that,' I said to Lady Hardcastle, 'how on earth did *you* know?'

It was her turn to grin sheepishly. 'Actually, I wasn't certain,' she said. 'It just seemed like the most practical solution. Was I right?'

'Dead on. Even down to the type of jam.'

'Everything in the kitchen is glued together with apricot jam. That much I do know.'

'I have learned something new and important, then,' said Harry. 'Now, sit yourselves down and let's talk about the case.'

'That's very kind of you, dear,' said Lady Hardcastle. 'I shall make myself comfortable in my own home. He's a gracious host, isn't he, Flo?'

'Most kind,' I said. 'But I need to go and sort something out first. Someone left our front door wide open.'

'Where have you two been today?' asked Harry through a mouth-ful of cake.

'Bristol Aviation, of course,' said Lady Hardcastle. 'It's what you asked us to do.'

'Good show,' he said. 'Just checking. Anything to report?'

'Only that you're still as uncouth as ever. Do you talk with your mouth full at home?'

'Good Lord, no. Jake would skin me.'

Harry's wife, Lady Lavinia, was Lord Riddlethorpe's sister and had been known since her schooldays as 'Jake'. The schoolgirl logic had taken her from Lavinia to Lav to Lavatory to Jakes to Jake. Lady Hardcastle couldn't bring herself to use the name most of the time, and preferred to stick to Lavinia, but Harry thought it a perfectly splendid name for his beautiful wife.

He took a swig of tea to clear his mouth. 'She's terribly fastidious about that sort of thing.'

'And yet . . .' said Lady Hardcastle, her eyebrows arched.

'Comfortable in your company, old horse. If you can't relax in your sister's house, then where?'

She harrumphed. 'Well, there is slightly more, as it happens. I'm more suspicious of Myrtle Matthews than I once was. I know that's not saying much, given that I didn't suspect her at all before today, but it's still a change worthy of note.'

'What changed your mind?'

Lady Hardcastle took a bite of Battenberg and declined to speak, indicating the fullness of her mouth.

I rolled my eyes. 'Something she'd said about John Milhouse,' I said. 'The accountant. You remember we told you she painted him as a lecherous old goat? He was nothing but polite and courteous when he met us. Obviously he might have just been on his best behaviour with a prospective customer—'

'Or you're not his type,' interrupted Harry.

'We've definitely considered that. But slightly more likely, given my undeniable gorgeousness and your sister's . . . whatever it is she's got going for her, is that she bears a grudge of some sort. For some reason it's important to her to paint him in a bad light. And that's never a good sign.'

'No,' he said, thoughtfully. 'No, I don't suppose it is. You've no idea what this grudge might be, though?'

'Give us time, dear,' said Lady Hardcastle, her cake now eaten. 'We're working undercover here. We can't just get out the rubber hoses and demand answers. Softly softly and all that.'

'Quite, quite.' He was still somewhat distracted. 'Anyone else?'

'I had a most illuminating conversation about aeroplane design and manufacture with Goff Parfitt,' she said. 'He really is rather dedicated to his work.'

'Any grudges?'

'None I could discern, dear. He loves the company, loves aeroplanes, loves his job.'

'But does he love his country?'

'Oh, Harry, don't be a goose. How would I be able to tell?'

'Did he express any cynicism? Any criticism of the government? Our relations with other nations?'

'Do you ever speak to anyone outside Westminster, dear?' she said, shaking her head. 'That's how all Englishmen talk about their country. They're cynical about everything. They think the government is useless and makes the most appallingly poor decisions on all matters at home and abroad. That's how one knows they're English.'

It was Harry's turn to harrumph. 'Look, I don't like to labour the point,' he said, 'and I know full well that you were both in this game while I was . . . how is it you always dismiss my early career? "Still making tea for Whitehall mandarins"? Anyway, you surely know that this whole matter is rather urgent and important. The Germans might have backed down over Morocco in the end, but we all nearly came to blows over that little lot. It was only a financial crisis at home that made them think twice. When the starting pistol is eventually fired – and everyone in Westminster is convinced it's a matter of when, not if – we're going to depend on companies like Bristol Aviation and their research teams to keep us in the running. We can't afford leaks. We can't afford setbacks to vital research. We can't afford to lose any more good men like Dickie Dupree.'

'We never did hear anything much about Dupree,' I said. 'Who was he? What did he do?'

'A splendid chap, by all accounts. Kind, generous, handsome as you like. Played rugby in the winter, cricket in the summer – dashed good at both. No one had a bad word to say about him. On top of all that, he was something of a rising star in the aeroplane world. The higher-ups at the War Office were keeping an eye on him. Destined for greatness, they thought.'

'What was his area of expertise?' asked Lady Hardcastle.

'Weaponry. It's being very much played down. The War Office won't officially recognize Bristol Aviation as part of the arms industry – they want to keep it on the QT. But he was working on ideas for mounting machine guns on aeroplanes.'

'All the official bumf you sent us said aeroplanes were being considered as unarmed observation platforms,' I said.

'Which is all very noble and gentlemanly right up to the point when the other chaps get miffed about you peering down on them from your lofty vantage point. It's at that moment that they'll start taking potshots at you, and the only sensible thing is to have a way of shooting back. Easiest thing is to mount a machine gun in front of the pilot – aiming is just a matter of pointing the aeroplane at the target. Problem is those blasted big propellers. Machine guns rip them to bits.'

Lady Hardcastle thought for a moment. 'Surely it's just a matter of synchronizing the gun to the propeller so that it only fires while the propeller blade isn't directly in the path of the bullet,' she said. 'Some sort of device driven by the rotation of the engine that only pulls the trigger when it's safe to do so would do the trick.'

Harry goggled at her for a moment. 'You need to have a word with some of the gun wizards at the War Office,' he said.

'Oh, they'll take no notice of me. What can a woman possibly know about guns?'

'Well, Dickie Dupree had gone down any number of dead ends in months of research, and you come up with a solution off the top of your head. He was looking at other methods of mounting the gun out of the way of the propeller entirely.'

'He's a loss to the country as well as poor Myrtle, then,' I said.

'Great loss. Which is why we need to get this whole thing squared away snappily. Any life lost is a tragedy, but in this day and age we can ill afford to lose brains like his. The traitor has to be stopped.'

'We'll get to the bottom of it, dear. We do take things a good deal more seriously than you give us credit for, you know.'

'I know. I'm sorry. It's just so dashed frustrating. It's all I can do not to tell you to get those rubber hoses out sometimes. How do you cope with the slow pace of it all?'

'Experience,' I said. 'We know that if we keep looking and listening, keep asking the right questions of the right people, it'll all become clear in the end.'

'As long as it all becomes clear before we all line up and start shooting at each other,' he said.

'It will, dear,' said Lady Hardcastle. 'We're working our way through the suspects. Flo spoke to his junior, didn't you, dear?' she said.

'I did,' I said. 'He's not quite the "odd fish" I was expecting after what Adam Whitman said, but he's not entirely ordinary, either. He's another one obsessed with his work. He's the sort who could spend three years at university in London and know nothing of the city because he was so engrossed in his studies.'

'How do you know?' said Harry.

'Because when I asked him about his time in London, he said he had no idea what the city was like because he'd been so engrossed in his studies,' I said with a smile.

'It's my own fault for asking,' he said. 'Any thoughts on your next steps?'

'We're planning a break-in,' said Lady Hardcastle. 'Milhouse has two safes in his office: one in plain view, the other concealed behind a ghastly portrait of a self-important man with side whiskers.'

'And you know there's a safe behind it because . . . ?'

'Because we've been doing this job for years – every idiot who ever had a secret to keep put his safe behind a portrait, though not always as attention-grabbingly ghastly as that one. We're betting that's where the "real" books are kept, so we'd quite like to take a look inside. Any other incriminating titbits we come across will be a bonus.'

'I'd also like a chance to have a proper nose round the parachute project in Hangar B,' I said. 'I thought I could spend an hour or so there, then nip into the office block and see what Milhouse keeps in his "secret" safe.'

'You're not planning to divvy up the jobs between you, then?' said Harry.

'It's a perfect division of labour,' said Lady Hardcastle. 'Flo does the clever stuff inside, I wait outside in the Rolls so we can make a quick getaway.'

'You're the experts,' he said. 'I've another little wheeze for you, too, if you wouldn't mind helping us out.'

'We live to serve, dear,' said Lady Hardcastle. 'Speaking of which: what's the news on supper?'

'Trout gutted and stuffed, ready for the oven,' I said. 'Potatoes out. Salad washed. Miss Jones has left me little to do.'

'Wonderful. Would you care to stay for supper, Harry dear? There are a couple of bottles of Sancerre to go with it.'

'I should like that very much. Thank you. I don't suppose . . . ?'

'Bed for the night? Of course. Do you want to let Lavinia know not to expect you home? The telephone's in the hall.'

'Oh, I already told Jake I was staying here. I . . . umm . . . I packed a bag.' He pointed to a leather Gladstone bag on the floor beside his chair.

'Of course you did,' said Lady Hardcastle. She turned to me. 'Is there a room made up?'

'There is,' I said. 'I make sure Edna keeps at least one of the guest rooms ready for just such an eventuality.'

'Then we shall dine, you shall make your impertinent request for further help, and Flo shall extract payment for your board and lodging by skinning you at cards.'

'Sounds like a perfect evening,' said Harry. 'Anything I can do to help?'

'You can fetch yourself a candle and pop down into the cellar for the Sancerre,' I said. 'That'll save me from getting dusty and dirty.'

'Get the 1908,' said Lady Hardcastle. 'I'd like to save the 1906.'

'Right you are,' said Harry.

We left Lady Hardcastle to make notes and sketches for her crime board while we prepared everything for dinner in the garden.

'I say. My compliments to the chefs,' said Harry. 'This is delicious.'

We were sitting at the rotting table in the rotting chairs and enjoying a meal in the summer evening sunshine.

'Wine's not bad, either,' he continued. 'Local vintner? Or do you have it sent down from London?'

'We use a local firm,' said Lady Hardcastle. 'Bristol's a port, dear. It has a long and illustrious reputation for importing wines and spirits. Why would we send to London when we have some of the best wine merchants in the country right here on our doorstep?'

'You must give me their address. I'm not above having a case or two shipped across the country if it's as good as this.'

'Take a couple of bottles with you. I'm sure Lavinia would love it.'

'Very kind. Thank you.'

'Always a pleasure,' she said. 'And now that you have us suitably relaxed with our own splendid wine, what horrible additional imposition do you wish to impose upon us?'

Harry laughed. 'Nothing more than you're paid for, old thing,' he said. 'You remember the business at Weston last year?'

'I'm not likely to forget, dear. I still bear the scars.'

She bore no scars, but I didn't correct her.

'Do you?' he said. 'Where?'

'Never you mind.'

'Right you are. But we tried a little ruse on that job that we'd like to repeat. Not a new trick, but a useful one. We'd like to plant some false information and see where it ends up.'

'Like putting dye in the water,' I said.

'Exactly like that, Strongarm. Exactly like that.'

'Where do we come in?' asked Lady Hardcastle.

'As always, I'm a bit short-handed and I rather thought you might keep an eye on a potential meet for me.'

'Hmm,' she said. 'What if we're spotted? Won't that make the rest of the mission somewhat problematic? We're going to struggle to carry on posing as potential purchasers of aeroplanes if we've already tipped our hand and revealed that we were working for you all along.'

'Then don't get spotted. I thought you were good at this sort of thing. And you're only in there to trace the leak, anyway. Once we know who's blabbing, your work at Bristol Aviation will be done.'

'We're looking into the murder as well.'

'Potential manslaughter,' he corrected. 'Chances are it's the same chap – selling secrets and setting Bristol Aviation back while others steal the march. Or catch up, at least.'

'Hmm,' she said again. 'We'd be putting a lot of faith in your hunch, though, wouldn't we? Once we've burned our bridges there, the investigation into the murder stops. If your leaker and your parachute-mangler aren't the same man, the murderer goes free.'

'It might just be involuntary manslaughter,' I said. 'The test was supposed to be with a dummy, remember? Myrtle Matthews told us. The wrecker might only have intended to spoil the test, not kill anyone.'

'Even so,' she said.

'I take your point, sis,' said Harry. 'But if I'm faced with the choice between the safety of the country and catching a killer who might or might not have intended to kill, I'll take care of national security first and worry about justice afterwards. We can't bring the poor chap back.'

'That's a cynical attitude, Henry Featherstonhaugh.'

He frowned. 'We're in a cynical business,' he said. 'You of all people should know that.'

She sighed. 'You're right, of course.' She thought for a moment. 'Yes, then, we'll lurk in the shadows to trap your leaker. That's all right with you, Flo?'

'It'll be a shame to miss out on bringing the killer to justice if it doesn't pan out like you think it will,' I said. 'But I'm happy to play along. Make sure we have more than just a few hours' notice, though.'

'You'll know exactly when you need to be in place. As soon as I have confirmation that the . . . that the . . . I want to say that the hook has been baited, but we're already talking about tracing leaks with dye and there are no hooks involved—'

'But anyway . . . ' said Lady Hardcastle.

'Quite, quite. Sorry. A time and place will be specified. We're confident that we have the method of communication figured out – we pieced it together before the last leak – but it's all rather cleverly done to conceal the identities of those involved. Once everything's in place, we'll send a message demanding new information, as though it has come from the foreign contact. The leaker, finding himself in fortuitous possession of a tasty titbit, will leap up, leak his leak, then leap back and return to his daily life as though no leaks were leaked. Or at least he'll attempt to. His contact won't be there, of course, but you'll be hanging around discreetly at the appointed meeting place to see who turns up. He'll just assume there's been a change of plans and slink back to his lair to await further instructions.'

'Child's play,' I said. 'Do you have a meeting place in mind?'

'Actually, no. We thought you might have some ideas there. Local knowledge and all that.'

'It needs to be somewhere we can lurk without causing suspicion,' said Lady Hardcastle. 'It'll be an evening meeting, one presumes? In a public place?'

'If that's the way these things are done,' he said, 'then yes.'

'A pub would be best,' I said. 'But he'll not want it to be too close to work, obviously. It'll need to be somewhere he can get to, but where he'll not be seen by anyone from the factory.'

'Know anywhere?'

'Not our area of expertise,' said Lady Hardcastle. 'It's pleasingly suburban and jolly between the factory and the edge of town, but I'm not familiar with the local hostelries. And if he doesn't at least have a bicycle, all the villages out this way will be a bit of a trek for him.'

'We'd stand out in a village pub, though,' I said, 'unless we drag him all the way out here. Everyone knows everyone else in a village pub – incomers attract a lot of attention. Especially unaccompanied women.'

'We'll think of something,' said Lady Hardcastle. 'It's what we're good at, after all.'

'We shall,' I said. 'More potatoes before we clear away?'

'Depends,' said Harry.

'On what?'

'On whether your cook has made anything for pudding.'

'Ah,' I said. 'In that case you might wish to save room for her delicious blackcurrant pie.'

'With custard?'

'I'm sure I can make you some custard. Would you like some, my lady?'

'Rather,' she said. 'Pie and custard all round. Then we can retire indoors and get the cards out.'

I cleared the table and went to the kitchen to make some custard.

Chapter Ten

Dawn broke on Thursday morning long before sensible people ought to be awake. For reasons known only to my own wilful brain I had woken not long afterwards. I had nothing to worry about – my life was calm and peaceful for the most part – but my beloved brain had decided that a life free of anxiety was a life wasted. To induce what it clearly considered to be the appropriate levels of dread and discomfort, it had trawled through recent events looking for something to fret over. Having found nothing, it had decided to catalogue every mistake I had ever made and every embarrassment I had ever suffered. In chronological order. That did the trick. Well done, brain.

So now, while the sensible folk slumbered, I was up.

The range was lit, and the kitchen cleaned. I had done my morning exercises.

I toyed with the idea of walking down the lane and seeing if the bakery was open. I knew Holman would be working – bakers always start early – but it was a while since I'd been into the village that early in the morning and I couldn't remember whether he opened the shop or just loaded up the basket on the front of his delivery boy's bicycle and supplied the neighbourhood with bread that way.

I decided not to take the early walk and just to wait for the delivery boy.

Then I wondered if Miss Jones ordered a bread delivery on Thursdays. Or did we have a delivery on Tuesday?

What if we had a delivery on Thursday but the lad's bicycle broke down and we didn't get any bread until lunchtime?

Even if there was a delivery today, would we have enough bread now that we had an unexpected houseguest?

I started making some bread and left it proving beside the range.

I wrote letters to Gwenith in Woolwich and Ellie in Annapolis.

I took photographs of a cat in the garden. We didn't own a cat. Cats must roam for miles.

I worried that the cat might be lost.

Back in the kitchen I put the bread on to bake and boiled the kettle.

I started to make some coffee.

Finally Miss Jones and Edna arrived.

'Hello, Miss Armstrong,' said Miss Jones. 'Is everythin' all right? Not like you to be up and doin' this time of the mornin'. Is that bread I can smell?'

'I put a loaf on,' I said. 'I couldn't sleep. Two loaves, actually. And some rolls.'

Edna chuckled. 'And cleaned the kitchen, too, by the looks of it.'

'I might have pushed a broom round. I thought since I was up . . .'

'Well, you sit down there and I'll finish off the coffee,' said Miss Jones.

'Thank you. We're one extra for breakfast, by the way. Lady Hardcastle's brother stayed the night rather than hare back to London.'

'We gots plenty to eat,' she said. 'Nothin' to worry about there.'

'When did he come?' asked Edna.

'Yesterday afternoon some time,' I said. 'Let himself in.'

'I didn't know he had a key,' she said with a slight hint of accusation in her tone.

'Nor did I,' I said.

''S funny. We locked up same as always.'

I smiled. 'It seems he's better at fieldwork than he lets on,' I said.

'Like on the farm?' said Miss Jones. 'How would that help him?'

'No, I meant . . . you know . . . the practical side of . . . things. His work. I always thought of him as more of an office Johnny.'

'Who's an office Johnny?' said Harry.

He was standing in the kitchen doorway.

'You,' I said. 'It's just been brought to my attention that you broke in yesterday afternoon. I didn't know you were handy with a picklock.'

'One has to keep at least a small part of one's light hidden under the old bushel,' he said.

'Well, quite,' I said. 'People might start asking you to help out on the dangerous jobs.'

'Can't have that. I'm an office Johnny, after all. But I did break in.'

'And left the door open. Probably best you don't do any fieldwork if you're going to be as clumsy as that.'

'Schoolboy error,' he agreed. 'Nearly got myself shot for my trouble.'

'Shot?' said Miss Jones. 'Is there a gunman on the loose?'

'More of a gunwoman,' said Harry. 'My darling sister was all set to plug me where I sat.'

'Oh,' said Miss Jones, now much less concerned. 'She wouldn't shoot you.'

'Who wouldn't I shoot?' said Lady Hardcastle.

She was standing, yawning, next to Harry.

'You wouldn't shoot no one, m'lady,' said Miss Jones. 'Not you.'

'I'll shoot this blessed idiot if he breaks into my house again. Don't think I won't.'

'Duly noted, sis,' said Harry. 'Duly noted.'

'Would you all care to take coffee in the morning room?' said Edna. Even after all this time, the informality of the Hardcastle household made her uncomfortable sometimes. She could just about cope when it was only Lady Hardcastle chatting in the kitchen, but guests were a step too far, even when they were family.

I got up.

'Coffee would be lovely,' I said. 'Come on, you two. We've got plans to plan, stratagems to strategize, and ruses to . . . to . . . something or other. What do you do with ruses?'

'Put them in your buttonhule?' said Harry.

'I say, Harry, well done,' said Lady Hardcastle. 'That was almost clever.'

I shook my head and ushered them out the door and towards the morning room.

I settled the Featherstonhaugh siblings at the table and returned to the kitchen to ask Miss Jones for breakfast for three as soon as she was able. She had finished making the coffee, so I took that back with me.

'. . . large government order,' said Harry as I re-entered the morning room.

'And you're sure the leaker will take the bait?' said Lady Hardcastle.

'Not "sure", no. It's exactly the sort of titbit the spy will be keen to pass on, though – exactly the sort of thing his masters will be asking him to be on the lookout for – so we're quietly confident, but nothing is ever certain in this game. You know that.'

I put the coffee tray on the table and sat down. 'Miss Jones is making a slap-up breakfast,' I said. 'There'll be toast in a few moments to tide us over.'

'Thank you, dear,' said Lady Hardcastle. 'We're discussing the ruse.'

'So I gathered,' I said. 'A government order for what?'

'Parachutes,' said Harry. 'Our nosy foreign friends are already interested in them, so we thought the best way to flush them out would be to offer something irresistible. Who wouldn't want to know that His Majesty's government is placing an order for a hundred of the things?'

'That many?' said Lady Hardcastle. 'Does the army even have a hundred aviators, let alone aeroplanes?'

'Actually, you might be surprised – things are getting a little interesting on that score. The Air Battalion of the Royal Engineers has just shy of two hundred officers and men on the strength. It's true they only have five aeroplanes at the moment, but that makes it all the more interesting, don't you think? Why would they be ordering so many parachutes? Are they placing more orders for aeroplanes? Is the Air Battalion preparing for war? Who could resist the urge to try to find out more?'

'Are they preparing for war?' I asked.

'You see? Everyone wants to know. If you were a spy you'd be champing at the bit to pass on news of a big order for parachutes.'

'I *am* a spy,' I said.

'And a damned fine one. But even you'd be drawn in by this.'

'I'm not so sure,' said Lady Hardcastle. 'Sometimes the reason for something seeming to be too good to be true is that it really is too good to be true. I think you're over-egging it.'

'What would you suggest?' he said.

'Cut the order back. Why not three dozen?'

'Because any number of dozens sounds like none at all. Thirty-five sounds like more than three dozen. Three dozen is an order for oysters.'

'Fifty?' I suggested. 'A large number, but not fantastically large.'

He sighed. 'I'll consult the Powers That Be,' he said. 'Though I do think we're quibbling over nothing. The point is that some disgruntled employee, fundless spendthrift, or dewy-eyed political idealist won't be thinking too hard about whether they've been sold a tweedle. They'll be straight on to their contact in search of praise or reward.'

'Ours is not to reason why,' said Lady Hardcastle. 'Ours is but to go to a village tea room and wait for skulduggery to unfold before us.'

'A tea room?' he said.

'It came to me this morning as I surfaced from my slumbers. Our leaker and his contact would rule out pubs near the factory lest they be seen by other Bristol Aviation employees. Pubs further away are better for them, but not for us – Flo makes an excellent point about how badly we would stand out. To be honest, though, they were probably ruled out by the leaker's contact for similar reasons – everyone notices strangers in their local pub. So why not a tea room? It would be acceptable to the spies – two pals could enjoy a cup of tea and a slice of cake in a village tea room without attracting attention – and it would suit us, too. Our leaker wouldn't think twice about seeing two ladies at a tea room while he waited for his contact.'

'Except that everyone you currently suspect has seen you and knows full well who you are.'

'If it were somewhere near here it wouldn't be so unusual.'

'But they'd be spooked,' he said. 'And I'd wager it's a huge change from their usual procedure. That would ring alarm bells even before they noticed the nosy customer and her maid sitting at the next table. And you already suggested it was probably too far for them to travel.'

'We're all overthinking it,' I said. 'I said it would be a pub yesterday because that's how we've always met our own informants. But it doesn't have to be anything like that. We don't know how the meetings are usually conducted, so anything we do will be a change. We need to make the change as innocent and commonplace as possible so as not, as you say, Harry, to spook them. It's summertime. The evenings are bright. People are out and about. Horfield Common is the place. It's halfway between the city and the factory, it's open, it's popular with evening strollers—'

'And vagabonds, footpads, cutpurses and assorted other ne'er-do-wells,' interrupted Lady Hardcastle.

'Even better,' I said. 'Wrong 'uns aren't going to go blabbing to the police about shifty characters handing over files – it'll draw attention to their own dastardly doings. And I think you'd be surprised, anyway. With the prison and the barracks nearby, I'm going to bet the common is quite a genteel place these days.'

'Horfield Common it is, then,' said Harry. 'We can say something ambiguous about it being a good meeting place. We can't talk about a change of plans in case it's their usual venue, but we'll need to reassure the leaker that all is well, just in case it does happen to be a radical change.'

'We shall leave that to you, dear,' said Lady Hardcastle. 'We have some breaking and entering to plan this afternoon.'

'Of course. Would it be putting you out too much if I were to stay another few nights? I'd like to be on the spot in case things turn ugly.'

'It's a pleasure to have you here. Edna can take care of laundry for you, and we can send to Chipping for sundries if you need anything.'

'You're the best sister a chap could wish for. Do you mind if I book a trunk call to London? I ought to tell Jake what I'm up to – I said I'd only be away for a couple of days.'

Edna and Miss Jones arrived bearing trays laden with a breakfast feast, which we attacked ravenously. Plotting is hungry work.

Before we could make further plans and arrangements, there were household matters to attend to. Miss Jones kept an excellent record of her orders with the local shops so it was easy to reconcile the neatly written entries in her notebook with the scrawled bills that had come with the latest deliveries. I put the cash into envelopes and gave them to Miss Jones to send with her next orders.

Harry finally got a call through to his home in London just before lunch. Lady Lavinia assured him that all was well, and that although she and baby Addie would miss him terribly, they'd surely survive without him for a couple of days while he visited his sister.

His sister, meanwhile, had disappeared into her study and hadn't been seen since breakfast. She emerged just as Miss Jones announced lunch.

'What have you been up to, sis?' asked Harry, as she joined us in the garden.

'Planning, plotting and preparing,' she said.

'Splendid.'

'Spiffing,' I added.

'Sp— No, I've got nothing,' said Harry.

Lady Hardcastle shook her head and sighed. 'I've been checking maps and whatnot for this evening's excursion,' she said. 'I'll show you both after lunch, but I think things should be reasonably straightforward.'

'I can smooth things over with the local rozzers if you get caught, but please don't. I'm having second thoughts about you blundering in there while we're trying to plug the leak as it is.'

'There's more going on there than just someone leaking—' she began.

I stifled a chuckle.

'Really, dear?' she said. 'Leaking? Really?'

'Oh, come on,' I said. 'Tell me you haven't wanted to smirk every time one of us talks about leaks.'

She frowned. 'There's more going on there than just . . . the theft of proprietary information,' she continued. 'Once you've caught your spies there might still be unsolved matters. What if the parachute nobbling is unconnected? What if the fraud has nothing to do with either the spying or wrecking the project? Once you and your Special Branch thugs go galumphing in arresting people, evidence will be destroyed. Or spirited away. Either way, we'll not find the answers to all our questions.'

'Which is why I'm not stopping you,' he said. 'I'm merely asking you to be circumspect.'

'I am the very soul of circumspection,' she said. 'I am careful, prudent and discreet. Flo, meanwhile, is positively wraithlike in her ability to flit unseen among the shadows. The police rejoice daily that she didn't turn to a life of crime. She would have been the most notorious sneak thief in all England. Caught, indeed! Whatever next?'

'You'd think less of me if I didn't say anything.'

'I couldn't possibly think any less of you, dear, you know that. How was Lavinia?'

'She's well and sends her love. Addie is sitting up on her own now and clapped for the first time yesterday.'

'How delightful. I shall take her to the theatre the next time we're in town. She'll be the perfect audience member.'

'You do that,' he said. 'Take something for her to chew on – she's teething.'

'So she'll be miserable, too? Absolutely the perfect audience member. She can complain loudly all the way through and then clap as though she's had the most marvellous time.'

'Sounds like every show I've ever been to. Can we steal your cook? This pork pie is delicious.'

'She is rather good, isn't she? I told her I'd support her if ambition drew her away from us, but she's content for the time being. She has an ailing mother in the village, so cooking for us part-time suits her well.'

Conversation flitted about like this until the summer pudding had been demolished and we returned to the dining room – the only room with a table large enough to display Lady Hardcastle's maps.

'These maps are a little out of date,' she said as she spread out three overlapping Ordnance Survey maps on the dining table. 'But I've added some of the new features in pencil, as you can see.'

'There'll be new ones next year,' said Harry. 'I saw a memo about it the other day.'

'Interesting,' she said, 'but unhelpful for the moment.'

'I was just saying.'

'I know, dear. Thank you. Perhaps you could secure us an advance set. I'll take the six inch and the twenty-five inch, please.'

'I'll see what I can do.'

'Now, then,' she continued, tapping on the map with her pencil. 'This is the site of the factory here, just north of the village of Filton. I've sketched in the new access road and marked the main buildings. Obviously we'll be coming from the north, and I've indicated the preferred route and our two main escape routes if, for any reason, we can't just drive back up the main road when we're done.'

'Very thorough,' said Harry. 'What's this?'

She looked where he had indicated.

'Jam, dear. These maps have seen plenty of activity. And cake. We're happy with the routes?'

'I'm not sure about getting through this lane in the dark,' I said, pointing, 'but if we end up having to drive down there in the middle of the night we'll have more problems than rutted tracks and overhanging branches.'

'Quite,' she said. 'But that's definitely a last resort. We might be better off abandoning the Rolls and heading off on foot, if it comes to it.'

She took a larger-scale map – twenty-five inches to the mile – and laid it on top of the others.

'I've tried to add as much detail as I can here,' she said. 'This is the new road. Here's the office block with the yard in front of it for parking. These are Hangars A and B. And this, I'm reasonably sure, is the extent of the aerodrome itself.'

As she spoke, she tapped the neatly drawn additions to the out-of-date map.

'I propose pulling off the main road here and parking the car in this little copse. I know that's still there – I remember seeing it the other day. From there, you can enter this field. At least, I'm assuming you can. It's all dairy farms along there as far as I recall, so it should just be pasture. Anyway, whatever terrain you have to navigate, you hug this hedge here, keeping an eye to your right for the edge of the hangars. Then onwards for another sixty-five yards—'

'Seventy-three Flosteps,' I said.

'Seventy-three what?' said Harry.

'It's her personal unit of measurement,' said Lady Hardcastle. 'Take no notice. When you reach the designated spot – however you choose to measure it – duck through the hedge and scan the fence for the badger gap. That's your entry point.'

'Wouldn't it be easier to do the whole journey between the hedge and the fence?' said Harry.

'More chance of being spotted if the nightwatchmen are paying attention to their jobs,' I said.

'But what if you can't get to the other side? A properly laid hedge can be damned tricky to get through.'

'They tend not to do that round here,' I said. 'They just plant everything nice and tight – they don't do any of that clever cutting and weaving they do in other parts of the country.'

'I live and learn.'

I curtseyed. 'But even so, it's me we're talking about. I'll find a way.'

'Of course you will,' he said. 'My apologies. I take it you already know there's a badger gap?'

'We scouted it last time we were there,' I said. 'They've dug a nice little trench under the fence. That's how we know how far I have to go.'

'How will you know when to start counting? How will you see the hangars in the dark?'

'He has a point,' I said. 'How will I see the hangars in the dark?'

Lady Hardcastle tapped the almanac she'd brought in with her.

'The moon,' she said. 'It's a full moon tomorrow so it'll be good and bright tonight as well. We'll be going in at about eleven and the moon will be to the south. It'll be behind you from the point of view of any observers at the aerodrome, so you'll be in the shadow of the hedge, but it will light up the hangars beautifully.'

'You've thought of everything,' he said.

'That's how we've managed to stay alive and mostly out of gaol for so long.'

'Mostly?'

'There has been some unpleasantness along the way,' I said. 'All in foreign parts, don't worry.'

'And I always got her out,' said Lady Hardcastle. 'Eventually. Where were we?'

'Badger trench under the fence,' said Harry.

'Ah, yes. That's where my planning takes a little break. Once you're in, it's up to you. I presume you have some ideas?'

'I do,' I said. 'It's all in hand.'

'Splendid. Getting out should be a simple matter of retracing your steps back to the Rolls. If nothing goes awry we'll just pootle back up the road to home and no one will be any the wiser. Sunrise is at a quarter to five, give or take, so we need to be on the road by no later than half past four, I'd say.'

'That's more than enough time,' I said. 'We should be home before anyone even knows we've gone.'

'I'll know,' said Harry. 'But I shan't wait up.'

'Talking of which,' I said. 'Would anyone mind if I had a nap? I've been up since heaven knows when this morning and if I'm going to be up until heaven knows when tomorrow morning, I ought to try to get a little sleep.'

'An excellent idea,' said Lady Hardcastle. 'You toddle off, and we'll amuse ourselves until dinner. I can show Harry the plans for the garden.'

'You're in for a treat there,' I said. 'If I'm not down by dinner time can one of you wake me, please?'

I was asleep within five minutes of lying down.

173

I made it downstairs, yawning and scratching, in time for scrambled eggs on toast. Without me to cook anything, and with Miss Jones being unable to stay late because of important business elsewhere, the Featherstonhaugh siblings had been at a loss.

'But I can scramble eggs,' said Harry, proudly.

He was right. He could.

We ate our supper in the garden once more, chatting inconsequentially until about eight o'clock, when the gathering gloom brought out the biting insects and forced us indoors.

'When are we leaving?' I asked, once we were all settled in the drawing room with a pot of coffee.

'It's going to take us about three-quarters of an hour to get there,' said Lady Hardcastle. 'And we'll need a few minutes of peace and quiet to get accustomed to our surroundings and make sure we're alone. Shall we say ten o'clock? That should see you on your way by no later than eleven.'

'Sounds good to me,' I said. 'I'll need to change.'

'Change?' said Harry. 'There's a dress code for burglary? I had no idea it was so formal.'

I indicated my unusually fashionable muslin summer dress. 'I'm not scrambling under fences in this,' I said. 'Someone in this household is careless with her clothes, but I can't afford to be so blasé. And these shoes look thoroughly swish if I'm strolling about the village, but they're no use for running. And certainly not climbing.'

'Point taken. Something a bit more utilitarian required, then, eh?'

'Don't worry,' said Lady Hardcastle, 'she has just the thing.'

She was right. I did.

We drank our coffee and talked about nothing very much until I excused myself to dress for the festivities.

I returned a short while later, transformed.

'I say,' said Harry. 'You weren't kidding, were you? You really do have just the thing. Chinese?'

'Inspired by our time in China, yes,' I said.

'We had my dressmaker knock it up for us last year when we allowed ourselves to be press-ganged back into active service,' said Lady Hardcastle. 'I have something just like it.'

I was dressed in a black suit fashioned from a soft but hard-wearing cotton. We had first seen the loose trousers and jackets on both men and women in Shanghai, and had worn them ourselves on several missions there. They were comfortable, quiet, and easy to move about in. The originals were made of lighter cotton, or sometimes silk, but we needed something more ruggedly suitable for nighttime skulduggery in the variable English climate.

On my feet were my trusty black plimsolls.

'No cap?' he said.

'Not tonight,' I said. 'I find they get in the way, so if I don't need to keep my face hidden I don't bother. I'll just tie my hair back in a braid.'

'Do you have the tools of your nefarious trade, dear?' said Lady Hardcastle.

I hefted a small haversack. 'Picklocks, a small jemmy, some cord, a length of rope, a flashlight, a knife, and a doctor's stethoscope. If I need anything else I'm scuppered. But I shan't. We've reconnoitred the place well enough. I know what I'm up against.'

'No gun?' asked Harry.

'No, never a gun. That's your sister's favourite toy. I'll be fine.' I pulled up my right sleeve to reveal the sheathed throwing knife strapped to my forearm.

'You really are rather scary. Wait. Did you just say stethoscope?'

'For the safe. If it's a combination lock I'll need to try to crack it. The stethoscope is for listening to the lock. I hope it doesn't come to that, though – it takes hours.'

'Fingers crossed, then, eh? What will you be doing while Flo's doing all the hard work, sis?'

'I'd like to read, but I can't risk a lantern. I shall have a flask of tea with me. Perhaps I'll have a nice snooze.'

'All right for some. If you weren't so insistent on always buying two-seaters I'd have come along to keep you company.'

'You're useful here near the telephone, dear. If we run into any difficulties with the local law, you can work your Westminster magic and free us before we have to resort to more Flo-like methods of escape.'

He frowned.

'But we're not going to get caught,' I said. 'The nightwatchmen will be idiots, the local coppers will be miles away, and I'll be in and out leaving no more trace than a summer breeze.'

'You'd better,' he said. 'Oh, one more thing, though. You don't have a watch. How will you know what time it is?'

'I'll be in the hangar or the offices – there are clocks everywhere.'

'Best be on the safe side,' he said.

He took his watch from his waistcoat pocket and handed it to me. 'Emily has her fancy Swiss wristwatch, but this is a reliable old thing. It'll see you right.'

'I'll keep it safe,' I said. 'Thank you.'

'Come along, then, Summer Breeze,' said Lady Hardcastle, standing up. 'Let's get you and your bag of tricks into the Rolls.'

We packed ourselves into the motor car, and Harry waved us off.

Chapter Eleven

Against my better judgement, I let Lady Hardcastle drive. I had to balance my desire to arrive safe and sound against the need for her to get her eye in. We seldom drove in the dark, and although the Rolls had powerful headlights, it was still a completely different proposition to driving in daylight. If we had to scarper in a hurry, I wanted her sharp and ready, not still trying to get used to the idea of driving by moonlight.

She seemed much less concerned by the darkness than I had imagined she might be. The absence of even the possibility of other traffic seemed to offset any worries she might have had about not being able to see where she was going. If there were to be no farmers or delivery men and their skittish horses in her path, what need was there for caution? The fact that she could only see two yards in front of her seemed merely to add to the fun.

'Soon be there,' she said cheerfully as we rocketed down the Gloucester Road.

'Or dead in a ditch,' I said.

'Or that. But at least we'll have died doing what we love.'

'I don't love being terrified.'

'You are funny. You're sure you have everything you need?'

'I'm sure. As I said to Harry – if I can't do what needs to be done with what I've brought with me, I probably can't do it at all.'

'It's quite frustrating not to be able to keep in touch with each other while you're in there.'

'If it all comes unstuck I'll try to make my way out to the main road. If I'm not back at the copse by half past four, set off for home and look for me by the side of the road. If I'm not there, assume I'm being held by the nightwatchmen and bring Harry.'

'Right you are, dear. But they'll have to be more than averagely impressive nightwatchmen to nab you. You'll be fine.'

'Of course. But we have a plan now, just in case.'

Before long we were driving past the great shadowy masses of the former airship hangars at Bristol Aviation. The moon, as Lady Hardcastle had predicted, was lighting them nicely. This was going to be easy.

Lady Hardcastle slowed to an uncharacteristically careful pace as we approached the point where she thought she might be able to turn right and into the small copse. Despite her reduced speed, she still managed almost to miss the gap in the undergrowth, and we turned with such ferocity that once again, two of the motor car's wheels left the road.

'I still haven't written to Fishy,' she said. 'I must remember to do that.'

I said nothing. When our Chinese guide, Chen Ping Bo, had taught me some of his fighting skills, he had also taught me some of the meditation techniques of his order. He insisted that a clear and relaxed mind was essential to the success of any undertaking, and I was following his guidance. I had almost achieved the required state of calm when a thought intruded: why hadn't I done this at dawn that morning when I found myself unable to sleep? That was going to irritate me all night.

'Here we are, dear,' said Lady Hardcastle. 'Time to go.'

I grabbed my haversack and hopped out of the Rolls.

The game, as a famous detective used to say, was afoot.

◆ ◆ ◆

Infiltrating the aerodrome was as straightforward as we had imagined it would be. The field was pasture and easily traversed. The hedge was a simple row of close-planted hawthorn and easily crossed. I didn't know it was hawthorn at the time, of course – Lady Hardcastle told me afterwards.

There was a panicked scurrying a couple of yards to my left as I pushed through the hedgerow, and I was just in time to see a hefty adult badger hurrying across the grass on the other side of the chain-link fence. I had counted my Flosteps with surprising accuracy, and friend Brock had finished the job by showing me exactly where the crossing point was.

I pushed my haversack through the gap and wriggled through behind it. Brushing the dirt from my jacket and trousers, I took up my bag and walked back the way I had just come, this time on the aerodrome side of the fence. Lady Hardcastle's predictions about the moon had proven correct – as always – and even had a nightwatchman chanced to look my way I'd have been naught but a shadow among the shadows. Of the presumed guardians of the aerodrome, though, there was no sign. Probably sitting with their feet up in reception smoking their pipes, sipping their tea, and yarning about their army days.

This posited a problem I hadn't previously addressed. I had assumed that such nightwatchmen as there were would be engaged on regular patrols and would thus be easy to evade. But what if they really were all taking their ease in the office block? I had intended to sneak in through the front door, but if they were there . . . It wasn't an insurmountable problem, but it was potentially tiresome.

I put it out of my mind as I approached Hangar B – sufficient unto the hour of the break-in are the nightwatchmen thereof and all that. For now I had to find my way safely undetected into the parachute office.

My original plan had been to enter the hangar through the side door we had used during Adam's tour. It was in between the two gigantic buildings, so my efforts would be suitably concealed – especially given the position of the moon – and I knew from having already given it the once-over on that first visit that picking the lock would be child's play.

So certain was I that this would be the ideal entry point that I hadn't even considered the vast hangar doors. Why would I? What sort of idiot would try to heave open a twelve-elephant door when there was a perfectly serviceable human-sized door just around the corner?

The main hangar doors were unusual beasts. The tops appeared to hang from a rail across the top of the building, but that would never support their weight – it was just there to attach them to the building. Their bulk was carried on two giant trolleys, with a latticework of supports to keep them upright. They looked like oversized cricket sight screens.

That much I had seen on our previous trips, but what I'd never spotted – because I'd never been looking – was that the right-hand door on each building had a small wicket gate set into it, close to the point where the two doors met.

I decided to try my luck.

Oh, frabjous day – it was protected by a hefty padlock of the sort that householders imagine will keep their precious possessions safe against all comers and which a half-decent burglar can pick in a heartbeat.

I picked it in slightly less than a heartbeat and slipped quietly inside.

I shut the little door behind me, belatedly hoping it would stay closed without the padlock to hold it. That's the problem with improvised plans – they introduce unforeseen variables. Ah, well. Too late now.

It was pitch dark in the hangar, and surprisingly eerie. It had the feel of an enclosed space, even though there was no way to see the walls or roof, but it lacked the echoey character of a cathedral. It was as though sounds were so exhausted by their long journey that by the time they hit the walls they couldn't be bothered to make the return trip and just gave up.

That's not to say there were no sounds, though. The soft breeze was making the distant walls creak, and there was a faint pitter-pat from dozens of tiny clawed feet scurrying about the concrete floor. Even in this temple of engineering, mankind's oldest houseguests had taken up residence. I wasn't troubled by rats and mice, but they were an unwelcome distraction. Now, as well as wondering where the nightwatchmen might be, I was also trying to fathom what on earth our rodent friends found to eat among the aeroplane components, oil, grease, and varnish. Discarded sandwiches, perhaps? Dropped biscuits? The bodies of overworked apprentices?

I reached into my haversack and found my flashlight. The batteries were fresh, and the light that leapt from the end of the thing was shockingly bright after all that time in the gloom. I panicked briefly that I might give myself away, but reason intervened. It was dark in here despite the bright moonlight outside because there were no windows. If light couldn't get in, then light couldn't get out.

My rodenty companions weren't nearly so sanguine about the whole thing and there was a noticeable increase in the urgency of their scurrying as they sought to get away from the human and her mysterious light.

The white-painted partitions of the parachute project positively gleamed in the glow of the flashlight, and I made my way stealthily to the locked door. It yielded once more to my trusty picklocks and I let myself inside.

◆ ◆ ◆

The parachute room looked different at night, but it was still familiar. The cabinets, the drawing desks, the two giant sewing tables – everything was where I expected it to be, just casting stranger shadows. The mannequin looked particularly menacing in the gloom. On the floor sat the three packed parachutes, but of the failed one there was no immediate sign. This wasn't good. The failed parachute was the only reason for my being there. I cast about, hoping to see it.

It wasn't elsewhere on the floor – not stuffed between the cabinets or kicked under the sewing tables.

I was about to give up in frustration when it belatedly occurred to me to inspect the pile of silk sitting on top of the nearest table. I had assumed it was a new parachute under construction, but a quick rummage revealed the handwritten sign I had seen before: 'Failed. Do not use.'

Someone had been examining the deadly device.

The long table made it easy to carry out my own examination, and I quickly found where it had ripped apart. As Mr Sandling had said, the gores were held together with a top-stitched felled seam. It was a tough, neat way of joining two pieces of fabric together and I'd never known one fail, but this one had split apart from top to bottom.

I looked closely at the failed seam, holding the flashlight close. There was something odd about the thread.

Draughtsmen used magnifying lenses, surely. There must be one in here somewhere.

Five minutes of searching turned up exactly what I wanted – a large bone-handled lens.

I returned to my scrutiny.

My suspicions were correct. When thread snaps, it leaves a ragged end where the different strands stretch and break at different points. A cut thread has clean ends, and at several points along the seam the thread had very obviously been neatly snipped, through both rows of stitching. The parachute had, indeed, been deliberately weakened.

I briefly regretted not bringing the little camera so that I could record the evidence, but it would have been no help. There was far too little light to capture the detail needed, even if I could persuade it to take a picture through a magnifying lens – and I was by no means sure I could.

But I knew what had happened and I'd be prepared to swear to it if needs be.

I put the parachute back as I had found it – or as close as I could manage. I doubted anyone would remember exactly how it had been left.

I returned the lens to its owner's drawing table.

There was nothing else I desperately needed to look at, so I double-checked that I'd left everything as it should be – and went back out into the main building, relocking the door behind me.

There was more frantic scurrying from my rodent friends as I picked my way back to the door, careful not to disturb anything on the way. It would probably be blamed on the rats if I did manage to knock something over, but a noise would be undesirable.

I reached the wicket gate and checked Harry's watch before switching off my flashlight. It was still only a quarter to midnight. Plenty of time.

With no windows anywhere, there was no way to check whether the coast was clear. I inched the door open and looked out on to the moonlit field. I waited for a moment or two to make sure there was no sign of movement, then opened it a little further so I could listen, too. I could hear nothing.

Opening the door only wide enough for me to slip through, I eased back out into the night and replaced the padlock.

Time to take a dekko at the office block and see how best to get to John Milhouse's office.

Keeping to the shadows as much as possible, I made my way across to the office building. All the lights were out on the side facing the hangars, so no one was on patrol inside. That was something, at least.

I crept along the end of the building and peered round towards the main entrance. This time there were lights and they were coming from the reception area. Instinct told me to get away and take my chances at the back of the block, but reason prevailed. I had to know what was going on in there so I knew what I might have to deal with.

A narrow strip of flagstones ran along the front of the block. I should have preferred not to be so close to the building. In an ideal world I'd have kept ten or twenty yards from the wall, well beyond the reach of any lights that might suddenly come on and where my options for flight were much more numerous. Beyond the path, though, there was only scrunchy, noisy gravel. Better to stay on the paving stones, keep below the windows, and hope for the best. I was doing a lot of hoping for the best that night.

I reached the first reception window and peered cautiously in. I could see no one.

I crossed in front of the door and looked through the window on the other side. It was difficult to get a good view without putting myself into a position where I must surely be seen myself, but I did manage to catch sight of two uniformed nightwatchmen of late middle age playing cards at Miss Matthews's desk.

That must be all of them. If there were a third, he would surely be playing cards with them. He wasn't patrolling the building unless he was doing it in the dark, and in all the time I'd spent out of doors there'd been no sign of anyone on picket duty in the grounds.

Two men, then. Playing cards. Drinking tea. Probably occasionally dozing. Almost exactly the sort of indolent sentinels I'd been hoping for. Aside from trips to the lavatory, I doubted they'd leave their present post until the first of the staff began to turn up next morning.

Their choice of venue for their card game was unfortunate, though. Life would have been much easier had I been able to use the front door and the main staircase to get to Mr Milhouse's office, but I'd accomplished trickier break-ins in my time. And it would be an entertaining story to tell Lady Hardcastle and Harry.

I padded back round to the other side of the building, still carefully, but with much less trepidation now I knew where my doughty opponents made their lair.

I moved further away, towards the hangars, to get a better view of the first floor. I couldn't quite remember the exact position of Mr Milhouse's office, but a glimpse of the aspidistra in the window gave its location away.

I scanned the wall. In the same ideal world where there was no gravel in front of the building, there would have been a drainpipe beside Mr Milhouse's window. The world remained steadfastly short of being ideal, but there was a drainpipe beside that of one of his neighbours. That was my route in.

I quickly crossed the grass and tested the cast-iron pipe. It would easily take my weight. It would take Lady Hardcastle's weight. Riding an elephant. I suddenly wished I had an elephant – I'd be most of the way to the window from the back of an elephant.

Hand over hand, I climbed the drainpipe. My rubber-soled plimsolls gripped the bricks of the wall and in just a few short minutes I was level with the first-floor windows. They were steel-framed, painted white and the one right next to me would open. Aggravatingly, it would open towards me. It was almost as if the architects were trying to make things difficult for burglars.

The windows didn't appear to be locked – there was just a handle to latch them shut – so getting this one open shouldn't be too tricky if only I could get to it. There was a narrow ledge, but it would be difficult to balance and work the latch.

I looked up.

There was a white-painted gutter running across the building above the windows. I continued my climb.

The guttering was a good deal less sturdy than the downpipe, but it wouldn't have to take my full weight, just steady me a little. I rummaged in my haversack for the rope and managed to loop it over the gutter so that both ends hung down below the window ledge. I checked that the gutter's supporting brackets were far enough apart that the rope would slide across to where I needed it, and shinned back down.

Taking both parts of the rope in one hand, I eased my right foot gingerly across on to the ledge. Steadying myself with the rope, I let go of the drainpipe and moved my left foot, too. This was altogether more precarious than I liked, but it was probably going to work. Probably.

I took the knife from my bag and worked the blade between the window and the frame. Steel windows are seldom an exact fit and there was room enough to get sufficient purchase on the latch to get the window open. I was in.

I pulled the rope in through the window so that it wouldn't be so easily spotted in the unlikely event that one of the building's stalwart guardians should leave his card game and venture outside, then closed the window as much as the rope would allow.

I was in an office decorated much like all the others, with the same aeroplane photographs on the same drab walls and the same utilitarian furniture on the same linoleum floor.

The door was locked.

I sighed and picked it.

Turning to my right, I quickly found Mr Milhouse's door.

That needed picking, too.

But I was finally inside.

As silently as I was able, I took a quick look through the filing cabinets by the light of my flashlight. As I'd predicted, they were filled with invoices, both incoming and outgoing, all neatly collated in manila folders. There might be something interesting in there but it would take a trained accountant with a lot of time on his hands to find it.

I contemplated the 'public' safe. Was it worth the time it would take to pick the lock? It wasn't a simple padlock or office door – it would require some serious effort to get into it. And would it be worth it? Presumably it wouldn't hold anything embarrassing, just things they wanted to keep away from thieves and competitors.

Last resort, then. I'd do what I came for instead.

I had a moment of doubt about the whole endeavour when the hideous portrait seemed to be too firmly attached to the wall to be concealing anything. I ran my fingers around the frame and soon came upon a very well-concealed catch. I pressed it, and the portrait swung away from the wall like a door.

It was a substantial safe, about eighteen inches square and large enough for all your underhanded needs. It had a combination lock, which was tiresome, but not dreadful. I had plenty of time – I'd need it – and I was reasonably sure I could crack it. Despite my bravado, locks opened by keys were sometimes harder to defeat, most especially the sort used by safe manufacturers. They were engaged in a constant battle with thieves who had known how to pick locks since shortly after the first locks had been invented, so locksmiths had always tried to stay one step ahead. The Yale combination lock was generally considered by the public at large to be uncrackable, but there were those who knew the way in.

I knew the way in. Some years earlier we had made use of a safe-cracker on a job in London and he'd been generous enough to share his not-so-ancient wisdom with me. I took out my stethoscope and fixed it in place with a small piece of plasticine. I settled against the back of Mr Milhouse's chair and began.

It was painstaking, frustrating work. I was listening for a particular combination of sounds that would indicate that the mysterious gubbins inside the lock were falling into the correct position. It takes hours. I took regular breaks to stretch my aching shoulders and back, and kept a weather-eye on the time. I had ages yet, but I didn't want to leave it too late and get caught in the pre-dawn light as I scampered back to my badger run and onwards to the waiting Rolls.

Two hours later it was a quarter past two in the morning and the secret safe was open. I switched on the flashlight and looked inside.

There were a few more manila folders. Several large bundles of five-pound notes. A Webley service revolver. And a neat stack of ledgers, outwardly similar to the ones on the shelves but, I was willing to bet, quite different on the inside.

This was where I hit the problem I had foreseen but not yet solved. It was one thing to know that the ledgers were there, and if needs be Harry – or some other agent of the law – could obtain a warrant and 'find' the dodgy books quite by chance during their search. But unless and until they were examined by that trained accountant (once he'd finished with the invoices), there wasn't a lot they could tell us. I could pinch one, of course, but it wouldn't be much use without the 'official' one to compare it with. Once again I wished there were some way to photograph everything.

My ponderings were interrupted by the sound of footsteps echoing along the corridor. The owner of the stepping feet was moving slowly and seemed to be trying each office door in turn, presumably to check that everything was still secure.

At least that solved my dilemma.

I took one last look at the contents, then quietly closed and locked the safe door. The hideous portrait snapped back into place with a soft click. I switched off the flashlight and ducked into the footwell of the desk, just as the handle turned and the door opened.

'Typical,' muttered a man's voice. 'I'll have to have words with that Mr Milhouse.'

The door closed and I heard a key in the lock.

I could still hear the nightwatchman talking to himself in the corridor.

'If I've told 'em once,' he said, 'I've told 'em a thousand times: they gots to lock their doors of an evenin'. T'i'n't secure leavin' everythin' open like this.'

He tried the next door. It opened.

'Oh, for the love of—'

There was a moment's pause when I thought I might have got away with it.

'Sid!' yelled the man. 'Sid, get up here!'

Another pause and then more footsteps. Quicker this time, but still not terribly urgent.

'What's the matter, Bert?' said a new voice. 'You found another mouse? Don't worry, I'll shoo 'im out for 'ee.'

I could hear no more of their conversation, which was taking place in the office now, but it was a fair bet that Sid had found my rope and they were deciding what to do about it. So much for bringing it inside to avoid detection.

I had to move fast. I had to get out of the office while Sid and Bert were still debating the presence of the rope and looking gormlessly out of the window for signs of the intruder. Sooner or later they'd wonder if someone were inside the building, and not long after that, Bert would remember that Mr Milhouse's door had been unlocked.

I cursed his efficiency in locking it, but it was the work of just a few moments to spring the lock again and open the door. I peeped cautiously along the corridor. Sid and Bert were still deep in confused conversation in the next room. I could hear them more clearly now, and the discussion had moved on to wondering how best to avoid blame for the break-in. They seemed keen on the idea of pretending it had never happened, and their first step would be to get the rope down from the gutter and shut the window. This should give me the time I needed.

Praying to Laverna – whom Lady Hardcastle had assured me was the Roman goddess of thieves – that my rubber soles wouldn't squeak on the linoleum floor, I ran on my tiptoes towards the stairs.

The door to the staircase was just closing behind me when I heard a shout.

'Oi! You there! Stop! You! Chinaman! Stop!'

I took the stairs three at a time and barrelled through the doors at the bottom.

The reception area was dazzlingly bright after the moonlit gloom upstairs, but I knew well enough where I was headed. Another two crashes of doors and I was outside the building and running hell for leather around the office block and on towards the shadows at the far end of the hangars.

I slowed as I reached their shelter. There was no sign of pursuit. Sid and Bert were not men of action, it seemed, and I had time to take stock.

Given their obvious inclination to pretend nothing had happened, it seemed unlikely that they'd call the police, but I considered it unwise to hang around and find out. Even if I managed to avoid detection and capture, Lady Hardcastle was something of a sitting duck in the Rolls – she had no plausible excuse for being there and nowhere to go once the rozzers were upon her. Obviously Harry would secure her release from the cells eventually, but he wouldn't be best pleased and he might let her stew for a while.

I needed to get out and get away.

The moon was still my friend and was still doing his best to create an area of gloom along the length of the perimeter fence. If I didn't draw too much attention to myself by unnecessary hurrying, I might just evade the vigilant gaze of Sid and Bert for long enough to find a way through.

I heard voices out in the open, but no accompanying sounds of pursuit. Time to make another move.

I rounded Hangar B and started along the line of the chain-link fence. If I was lucky, then . . .

Yes. Brock and his family weren't the only ones to have dug their way under the wire. About halfway along the side of the hangar was evidence that someone else – a fox perhaps – had created their own little entrance to the field.

Gratefully, I shoved my haversack under and wriggled through after it.

The hedge was thinner here, and I was out into the neighbouring pasture and trotting down to the copse in no time.

Lady Hardcastle was snoring when I arrived.

I jumped in beside her and she woke with a startled snort.

'You're home early,' she said, sleepily. 'Did you get everything?'

'I'll tell you later,' I said. 'For now, just start the motor and get us out of here. Turn right towards town – we don't want to go past the entrance road just yet.'

She pressed the starter button.

'Trouble?' she asked as she drove off.

'Nothing to worry about. But let's not hang around, just in case.'

'I'll take Route B. I knew it was worth looking at those maps.'

Chapter Twelve

Harry had been – rather sensibly – in his room and fast asleep by the time we arrived. I had already told Lady Hardcastle everything on the slightly longer journey home, so we retired immediately. I slept through until almost ten. Not quite a full night's sleep, but an uninterrupted one nonetheless. I ought to go out burgling more often.

By the time I stumbled blearily down the stairs, the house was filled with the smell of coffee and breakfast. Lady Hardcastle and Harry were in the morning room.

'Here's the woman of the hour,' said Harry as I entered and sat down. 'Em tells me you had a close shave.'

'Close enough,' I said. 'But whatever Bristol Aviation is spending its money on, it's not nightwatchmen.'

'Were you seen?'

'They caught a glimpse, but even if they report the incident to their employers – and I'm not at all certain they will – the mysterious burglar will be described as a fleet-footed Chinese man.'

'A Chinese man?' said Harry with a chuckle. 'I can see the Chinese – what with the clothes and the pigtail. But a man? That's not terribly flattering. You poor old thing.'

'They only saw my back disappearing down the stairs, and with the perennial assumption that burgling is men's work, they put two and two together to make ninepence ha'penny.'

'I'll keep an eye on police communications for a few days. We don't want to start a diplomatic incident by accusing the Chinese of spying on our aeroplane factories. They've got problems enough at home without the British authorities suggesting they're up to no good abroad.'

'I doubt it'll come to that,' I said. 'Sid and Bert seemed mostly to be focused on avoiding trouble for themselves. I suspect they'll have taken a look round, satisfied themselves that nothing was stolen, and carry on as if nothing had happened.'

'Even so, it pays to be careful. Em said you'd found evidence of deliberate damage to the parachute. And fraud.'

'It was definitely human intervention rather than material failure,' I said. 'The parachute stitching had been neatly cut with something very sharp. A razor, perhaps. As for fraud . . . No proof, as such, but the existence of a second set of books is very suggestive.'

'It certainly is. Cash and a gun in there, too?'

'Yes. Quite incriminating, wouldn't you say?'

'I most definitely would. Even just having a secret safe speaks volumes on its own.'

'Oh, that's common enough – lots of management types have secret safes. And it wouldn't have been secret within the firm. It's set into the brick wall, so the back of it must be hidden behind a partition in the next room.'

'I suppose so. But I'll wager no one else knows what's in it. You've done a wonderful job there. Thank you.'

'I'm glad to be of service.'

'I'm just glad you're on our side,' he said. 'If the other lot were even half as good as you, we'd stand no chance.'

I accepted the compliment with a smile, and tucked in to a heroic helping of breakfast. Burglary was hungry work.

'What's our next move?' asked Lady Hardcastle.

'As soon as that trunk call comes through,' said Harry, 'I shall report back to London. I'll ask for confirmation that the order is in and that the message was left for the leaker, too.'

'You never did say how you were doing that, dear,' said Lady Hardcastle.

'The old-fashioned way, sis – advertisements in the personal column. Hardly original, but infuriatingly anonymous. We're still not absolutely certain of the way they encode all the details, but we think we've got it right. Risky business, obviously – the real spies will know something's up straight away. We just have to hope they don't have a way of alerting the leaker that he's been rumbled.'

'It's not likely they'd have a more secure second channel, though, is it?' I said. 'They'd be using that for everything if they did.'

'That's certainly what we're banking on.'

'There's nothing much for us to do until your chaps in Whitehall have pondered and pronounced, then,' said Lady Hardcastle. 'If neither of you mind, I shall spend the morning in the orangery. I received some helpful information from one of my correspondents the other day and I'm dying to try something.'

'To do with your moving pictures?'

'Not at the moment, no. Weaving.'

'Weaving?'

'She has a loom,' I said. 'She told you last time we were in London.'

'You never listen to me,' said Lady Hardcastle.

'Ah,' he said. 'Well . . . now . . . you see . . . the thing is . . . you say so many fascinating things over the course of a weekend, sis – it's impossible for me to remember every single little thing.'

'Hmm. Well, I shall be looming unless anyone needs me.'

'Loom away, old thing. I'll try to get that trunk call organized.'

'What shall you do, Flo?' asked Lady Hardcastle.

'I hadn't given it much thought,' I said. 'I might just read.'

'It seems we all have something enjoyable to do, then,' she said. 'Shall we meet in the garden for lunch at one?'

◆ ◆ ◆

I tried to read but I fell asleep in an armchair in the drawing room and had to be gently woken by Edna, who had been sent to find me when I hadn't arrived at the lunch table.

'Are you all right, dear?' asked Lady Hardcastle when I wandered, still yawning, into the garden.

'I was just more tired than I thought,' I said. 'And our armchairs are surprisingly comfortable. What have I missed?'

'I made some absolutely delicious fabric,' she said. 'If I can make a few yards of it, I might get Cridge's to turn it into something fancy for me.'

'What sort of fabric?'

'Heavyish wool. It would make a splendid overcoat. It's green.'

'Is it, indeed? I look forward to seeing it.' I turned to Harry. 'What about you? Did you manage to make your call?'

'I did, as a matter of fact. Just now. I'm surprised I didn't wake you – there was a lot of shouting.'

'Acrimonious dealings with your staff?' I said.

'No, not this time. It was the line. Terrible. We were both having to yell.'

'Other than that, dear,' said Lady Hardcastle, 'what happened?'

'Well,' he said, helping himself to an extraordinarily large lump of cheese. 'Let me see. I gave them a brief description of Flo's discoveries from last night and asked them to ready a report for the

196

Inland Revenue people – the extra set of books and whatnot. I don't want them to send it yet, but there's bound to be some sort of stink when they find we've been sitting on evidence. It would be nice to minimize the delays once we know it's not going to compromise our operations if they go galumphing in there with their stern expressions and abacuses. Abaci?'

'If you're an ancient Roman, by all means abaci,' she said. 'But abacuses will do fine if you're English.'

'I'm reasonably sure I am. I asked them to prepare a report about the nobbled parachute as well, but we'll sit on that, too. Same reasons, but replace abacuses with truncheons and handcuffs – different set of galumphers. Meanwhile, there's no news on any of our other enquiries.'

'What about the newspaper advertisement?' I asked.

'All done. Went into today's edition of the *Bristol News*. Coded instructions for a meeting on Horfield Common. At six pip emma.'

'Six p.m. when, dear?' said Lady Hardcastle.

'Ah,' he said. 'Disappointed you asked that. The . . . ah . . . the code they use is a little non-specific. It's one you've used yourself, I imagine. It can specify a time and place, but not an actual day. Flexible, you see? "Meet me here when you can" sort of thing.'

'Oh, how very tiresome. So you'd like us to be there every day until someone turns up?'

'If you'd be so kind,' he said. 'It's lovely weather for it. Obviously I'd come with you, but . . . you know . . . office Johnny and all that. And you've only a two-seater, anyway.'

'We could strap you to the back,' I said.

'Or put you in a trunk,' said Lady Hardcastle. 'We have a large one we used to use for ocean voyages. You'd fit into that nicely. Safer than just lashing you to the luggage rack.'

'I'll pass,' he said. 'But thank you both. I'll stay here and man the fort.'

'As you wish, dear,' she said. 'But the offer remains open.'

'How would you like to play it this evening?' I asked.

'I don't think it's the sort of thing that requires any sort of elaborate ruse,' she said. 'I thought we might just take an evening stroll on the common. Did your lackeys specify a location for the meeting, Harry?'

'We learned that there's a bench,' he said. 'For reasons unknown it looks towards the road and a handful of houses on the other side. I'm sure if I'd placed a bench on a common I'd have had it looking the other way, towards the common and what I'm told are the magnificent views of the city beyond. But there you are. The advantage is that you can take your stroll and the leaker will be sitting with his back to you. You should be able to keep an eye on the comings and goings without his noticing you.'

'Splendid,' she said. 'Summer frocks and strolling hats, then. No one from the factory will recognize you out of your uniform, Flo, so we'll be reasonably invisible even if they do glance our way.'

'Right you are,' I said. 'Departure time?'

'We ought to be comfortably in place a while before six. What say we set off at around half-past four?'

'I'll be ready,' I said.

'Good-o,' said Harry. 'I don't suppose there's any more of this cheese, is there?'

At half past four on the dot we were aboard the Rolls and tootling merrily back in the direction of Bristol. The weather was still gloriously summery and warm, and I had elected to drive.

'Are you afraid we might arrive too early?' asked Lady Hardcastle as we took a corner on all four wheels.

'I was afraid we might arrive too dead,' I said. 'And isn't this steady pace just wonderful in this weather? We can hear the birds in the trees, smell the flowers in the hedgerows. And look there – that's what farmers look like when they're not shaking their fists at us.'

She harrumphed. 'Grandma,' she said.

'Hooligan.'

'Are there tennis courts at the common, do you know?'

'I've no idea. Why?'

'There's only so much strolling one can do on a patch of grassland without looking as though one has other reasons for dawdling about. I thought a game of tennis might keep us amused and give us a better reason for being there.'

'It will be fine,' I said. 'But if you want to turn back and get our racquets, I can.'

'No, dear, it's all right. I should have thought of it sooner. Oh, we could have borrowed Jagruti Bland's dog.'

'Hamlet? In here? Where would we put him?'

'We could fasten a basket on the back there. He'd love it.'

'He'd need goggles,' I said. 'He'd be exposed to the wind.'

'That would look precious, wouldn't it? And a little leather cap.'

'Something for us to bear in mind the next time we're called upon to carry out surveillance in a public park.'

'I shall speak to the vicar. We'll be seeing them tomorrow. You haven't forgotten the rehearsals?'

'I've not forgotten the rehearsals, no,' I said.

I'd been trying to forget the blessed rehearsals, to cast them entirely from my mind. But they were in there, nagging away at me. Why had I let Daisy talk me into her terrifying comedy act? I could just throw a few knives at Lady Hardcastle while playing the banjo and be done with it. But no. Animal noises. That it should come to this.

In slightly more time than it would have taken us with Lady Hardcastle at the wheel, we arrived at Horfield Common.

'There's the bench,' said Lady Hardcastle. 'Facing the houses, like Harry said.'

'I'll try to find somewhere discreet to park,' I said. 'The Rolls has been outside the Bristol Aviation office quite a lot – the leaker might recognize it.'

'Turn left here,' she said. 'It looks like we can get round to the other side of the common that way.'

I drove down the lane and found a convenient spot a few hundred yards from the main road and the bench.

'This will do nicely,' said Lady Hardcastle. 'We can stroll from here as slowly as we please, and keep an eye on the bench all the while.'

I cut the engine and clambered out, then walked round to join her on the yellowing grass.

'No sign of any tennis courts,' I said.

'No. What a shame. They'd be a nice addition.'

We set off on our slow amble uphill across the common.

Lady Hardcastle checked her watch.

'It's just after six,' she said. 'And still no sign of anyone.'

'It's not those two old ladies, then?' I said, indicating the current occupants of the bench.

'I'd never rule it out. Quite a few people have come unstuck saying "It can't be those two ladies" shortly before we did something unspeakably beastly to them and nicked their secret whatnots. But no, not those two old ladies. One of them is eating a meat pie from a paper bag. I don't think spies do that.'

'Or do they? Maybe we should start eating pies while we're working. It seems to throw people off the scent.'

'I can think of less fattening ways of throwing people off the scent. They're leaving now, anyway. Oh, and she's just thrown the empty bag on the ground. Some people are so uncouth. I mean, really. It wouldn't take— Hello.'

'Seen something?'

'Yes, over there.' She nodded towards the road, where a man was making an awkward but determined beeline for the recently vacated bench. He was struggling to hold a bunch of flowers without ruining them as he pushed a reluctant bicycle along the path.

'Is that . . . ?' I began.

'I believe it is,' she said. 'He looks even dapperer outside his dreary office. It seems everything is tying up rather nicely.'

'Dapperer?'

'Shush. Just watch.'

The man with the bicycle was John Milhouse, the chief accountant.

The obvious problems of his recalcitrant bicycle notwithstanding, he seemed perfectly at ease. He didn't look furtively about, but didn't try to shrink himself and keep his head down, either. Perfect behaviour for someone indulging in a bit of espionage. He was a very cool customer indeed.

He arrived at the bench and propped his velocipede against it. He sat with one arm along the back of the bench and the flowers in his lap. He was a man taking his ease after a hard day at the office, not some sly leaker of confidential information.

'He's very good,' said Lady Hardcastle. 'If one didn't know he was a traitor betraying his employer and his country, one might think he was just here to meet a lady friend.'

'He is meeting a lady friend,' I said. 'Look.'

Waiting for a horse and cart to pass before crossing the road was an attractive blonde-haired woman, close to Milhouse's own age. She waved to attract his attention, and when he waved back she smiled happily.

'He's not our leaker,' I said.

'I rather think not,' said Lady Hardcastle. 'And I'm going to go out on a limb and suggest that she's not an agent of a foreign power any more than the two old dears we saw a moment ago.'

'Despite your comments about unlikely-looking women being the ones who'll do you a mischief and steal your secrets?'

'Even so,' she said.

'I confess I do think it's unlikely.'

The woman had crossed the road and Mr Milhouse had stood to greet her.

'No foreign agent has ever kissed me like that, either. I say. Steady on, old girl, you'll frighten the horses.'

I chuckled. 'What about that one in—' I began.

'Not even then,' she said, quickly. 'It's nice to see a husband and wife still so much in love.'

'Oh, that's not his wife.'

'How can you tell? Are you so cynical that you don't think married couples carry on like that?'

'No,' I said. 'I've seen a photograph of his wife – he keeps it on his desk. She has dark hair and stands a good three or four inches shorter than that long-limbed goddess.'

'She is rather stunning, isn't she?'

'His wife's not bad-looking, either, mind you.'

'Well, well, well,' she said. 'It seems there was something in Miss Matthews's accusations of goatishness after all.'

Mr Milhouse had retrieved his bicycle from the end of the bench and was demonstrating the problem with the front wheel.

The woman laughed delightedly. They began to walk back towards the road.

'What now?' I said. 'Do we follow them, or is that more in the realm of voyeurism than counter-espionage?'

'We ought at least to keep an eye on where they go,' she said. 'It might well be a coincidence, but assuming Harry's underlings placed their advertisement correctly, we're further assuming that a naughty employee of Bristol Aviation will turn up here, sit at that bench and wait to be contacted. It would be remiss to ignore the chief accountant just because we think he has an entirely different sort of naughtiness in mind.'

We started to follow.

The couple stopped at the edge of the road, waited for yet another cart to pass by, then crossed. They walked along the pavement opposite for a few yards before stopping in front of one of the houses. The woman put her hand on Mr Milhouse's chest and kissed him. Quickly she darted through the front gate of the house and up to the door, where she let herself in while Mr Milhouse propped the bicycle against the wall.

She emerged a few moments later, looked quickly up and down the street, then beckoned Mr Milhouse to join her. He hurried up the path and into the house, closing the door behind him.

'I'm not shinning up the drainpipe to check what they're up to,' I said.

'I think we can safely assume what they're up to. And I don't think he's our man.'

'Do you think we should wait, just in case?'

'No,' she said. 'It's half past already. You remember the rules – the meeting happens at the appointed hour or not at all. No one hangs about waiting to get caught.'

'True,' I said. 'Well, that's that, then. Home?'

'Home. We can see what Harry's prepared for supper.'

We walked slightly more swiftly back to the waiting Rolls and I took us home.

'Well, well, well,' said Harry with a chuckle when we told him the news in the drawing room that evening. 'Old John Milhouse is having an affair, eh?'

'Don't sound so gleeful,' said Lady Hardcastle. 'A man's being unfaithful to his wife, not walloping an injudicious yorker over the bowler's head for six at Lord's.'

'Yes, sorry,' he said. 'I confess I had him down as our leaker, but he wouldn't have arranged to see his lady friend if he'd seen the instruction to meet his contact there.'

'Unless he was killing two birds with one stone,' I said. 'The code doesn't specify a day. What if he saw the message and arranged to meet his mistress at the same time? He was going to be in the area anyway; why not have a bit of fun after passing on his gossip? He wouldn't have been surprised that his contact wasn't there – he'll just try again tomorrow. And if her husband's out again, he might get an extra bit of fun then, too.'

'Husband?'

'She double-checked that the coast was clear before inviting him in,' said Lady Hardcastle. 'She might have been making sure her landlady was out of the way, or that the parlour was fit for visitors, but she might also have been taking a quick gander to make sure her husband hadn't come home unexpectedly while she was over the road kissing Milhouse.'

'That was my thinking,' I agreed. 'She definitely checked who was at home before inviting her paramour in.'

'Well, anyway,' said Harry with another little chuckle, 'now we've found that he's betraying his wife, not his country, it's a bit of an anticlimax.'

'There's still the little matter of defrauding the Treasury,' I said. 'It's not quite so easy to snigger at creative bookkeeping.'

'I don't know,' said Harry. 'I've done more than my fair share of sniggering at "double-entry bookkeeping". But you're right, he's not off the hook even if we can clear him of selling secrets.'

'How do you wish us to proceed?' said Lady Hardcastle. 'Are you ready to move on Milhouse and Sandling?'

'Not yet, no. We're still awaiting word from Scotland Yard and the Treasury on the whole tax fiddle thing, if that's what it is. And I'd resist any moves until we've flushed out our leaker, anyway. I want to catch him, not spook him. There's a danger he'll go to ground and we'll never nab him or his handlers.'

'Do we have any thoughts on the matter of the wrecked parachute?' I said.

'I've been mulling on that while you were out,' he said. 'I'm still very much of the opinion that it's the work of the leaker. It makes sense to me that our unknown foreign friends might wish to set the project back a bit while they have another go at getting hold of the plans. It'll give them a better chance of catching up when they finally have them if Bristol Aviation have been sitting on their hands for fear of another accident.'

'And why haven't they tried again?' I said. 'You intercepted their courier, so they don't yet have the parachute plans, but they don't seem to have made much effort to have another go.'

'We're presuming they're lying low,' he said. 'Obviously the leaker has no idea what happened, but his handlers must have a pretty shrewd idea by now. I'd play it pretty cagey for a while if I were them, wouldn't you? That's why we thought it safe to place the advertisement, you see? They're unlikely to be placing competing messages, so we've got the field to ourselves for the time being.'

'Except you've shown them you know how it's done and that you're trying to flush out their source,' said Lady Hardcastle. 'You've put him in considerable danger. It was fine when we thought he might turn up this evening, but every day he delays gives them another day to do him in.'

'It's a dangerous game, treason.'

'We know the risks because it's our game,' she said. 'But he's either a greedy fool or an idealistic traitor. Either way I'd wager it never occurred to him he might get killed for his trouble.'

'At the risk of incurring accusations of callousness or cynicism, "hard cheese". If you're going to step up to play with the First XV, it's really rather your own responsibility to look into the possibilities of getting mulched by some heavy chaps on the other team. High treason is still a hanging offence.'

'After a trial in a court of law,' she said. 'Having his throat slit in a back alley is hardly the sort of justice we like to imagine we're fighting for.'

'You've killed plenty of people in your time. Both of you.'

'All of them paid-up members of the fraternity and all in self-defence. I'm not saying it's not a deadly occupation or that our hands are clean, but this leaker is just one step up from being a civilian.'

'What's done is done,' he said. 'In truth I don't like it any more than you do, but the cards have been dealt.'

'We'll just have to get to him before the opposition,' I said. 'We'll go down to Horfield Common every evening at six and hope we can pull him in before they do him in.'

'We can do no better than that,' said Lady Hardcastle. 'Now, then, brother dearest, what's for supper?'

'I'm glad you asked,' he said. 'Using my considerable charms and a small quantity of cash, I persuaded young Miss Jones to stay on for an extra hour and she has prepared a most excellent repast. I was going to claim credit for it myself, but you'd have seen through that little deception in a moment. It'll be ready in about half an hour.'

Dinner, eaten in the garden again, was delicious and no one, not even someone who didn't know him particularly well, would ever have believed that Harry had been responsible.

We retired to the drawing room where Lady Hardcastle played the piano while Harry and I set up the parlour croquet set. I allowed him to beat me heavily and then begged for a sudden death rematch for the championship. He agreed.

'Why not make it interesting?' he said.

'How interesting did you have in mind?' I said.

'A shilling?'

'That's not as interesting as you might suppose. Make it a guinea and you're on.'

'A guinea, Strongarm? Are you sure?'

'Of course.'

'Don't do it, Harry,' said Lady Hardcastle.

'Protecting your pal's money, eh?' he said.

'No, dear, yours.'

'Oh, I'm in no danger. A guinea it is.'

'Suit yourself,' she said, and returned to her ragtime experiments.

Obviously, I thrashed him.

'I feel I might have been taken for a fool here,' said Harry as he handed over my winnings and we packed up the croquet set.

'I did warn you,' said Lady Hardcastle. 'She's an astonishingly good player. I've not beaten her once since we bought the set.'

'And I didn't make the bet,' I said. 'That was your idea.'

'I know, I know,' he said. 'Is there any brandy? I think I need one.'

I poured a round of brandies and we spent the rest of the evening playing cards.

By the time we all retired for the night, I was quite a bit richer and the Featherstonhaughs were plotting my assassination.

Chapter Thirteen

Harry was already up and dressed by the time I arrived in the kitchen on Saturday.

'Good morning,' I said, cocking an eyebrow.

'No need to look so shocked,' he said. 'I can get up early when I need to. My dog cart chap is picking me up at seven.'

'Not shocked. Surprised, perhaps. I thought you Feather-stone-huffs were congenitally incapable of rising early.'

'We are – we inherited it from Mother's side of the family. It used to drive Father batty. He'd be raring to go on whatever trip or adventure he'd planned. Meanwhile she'd still be in bed and Nanny would be trying to stuff us into our clothes while we were still half asleep.'

'You miss the best part of the day.'

'It's all a matter of perspective, old thing. For me the best part of the day is getting home to Lavinia and Addie, the day's work done. Nothing beats the feeling of closing the door on the troubles of the world and spending the evening in the company of my loved ones.'

'When you put it like that . . .' I said.

There was a knock at the door.

'And speaking of my loved ones,' he said, 'that'll be Dog Cart Man to hasten my journey towards them. If we hurry I might even catch the earlier train.'

'Have a safe trip,' I said. 'Give our love to your girls.'

'Thank you. I'll be back on Monday.'

I saw him out and tried to decide on what to do while I waited for Lady Hardcastle to stir. I settled on the idea of taking my daily exercise in the garden, at one with unidentifiable nature just as my Chinese instructor had intended. I used the quiet time to clear my mind, but it kept straying back to the current goings-on.

With Harry returning home and the aeroplane factory closing for the weekend at lunchtime, there was nothing useful we could do to further the investigation, but we were planning to walk into the village at some point to help with the preparations for the show.

There was only a week to go, so rehearsals were in full flood and the village hall was being readied. Lady Hardcastle had volunteered her services as accompanist for any musical acts who wanted a run-through, and I'd said I'd happily lend a hand with any fetching and carrying that needed to be done.

I had also arranged to meet Daisy. We still hadn't worked out our act, and she said we should get together so that she could hear what I could do and then write some patter to go with it. I was dreading the whole thing, but Daisy had a knack for the comical so we might scrape by.

Lady Hardcastle surfaced at about nine o'clock and found me in the morning room with a round of toast and some urgent mending.

'Sorry to keep you, dear,' she yawned. 'Have you eaten?'

'No, I was waiting for you,' I said. 'I'll tell Miss Jones we're ready.'

I returned a moment later.

'She'll be a few minutes,' I said.

'Thank you. Where's Harry?'

'Gone home.'

'Gracious, he was up early.'

'I had that very conversation with him a couple of hours ago before he trundled off to Chipping to catch his train.'

'We could never get him out of bed for family trips.'

'He said much the same about you.'

She laughed. 'Yes, I'm sure he did. Oh, is that my dress? Thank you.'

I held it up to display my handiwork. 'You'd hardly know it had ever had an eight-inch rip in it,' I said. 'I'm rather pleased with that.'

'You work marvels, dear. I'm very grateful.'

'Out of curiosity, how did an afternoon dress get an eight-inch rip in it in the first place? Actually, it's more of a slash than a rip. Was some sort of blade involved?'

'It is an epic tale of struggle and woe,' she said. 'Of razor blades and puppet mice. Of looms and celluloid film. Of—'

'You slipped in the orangery while you had a razor in your hand.'

'In a nutshell. Actually, I dropped it, but the effect was the same.'

'You're lucky you didn't slice your leg open.'

'Just one of the many things I'm grateful for. I'm a very lucky lady.'

'A very clumsy lady,' I said.

'That, too.'

Miss Jones appeared at the door with the breakfast tray.

'And here's something else to be grateful for,' said Lady Hardcastle. 'Thank you, dear.'

'Always a pleasure, m'lady,' said Miss Jones. 'Can I get you anything else?'

'No, this will be splendid. Shall we see you at the rehearsals this afternoon?'

Miss Jones seemed uncharacteristically embarrassed for a moment. 'Umm . . .' she began. 'Yes . . . Yes, you might.'

Lady Hardcastle smiled. 'But you'd prefer we didn't?'

'Something like that, m'lady.'

'You've nothing to worry about – I'm sure you'll be wonderful.'

She was still blushing. 'No, it's not that,' she said. 'It's just . . . well, the girls have it in mind to do a dance while we sing an old Marie Lloyd song.'

'That sounds delightful. '"Oh! Mr Porter", perhaps? "The Boy I Love Is Up in the Gallery"?'

The blush deepened. '"She Sits Among the Cabbages and Peas",' she said.

Lady Hardcastle's laugh could brighten any room at the best of times, but the explosion of mirth occasioned by this revelation would have made even Hilda Pantry – the perennially miserable proprietrix of the grocer's in the village – beam with joy.

'That's quite the best idea I've heard,' she said, still chuckling. 'Do promise you won't get cold feet, won't you. I'm already looking forward to the reaction of certain members of our little community.'

Miss Jones smiled at last. 'You don't think it's a bit . . . you know . . .'

'I think it's very "you know" – which is exactly why you must do it. With gusto. I'm on accompanist duty with Mrs Bland – if you can, promise me you'll wait until it's my turn to play – I'd love to hear you.'

'I'll see what I can do, m'lady,' said Miss Jones.

She left us to our breakfast.

Lady Farley-Stroud would have made a magnificent regimental sergeant major. I'm sure she imagined herself a field marshal, or a general at the very least, but her parade-ground manner marked her out as ideal senior NCO material.

We found her in the vestibule of the village hall with a large notebook in her hand, bellowing terse orders in all directions. Those inside the hall were being told exactly how she wished the stage to be set up, while those delivering goods and material to the outside were left in no doubt as to precisely where she wished things to go.

'Emily, m'dear,' she barked, her parade-ground voice still fully engaged, 'splendid of you to come over. What have we got you down for?'

'I'm the accompanist's apprentice,' said Lady Hardcastle. 'Jagruti Bland and I are sharing piano duties for the rehearsals.'

Lady Farley-Stroud consulted her notebook.

'So you are, m'dear,' she said. 'So you are. We've had the piano tuned for you – I know how fussy you are.'

'You're so thoughtful, thank you. I do love a properly tuned piano.'

'What about you, Queen Florence? Hector's still banging on about that, you know.'

'I just signed up as general dogsbody,' I said.

'Oh, I think we can make better use of you than that, m'dear. Someone of your abilities. Let me see . . . We need someone to oversee the scenery painters, if you don't mind? Just a few ladies from the village. They're enthusiastic, but a bit haphazard. They need someone to whip 'em into line.'

'That sounds fine as long as I'll not be required to actually paint anything,' I said.

'No need for that, m'dear. We just need a sympathetic overseer. Someone who can look at the plans and make sure everybody's doing what they should be.'

'I'd be happy to.'

'D'you have a rehearsal slot booked?' she said, looking at another list.

'No,' I said. 'Daisy Spratt and I are still working out the details of the act. We were hoping to find a quiet room somewhere after the butcher's closes.'

'I'll make sure there's a room free for you at one o'clock. Follow me.'

I left Lady Hardcastle to find the piano and followed Lady Farley-Stroud to the stage. She introduced me to the painting crew – all of whom I knew anyway – and left us to our important labours.

◆　◆　◆

The painting ladies were a wonderful little gang and we had a very jolly time. They didn't mind my lack of skill with a paintbrush and were actually rather relieved to have someone to tell them what to do. I was almost sorry to have to leave them at one o'clock, when Daisy bowled in.

'All right, Flo?' she said. 'You ready to make music hall history?'

'As ready as I'll ever be,' I said. 'Lady Farley-Stroud promised us a room to work in.'

'I seen 'er when I come in,' she said. 'I knows where we're goin'.'

She led the way to one of the side rooms and we shut the door behind us.

'Right, then, me old mate,' said Daisy as she sat on a chair at the table that almost filled the room. 'Show me what you got.'

'Do you have any idea what we're going to do?' I said.

'I got some ideas. We could try one where you always gets it wrong. Like, I tells a story and you does the noises, but they's always the wrong one. Sommat like . . . Here comes old Farmer Brown with 'is faithful dog, Rover.'

'Miaow.' I've always been rather proud of my cat sounds.

'That's it,' said Daisy with a grin. 'And who's that trottin' across the field to see 'im? Why, it's 'is favourite sheep, Flossie.'

'Baa.'

'No, you's supposed to get it wrong, remember?'

'I did,' I said proudly. 'That was a goat.'

'Do it again.'

'Baa.'

'That's definitely a sheep.'

'No,' I said. 'This is a sheep. Baa.'

'Do the goat again?'

'Baa.'

'And the sheep?'

'Baa.'

'Blow me,' she said. 'They are different, i'n't they? I'm gonna 'ave to do sommat with that. That's really clever. Anyway . . . Look over yonder, a lark singin' 'is song in the field.'

'Caw.' My crow was always a big hit.

'This is gonna be a scream,' she said. She started making notes on a scrap of paper with a scrap of pencil.

We carried on like this for some time. She was much more amused by it than I was, but we had a week to work on it and I trusted her to come up with something properly funny. It seemed to me that the key was going to be getting the sounds wrong in the right way, and I was sure we'd get it spot on eventually.

By the time Lydia and Mo from the painting team poked their heads round the door to ask where they might find some more turps, I was feeling slightly better about having to do the act. I wasn't looking forward to it by any means, but I was dreading it less. A little less, anyway.

I hugged Daisy and returned to the stage.

The rehearsals provided a pleasing accompaniment to the painting, but everyone stopped to listen to the village greengrocer, Lawrence Weakley. He was a quiet, polite, unassuming man, whom one would never suspect of even saying so much as a respectful hello to a goose, let alone, 'Boo.' It came as something of a surprise to everyone in the village hall, then, to find that he had the sweetest, purest tenor voice I'd ever heard outside a professional concert hall.

By the time he'd finished the old sentimental song – to enthusiastic applause from all present – even one or two of the burlier farmhands who had been helping build the scenery were wiping tears from their eyes.

Lady Hardcastle folded the music and put it on top of the piano. She motioned for me to join her on the hall floor.

'Time we were off, dear,' she said. 'We have that appointment, remember?'

I did remember. Another pointless trip to Horfield Common to watch ladies walking their dogs and young men practising their golf swings.

We walked briskly back to the house and jumped straight into the Rolls. No need to dress up to stand on the common for half an hour.

It was Saturday afternoon, so there were fewer delivery wagons for Lady Hardcastle to overtake at speed to the fist-shaking fury of their drivers.

'How was the rehearsal?' she said, somewhere around Almondsbury.

'Not wonderful,' I said. 'But not utterly dreadful.'

'Oh dear. What was wrong with it?'

'The act's just not funny. Well, no, that's not true. It's not funny to me. Daisy seems to think it's an absolute hoot.'

'Funny is in the ear of the beholder,' said Lady Hardcastle sagely.

'Oh, I know. But I'm terrified.'

'What exactly is it you're doing?'

'You know those music hall acts where some old chap in a rumpled dinner suit performs a rambling, whimsical monologue about taking a walk in the country where he meets a charming assortment of birds and animals, which he impersonates with great skill?'

'I know them well,' she said. 'Tiny Tommy Tucker and his Imaginary Menagerie is one I remember most fondly.'

'Indeed. Well, it's that, but with me doing the wrong noises.'

'Oh, that sounds precious. Did you do the goat-sheep thing? I love it when you do that.'

'I did. It took her ages to hear the difference.'

'Do one now.'

'Baa.'

'Goat.'

'Yes.'

'You're so clever,' she said.

'We might need you in the audience explaining how clever I am.'

'It'll be fine.'

'I might pop out one night in the week and burn down the village hall.'

'It'll do you no good, dear. In this weather they'll just do the show in the open air on the green.'

'Then I'll have to get Toby Thompson to let his herd loose on it again. I'm not beaten yet.'

'That's the spirit.'

We parked by the common and took our half-hour stroll among the courting couples and a small gang of rampaging children.

Of the leaker there was no sign.

We gave it until twenty past six and called it a night. Time to head for home.

◆ ◆ ◆

After breakfast on Sunday morning we went out into the garden for some air, and I was somewhat surprised to find that new furniture had been delivered.

'Oh, good,' said Lady Hardcastle. 'I'm glad this has arrived before the good weather's over.'

'When did you order it?' I said. 'And how? We've not been out.'

'By telephone. I saw an advertisement in the Bristol News and it looked like exactly what we were after, so I just went ahead. You're not disappointed not to have been involved?'

'Honestly? No, not at all. I can't imagine many shopping trips I'd find more tedious than one devoted to the purchase of garden furniture. Well done, you.'

'Jed had already built his little paved area, so it seemed the time was right. We can get it all set up today, if you're game.'

I was, and we did.

We stacked the old furniture with the rotten legs against the wall and arranged the new table and chairs on the stone slabs in the shade of the apple tree. By the time we broke for lunch we had built a family dining area fit for a Tuscan villa.

'It's a shame we'll only be able to use it for a few weeks in the year,' said Lady Hardcastle. 'But they'll be much more enjoyable weeks now.'

'They will,' I said. 'Thank you.'

'For what, dear? I just picked up a telephone.'

'Well, thank you anyway. Would you like some lunch?'

'A splendid notion. I'll help.'

'You'll get in the way.'

'It's my special gift. Would you rather I didn't?'

'I'd rather you found a bottle of something nice while I got on unhindered.'

'An excellent division of labour. You're a natural manager, it seems. I saw how you handled the village women yesterday. I was very proud.'

I curtseyed. 'Thank you,' I said. 'Now get the wine.'

'Yes, ma'am,' she said, knuckling her forehead.

The afternoon passed in a blur of pottering, chattering and not remembering the names of plants. Well, it did for me, anyway. She had no trouble remembering, nor any lack of patience with telling me. Over and over again.

'To me,' I said, 'they're just green things. Some of them have pretty flowers. Most of them don't belong here, but that's all right because you and Jed take great pleasure in battling against Nature to keep them alive.'

'Battling against Nature?'

'Of course,' I said. 'Isn't that what gardening is? I've read Darwin. I think I understood him. Most of the things we plant in our gardens wouldn't survive without our intervention, so they're clearly not adapted to being there. Gardening isn't working with Nature, it's a constant struggle against it.'

'That's one way of looking at it, I suppose,' she said. 'I prefer thinking about the pretty flowers.'

'I'm not opposed to pretty flowers,' I said. 'Nor to you and Jed pottering about, clipping this, pulling up that, sheltering the other thing from the wrong kind of weather. It clearly makes you happy.'

She laughed. 'It does. Shall we take a cup of tea before braving the common?'

I groaned. 'I'd forgotten the stupid common,' I said. 'Tea and a slice of cake, then. I need my strength for another wasted journey.'

It was a wasted journey, too, though we did happen upon some goings-on in the bushes that made us both laugh.

◆ ◆ ◆

Back at the house we decided that Sunday evening would be perfect for a game of cards. I made sure there was a tray of refreshments near at hand while Lady Hardcastle prepared the card table.

'Do you think anything will come of all the political shenanigans on the Continent?' I said as she dealt the first hand.

'Harry seems to think so,' she said. 'Alliances are being formed. It seems like the early stages of a game of chess, with both sides putting their strategic pieces in place. And the German Kaiser is a warlike chap. All that strutting around in a uniform and sending his army out on manoeuvres. He's in charge of the most highly developed and prosperous country in the world, but he gives the impression that nothing would please him more than picking up his sabre and going out and cutting off a few heads like they used to in the good old days.'

'I thought ours was the most highly developed and prosperous country in the world,' I said.

'That's what we like people to think, but we've been punching above our weight for some time now. We might have sparked the Industrial Revolution, but we've been left behind. It's all German chemicals and optics these days. What have we got? Hargreaves's spinning jenny and Arkwright's mechanical whatnot.'

'So we're doomed if it all turns nasty?'

'Oh, I wouldn't say that. What we have in spades is an unshakeable self-belief: the sure and certain knowledge, no matter how ill-founded, that the world is ours and everything that's in it. He'll have a fight on his hands if he tries to start a war with Britain – it'll never occur to us that we're not entitled to win by divine right.'

'Do you think he will pick a fight?'

'It would be nice to imagine he'd have more sense, but no one ever made any money betting on the good sense of kings and princes.'

'Nor on a hand like yours,' I said. 'My game, I think.'

She looked down at the cards. 'You have the luck of the Devil,' she said.

'I have the skill of a wily, card-playing fox,' I said. 'You allowed me to lure you into my trap. I know you never concentrate on the game while you're pontificating. All I need to do is to set you off on one of your pet subjects and I can win every time.'

'Well played, Miss Armstrong. But you've revealed your secret now. It won't work again.'

'We'll see,' I said, and dealt another hand.

'At least we're keeping up with some of the new technology,' she said as she examined her cards. 'We'll have aeroplanes, at least.'

'Aeroplanes with exploding engines.'

'You never know – that might be part of the plan. We develop the exploding engine and sell it to all our potential enemies. War breaks out, their aeroplanes take to the skies and . . . bang! Down will come the naughty bad men, aeroplanes and all.'

'You credit our leaders with far greater powers of forward planning than they've exhibited to date.'

'Perhaps. You know things might get dicey for us if the situation worsens, don't you?'

'Of course,' I said.

'And you don't mind? We retired once – we can retire again.'

'I don't mind. I knew what I was letting myself in for. I was reluctant when Harry first mentioned dragging us back into it, but things are different from the way they were three years ago when we came out here. When we gave it all up the first time, it seemed to me we were putting ourselves in harm's way just for the sake of it. As though we were part of some game being played by rich and powerful men for their own amusement.'

'We are now, to some extent.'

'But now, with the way things are so very obviously heading, the stakes are a good deal higher. If all this ends in war, it'll be our village cricket team with guns in their hands, risking their lives for king and country. We owe it to Davey Bishop and the lads in the cricket team who'll join up as soon as there's a scrap, and my Gwenith's husband in the Royal Artillery, and Daisy's brother in the merchant navy – they're worth protecting. And if we can delay a war – or stop it altogether – by getting into a bit of trouble of our own, then it's worth it.'

She looked up. 'You're a remarkable woman, Florence Armstrong,' she said.

'I'm a bloody good cards player, too,' I said, laying down my winning hand. 'A wily, card-playing fox. I got you again.'

'I will, it seems, never learn.'

'I do hope not. You're my pension plan. I'll put my winnings in the book.'

'I'm going to burn that blessed book. What say we abandon the cards and try our hands at some music before bed?'

'Something you're good at, you mean?'

'Something I'm good at, yes. Fetch your banjo, tiny one, I feel some ragtime coming on.'

We tidied away the cards and spent the rest of the evening making music and laughing, the troubles of the world, and the imminence of the terrifying village show, temporarily forgotten.

Chapter Fourteen

Harry caught one of the first trains out of Paddington on Monday morning and was with us not long after lunchtime. I welcomed him back and helped him with his bags.

'How's Lady Lavinia?' I asked as we plodded up the stairs.

'Uncommonly well,' he said. 'She sends her love and wonders when you'll next be coming down to see us.'

'I'm not the one to ask, you know that.'

'She knows her own mind, my sister.'

I opened the door to the guest room he'd been using and then followed him in.

'She teases me for never making decisions,' I said, 'but the truth is there's seldom any point anyway. She'll always have a better idea.'

'Well, your visit is overdue. Addie needs an Aunt Emily in her life. Jake and I do our best, but we're a bit ordinary. I feel she needs a bad influence.'

'Aunt Emily can certainly provide that,' I said.

'What can I provide?' asked Lady Hardcastle.

'Great Scott!' said Harry. 'You frightened the life out of me. Where did you come from?'

'I'm not entirely certain,' she said. 'Mother was always a little vague on the subject. But what is it that I can provide?'

'A bad influence on baby Addie,' I said.

'That's certainly my plan. Hello, Harry dear. How was your journey?'

'There were trains and then a man with a dog cart. I didn't really pay it much attention, I'm afraid. The man with the dog cart told me at some length about his wife's legs.'

'Were they particularly fine, these spousal legs?' she said.

'They may once have been the talk of the town, but now they "play 'er up sommat rotten", apparently.'

'The poor love. Have you eaten?'

'I was rather hoping to scrounge something here,' he said with a grin. 'No point bringing sandwiches wrapped in greaseproof paper when the finest cook in the West Country waits at the other end of the journey.'

'Good thing I asked her to save you something, then,' I said.

'Join us in the dining room when you've unpacked,' said Lady Hardcastle. 'We're looking at the board.'

Lady Hardcastle and I were enjoying a postprandial coffee in the dining room when Harry finally arrived with his briefcase.

'Oh, look out,' said Lady Hardcastle. 'Best behaviour – it's the guv'nor.'

'I dream of the day when you might take me seriously enough to be on your best behaviour when I'm around,' he said.

'You were just saying how you need me to be a bad influence. You can't have it both ways.'

'True, true. I say, is that for me?' He indicated the dishes of food on the table.

'All yours, dear,' she said. 'We've eaten. You don't mind if we contemplate the case while you strap on the nosebag?'

'Carry on, old thing. Much prefer that to you watching me eat.'

He attacked the food while we contemplated the crime board, which I'd carried through from the drawing room earlier.

'We were wondering whether to include any of the other drawing office staff,' I said. 'There was space for a few other teams in there, but when we visited they were all away.'

'Visiting the War Office,' said Harry. 'Already know about them. Spotter plane project. They've been with the Air Battalion at Larkhill for a while now. They're all in the clear.'

'How can you be sure?' said Lady Hardcastle.

'They were all sunning themselves on Salisbury Plain when the files went missing from Bristol.'

'That gives us less to worry about, then,' I said. 'So our list of runners and riders is complete?'

He looked up from his food. 'You tell me,' he said. 'I've forgotten who everyone is.'

'Managing director Walter "everybody calls me Walt" Sandling,' began Lady Hardcastle. 'Nice enough chap, might be fiddling his tax returns.'

'Our checks came up clean,' said Harry. 'Nothing suspicious in his life at all.'

'You sound disappointed,' I said.

'I live for the thrill of a little salacious tittle-tattle. Where's the fun in rootling through a chap's private life to find that he barely even swears? Clean as a whistle, that boy.'

'Aside from a possible fondness for cheating the Revenue.'

'We'll get to that in a moment,' he said. 'But even if he were up to no good there, it's not really scandal-worthy. Not the sort of thing that might see him being blackmailed by foreign powers.'

'Fair enough,' said Lady Hardcastle. 'Senior engineer Godfrey "Goff" Parfitt. Another pleasant chap. Slightly duller than ditch-water outside work, I'd wager, but utterly fascinating when you get him talking about his passion.'

'Aeroplanes?' said Harry.

'Lives for them. Keep an eye on him – he's going to design some breathtaking aircraft if he's given the chance.'

'Duly noted. He came up clean, too. There was a drunken incident with a statue and a small quantity of dynamite while he was up at Oxford, but we're writing that off as youthful high jinks.'

'Dynamite?' I said. 'That's quite the high jink.'

'They were engineering students. They'd calculated precisely the quantity needed to topple a statue of some notable or other without damaging it. They had some sort of elaborate wheeled contraption of ropes, pulleys and nets to capture it as it fell. Then they moved it and set it up to block the main steps of the Radcliffe Camera. Hilarity ensued, naturally. The university was all for sending them down, but their tutor stepped in and pointed out the accuracy of their calculations and the ingenuity of their statue-transporting carriage. It demonstrated what extraordinary engineers they were, he said, and argued that the university should be proud of them. They were let off with a fine.'

'It does rather put your own efforts in the shade,' said Lady Hardcastle. 'Your most notable prank at Cambridge was leaving One-Shoe Wilson tied naked to a tree in the Botanic Garden.'

'Those were the days,' he said, wistfully. 'Anyway, Parfitt is dismayingly law-abiding and scandal-free.'

'What about his miraculously paid debts?' I said.

'Oh, yes, good point. It was prize money, apparently. He's one of those motor-racing Johnnys. His team won some competition or other. Did rather well out of it.'

'He did mention some wins,' I said, 'but he played it all down.'

'He's that sort of chap.'

'His assistant is Paul Curtis,' I said. 'We told you about him, didn't we?'

'You did,' he said. 'On that first evening, just after Em nearly shot me.'

'I never nearly shoot people, dear,' said Lady Hardcastle. 'They're either shot or not shot. You were not shot.'

'The nightmares haunt me nonetheless,' he said. 'He's something of a nonentity, though, young Curtis. No police record to speak of—'

'He's not the youthful high-jinks sort,' I said.

'Evidently not,' continued Harry. 'Meanwhile his university records are all pukka and above board, but such was his blandness that no one we've spoken to has any lasting memory of him. Just melted into the background. The sort of chap who turns up to tutorials, hands in his work on time, and never leaves a trace of his presence. One tutor said he vaguely recalled a blond chap who could well have been called Curtis, but that was it.'

'Nothing since?' said Lady Hardcastle.

'No, he went straight from the University of London to Bristol Aviation and has continued to fail to make waves ever since.'

'Did you get anything on Myrtle Matthews?' I asked.

'Not much. Youngest daughter of a reasonably well-to-do family in Bristol. Worked as a secretary in a shipping company for a while. Active in the WSPU, as you said, but no arrests and no other political affiliations. Pays her bills. No serious suitors other than the late Dickie Dupree.'

'She seems to have it in for Milhouse,' I said.

'Perhaps. But other than that, she's as unremarkable as the others.'

'And what about Milhouse?' said Lady Hardcastle.

'So far, he's the only properly interesting one,' said Harry. He put down his knife and fork and rummaged in his briefcase. 'I have the report from the accounting wizards and they're certain he's not defrauding the taxman.'

'Why all the palaver with the two sets of books, then?' I said. 'I definitely saw them.'

'He'd need them,' he said. 'Our chaps have completely dismantled the accounts. "Fine-tooth comb" doesn't even begin to convey the thoroughness of their painstaking work. Now, I'm not at all convinced I understand what they're telling me, but they assure me that every penny the company has earned has been reported for the purposes of corporation duty. But hundreds of pounds just disappear into some sort of financial thin air elsewhere in the calculations. The Inland Revenue gets its due, but somehow not all the money the company might think it has ends up in its own accounts.'

'So he's embezzling,' said Lady Hardcastle.

'Quite spectacularly. It's no wonder the company is struggling. Our wizards say it's a very clever scheme. By making sure there's no reason for the authorities to investigate, he might have kept it hidden until he had enough to retire to the South of France. It was only by chance that one of our chaps caught sight of something that didn't quite add up.'

'And how does your department feel about the idea that he might be the leaker?' I asked.

'Not entirely certain, but we're inclined to think not, given the way he behaved on Friday evening. You painted a picture of someone rather more intent on a horizontal turkey-trot than high treason. He might be fleecing the company as an act of revenge for some perceived slight, in which case he might also feel inclined to flog its secrets to the highest bidder. On the other hand, he might just be a greedy blighter who wants to supplement his salary to fund his lavish, infidelity-laden lifestyle.'

'And your preferred course of action?' asked Lady Hardcastle.

'Nick him. Let's get him in custody and charged with misappropriating company funds and see what happens.'

'Urgently?' I said.

'We don't want to leave it too long. Today would be nice. You have a tame policeman in Bristol, I seem to remember.'

'Inspector Sunderland?' said Lady Hardcastle. 'I can telephone him now, if you like. If he's not busy we can do it this afternoon on our way to hang around Horfield Common like a couple of street-walkers.'

'It would be nice to get things moving,' he said. 'If you wouldn't mind.'

'It might help us,' I said. 'If the leaker is beginning to wonder why we're always there asking questions, it would be good to make it seem as though we were on the trail of an embezzler all along. It might make him lower his guard.'

'I'll make the call,' said Lady Hardcastle. 'Would you like a cup of coffee?'

'I'd love one,' said Harry. 'The pot's empty.'

'The kettle's in the kitchen,' she said, and went into the hall to make her call.

◆ ◆ ◆

I had imagined our old friend Inspector Sunderland – if he had even been in the office to take Lady Hardcastle's call in the first place – politely telling her that he had far too much on his plate to be bothering with an embezzler on someone else's patch. I thought he might go on, in the kindest possible way, to invite her to take a running jump at herself. Instead he had been only too happy to drive out to Bristol Aviation to make an arrest. I expressed my surprise to Lady Hardcastle as we bowled along the now familiar route to the aerodrome.

'I got the impression that he's rather stumped by an ingenious burglary at a jeweller's shop in the middle of town,' she said. 'There was something about clearing out the cobwebs with a drive to the suburbs and how making an arrest – "Any old arrest," he said – would shut his superiors up for a bit.'

'Well, it'll be lovely to see him.'

'It will indeed. We ought to take him and Dollie out for supper again soon.'

We had known Inspector Sunderland since not long after arriving in Littleton Cotterell, and had become friends with him and his wife, Dollie. We always felt it was too far to invite them to dine at the house, and Lady Hardcastle was insistent that Mrs Sunderland shouldn't have to cook for us, so we took them out to dinner in Bristol once in a while.

'Did he say how long he'd be?' I asked.

'"As soon as I can, my lady" was the best I could get him to commit to. My plan is to have a quiet word with Sandling before the inspector gets there. We can sound him out a little and prepare the ground. If we're going to be hauling his chief accountant out of the building in handcuffs, it seems only polite to tell him before rather than after.'

'You're assuming he doesn't know,' I said. 'That he isn't in on it himself.'

'I am, it's true. But even if he is, what's he going to do about it? The evidence is locked in Milhouse's safe so he can't destroy it before the inspector gets there. He's not going to do a bunk while you're there to stop him. I think a discreet word in his shell-like will be just fine.'

We soon arrived and parked in what had become our usual spot. We went straight in.

Miss Matthews was surprised to see us.

'Good afternoon, Lady Hardcastle,' she said. 'And Miss Armstrong. Don't you look nice out of your uniform?'

'Thank you,' I said.

'What can we do for you? Are we expecting you?'

'No, dear, I shouldn't think so,' said Lady Hardcastle. 'But I wonder if it might be possible to have a word with Mr Sandling.'

'He's in his office.' She consulted a large diary on her desk. 'And he has no appointments this afternoon, so he's definitely free. I'm sure he'd be delighted to see you.'

'Would you be so kind as to announce us, then, please?'

'Of course.'

She made the call. From the half of the conversation we were able to hear, it seemed Mr Sandling would indeed be delighted to see us. I wasn't entirely certain how delighted he'd be by the time we left him, but even a little bit of delight in the day was more than many could hope for.

'Mr Sandling is free now, if you'd like to go up,' said Miss Matthews as she hung up the phone. 'I'm happy to take you if you'd like.'

'Thank you, dear,' said Lady Hardcastle, 'but we know the way by now. It's a shame to drag you away from your work.'

'Always happy to help a friend of the WSPU.' She flipped the lapel of her jacket to flash her badge again.

I turned towards the door that led to the stairs, but Lady Hardcastle hadn't finished.

'I've arranged to meet a business associate here,' she said. 'Oliver Sunderland. Would you be kind enough to bring him up when he arrives, please?'

'Of course.'

'Thank you.'

She turned and we set off again. There was a potted palm in the corner of the room and I noticed some scuff marks on the door where I had slammed it into the large pot. Closer inspection revealed a substantial crack in the pot, too. I wondered if the Chinese burglar were still a secret.

Mr Milhouse's door was open and he gave us a smile and a wave as we went past. We both waved back and carried on down the corridor.

Mr Sandling stood as we entered.

'Good afternoon, Lady Hardcastle,' he said warmly. 'Good afternoon, Miss Armstrong. To what do I owe the considerable pleasure? Have you come to place an order?'

I shut the office door before taking my seat on one of his visitors' chairs.

'Do you know, I may yet end up doing just that one of these days,' began Lady Hardcastle. 'But no, I'm afraid not. Not today.'

'Then how may I help you?'

'How well do you know John Milhouse?'

'He's my right-hand man. The company would be lost without him. I would be lost without him. My own background is in engineering. I can lead the way in the design and construction of groundbreaking aeronautical technology, but I have absolutely no grasp of the complexities of accountancy and finance. That's John's domain. Without him we'd be sunk.'

'Then I'm afraid I have some very bad news for you. You see . . . well, now . . . how best to put it? Your right-hand man is robbing you blind.'

'He's what?'

'I'm sorry to be the bearer of bad news, Mr Sandling, but there it is. John Milhouse has embezzled hundreds of pounds from the company.'

'How on earth can you possibly know that?'

'A team of government experts has examined the accounts submitted to the Inland Revenue in very fine detail, and a great deal of money seems to evaporate before it actually reaches your bank.'

'The Inland Revenue? But how would you know that?'

'We have certain . . . contacts in Westminster.'

'Do you? Do you, indeed?' He seemed too shocked to speak for a moment, but only the shortest of moments. 'Great Scott,' he exclaimed. 'Does this mean we've defrauded the tax man?'

'You're in no trouble with the tax man,' she said. 'But Mr Milhouse is about to be arrested. We thought it best to let you know before he is taken away. You deserve that, at least.'

'How long have you known?'

'We've suspected for a while, but we had it confirmed this morning.'

'You work for the government, then?'

'In a manner of speaking.'

'And you've been investigating us the whole time?'

'We have, yes.'

'You have no intention of buying a Dunnock, do you?'

'Actually,' she said, 'that part was never a lie. I genuinely am very interested in the Dunnock and I am very seriously thinking about buying one.'

'We might need you to if your claims are true. I could never quite fathom how we seemed to have so little money when business appeared to be so good. John assured me . . . Well, we know he was lying now, don't we?'

'I'm afraid so.'

'And you're sure? You have proof?'

'We have the company accounts.'

'But proof that John has been embezzling? Proof that it was him?'

'We shall very soon.'

There was a knock at the door.

'Mr Sunderland to see you, sir,' said Miss Matthews as she ushered him into the room.

'Inspector Sunderland, sir,' he said. 'Bristol CID.'

Mr Sandling stood to shake his hand.

'How do you do?' he said dejectedly.

Miss Matthews departed, leaving the office door open.

'I take it from your demeanour that Lady Hardcastle has explained what's going on?' said the inspector.

'John Milhouse has been fiddling the accounts,' said Mr Sandling. 'You're here to arrest him.'

'That's right, sir, yes.'

'Will we ever get the money back?'

'I'm afraid I couldn't say. I'm here to make the arrest, that's all. The investigation has been undertaken by men far senior to me.'

'I see. Well, we'd better get it over with, then, I suppose.'

I caught sight of one of the photographs on the office wall. I'd never really paid it much attention before. All the others were of aeroplanes, but this one was just a row of houses and it hadn't seemed nearly so interesting. Until now.

'Excuse me, sir,' I said. 'Is that Horfield Common?'

'What?' said Mr Sandling. 'Oh, yes. That's our house there in the middle. I took it when we bought the place. There's no place like home and all that. You know the common?'

'Rather better now than I used to,' I said.

Lady Hardcastle looked at me. I widened my eyes and gave a little shrug. Now was probably not the time to tell him what we'd seen.

She led the way back down the corridor to Mr Milhouse's office.

◆ ◆ ◆

Lady Hardcastle breezed confidently into Milhouse's office, then stopped sharply. I was two steps behind her and I, too, drew to a sudden halt.

'Stay outside, gentlemen,' I said.

'I will not,' blustered Mr Sandling, seemingly keen to assert his authority in front of his soon-to-be-disgraced chief accountant. 'This is my company and I'll jolly well go where I please. If what you say is true—'

'Shut up, and stay where you are,' I said firmly. The timidly deferential lady's maid is such a useful role, not least because it makes that sort of assertive behaviour so shocking.

'Now look here—'

'If I had a shilling for every time a man who doesn't know what's going on had told me to look there,' I said, 'I'd have long since retired to a cottage by the sea and I wouldn't be facing a frightened accountant with a Webley Service Revolver. Now shut up, and stay where you are.'

'You shut up as well, you little—' began Milhouse.

'There's no need for that,' said Lady Hardcastle. 'Lower your gun and we'll talk about this.'

Milhouse was standing beside the open safe, the accounts books and a bundle of fivers held tight to his body with one arm while the other hand pointed the pistol at Lady Hardcastle.

'No. You're all going to step out of my way and I'm getting out of here. There's no need for any unpleasantness. Lilly and I will just quietly disappear and no one will get hurt.'

'Lilly?' yelled Mr Sandling. 'Why, you perfidious—'

There was a slight scuffle outside, where I presumed Inspector Sunderland was restraining Mr Sandling. At least we were spared the uncomfortable task of telling him about his wife's affair, though I'm sure we'd have made a more compassionate job of it.

'No, dear,' said Lady Hardcastle calmly. 'We're not going anywhere and you're not shooting anyone. Put the gun down. It's all over.'

'It's not over till I say it's over,' said Milhouse. 'The man with the gun makes the rules, not some jumped-up totty with more money than sense who thinks she can fly an aeroplane for a lark. Now get out of my way.'

'As you wish, dear,' she said, stepping across in front of me to allow him to pass alongside us. 'But it's not going to end well. You must know that.'

He started to push past us, his gun nervously flicking between Lady Hardcastle and the open door to the office.

Obviously, I wasn't going to allow him to get out there with the evidence – I'd dangled from the side of the building in the middle of the night to find that, and I wasn't about to let him wander off with it.

As he drew alongside me, I lifted my left leg and leaned over on my right to counterbalance myself. I kicked across his body and into his wrist with all my might. I'd tried exactly this move during a case a few years earlier and I remembered the potential consequences only too well. Sure enough, there was an unpleasant crunch of breaking bone as the heel of my shoe made contact, followed by an almighty bang. The Webley went off as it spun out of his hand. The recoil from the loosely-held pistol inflicted further damage on his wrist and he screamed.

I saw the pain and rage in his eyes and was braced for a frenzied retaliation, but he suddenly froze. Lady Hardcastle was holding her little pistol to his head.

'I did tell you it wasn't going to end well, didn't I?' she said.

'It's safe to come in now,' I called. 'He's been disarmed.'

There was another scuffle in the corridor and instead of the calmly reassuring figure of Inspector Sunderland, the first person through the door was an enraged Mr Sandling.

He launched himself at the now whimpering Milhouse and landed a punch Jack Johnson would have been proud of. Milhouse hit the ground like the proverbial sack of spuds.

'John Milhouse,' said Inspector Sunderland, 'I am arresting you in accordance with this warrant issued by . . . Well, I'll tell you later. You have the right to remain unconscious. Mr Sandling, you're going to need that hand looking at – you might well have broken something there. Never hit someone in the face with a closed fist if you don't know what you're doing. Now, Miss Armstrong here can smack people about all day long – she's rather good at it – but you? Well, you should be more careful. I take it the ladies are all right?'

'Tidy,' I said.

'Quite well, thank you, Inspector,' said Lady Hardcastle.

'Good,' he said. 'I'm going to have to get some help out here now. I thought this was going to be a simple collar of a respectable gent on a fraud charge. I wasn't expecting firearms and fisticuffs.'

He took a pencil and a scrap of paper from Milhouse's desk and scribbled something on it.

'Mr Sandling, if you'd be so good as to ask your secretary to call this number. Ask to speak to Inspector Harvey. Tell him I'm here, tell him what's happened, and ask him if he'd be kind enough to send two lads and a wagon to collect this Milhouse character. I'll take care of things here.'

He picked up the pistol while Mr Sandling set off for reception, nursing his injured hand.

'I'd like to handcuff him,' said Inspector Sunderland as Milhouse started to come round. 'But he seems to have broken his wrist.'

'I'm sorry,' I said. 'It seemed the most effective thing to do under the circumstances.'

'You bloody kicked me,' mumbled Milhouse.

'You were pointing a gun at her,' said Lady Hardcastle.

'To be fair, he was pointing the gun at the open doorway,' I said. 'But it's still not polite to wave guns about.'

'I'll bloody get you for this,' he mumbled.

'We'll have none of that talk,' said the inspector. 'You just behave yourself. You're under arrest.'

He reached down and took the accounts books and money from the stricken accountant.

'I'll take these, too,' he said. He shook his head. 'I honestly thought this was going to be a straightforward one.'

'We'll help you with the paperwork,' said Lady Hardcastle. 'We need to be away by half past five but we can get started on writing our statements now, if you like.'

'That would be most helpful,' he said. 'And do you know where we can get a cup of tea?'

'I'll see what I can find,' I said, and went to speak to Miss Matthews.

By the time we arrived back at the house after our daily trip to Horfield Common, Harry was fast asleep in an armchair in the drawing room.

Despite our best efforts to be quiet, he snuffled awake as we tried to sneak out of the room.

'Evening, girls,' he yawned. 'Congratulations on another skirmish won.'

'You heard, then?' said Lady Hardcastle.

'Sunderland telephoned not long after you'd left him for your other important engagement. I take it you had no joy at the common?'

'Another no-show,' I said. 'I'm beginning to think we've spooked him somehow.'

'Or you have,' said Lady Hardcastle to Harry. 'Are you sure you got the message format right?'

'As sure as we can be,' he said. 'Give it another couple of days, then we'll try to come up with something else.'

'Did the inspector tell you who Milhouse has been tupping?' said Lady Hardcastle.

'No?'

'Lilly Sandling, known more formally as Mrs Walter Sandling.'

Harry laughed. 'What a piece of work,' he said. 'Not content with stealing from the company, he was diddling the boss's wife. How did you find out?'

'Sandling has a photograph of his house on his office wall. I recognized it as the house the lovers went into the other evening.'

Lady Hardcastle looked at Harry. 'Now I come to think of it,' she said, 'how did you *not* work it out?'

'How on earth would I?' he said.

'I thought you'd thoroughly vetted Sandling.'

'We did.'

'So you knew his address?'

'We did.'

'So when we told you what we'd seen, why didn't your little civil service brain whir into action and say, "Hold on a moment, Harry, old bean, that's where Walter Sandling lives"?'

'Why would it?'

'Because you knew his address.'

'I certainly did, but I hadn't got the foggiest where that was. I had an address in Bristol. Could have been by Horfield Common. Could have been in the middle of town. Could have been a cave at the bottom of the Avon Gorge for all I knew.'

'Well, anyway,' I said. 'It saved me from having to restrain Milhouse – Sandling knocked him out cold.'

'Ah, so that's what happened. It all makes sense now. Sunderland said something about Sandling having another go at Milhouse as the gendarmes hauled him off. He said you'd explain why. He can be quite the prude for a copper.'

'I prefer to think of him as a true gentleman,' said Lady Hardcastle. 'Not given to salacious tittle-tattle.'

'All the gentlemen I've ever met absolutely live for salacious tittle-tattle,' said Harry. 'But there's an old fashioned charm about it, I'll grant you that.'

'What happens to Milhouse now?' I asked.

'Our lads will take a look at the second set of books to double-check that we don't want to refer the case to the tax bods – and to make sure he's not involved in anything that might more directly concern us, of course – then we'll hand the whole thing over to the rozzers. "Local Police Trap Embezzler". Let them have their day.'

'Did the inspector ask any awkward questions about our involvement?' said Lady Hardcastle.

'No, Strongarm's burglary remains officially unreported. He's no fool, though – he laid heavy hints that he's pretty sure exactly what went on. He's known you both for a few years, after all. But nothing will come of it and no one at Bristol Aviation has any idea what you're up to.'

'So we're free to carry on with not getting anywhere with the main case, then,' I said. 'What have you made us for dinner?'

'Coq-au-vin,' he said. 'Boiled new potatoes, which I have scrubbed, not peeled. And . . . and . . . something green. Don't tell me, it'll come to me . . .'

'Did Miss Jones leave me any instructions?' I asked.

'Other than suggesting you don't peel the potatoes, no. It's something she's trying.'

'I'll go and finish her – sorry, your – work.'

'I'll take a trip down the cellar,' he said. 'It's the least I can do.'

Chapter Fifteen

Harry had brought a dismaying amount of paperwork with him, and set himself up in the drawing room the next morning after breakfast. Edna and I kept him supplied with tea.

'Thank you, Strongarm,' he said as I brought in yet another cup just after eleven. 'The civil service runs on tea, you know.'

'I'd be happy to bring it in a chipped cup if it would make it feel more like your office in Whitehall,' I said.

'I don't believe Em would keep any chipped cups.'

'Ah, but you underestimate my ingenuity. I'm reasonably sure I could contrive to chip a cup if it were important for the smooth running of the Secret Service Bureau.'

'I'm sure you could at that. I don't say it often enough, old sport, but your efforts are greatly appreciated by the Bureau. Yours and Emily's. There was a good deal of opposition from some of the bigwigs to the idea of having women on the strength. "Not cut out for that kind of thing, what? Too emotional. And what happens when things cut up rough? How they gonna cope then, eh?" It didn't matter that you already had a glowing reputation and that their predecessors had seen fit to employ you on a number of jobs where men would have fallen at the first jump.

You're invaluable, the pair of you. But mostly you. Em's a living nightmare, obviously.'

'Why, thank you, Mr Feather-stone-huff. You're very kind to say so.'

'But don't get complacent. We still haven't caught our leaking parachute nobbler.'

'*The Leaking Parachute Nobbler*,' I said. 'That's a painting I'd pay to see.'

'I rather envisaged it as a West End show. A musical comedy.'

'No, it would be in the style of a dark Jacobean drama.'

He laughed. 'Perhaps you're right,' he said. 'But we still have to nab him.'

'*The Nabbing of the Leaking Parachute Nobbler* would definitely be a musical comedy. And we'll keep going to Horfield Common until you tell us otherwise.'

'Thank you.'

Lady Hardcastle popped her head around the door.

'Ah, there you both are,' she said. 'I've had Edna in the study telling me about her Dan's new bicycle and wondering what we'd like for lunch. It seems Miss Jones wants to know because she'd like to get away early to take her mother to a rehearsal for the show. I said not to worry and that we'd dine at the pub, but could they make sure we could cobble together a cold collation for supper. She was most apologetic for bothering me and said she'd have asked you, Flo, but she couldn't find you. Then we returned to the matter of two-wheeled personal transport.'

'I told her I was bringing tea for Harry. She was with me in the kitchen while I made it.'

'Then she must just have wanted to talk about bicycles. We should have bicycles. We could lash them to the back of the Rolls.'

'Wouldn't they be somewhat redundant if you were already travelling by motor car?' said Harry.

'We'd take them somewhere nice and cycle around when we got there,' she said.

'Why on earth would you want to do that?'

'For the pleasure of it, dear. You can be so obtuse at times. Now, then, what have I missed?'

'Missed?' he said.

'Well, you two are in here, thick as thieves, and I know you're not talking about bicycles – you're not interested in bicycles.'

'Harry was telling me how marvellous we are as a way of buttering us up so we'll trek over to Horfield again to look for his leaker.'

'We'll do that anyway,' she said. 'It's going to be another lovely evening stroll. But I'm beginning to wonder why we don't just haul in Molly Mumbles the secretary and the invisible Paul Whatnot from the drawing office. They're the only ones left on our list.'

'And Rupert Gilbert Hubert Herbert,' I said.

'Oh, the dashing pilot, yes,' she said. 'I'd forgotten him. So there are still three in the race, then – it might get a bit crowded if you pinched them all. Not to mention the complete lack of evidence. Forget I said anything.'

'How well do you know Adam Whitman?' said Harry.

'Hardly at all. We met him for the first time a few weeks ago when he and Clarissa came to visit Grandma Gertie. I presume he's been vetted, though. You said you were keeping an eye on anyone working for foreign companies.'

'Foreign companies involved in businesses with a military potential, yes. If they want to work in a *bar tabac* or dance at the Folies Bergère we're not going to stop them.'

'Do you remember Fifi Charpentier?' I said. 'From the Moulin Rouge.'

'Oh, yes,' said Lady Hardcastle. 'Lovely girl. Beautiful dancer.'

'You're going to tell me she was a spy,' said Harry. 'To prove me wrong.'

'Oh, no,' I said. 'Not a spy, not our Fifi.'

'She was an assassin,' said Lady Hardcastle. 'Used a blowpipe concealed in a silver-handled parasol. Poisoned darts. Deadly at ten paces, but we saw her hit a target from twenty.'

'And yet still we're ignoring dancers and waiters for the time being. Anyway. We found nothing to ring any alarm bells in Whitman's history, but a personal perspective is always helpful.'

'He seems an ordinary, decent sort of chap,' she said. 'Quietly charming in his own way, and with the patience of a saint.'

'How so?'

'You'd not have to ask if you'd met Clarissa when she was younger,' I said. 'She's grown up a lot since we first met her in '08, but . . . she was . . . well . . .'

'She was a ninny,' said Lady Hardcastle. 'A flighty flibbertigibbet. She's sweet enough and she seems to have made something of a career for herself in the world of magazines, but she's not one of Mother Nature's great intellectuals. I do sometimes wonder what Adam sees in her.'

Harry flashed his schoolboy grin.

'She'd have to be particularly skilled if that's all it was,' said Lady Hardcastle.

'We may never know,' he said. 'But you don't suspect him of skulduggery.'

'No, I think you can rule him out, too. Is it lunchtime yet, do you think?'

'No,' said Harry, 'but I'm dashed bored of all this bumf I've got to wade through. What say we take a stroll into the village and end up at this pub of yours? Good there, is it? The nosh, I mean.'

'You've never seen doorsteps thicker, nor pies more generously filled,' I said.

'Then give me a few moments to finish off here and I shall treat you both to a slap-up feed.'

◆ ◆ ◆

The weather was still wonderful and our walk was as pleasant as any walk has ever been. Lady Hardcastle and Harry bickered like only brothers and sisters can, and I wished I'd had a chance to fly the Dunnock. Our investigation must surely be nearing its end, and unless Lady Hardcastle walked into Bristol Aviation with a cheque in her hand, it was unlikely that anyone there was going to continue to indulge the pretence that she was a serious buyer.

Village life continued, as village life always does, completely oblivious to the dark goings-on elsewhere in the world. The shop-keepers were busy selling their wares, children were playing on the green, and the vicar's wife's dog was chasing woodpigeons. The pigeons – who always struck me as the most dimwitted of all the birds – were, at least, sensible enough to keep out of his way. Little did they know that if he caught them he would do them no deliberate harm but would only try to enlist them in one of his exuberant games.

Our route brought us back past the pub, where business was booming. The lunchtime crowd of farm labourers was enjoying sitting outside, and the mood was summery and festive. There was one table spare and I urged the others to nab it while I went inside and ordered our food.

Daisy was behind the bar and was chatting to a couple of the younger farmhands. She saw me, smiled, waved, and then excused herself from her conversation so she could serve me.

'All right, Flo,' she said warmly. "Ow bist?'

'Passing well, thank you, Daisy dear,' I said. 'You're busy today.'

'It's been like it for a few days now. Word got round about Old Joe's outside tables and everyone and his dog has come down to sup their cider in the sunshine.'

'He must be pleased.'

'He's thrilled. Course, that's cos he don't have to serve 'em. He's out the back seein' to the pies and sandwiches. He's very particular about his pies and sandwiches, specially when it means he don't have to run around behind the bar. What can I get you?'

'We'll take three pies, please, and two pints of cider, and a ginger beer.'

'You got a guest?'

'Lady Hardcastle's brother,' I said.

'Ooh, is he as good-lookin' as she is?'

'There's a family resemblance.'

She grinned. 'I'll bring your pies out personally,' she said.

'He's married.'

'A cat may look at a king. I mean, look at what I've got to choose from round here. My eyes needs a little treat once in a while.'

'As long as the cat doesn't start batting her eyelashes at the happily married king, she'll be fine.'

'Right you are, Miss Armstrong. Right you are.'

She paused in her drink-pouring for a moment and looked pensive.

'Something the matter, Dais?' I said.

'Sort of,' she said. 'I . . . well . . . you see . . . the thing is . . .'

'It's better out than in, as my mother always used to say.'

'How upset would you be if we didn't do our act at the show? Only . . . I've been asked to join in a dance number with a couple of girls from the village . . . and . . . well, I know you wasn't all that keen anyway, so I said I'd ask if it was all right. I mean, I'll still do ours if you wants. I mean, a promise is a promise and all that. But . . . you know . . . I said I'd ask.'

'Oh, thank goodness for that,' I said. 'Please, please, join your dancer friends. You've no idea how relieved I am.'

'Really?'

'I've faced crazed assassins and lunatics with rifles bent on revenge. Yesterday I faced down a lecherous accountant who threatened to shoot us so he could run off with his boss's wife. But I have never been more terrified than by the thought of getting up on the stage in the village hall and doing animal impressions, no matter how funny you would have made it.'

'Oh, Flo, you twit. You should have said sommat. I thought you were a born performer. You always talk so fondly about the circus.'

'I was just a little girl then,' I said. 'And everyone loves a little girl with a knife in her hand.'

'They do if they knows what's good for 'em.'

'Well, quite. But our act . . . I was dreading it.'

'Then you's off the hook, my old mate.'

'Just one thing, though,' I said. 'You told me you have two left feet.'

'Oh, I does. Lord, but I does. But it's a comic song, so it don't matter. Me, Blodwen, and Rosy, it is.'

'Blodwen Jones?' I said. 'Our Blodwen?'

'I'n't no other Blodwens round 'ere.'

'"She Sits Among the Cabbages and Peas"?' I said.

'You wants to keep that to yourself,' she said with a laugh. 'People will talk.'

'Miss Jones told us about the song. It'll be a hoot.'

'I reckon it might at that,' she said. 'Does that mean you won't be doin' nothin', though?'

'I do hope so,' I said. 'I might help out as Lady Hardcastle's page-turner, but that's about as far as I'll go.'

'You are an old twit. Get out with your dinin' companions. I'll bring your food out when it's ready.'

I carried the drinks out to the table and sat down.

'You look pleased with yourself,' said Lady Hardcastle. 'What have you been plotting in there with your pal?'

'My escape,' I said.

'Escape?' said Harry. 'Don't tell me you've finally seen sense and you're going to abandon my idiot sister to her fate. You've been propping her up for far too long, you know.'

'No, my escape from the village show. Daisy has been asked to join another act so we've scratched the comedy routine and I'm free to enjoy Saturday's show without fretting about having to perform.'

'Excellent news,' said Lady Hardcastle. 'Does this mean the knife-throwing act is back on? I still have time to get a spangly leotard.'

'That's an image that will haunt my nightmares,' said Harry. 'Do make sure she never appears in public in a leotard, Strongarm, spangly or otherwise.'

'It's all under control,' I said. 'Have no fear.'

Lady Hardcastle harrumphed. 'I'll have my moment of glamour, you killjoy curmudgeons. You just wait.'

Old Joe had the pie situation under control, too. Given the volume of lunchtime trade, I'd been expecting to wait a while for our food, but here was Daisy with three pies on a tray.

'Here you go, my loves,' she said. 'Three pies.'

'Thanks, Dais,' I said.

'Yes, dear, thank you,' said Lady Hardcastle.

'My pleasure,' said Daisy. 'Is everythin' all right for you, sir?'

Harry smiled. 'It looks smashing, thank you,' he said.

Daisy caught my eye and flicked her head towards Harry.

I sighed. 'Harry,' I said, 'please allow me to introduce my good friend Miss Daisy Spratt. Daisy, this is Harry Featherstonhaugh, Lady Hardcastle's brother.'

'Pleased to meet you, I'm sure,' said Daisy.

'How do you do?' said Harry.

Daisy caught my eye again and mouthed, 'He's gorgeous.'

I rolled my eyes. 'But don't let us keep you, Dais,' I said. 'I'm sure you've got lots to be getting on with.'

'What? Oh, yes, right you are. I'd best get back behind the bar.' She gave me a wink and swished back inside.

'She seems like a nice girl,' said Harry as he tucked into his pie.

Lady Hardcastle and I both laughed.

'What?' he said. 'What have I done?'

'Nothing, dear, nothing,' said Lady Hardcastle. 'You just eat your pie.'

'It's a fine pie,' he said.

'Yes. Yes, it is.'

After our prolonged lunch, we took Harry home and settled him in the garden with his papers and a pot of tea. He wasn't delighted about being pushed back to work, but his sister patted his head and told him he was a brave boy, and we left him to it.

We readied ourselves for another trip to the common, and I once again suggested the idea of taking a couple of tennis racquets and a ball.

'It would make keeping an eye on the bench much easier,' I said. 'I know there's no tennis court, but it would mean we could stand still without attracting too much attention.'

'Two idiots batting a ball about?' said Lady Hardcastle. 'I should think that'll draw quite a bit of attention.'

'But it's the sort of thing people do on commons. They might find our efforts comical, but they won't think us odd for standing there.'

'You have persuaded me, tiny servant,' she said. 'Bung the necessary in the boot.'

It was my turn to drive again, so we set off in plenty of time. We parked in our usual spot with fifteen minutes to spare and began our slow stroll up the hill towards our vantage point.

'If nobody shows this evening,' she said as we looked for a suitably flat patch of grass, 'I'm going to call a halt to this nonsense. Harry and his gang of wizards are going to have to come up with a new way of plugging their leak.'

'I can't say I disagree,' I said. 'It's not the most rewarding surveillance we've ever done.'

'It isn't, is it? I much preferred that time in Venice. Do you remember? Sitting outside that little trattoria near St Mark's Square, waiting for that Hungarian chap to appear and meet the Italian agent in the building opposite.'

'I do remember. That was much more fun.' I looked around. 'I'd completely overlooked a rather obvious problem with my tennis plan.'

'I wasn't going to mention it, but I think I know what you mean. This grass isn't quite the ticket, is it? Too long. They should graze some sheep here, perhaps – keep it all a bit shorter.'

'Ah well. At least holding the racquets we look like we have a purpose.'

'We could try volleys?' she suggested.

'It'll certainly pass the time.'

We paced out a sensible distance between us and began lobbing the ball back and forth. Against my expectations, it turned out to be rather entertaining. I was just beginning to get properly engrossed in the new game and was trying to devise a scoring system when Lady Hardcastle took her eye off the ball and let it sail past her. I was about to remonstrate, but she held up her hand to stop me and nodded towards the bench.

Paul Curtis really hadn't mastered the art of nonchalance. He clutched a manila folder tightly to his chest and looked nervously this way and that. He walked past the bench, then turned and walked back, his head still jerking around as he scanned his surroundings. If you were giving a lecture on how to behave furtively, you'd want him in the hall to demonstrate for you.

Lady Hardcastle had returned to stand beside me. 'Thank heavens for that,' she said. 'I really thought we were wasting our time.'

'Apparently not,' I said. 'There's no doubt it's him, is there? He's got a file and a guilty look. He's our man.'

'He almost certainly is. Do you think he's seen us?'

'He's seen everyone,' I said. 'But I doubt he's noticed any of us. He's so nervous he's not taking it in. Look at the way he's jiggling his leg.'

'And looking at that watch. He'd be better off not putting it back in his pocket every time if he's only going to get it out and look at it again a few seconds later.'

'How long do you think he's going to wait?'

'I don't think it matters,' she said. 'Do you? We know the meeting's a fake so we know there's no one coming to meet him. We know who he is and where we can find him. I suggest we just jump in the Rolls and head back to the house. We can pass the intelligence on to Harry and return to enjoying the summer. Our work is done. Our part played.'

'Cold collation and white wine in the garden, then,' I said. 'That sounds like a much better evening. Do you think Harry will have set the table?'

She laughed. 'How long have you known my brother? Do you really think that's likely?'

'I suppose not. Do you want to drive?'

'You don't want to?'

'I just thought it would be quicker if you did. I'm fed up of Horfield Common.'

We set off for home.

◆ ◆ ◆

'I have good news,' said Harry as I opened the front door.

'Have you been standing there waiting for us?' said Lady Hardcastle.

'I heard the motor car arrive. I was in the garden laying the table.'

'Well, that is good news,' I said. 'Thank you.'

'You're welcome,' he said. 'But that's not the good news. The good news is that I know who the leaker is.'

'Oh, we all know that,' said Lady Hardcastle.

'Yes,' I said. 'It's Paul Curtis.'

'You saw him?' said Harry. He seemed a little disappointed.

'We did,' said Lady Hardcastle. 'How did you find out?'

'The office called while you were out,' he said.

We both sighed.

'You mean we could have saved ourselves a trip?' said Lady Hardcastle.

'I've scuffed my shoes,' I said. 'Look.'

'I'm sorry about all that,' he said. 'But it's nice to have it confirmed. Thank you.'

'We saw him waiting to meet his contact,' I said. 'How did your minions find out?'

'They kept on digging. You remember you said something about him being up at the University of London but never seeing anything of the city? And then my chaps asking around and no one remembering him? It all seemed a bit fishy, so they took a proper look at the university records. Forged. It was an extremely competent job. It was good enough to fool a harassed university administrator when he was asked to confirm something by a sinister government official, but not good enough to fool the sinister government officials when they took a look for themselves.'

'Interesting,' said Lady Hardcastle, 'but hardly conclusive.'

'True. But once my boys knew that, they were off like whatsits after a thingummy. You know. Some sort of hunting simile. Probably has dogs in it. Or ferrets. Fill in the blanks.'

'A conversation with you is just a box of parts we have to assemble for ourselves, isn't it?' she said.

'I was just trying to add a bit of colour, but it ran away from me. But anyway. The boys dug a little deeper. Like ferrets. Yes, definitely ferrets. A hotel register here, a ship's passenger manifest there – you know the sort of thing. Paul Curtis is actually Kurt Pohl from Hamburg. We asked our man in Berlin and he did some digging of his own. A Kurt Pohl of about the right age studied engineering at the University of Rostock. He was a bit of a fanatical nationalist, by all accounts. Our man's contact says he was turned down by the army for being a bit bonkers, but their equivalent of the Secret Service Bureau wasn't above putting him to work for them. They forged some university records and got him a job at Bristol Aviation.'

'They didn't give him any espionage training,' I said. 'I've never seen a worse attempt at a clandestine meeting.'

'He's not on the strength, so they wouldn't have bothered. As long as he kept the information flowing, that was all that mattered.'

'Do you think they'll try to extract him?'

'I think they'll just cut him loose. My guess is they know we worked out their newspaper advertisement code and reckon it's only a matter of time before we nab him. That's why they've gone quiet.'

'Is he in danger?' asked Lady Hardcastle.

'Potentially. We all are, if you want to take a properly bleak view. But he's no threat to them. What does he know, after all? He doesn't have any means of contacting them, so he almost certainly doesn't know who anyone is. They'll just leave him to face the music and pretend they've never heard of him.'

'He almost certainly saw us. He might scarper.'

'He won't get far. But he's a fanatic, remember? He'll stick to his mission no matter what.'

'Will you pick him up?' I said.

'Tomorrow morning. I asked your pal Sunderland to help us out again. He's a good chap, that one. I like him.'

'We like him, too,' said Lady Hardcastle. 'Have you thought about the logistics?'

'As a matter of fact, I have. Sunderland's coming out here in his shiny motor car and we'll head to the aerodrome together. You two can go in your own motor, and we'll meet his men and their wagon at the factory.'

'It seems you've thought of everything.'

'One does try. Now what say we move out to the garden for a spot of dinner? I've been to a lot of effort over that.'

'You carried a few things out to the garden and put them on the table,' said Lady Hardcastle.

'That's a lot of effort for a chap like me, Em. I even opened the wine.'

'Then let's go and eat.'

Chapter Sixteen

Wednesday dawned without any of us noticing, but we were soon all up and about. I managed to sleep through to a sensible hour while the usually late-sleeping Featherstonhaughs were up earlier than usual. This meant that we were all shambling blearily about the place at the same time, getting under each other's feet. I told Edna and Miss Jones that we would be out for lunch, and that I'd try to persuade the others it would be a great idea to have dinner out.

'We're going to be busy all day,' I said, 'so by all means leave as soon as you've got everything done.'

'I've got the downstairs to do today,' said Edna, 'but I wouldn't mind nippin' off a bit early. My Dan's come off his bike and hurt 'is arm so I'd like to get back to him, even if it's only to tell him what an idiot he is.'

'He keeps damaging himself,' I said, remembering how he broke his leg a couple of years earlier.

'Always been an active man, my Dan. Active and clumsy. Dangerous combination.'

'If there's no cookin' to be done,' said Miss Jones, 'I can do the books and the orders for next month. I was worryin' I'd not get time.'

'Then it's working out perfectly,' I said. 'Do you both have everything you need? Is there anything I can do?'

'No, miss, you go off and save the country,' said Edna with a wink.

'All in a day's work, Edna.'

'Breakfast will be ready in about a quarter of an hour,' said Miss Jones.

'Thank you,' I said. 'Oh, can you do a little extra just in case, please? We're expecting Inspector Sunderland and it would be nice to be able to offer him something.'

'I'll see to it,' said Miss Jones.

I went through to the morning room with a pot of coffee and found Lady Hardcastle and Harry already sitting at the table, deep in discussion.

'. . . do please try to find out why on earth he killed poor Dupree,' Lady Hardcastle was saying. 'It just doesn't make any sense. And poor Myrtle Matthews deserves an explanation.'

'We'll definitely be asking him. At the very least, we need to know whether it was his own idea or if it came from his masters in Berlin.'

I was about to sit down when the doorbell rang.

'That'll be Inspector Sunderland,' I said. 'I shan't be a moment.'

I let the inspector in and brought him back to the morning room.

'Ah, Inspector,' said Lady Hardcastle. 'How lovely to see you. We're about to have breakfast – would you care to join us?'

'That would be most agreeable, my lady,' said the inspector. 'Thank you. I barely had time to drink my cup of tea this morning, let alone eat anything.'

'Morning, Sunderland,' said Harry. 'What's the news on Milhouse?'

'The magistrates committed him for trial at the next assizes and he's out on bail.'

'Silly man,' said Lady Hardcastle.

'Will the company get its money back?' I asked.

'As a matter of fact,' said the inspector, 'that's the main reason he was granted bail. He'd been stashing the money away so he could make a run for it and start a new life with Mrs Sandling. Normally in cases like that they've spent it all on wine, women and song. He offered to pay back everything he still had – there had been some wine and women-related expenses, you understand – so the magistrates took it as a sign of remorse and sent him home to face his wife.'

'Him not having the oof to make a run for it would have helped them with their decision,' said Harry.

'Well, that was a consideration, of course.'

'Splendid, splendid,' said Harry. 'Well, that's one down, but not the one we really wanted. That's today's little jaunt. Thank you for coming out again – much appreciated.'

'My pleasure, sir,' said the inspector. 'I always enjoy a trip out to the countryside.'

'Good show. Your chaps haven't made a fuss about your being involved? Wouldn't want to make things awkward for you.'

'Of course they have. There was a good deal of huffing and puffing from the chief super and he was all set to give me what for, but then a call came in from a fellow in Whitehall and suddenly I was the hero of the hour and a shining credit to the Bristol force. Being involved with the Secret Service Bureau is quite a feather in his cap, even if it's not actually him who's doing the work.'

'Oh, that's splendid. It shouldn't be too much work today, though. Our man is more of a weaselly boy. He won't present any danger.'

'Don't get cocky, dear,' said Lady Hardcastle. 'Picking up Milhouse was going to be a stroll in the park and he ended up pointing a gun at us.'

'Ah, but this one doesn't have a secret safe with a pistol in it. It'll be fine.'

Breakfast arrived before she could say anything, but her scowl spoke volumes.

◆ ◆ ◆

'I shan't miss having to make this trip every day,' I said as I drove once more along the sun-baked Gloucester Road.

'I quite agree,' said Lady Hardcastle. 'I couldn't trudge into the same old place day after day, no matter how invigorating the job was.'

'Soon be over, though,' I said. 'We'll just lift Paul-Kurt-Curtis-Pohl and then the summer's our own once more.'

'And we still have the village show to look forward to.'

'I'm certainly looking forward to it now.' I gave my best crow impression. 'I think the good folk of Littleton Cotterell can live without hearing that and I can relax and enjoy myself.'

'You still have a spot in the programme if you change your mind. I stand ready to be a target for your knife-throwing.'

'You know the trick is to miss the assistant, don't you?' I said. 'You'd not be a target.'

'Anything for the show, dear. I don't mind a few cuts and scrapes if it gives the audience what they want.'

'We'll see. For the moment, though, definitely not.'

'As you wish. And after that . . . what?'

'We could go and see Harry and Lady Lavinia,' I suggested. 'It's been a few weeks.'

'Oh, that would be marvellous. We could take Addie to the zoo. You and Harry could go and see one of your silly shows while Lavinia and I do something worthwhile. Lunch at the Ritz. I do love London in the summertime. I shall make plans.'

'We need our minds on the job now, though,' I said. 'There's the hangars. It's almost showtime.'

We parked the Rolls, not in our usual spot, but next to Inspector Sunderland. He had set off after us but had arrived first, having overtaken us soon after we turned on to the main road. The police wagon and two constables were also there.

'You drive like my grandmother,' said Harry as we disembarked.

'So I've been told,' I said. 'Often. Shall we go in?'

With Lady Hardcastle and me leading the way, we marched up to the office doors.

Once again, Miss Matthews was surprised to see us. Her surprise turned to white-faced shock when she saw that we were accompanied by Harry, the inspector, and two uniformed constables.

'Lady Hardcastle,' she all but stammered. 'What . . . what's going on?'

'Nothing to worry about, dear,' said Lady Hardcastle. 'We just need a word with—'

'Mr Sandling isn't here,' said Miss Matthews. 'He sent word that he'd be late. He has . . . matters to attend to at home.'

'I'm sure he does. It must be dreadful for him.' Lady Hardcastle paused for a moment. 'You knew, didn't you?'

'About what?' She sounded defensive.

'About the affair. That's why you dislike him so much, isn't it?'

'Oh,' said Miss Matthews. 'I did. He made a pass at me, too. While he was having it away with Mrs Sandling. I've never felt so cheap. Dreadful man.'

'I'm so sorry. But we wish to speak to Paul Curtis. We shan't be a moment. This way, gentlemen.'

She turned to lead the men towards the drawing office, but Miss Matthews spoke up again. 'He's not there, my lady. He went out with some files about ten minutes ago.'

'Did he say where he was going?' asked Harry.

'Out to the hangars,' she said. She was regaining her composure. 'I'm sorry, sir. The other gentleman I know – he was here to arrest Mr Milhouse. But . . . ?'

'Featherstonhaugh,' said Harry. 'I'm with the ministry.'

'Which ministry?'

Harry said nothing.

'Back out the way we came,' said Lady Hardcastle. 'Follow me.'

She swished out through the main doors and led us off around the office block towards the hangars.

'My goodness,' said Inspector Sunderland as the gargantuan buildings hove into view. 'I've seen them from the road, of course, but I never quite realized how enormous they are. You must be able to fit—'

'Two,' I said.

'Two what?'

'Two football pitches.'

'How did you . . . ?'

'It's always football pitches,' I said. 'Apparently it's the new standard measure of area. They're twelve elephants high, in case you were wondering.'

'Are they? Are they, indeed? You never cease to amaze me, Miss Armstrong.'

I smiled.

'She's one of our best,' said Harry.

'Oi!' Lady Hardcastle was affronted.

'I did say, "One of our best", sis. You're one of our best, too.' He was a pace or two behind his sister. With a wink and a grin he shook his head and pointed at me. 'She's the best one,' he mouthed silently.

The inspector and I both laughed.

In the middle distance we could see two mechanics on the field, fussing over a Dunnock. They appeared to be readying it for flight. We were still some way from the hangar when a man in flight overalls came hurrying out through the main doors towards the aeroplane.

'I don't think our man Curtis is going anywhere,' said Harry. 'And he'd have to come back towards us if he did. Let's stop a while and watch this. I've been working on this aeroplane case for months now, and I've still not managed to see one of the blessed things in flight.'

'Flo?' said Lady Hardcastle. 'Heebert Fleebert doesn't have blond hair, does he?'

'No,' I said. 'Very dark.'

'Then I fear you might not get your chance to stand about and admire the majestic flight of the Dunnock, Harry dear. I rather think our man Curtis is doing a bunk.'

'Oh, for pity's sake. Sunderland, old chap, would you mind getting your chaps to sprint over there and collar that fair-haired fellow before he scarpers?'

'You heard him, lads,' said the inspector. 'Best foot forward.'

The two constables took off their helmets and headed towards the aeroplane at a gentle trot.

'Quicker than that,' called Sunderland.

They sped up, but only slightly. The day was already hot and they were in their heavy serge uniforms. I'd have been reluctant to sprint dressed like that.

The sound and sudden movement had caught Curtis's attention. He spoke animatedly to the two mechanics and struggled into the Dunnock's cockpit. He yelled something at them, apparently angered by their reluctance to share his sense of urgency.

The two policemen noticed the activity and increased their pace.

The Dunnock's engine spluttered to life and Curtis opened the throttle, forcing the man who had spun the propeller for him to leap clear as the aeroplane began to lumber forward.

The two policemen ran faster. The Dunnock wobbled alarmingly at first without anyone holding on to its wings, and then steadied itself as its speed increased.

The policemen were sprinting now, but the aeroplane was already moving faster than a man could run. They slowed to a halt as the Dunnock took to the air.

'Well, that's dashed inconvenient,' said Harry.

'All is not lost,' I said. 'I have an idea.'

'I do hope it's the same idea I just had,' said Lady Hardcastle with a grin.

'I suspect it is. You three get back to the inspector's motor car and try to follow him as best you can from the ground. I'm going to the hangar.'

'Right you are, dear,' she said. 'Come on, chaps, follow me.'

Inspector Sunderland instructed the two constables to wait at the factory and we all went our separate ways.

◆ ◆ ◆

I ran towards Hangar A. It wasn't my best thought-through plan, but if it worked it was going to be one for the annals. I sprinted in through the main doors and blinked for a few seconds in the sudden gloom.

The plan was beginning to come together. A few yards inside the hangar stood a second Dunnock, surrounded by mechanics and engineers. To my untutored eye it looked ready to fly.

I approached quickly.

'Good morning, gentlemen,' I said. 'Is Mr Herbert about?'

'Rupert?' said one of the men. 'No, but he should be. 'E's late.' He chuckled. 'What's 'e been up to now?'

I ignored the question. 'Is this Dunnock flyable?' I said instead.

'It is,' said the man. 'That's what we needs Rupert for. Test flight booked for this mornin'.'

I cursed.

The men looked scandalized.

Suddenly I saw my potential saviour.

'Mr Whitman!' I called. There was no reaction. 'Adam!' I called, slightly more loudly.

He looked up at the sound of his name. He seemed baffled for a moment, but then he saw me and waved.

I motioned him to come over.

He sauntered towards me with an infuriating lack of haste, so I trotted over to meet him halfway.

'What ho, Florence,' he said. 'Fancy seeing you here. I heard about your exploits the other day – I thought you were done here now.'

'Not quite,' I said. 'Just tying up a few loose ends. You said you've flown one of those.' I indicated the shiny new Dunnock, and turned back the way I had come, forcing him to quicken his pace to keep up with me.

'I have,' he said. 'Quite a nice little aeroplane, actually. Not a patch on the latest from Vannier, of course. Do you know—'

'Splendid,' I said. 'Can you persuade that lot to let you take this one out?'

'Well, I—'

'Right now, Adam. Right now. Without delay.'

'Oh,' he said. 'So this is to do with your . . . you know . . .'

'It is, yes. And I really am in the most tearing hurry.'

'Right you are,' he said with a grin. 'How exciting.'

He hurried off towards the waiting aeroplane and the mechanics.

Within only a minute or so, we were aboard a Bristol Aviation Dunnock with Adam at the controls and me sitting in the rear seat as observer. We trundled across the grass and then with a delightful stomach-turning lurch we were in the air.

I had told Adam that Curtis had taken off towards the city, and we banked gracefully round to follow him. We were able to talk using the 'blower' – the speaking tube connecting the two compartments.

'I'm going to try to get some height,' shouted Adam. 'We should be able to get a better view from up there. He's got a few minutes' start on us, but on a day like today we'll be able to see for miles if we can get high enough.'

'Righto,' I yelled.

To be honest, at this point only part of my attention was on the chase. For the moment, I was completely enraptured by the flight. It was like looking down on a living map. Roads and settlements I knew well stretched out below me in a familiar – yet still oddly unfamiliar – tableau. It was cold without a decent coat on, but I was so excited I didn't really mind.

I spotted Inspector Sunderland's motor car some way ahead of us on the main road, so I knew we must be heading in the right direction. That or we were all wrong in exactly the same way.

We had been climbing for an age, but eventually we levelled off. Flying level I had a much better view. I could see city landmarks in the distance. There was the Clifton Suspension Bridge. So that must be the cathedral. And that must be . . . That must be Curtis.

'Over there!' I yelled. I pointed.

'Over where?' he said.

I was sitting behind him and he couldn't see where I was pointing.

'Ahead and to the left a bit,' I said. 'Quite a way ahead, and a few hundred feet below us.'

'I have him,' he said.

We turned slightly leftwards and began to descend.

'This one has the new engine,' called Adam. 'It's a few knots faster. Actually, did you know—'

'Will we catch him?' I interrupted.

'What? Oh, yes. With the quicker engine and the extra speed we'll get from this dive we should be on him in a few minutes.'

I relaxed and enjoyed the ride.

We overtook the police car and I saw Lady Hardcastle leaning out of the window, clutching her hat and waving like a maniac. I couldn't see it from that distance, but I could imagine the grin on her face. I waved back, but I didn't imagine I'd be visible. We pressed on.

A while later, Adam levelled off again. We were still above Curtis and he was just a few hundred yards ahead of us now. We cleared the southern suburbs of the city and were out above Somerset farmland.

Suddenly, there was a colossal bang from ahead, and I was afraid for a moment that the idiot lad was shooting at us. The plume of black smoke from the engine of the other Dunnock told another story. His engine had blown.

He wobbled slightly and began to lose height. As everyone at the factory had assured us, he was able to glide quite smoothly, but his descent was a good deal more rapid than would have been comfortable if you were already panicking about the loss of power and the black smoke coming from the engine.

He had slowed considerably and we soon overtook him.

Adam banked our Dunnock and circled back in time to see him coming to a bumpy, wing-shattering halt in a field of cows. Of course it was cows. Stupid man. The aeroplane was upside down in a tangled mass of broken spars and ripped canvas.

Adam circled again and came to a much more elegant stop in the next field.

We disembarked as swiftly as we were able and I sprinted towards the downed Dunnock.

I vaulted over the sturdy wooden gate that separated the two fields to be greeted by a most disturbing sight. Cows, it seems, are curious creatures. I had expected them to be terrified by the clattering, banging, snapping, ripping mess of the crash, and perhaps they were. But by the time I arrived they were plodding slowly towards it, their evil Cow Empress leading the way, intent on finding out more.

There was a groan from the still-ticking wreckage and a hand emerged, holding a German automatic pistol. I was getting really fed up of frightened men with guns.

The rest of the frightened man began to wriggle free, but I was upon him before he could do anything with the broom-handled Mauser. I was getting really fed up of those, too. For some reason they were extremely popular with the wrong 'uns in our lives.

I stood on his wrist and bent to pry the pistol loose from his grip.

He snarled something terribly uncomplimentary in German and I replied in the same language, telling him to mind his manners.

I hauled the rest of him free of the mangled aeroplane. I tried to check him for injuries but he snarled again, so I left him to recover his wits.

Adam joined me.

'Paul Curtis?' he said in astonishment. 'He stole an aeroplane?'

'An aeroplane, a load of secret files – you name it,' I said. 'He's quite the lad, old Curtis. Or Kurt Pohl as they call him at home. He even killed Dickie Dupree.'

This made Curtis stop glowering. He looked genuinely offended.

'I didn't kill him,' he said. 'No, no, not that. I only ever . . . I never would have . . . I couldn't . . .'

'You pointed a gun at me,' I said.

'It's not loaded,' he said. 'I was just trying to frighten you.'

I checked the pistol. He wasn't lying.

'I say,' said Adam. 'How do you know how to do that?'

'It's just one of those things one picks up,' I said.

'Not in my line of work.'

'Lady Hardcastle's the one to talk to if you really want to know about guns,' I said. 'I'm more of a smack-in-the-chops sort of girl.'

Curtis's mind was still on the recent accusation of murder.

'You see?' he said, plaintively. 'I'm not a killer. I'm a patriot, not a murderer.' He seemed to be over the shock of the crash and, with a struggle, was able to stand.

'But now I find that I am being held prisoner by a tiny woman and a timid engineer,' he said, 'I am not so sure I need a gun.'

He took a swing at me. To give him his due, there was a lot of youthful force behind it and it might have worked if he'd chosen to hit Adam rather than me, but I'm afraid I saw it coming. I blocked the punch, stepped inside his reach and delivered a couple of tidy little blows of my own, the result of which was Curtis lying winded on the grass.

The cows were inquisitively licking the aeroplane.

'Don't do that again, Herr Pohl,' I said in German. 'It's really not polite and you'll only get yourself hurt.'

There was more German swearing, but he made no further effort to get up.

'I say,' said Adam again. 'You weren't kidding, were you? I had no idea you were so terrifying.'

'It's not the sort of thing you mention over afternoon tea,' I said.

'No. No, I suppose it isn't.'

Curtis snarled some more unpleasantness and made to get up again.

'I'd stay there if I were you,' I said. 'You're an intelligent chap. You've seen what I can do and I'm sure you can imagine how badly I could hurt you if I put my mind to it. I don't really want to because underneath this sweet and adorable exterior I really am sweet and adorable. But that doesn't mean I won't leave you crying for your *Mutti* if I have to. So lie back and relax. You've had an exciting morning and you could do with a rest before the real trouble begins.'

He glared but said nothing more. Instead he sullenly put his hands behind his head and crossed his ankles as though settling for a snooze in the sun.

'Thank you,' I said. 'Adam? Can you remember the way back to the road?'

'It's just over there,' he said, pointing. 'Couple of hundred yards at the most.'

'Excellent. Go and look out for the inspector's motor car. They weren't too far behind and they'll have seen what happened. They'll work out where we are eventually.'

'Right you are,' he said. 'You're sure you'll be all right with chummy there? Of course you will. Stupid question. On my way.'

It took them two hours to find us. By the time they arrived, Curtis was fast asleep and the cows had been retrieved by the angry farmer. He was a portly man with a ruddy face and a belligerent attitude, and had complained most bitterly about having 'one o' they flyin' machines' in his best pasture. He hadn't been impressed by my reassurances that everything would be properly cleared away, but when I hinted that there might be some financial recompense for his trouble, he calmed down a little.

'Sorry it took us so long, dear,' said Lady Hardcastle as we accompanied them back to the motor car. Harry and the inspector were leading the sleepy Curtis between them while she, Adam and I walked along behind.

'We got across the suspension bridge all right, but then we lost sight of you,' she said. 'We ended up stopping everyone we passed to ask them if they'd seen two aeroplanes landing nearby. All of them had, of course, but no one was able to pinpoint exactly where. Eventually we saw young Adam sitting on a gate, and here we are.'

Harry turned his head. 'You should have popped back up in the Dunnock and shown us the way, old boy,' he said.

'It did occur to me,' said Adam, 'but we'd have had fresh problems then. I've got just about enough fuel to get us back to Bristol Aviation. If I'd buzzed about looking for you we'd have had to leave it here while we went in search of more fuel.'

'Ah,' said Harry. 'Good point. All's well that ends well, though, eh? We've got our leaker and our murderer and we can all be home in time for tea and medals.'

'I'd not be so sure about that if I were you,' I said. 'He denies killing Dupree and I'm rather inclined to believe him. He's an absolute idiot, but he's not a killer.'

'Then who . . . ?'

'I have a good idea who,' said Lady Hardcastle. 'I take it you two are flying back to the aerodrome?'

'I only borrowed the aeroplane,' said Adam. 'I ought to get it back to them.'

'We'll meet you there, then,' she said. 'Fly safely.'

Chapter Seventeen

Freed from the need to keep an eye out for fleeing leakers, the journey home was a much more relaxed affair. At my insistence, Adam had flown under the suspension bridge (if Lady Hardcastle could do it, so could I) and then, as we neared Bristol Aviation, his voice came from the blower.

'Fancy taking the controls?' he said.

'Really?' I said.

'I trust you.'

With surprising succinctness he explained the controls and what they did, and then suddenly I was in charge of an actual flying machine. I took us up, I took us down, I took us on a long, slow loop around the landing field. I was about to go round again but his voice came out of the tube again.

'I'll take it from here,' he said. 'We need to get this old girl on the ground before the fuel runs out completely. I have the controls.'

We landed smoothly and rumbled across the grass to the hangars. Stern-faced men were waiting for us as we drew to a stop and jumped out.

I fended off their angry questions as well as I could, but in the end I had to resort to telling them that it was official government business and that we'd explain it to Mr Sandling in due course. They grudgingly accepted this, though I sensed they were still dubious.

I'm not proud of it, but I'm afraid I abandoned Adam to explain the fate of the other Dunnock while I went to wait in the Rolls for the others to arrive.

This time I didn't have long to wait. This time they knew where they were going.

The inspector's car rolled to a stop and Lady Hardcastle jumped out of the passenger door. She bustled over to the Rolls and climbed in beside me.

'Are you well, dear?' she said. 'No ill effects from the shenanigans?'

'None whatsoever,' I said. 'It's a bit chilly up there, but I've warmed up now. Our flight was a great deal smoother than Curtis's, too. No crashing in a field for us. Oh, and I took the controls on the way home.'

'How utterly splendid. Was it everything you hoped for?'

'And more. Are we buying one?'

'Perhaps,' she said. 'But not until they've sorted that engine out. "We've checked them all and everything is in tip-top order" my eye.'

'They were right about it being able to glide safely to the ground, though,' I said.

'Up to a point. "Upside down and mangled" is a rather loose interpretation of "safely on the ground".'

While we were talking, Harry and the inspector were handing Curtis over to the two waiting constables. Once everything was arranged and the young leaker was on his way to the local police station, Harry and Inspector Sunderland joined us at the Rolls.

'You were saying you know who the killer is, sis?' said Harry. 'Is he here?'

'I know who damaged the parachute, yes,' said Lady Hardcastle. 'As for whether that person is a "killer" . . . Well, we shall have to let the courts decide.'

We both climbed out of the motor car and led the way back towards the office.

'The only thing I ask,' she said, 'is that you both remain calm. And quiet as well, please. It would be most helpful if you didn't interrupt.'

The two men exchanged puzzled glances, but didn't demur.

Miss Matthews was hard at work behind her reception desk. She looked up when she heard us come in.

'Oh, thank goodness you're all right,' she said. 'With all the comings and goings and Paul stealing the Dunnock I didn't know what to think.'

'We're all quite well, thank you, dear,' said Lady Hardcastle. 'Mr Curtis is unharmed, too, but in custody.'

'Unharmed? Arrested?'

We briefly outlined the events of the day, including an incomplete account of Paul Curtis's misdeeds. We said only that he had been selling commercial secrets, not that he was an agent of a foreign power.

'And did he damage the parachute?' said Miss Matthews. 'Is he the one responsible for Dickie's death?'

Lady Hardcastle looked at her kindly. 'No, dear,' she said. 'But you know that, don't you?'

Miss Matthews began to cry.

'Good Lord,' said Harry. 'Do you mean—'

Lady Hardcastle held up her hand to silence him and gave him an angry scowl.

'Sorry,' he said. 'Carry on.'

'I know you didn't mean to harm your fiancé,' said Lady Hardcastle. 'I know you were trying to protect him.'

Miss Matthews wiped her eyes on her handkerchief. 'I didn't do it.'

Lady Hardcastle held up her hand again. 'You did, dear. Dickie had told you about the tests, hadn't he? You might even have seen them out on the field with the balloon. They were going well. So well that they were almost ready to proceed to testing with a human volunteer. He told you he wanted to try it. You begged him not to, but he was adamant. It was safe, he told you. They'd dropped dozens of dummies. They were ready for a live test. They just needed one more dummy drop to double-check a few things, then it would be his turn.'

Miss Matthews blinked away some tears, then blew her nose noisily on the handkerchief. I noticed the EH monogram and remembered that Lady Hardcastle had given it to her when we had chatted over coffee in the almost-comfortable chairs in reception.

'He wouldn't listen to you. He thought your fears were unfounded. Silly, even. So you decided to make sure the next dummy test failed. You make your own clothes – you told us about that beautiful blouse you were wearing – so you know your way round a . . .'

'Top-stitched felled seam,' I said.

'Thank you. You knew you could weaken the seam in a way that no one would notice but that would cause the parachute to fail. Once the dummy had crashed shockingly to earth, the live test would be postponed until they could fix the problem, giving you more time to persuade Dickie that the whole thing was far too dangerous.'

Miss Matthews said nothing. She looked shocked, but oddly relieved that the truth was finally being told.

'What you didn't know – what nobody but Mr Sandling and Milhouse knew – was that the company's finances were in the direst straits. Milhouse had been stealing money left and right and the coffers were all but empty. If they didn't secure a large government order for the parachutes as quickly as possible, the whole enterprise might go under. And so they brought the live test forward. Why wouldn't they? With dozens of near-perfect dummy drops under their belts, all they needed was one live drop to prove their product worked, and all their problems would be over.'

'I didn't know,' said Miss Matthews. 'I had no idea what they were going to do.'

'Of course not. You'd have stopped them. But the first you knew about it was when the news of his death reached you.'

'I just wanted them to stop the live test,' she said. 'I just wanted Dickie not to jump.' Miss Matthews began sobbing again.

Inspector Sunderland stepped forward and put a kindly hand on her shoulder.

'I'm sorry, miss,' he said, 'but I'm going to have to take you in and take a formal statement. It'll be up to the magistrates to decide what happens next.'

'I'll speak up for her if it comes to it,' said Lady Hardcastle. 'We can make a good case for involuntary manslaughter, I think. And we can almost certainly lay some of the blame at Milhouse's door. Do you have a solicitor, dear?'

'My father has one,' sniffed Miss Matthews.

'Then contact him as soon as Inspector Sunderland allows.'

'I'll make sure of it,' said the inspector. 'Come along, miss.'

They left together.

'We'd better go and tell Sandling the news,' said Harry. 'Do you know the way?'

◆ ◆ ◆

Mr Sandling was in his office, staring forlornly at an accounting ledger. He looked up as we knocked on the doorframe.

'Ah,' he said. 'Lady Hardcastle. And Miss Armstrong. Hello. And . . . ?'

'Featherstonhaugh,' said Harry. 'Foreign Office.'

'The Foreign Office? Good Lord. What now?'

'May we come in?' said Lady Hardcastle.

'Of course, of course. Make yourselves comfortable. Shall I get Miss Matthews to bring us some coffee?'

'I'm afraid that won't be possible,' said Lady Hardcastle. 'Miss Matthews has had to go to the police station.'

'About the Milhouse business? She had nothing to do with it, I'm sure.'

'No, I'm afraid it wasn't that.'

She went on to explain what had happened.

'Good heavens,' he said. 'That poor girl. I mean, poor Dickie, too, but . . . well . . . she was acting out of love, wasn't she? Will she need a character witness?'

'I'm sure she'll be grateful for all the support and help she can get.'

'I gather you were involved in this morning's spot of bother with Paul Curtis and the Dunnock. Stupid boy. If he'd asked we would have arranged for him to take a flight. We can ill afford a loss like that, but thank you for trying.'

'Actually,' she said, 'there was a little more to it than just a silly boy taking an aeroplane for a spin. I'll let my brother explain.'

'Your brother? Oh, I see the family resemblance now. Good heavens. A brother in the Foreign Office, eh? You're a good deal better connected than we imagined.'

'You're aware of your existing obligations to keep things under your hat?' began Harry.

'Official Secrets and all that?' said Mr Sandling. 'Yes, I had the lecture when we began doing bits of work for the War Office.'

'Good. Consider everything I'm about to tell you to be covered by the same lecture.'

Now it was Harry's turn to recount the extraordinary circumstances of Kurt Pohl's infiltration of the company as Paul Curtis. I filled in the missing details at the end, explaining the crash and Curtis's detention.

'He handed over our files to a foreign power?' said Sandling when we had finished.

'He certainly tried to,' said Harry. 'We intercepted one batch, but we've no guarantee until we've questioned him that he didn't hand over more before we were on to him. He had files in his possession today, but we retrieved those, too. I'll let you have them back as soon as I can.'

'Where does this leave my company? How do we stand with the War Office?'

'I can't say for certain. I shouldn't imagine they'll be terribly impressed by your crooked accountant, your love-struck secretary and her misfiring attempt to save her fiancé, and your junior engineer feeding secrets to our potential enemies . . .'

Mr Sandling looked crestfallen at having his recent troubles spelled out so bluntly.

'. . . but you have a good deal going for you. You have an excellent aeroplane – exploding engines notwithstanding – and your parachute design is the best anyone has seen. You might have to put up with some increased scrutiny, and I shouldn't be surprised if they put one of their own men in the company to oversee things, but they'd be cutting off their noses to spite their faces if they turned their backs on you now.'

'I do hope you're right,' said Mr Sandling forlornly. 'Oh. If Mr Featherstonhaugh is your brother, Lady Hardcastle, I suppose you're not really a potential client, after all. I confess I was still rather hoping you might buy one of our Dunnocks.'

'I actually was a potential client,' she said. 'That's why it was so easy to persuade me to come down here to see what was going on.'

'But?' he said. 'It sounds as though there's a "but" coming.'

'But you have a bad case of exploding engine syndrome. The one Miss Armstrong flew this afternoon with Adam Whitman seemed more reliable—'

'It's a new design,' he interrupted. 'More powerful, too.'

'Quite. Well, if it survives a few more hours in the air without its pilot ending up having to crawl out of the wreckage in a field of dairy cows, I might think about it.'

'For now, though,' said Harry, 'we ought to leave you to your work. You have a lot of things to straighten out before someone from the War Office gets here.'

'I need to arrange for the retrieval of the wrecked Dunnock first. I don't suppose you remember where it crashed?'

Lady Hardcastle showed him the field on a map and we said our goodbyes. I lingered until the other two were out of earshot, then had a quiet word with Mr Sandling on my own. There were one or two things I wanted to say.

Just outside the main doors, Harry stopped dead.

'How am I going to get back to your place?' he said. 'My lift has gone off to a police station somewhere.'

'I've thought of that,' said Lady Hardcastle. 'You see, the other day, Flo and I were musing upon the notion of getting a dog. We wondered if it might be possible to fashion some sort of platform on the back of the Rolls where it could sit, but we had no idea if it would be safe to have anything riding back there. You can test it out for us.'

'Because live testing with human subjects has such a terrific record round these parts.'

'Oh, don't be such a baby. You'll love it.'

By the time we arrived at the house, Harry was alive and well but looking more than a little bedraggled. We stopped in the lane and I helped him down from the back of the motor car so that Lady Hardcastle could put it in the garage without us getting in her way.

'Thank you, Strongarm,' he said. 'That was . . . bracing.'

'You might have been a bit more comfortable had I been driving,' I said, 'but only a bit.'

'I'll bear that in mind for next time.'

Lady Hardcastle had joined us.

'I think you might have a slight problem with your motor car, old girl.'

'Oh?' she said. 'Really?'

'Seems like a suspension issue to me,' he said. 'I'm sure it's not supposed to go round corners on two wheels like that.'

'You see?' she said triumphantly. 'I told you there was something wrong with it.'

I said nothing.

Back inside the house we left Harry to tidy himself up while I checked that there had been no issues during our absence. All was well, and Miss Jones had left a note saying that everything was in hand and that she'd see us in the morning.

'Do we have any plans for dinner?' asked Lady Hardcastle.

'I have a plan,' I said. 'I rather thought we could stroll into the village and see if we can get anyone to take us into Chipping for dinner at the Grey Goose. There's bound to be someone with a dog cart loafing about, hoping for business. We can have a slap-up feed, a couple of bottles of the landlord's finest wine, and then come home safe in the knowledge that we're not driving the Rolls while tipsy and that Harry won't fall off the back.'

'Fall off the back of what?' said Harry. He had returned, looking as dapper as ever.

'Not to worry, dear,' said Lady Hardcastle. 'We're planning a trip to Chipping Bevington for supper. But come to think of it, you might need to get home.'

'No, I need to be here for a few more days to tie up all the loose ends,' he said.

'What about Lavinia and Addie?'

'Ah . . . well . . . now . . . you see . . . the thing is . . . how would you like to have a couple more houseguests? Nanny needs to get away for a few days to visit her ailing father, I've got to stay here . . . so I was wondering if it might be a good idea for them to come down here together and get some country air.'

'Oh, how wonderful,' said Lady Hardcastle. 'By all means, yes. Invite them at once.'

'I'm so glad you feel that way,' he said. 'They'll be here tomorrow lunchtime.'

Harry's regular man had been supping at the Dog and Duck and we were able to persuade him to undertake the round trip for us, suggesting that the Hayrick in Chipping was as good a place as any for him to spend the evening. He agreed – the Hayrick was his local anyway.

The staff at the Grey Goose recognized us and welcomed us warmly.

'We have your usual table if you'd like it, my lady,' said the head waiter.

'That would be lovely,' she said. 'Thank you.'

We ate, we drank, we yarned. We managed to avoid most of the evening's forbidden topics: aeroplanes, parachutes, and the worsening political situation on the Continent.

One forbidden topic could not be avoided.

'Would you and Lavinia like to come to the village show on Saturday evening?' said Lady Hardcastle.

'I thought we weren't talking about the blessed show,' I said.

'Oh, this is just a little domestic housekeeping,' she said. 'We're not talking about the show, just making sure our guests know they're welcome to come along if they want to.'

'I'm sure we'd love to,' said Harry. 'We might have to bring Addie. No nanny, you see.'

'The hall will be thronged with infants of all ages,' said Lady Hardcastle. 'Village events are like that. No one out here has nannies.'

'Then I look forward to it. Are you two performing?'

'That's something of a sore point,' she said. 'I still intend to give my rendition of a few ragtime favourites on the old joanna, but I've yet to hear if young Flo here has found alternative employment since she was so cruelly sacked from her comedy act by her pal Daisy.'

'I wasn't cruelly sacked—' I began.

'Cruelly. Sacked,' said Lady Hardcastle. 'Abandoned by her dear friend when a better offer came along. She's bereft, the poor thing. You can tell.'

I made a face and took a bite of my dinner.

'You can sit with us, old girl,' said Harry. 'We'll look after you.'

'You're too kind,' I said.

'Well, now that we've broken one of our self-imposed taboos,' said Lady Hardcastle, 'I'd like to break another one.'

'In for a penny,' said Harry.

'Will you be requiring our services over the next few months?'

'We've nothing in the works,' he said. 'We've seen an increase in activity among our friends and foes, both at home and abroad, but we're just keeping an eye on things for the time being. Why? Do you have plans?'

'No, not really. I just wanted to know. I've rather enjoyed this little caper.'

'We did have plans,' I said. 'We were going to visit you.'

'Then you invited your whole family down here,' she said, 'so there's no need for that. But we're available for work, should anything turn up.'

'I'll keep you in mind,' he said.

The second bottle of wine was followed by a dessert wine with the hotel's sickly-sweet and thoroughly delicious Chocolate Something-Or-Other – the pudding's actual name. There was port with the cheese and brandy to follow.

By the time we were done we were all pleased none of us had to drive home or balance on the back of the Rolls. Our charioteer was slightly reluctant to be dragged away from his game of skittles with his pals, but the offer of hard cash soon brought him round.

Safely home, we all retired immediately, promising that there was no need to get up in a hurry in the morning.

Chapter Eighteen

Despite still feeling slightly groggy after our overindulgence of the night before, I had errands to run on Thursday morning and even had to go out on my own in the Rolls for one or two things, but I was back at home by the time Lady Lavinia and Addie arrived just after lunch. We spent the afternoon in the garden and the evening in the drawing room, where the ladies played piano duets while I thrashed Harry at carpet croquet. Some people never learn.

Jed arrived on Friday morning with a wheelbarrowful of horticultural mysteries and two bird boxes he had fashioned from the remnants of our old garden furniture. He busied himself with whatever it is gardeners do while we tried our best to keep out of his way.

By eleven, though, Lady Hardcastle thought it was time for tea and scones in the garden and we all trooped out to interrupt him. He tried to leave.

'No, Jed, dear,' said Lady Hardcastle. 'Do please stay. Join us, won't you?'

'No, tha's all right, my lady,' he said. 'I'll leave you and your friends to it.'

'Nonsense,' she said. 'This is my brother, Harry, and his wife Lavinia. Oh, and the little moppet in the blue frock is Addie. You've done such a wonderful job out here, it would be lovely to be able to share it with you. Tea and scones are on the way.'

'Miss Jones's scones?' he said. 'Well, that does make a difference. If you're sure you don't mind.'

'Not at all, old chap,' said Harry. 'The more the merrier.'

We sat on the new furniture and enjoyed another excellent batch of scones as we talked about the garden. Addie was utterly fascinated by Jed and he patiently indulged her urgent wriggling entreaties to sit on his lap. In a soft voice he sang her an old Yorkshire folk song and she was completely entranced.

'You should join in with the village show,' said Lady Hardcastle. 'You'd be so very welcome.'

'And so very popular,' said Lady Lavinia. 'Look at the effect you've had on little Addie.'

Jed chuckled. 'I don't think so,' he said. 'It's one thing singin' to a bairn in the garden, but I can't think of nothin' more terrifyin' than singin' to a crowd of full-grown folk in a village hall.'

'Do at least say you'll come along, though, won't you?' said Lady Hardcastle.

'Saturday night?'

'Yes. It would be lovely to see you. Everyone will be there.'

'I'll see,' he said with a smile, and returned to allowing himself to be minutely examined by his new friend.

Jed returned to his work once the teapot was empty, and we left him in peace. Addie was none too pleased at being dragged away from the fascinating leathery man, but he promised to see her later and that seemed to satisfy her.

◆ ◆ ◆

The afternoon was devoted to enjoying the sunshine. A walk into the village turned into a walk in the woods. With its enormous wheels and massive suspension springs, Addie's pram proved remarkably capable on rough ground and we were able to explore more of our surroundings than I would have thought possible with an ankle-biter in tow.

We returned via the village to find the place in uproar. A chain of villagers had formed on the green, passing buckets from the pub to the village hall, which, to our collective horror, was on fire.

'Great Scott!' said Harry. 'Look at the damage.'

'Oh, my word,' said Lady Lavinia. 'I do hope no one was hurt.'

'I see no obvious signs of casualties,' said Lady Hardcastle.

'I feel terrible now,' I said. 'I joked about burning the place down last weekend.'

Harry chuckled. 'To get out of doing the show?'

'Exactly,' I said. 'There's no need now I've been sacked, but I still feel like I've jinxed it. We'd better go and see if we can help.'

'We better had,' said Lady Hardcastle. 'Do you want to take Addie back to the house, Lavinia? She doesn't want to be here with all this smoke.'

'I feel I should,' said Lady Lavinia. 'But I'd also like to help, if I can.'

'Nonsense, dear. They also serve who only stand and look after the little ones and all that. We might not be any help here ourselves, after all, then you'll be the only useful one among us.'

Having ordered Harry to take the utmost care of himself, Lady Lavinia reluctantly pushed the pram back across the green and up the lane, while the three of us set off towards the fire.

Lady Farley-Stroud was directing the relief effort.

'Hello, Gertie,' said Lady Hardcastle as we approached. 'Is there anything we can do?'

'Afternoon, m'dear,' said Lady Farley-Stroud, sadly. 'Thank you, but not for the moment. We have things more or less under control now, as you can see, and no one has been hurt, thank goodness. Dashed bad luck the day before the big show, though.'

'What happened?'

'The stupidest thing. A couple of gels were stung by wasps yesterday while they were up in the attic looking for decorations. Found an enormous wasps' nest. Screamed the place down. Everyone had their own idea of how to get rid of the wasps but then one of the lads from the pub said, "Smoke 'em out. That's the way." Everyone muttered about having heard that somewhere and off they went to fetch wet wood to make a smoky fire. You can guess the rest.'

'Oh dear,' said Lady Hardcastle. 'And is there much damage?'

'Half the roof's gone, as you can see. We'll know more about the structure once we've had a surveyor in, but the show's off, obviously.'

'Not necessarily,' I said, remembering Lady Hardcastle's dispiriting prediction of the weekend before. 'You . . . we could hold the show on the green. I'd bet the lads could knock up a stage' – I looked around – 'over there by the cricket pavilion. Put up some screens to create a backstage area and we could use the pavilion itself as the dressing rooms. How are the sets? Did the piano survive?'

Lady Farley-Stroud frowned thoughtfully. 'Some of the stage caught, some has been damaged by all the water,' she said. 'But some survived. We could make something of what we have left, I think. The piano, though, is beyond repair – smashed by a falling roof beam. There's one in the Dog and Duck, but . . .'

'Good Lord,' said Lady Hardcastle. 'Don't even think of using that dreadful thing. No offence to Old Joe, but the pub piano is an abomination. If you can find a few big strong boys and a suitable trolley, we can get our piano up here in a twinkling.'

Lady Farley-Stroud looked hopeful for the first time. 'D'you really think we could?' she said.

'Of course,' I said. 'Look at the way the whole village has come together to help put out the fire. You'll have a job to stop them pitching in. It was a long time ago, but I still remember a thing or two about putting on a show out of doors. We had a tent, of course, but the principles are the same. It might be difficult to hear some of the acts in the open air, but we can work round that.'

'Then you're in charge, m'dear,' she said. 'Tell me who and what you need and I'll make sure you get 'em.'

And so it came to pass that I made the next step of my journey from reluctant performer to relieved audience member to outdoor theatre manager.

◆ ◆ ◆

Friday evening was spent outside the Dog and Duck in conference with Lady Farley-Stroud and several members of the village show committee, discussing what could, and could not, be done in the time available. We tracked down the village carpenter and I explained what I had in mind. We made some rough sketches and he assured me that he and his lad would be able to build what we needed in a few hours if he had some help from a few of the farmhands.

Lady Lavinia had returned with a wide-awake Addie and they were sitting at another table with Lady Hardcastle and Harry. I joined them for a few minutes and supped at the pint of cider they had bought for me while I made a list of everything that needed to be done. I added estimates of the time each job might take. Some of the tasks could be undertaken simultaneously, of course, and I soon arrived at the conclusion that, yes, it was more than possible to complete them all in time for the show the next evening.

'The only problem,' I said, 'is going to be lighting. We were fine when we were indoors, but look – it's dark already and it's only just gone eight. We'll never light an outdoor stage with lanterns, no matter how many we get.'

'And you might burn the stage down,' said Harry.

'Well, there's that, too,' I said.

'Are you sure we can't get enough light on the stage?' said Lady Hardcastle. 'It's a village show, not a West End production.'

'Perhaps,' I said, 'but I have a better idea. Will you come with me while I put it to the committee? Lady Farley-Stroud is inclined to take me seriously, but I'm not sure about the others. If you're there they'll at least be afraid of mocking me.'

'I'm afraid of mocking you whether Emily's there or not,' said Harry. 'More so when she's not, actually – I like to imagine she might protect me.'

'That's because you've an idea of how many different ways I could kill you,' I said. 'Although you're underestimating wildly. But they have no idea what fate might befall them should they cross me.'

'And I'd not protect you, dear,' said Lady Hardcastle. 'If you'd upset her enough that she felt a need to kill you I'd be holding her coat and cheering her on.'

'I'll bear it in mind,' he said.

Lady Lavinia laughed and we left them to fuss over Addie as we returned to the show committee.

'Well, m'dear?' said Lady Farley-Stroud. 'Can it be done?'

'It can,' I said. 'With time to spare. But I have an idea that might make it even easier. What would you say to postponing the show until Sunday afternoon? We'd have the light, and we could turn it into more of a social event. We could encourage picnicking. The children could come. Perhaps they might watch the show, perhaps they might play on the green.'

'Nonsense,' said a florid-faced farmer I'd never met before. 'It's an evenin' show. It was always intended to be an evenin' show. Afternoon on the green, indeed. With children. I've never heard so much—'

Lady Farley-Stroud held up a hand to silence him. 'No, Mr Higgins, I think she's on to something,' she said. 'It wouldn't be at all what we'd planned, but with the hall out of commission it could never be what we'd planned. If we try to replicate the hall show on the green it will always feel like second best. Let's embrace the new situation. If we have to be outdoors, why not be outdoors on a beautiful late summer's afternoon?'

'And it'll give us Sunday morning to add the finishing touches,' said Miss Grove, the vicar's housekeeper. 'As long as we're done before evensong, mind.'

'I envisaged starting at about two o'clock,' I said. 'Three at the latest. The Sunday evening service is at half past six, isn't it?'

Miss Grove nodded. 'That's right,' she said. 'In that case, I think it's a splendid idea.'

'I'll take that as seconding the motion,' said Lady Farley-Stroud. 'All in favour of moving the show to Sunday afternoon, say, "Aye."'

'We're not quorate,' said the ruddy-faced farmer.

'Very well,' she said. 'All in favour of reducing the quorum under these exceptional circumstances, and sacking Mr Higgins from the committee, say, "Aye."'

There was a chorus of 'Aye's and one, 'Well, of all the—'

'Motion carried. Thank you for your service, Mr Higgins. Now . . . moving the show?'

Another chorus of 'Aye's and one, 'To the devil with the lot of you.'

The motion was carried and Mr Higgins stalked off.

'Well done, Florence,' said Lady Farley-Stroud. 'You've saved the show.'

'Oh, one more thing,' I said. 'I know you'd intended to include a competition element – a prize for the best performance, I think?'

'That's right, m'dear.'

'I wonder if it might be a good idea to quietly forget about that. What with one thing and another, it would probably fit the mood better if it were just a village celebration.'

'Another splendid point,' she said. 'You really ought to be on the committee, you know. A seat has recently become vacant.' She grinned.

'I'll think about it,' I said. 'Let's get this one done for now.'

'Right you are, m'dear, but the offer will remain open.'

Lady Hardcastle and I returned to our table.

◆ ◆ ◆

I rose early on Saturday and made sure my lists were up to date. I knew people would be keen to work and that motivating them would present no problems, but I also knew that without proper direction they'd go at it like a bull at a gate and the whole project would descend into chaos. Someone had to know exactly what was going on, and that someone was going to have to be me.

I had jobs for everyone in the household, including Addie, though her principal duties involved having to 'be adorable' and 'giggle a lot'. I gave them their instructions before leaving for the green.

Lady Farley-Stroud and her committee had managed to get the word out about the change of venue and date for the show, as well as appeal for volunteers to help make it happen. By the time I arrived, some of my crew were already there.

The village carpenter, Charley Hill, had spent several hours the night before working on proper drawings for the stage design, and was confident that with a few extra hands he could get the stage and backstage screening built by mid-afternoon. I left him to it, with instructions to see me at once if he needed anything.

My set decorators were already sorting through the fire- and water-damaged sets and props to see what they could salvage. I organized them into teams and set them to work.

Other volunteers arrived during the morning and it wasn't long before we were transforming the village green into an outdoor theatre.

We broke for lunch, with food and drink kindly donated by Old Joe and served by the trusty staff of the Dog and Duck. Or 'Daisy', as she was known to her friends.

'You're the talk of the village, you are,' she said as she handed me a ginger beer and a cheese doorstop.

'And not for the usual reasons,' I said.

'Well, no, but none of that was ever proved, was it? And there weren't no witnesses.'

'I never leave witnesses.'

'But there's witnesses to this,' she said. 'You'll not be forgotten for savin' the show.'

'Don't be silly. Anyone would have done it.'

'There's many as wouldn't. Hilda Pantry wouldn't give you the skin off 'er rice puddin', let alone put 'erself to all this trouble. And even among those who would have, there's not so many as could have. Can you imagine half this lot tryin' to organize a booze-up in a brewery? You're the star of the show, Florence Armstrong.'

'And I didn't even have to give my horse.'

'I didn't even know you could do a horse.'

'Neigh.'

'They missed out on a treat when I was dragged into the dance troupe.'

'How's that going?' I asked.

'Blimmin' terrible. Turns out we've all got two left feet and i'n't one of us can keep in time with the music. But the song's a laugh and a promise is a promise. It saved you from bein' unhappy an' all, so it's all good.'

'I shall be cheering all the louder for that. Thank you.' Out of the corner of my eye, I saw one of my painting crew hastening towards us. 'Looks like lunchtime is over for me, Dais,' I said. 'Thanks for bringing it out, but I rather fear I'm going to be asked to deal with something. Something urgent from the look on her face.'

'I'll see you later,' said Daisy, and left me to my labours.

By eight o'clock on Saturday evening everything was ready and there was a carnival atmosphere on the village green. The food stalls we had set up for Sunday were already doing a roaring trade, but I was too tired to join the party.

Instead I returned home to find that Miss Jones had spent the afternoon at the house rather than taking her leisure, and had prepared a sumptuous feast. I was feted once more as the saviour of the village show.

'I haven't saved it yet,' I said. 'I've just bossed a few people about. The proof of the pudding will be in the music and dancing.'

But my companions weren't having any of it. They had their own party, still singing my praises, while I went off to collapse.

Next morning there were a few more errands to run and I disappeared in the Rolls before the revellers were abroad. A couple of hours later I was back at the house.

'Good morning, Flo,' said Lady Lavinia. 'You've missed breakfast, I'm afraid. Harry and Emily are in the garden playing with Addie and I'm on the hunt for something to get the jam out of this dress.' She indicated a tiny pink handprint on her skirt.

'I have just the thing for that,' I said. 'Follow me.'

In the kitchen I restored her summer frock to its former glory while Edna made a fresh pot of coffee and cobbled together a sandwich from some leftover bread and sausages.

Lady Lavinia and I went out to the garden.

'What ho, Strongarm,' said Harry. 'Where the devil have you been? You've been missed.'

'Hither, thither and, to a lesser extent, yon,' I said. 'Village show business.'

'Important stuff, then,' he said. 'You're forgiven.'

'Thank you.'

'Is all well, though?' said Lady Hardcastle.

'Spectacularly well, thank you,' I said.

I sat on one of the new chairs watching the game unfolding on the grass and eating my delicious sandwich.

'What time do we have to be off?' asked Lavinia. 'Does madam here have time for a snooze before we go?'

'The show starts at two,' I said. 'I imagine people will start bagging a pitch for themselves and their families from about noon.'

'Plenty of time, then,' she said. 'Come along, Miss Featherstone-huff. Time for bye-byes.'

She bent to pick her daughter up and Addie raised two squidgy arms in response. They went indoors.

'I need to sort some things out before the show,' I said, 'so I'll not be coming with you. I'll meet you all there. Save me a space and get me a cider.'

'Busy bee,' said Harry.

'The busiest and bee-iest,' I said. 'I'll need the Rolls, if that's all right.'

'Of course, dear,' said Lady Hardcastle. 'I can drive you, if you like.'

'No,' I said, rather too quickly. 'I'd prefer to get there alive. But thank you.'

'Think nothing of it. Is there more coffee in that pot?'

◆ ◆ ◆

The others were long gone by the time I set off in the Rolls. I had batted aside their many questions with much nose-tapping and 'wait and see'-ing. They hadn't been happy to be kept in the dark, but they soon worked out that pestering me wasn't going to get them anywhere.

It wasn't a long drive, though it was too far to walk, and I was soon standing with Adam Whitman in a level pasture that formed part of The Grange's estate.

'This is a very exciting idea,' he said as I put on my goggles. 'Walt Sandling's eyes lit up as he contemplated the commercial possibilities.'

'Let's see if it works before we start trying to make our fortunes from it,' I said. 'Is everything ready?'

'Ready and waiting. I'll need you to help me start her up, then we can get under way.'

With Adam safely in the pilot's seat, I swung the Dunnock's huge propeller and the new engine coughed to life. I jumped clear of the deadly blades and trotted round to take my place in the rear seat.

We trundled across the bumpy field, slowly gathering speed until with a delicious lurch, we were airborne.

Adam flew in a lazy spiral as he gained some height, then turned towards Littleton Cotterell.

From our lofty vantage, I could see the village green in the distance and could just about make out the little stage and the gathering crowd. News had spread fast, and it seemed that villagers from miles around had decided to spend the afternoon at Littleton. There would be many more in the audience than would have been possible in the little village hall.

My role in the aeroplane was not just that of passenger. I had an important job to do, and as we neared the village I shifted in my seat to prepare myself for action.

'All set back there?' came Adam's voice from the speaking tube.

'Just waiting for your signal,' I said.

'Right you are. Ready . . . steady . . . go!'

I pulled a handle attached to what the engineers at Bristol Aviation told me was called a ripcord. There was a jolt, and the aeroplane shuddered a little. The engine laboured, but then settled.

Adam aimed for the village green.

I was worried for a moment that my plan would come to nothing and that no one would even notice. But then a girl in the crowd caught sight of us. I could see her pointing. Others looked up and began pointing, too. Then clapping. And waving. Even from several hundred feet in the air we could hear the cheers.

The ripcord had pulled a pin that had been holding a package closed at the back of the aeroplane. The contents had unfurled until we were towing a long banner of white silk, upon both sides of which the boys at the factory had painted, 'Littleton Cotterell Village Show 1911'.

We made two more passes over the green, to the increasing excitement of the crowd, all of whom were now on their feet, cheering and waving, before heading back to our makeshift aerodrome at The Grange.

We parked up and hurriedly changed into more presentable clothes.

I drove us both back to the village.

The show was well underway by the time I finally found my spot on the picnic blanket with Lady Hardcastle and the Featherstonhaughs.

'Absolutely marvellous, Strongarm, old girl,' said Harry as I sat down.

'Best opening to a village show I've ever seen,' said Lady Lavinia.

'Well done, indeed,' said Lady Hardcastle. 'And even weller done for not letting the cat out of the bag. It was enhanced a hundredfold by the surprise. Whenever did you have the time to arrange it all?'

'I have to do something while you lot are lying in,' I said. 'Now shush – people are trying to watch the show.'

On stage was one of the village policemen, Constable Hancock, who was playing a selection of popular tunes on the trumpet.

Up next was the unlikely pairing of Old Joe and the vicar, who gave us a new version of the crosstalk act they usually performed at the Christmas show at The Grange.

Butcher's wife Eunice Spratt and our own Edna Gibson sang a sentimental duet and a rather bawdy music hall number before Daisy and her friends treated us to their own uncoordinated but delightfully risqué performance.

The dancing was every bit as awful as Daisy had promised, but her comic instincts made the song all the funnier and the crowd loved it.

Sir Hector Farley-Stroud was up next, continuing the theme with quite the smuttiest, most innuendo-laden monologue it was possible to imagine. I could see his wife glaring daggers at him, but such was the positive reaction from the audience that she didn't try to stop him.

Lady Hardcastle missed Sir Hector, having gone backstage to prepare for her own turn. As he left the stage with the laughter still ringing round the green, she stepped out of the wings to her own round of applause and quite a few gasps of admiration.

She wasn't the only one who could sneakily order things by telephone. One of my trips on Thursday – as well as checking on the production of the banner at Bristol Aviation – had been to pick up a dress I had ordered for her. As much as I would have loved to see her in a spangly leotard, I couldn't in all conscience inflict such a sight on the good people of Littleton Cotterell, but I did know a dressmaker who could knock up a spangly frock.

She looked amazing as she sat down at her beloved piano and belted out a few ragtime songs that got the whole crowd dancing.

Such was the enthusiasm of the response that she was required to give two encores, but it was soon time for Lawrence Weakley, the greengrocer, to close the show. He sang the heartbreaking ballad that had reduced the rehearsals to tears, and while everyone was still wiping their eyes, followed it up with a rousing medley of jollier music hall songs that had everyone joining in.

As the applause faded away, Lady Farley-Stroud took to the stage with a large tin megaphone and addressed the crowd.

'Ladies and gentlemen,' she began. 'Thank you all so very much for coming to our little show this afternoon. I see a lot of familiar Littleton Cotterell faces among you, but also many friends from our neighbouring villages. Thank you. You all know, I'm sure, that the show very nearly didn't go ahead. The damage to our beloved village hall very nearly put a stop to it. But one woman stepped into the breach. She moved to Littleton Cotterell little more than three years ago, but in that short time she and her friend Emily Hardcastle have become an essential part of our village life. It was Florence Armstrong who decided the show should go ahead out here on the green, and she who made it happen. I have it on good authority from my son-in-law that she was also responsible for the glorious air display that opened the show. Come up here, would you, m'dear, I think the village wishes to thank you properly.'

So much for avoiding the stage. I looked to Lady Hardcastle for support, but none came.

'You'd better get up and take your bow, dear,' she said.

'You really should,' said Harry. 'You've earned the thanks of a grateful nation, Strongarm. Or a grateful Gloucestershire village at any rate. Off you trot.'

'He's not often right,' said Lady Lavinia, 'but I can't disagree with him here. None of this would have happened without you.'

The villagers cheered, and even Addie was laughing and clapping.

Reluctantly, I made my way to the stage.

Author's Notes

The Bristol Aviation and Aeronautics Company is fictitious, but Bristol does have a long and illustrious history as a centre of aeroplane design and manufacture. It was the home of the British and Colonial Aeroplane Company, later known as the Bristol Aeroplane Company, and its works at Filton, a few miles north of the city, produced many famous aircraft until the firm's closure in 1959. Aircraft design and building continued at Filton, which played a part in the development of Concorde, the only successful commercial supersonic aeroplane. Filton's runway had been extended in 1949 for the Bristol Brabazon (a giant prop-driven plane) and was one of the only runways in the country, other than those at busy airports, suitable for the testing of Concorde. The very first model, Prototype 001, was built in France and flew from Toulouse (as did all the other French-built models), but Filton was the site of the maiden flights of every British-built Concorde. The last one ever to have flown is now housed in a museum there, Aerospace Bristol.

Similarly, Aéroplanes Vannier is also fictitious. Louis Blériot, the Channel-crossing aviation pioneer is real, though. Obviously.

Modern parachutes have been around in one form or another since the end of the eighteenth century but they were, as Harry says, cumbersome and awkward. Wearable parachutes began to appear around 1907, but the first parachute carried in a knapsack was designed in 1911 by a Russian gentleman by the name of Gleb Kotelnikov. I have taken the liberty of having the fictional Bristol Aviation Company invent it independently (and secretly) at about the same time.

Despite the many complaints I've had over the years, 'my lover' really is a generic West Country term of endearment. 'Lover' was commonly used in English to refer to someone who felt fondness for another (a friend), but its other sense (a sexual partner) has become the only modern sense. Except in the West Country. It's slowly falling from use as mass communication homogenizes the language and chips away at all the splendid local quirks that exist around the country, and one day it might be gone for good, but it can still sometimes be heard in the Bristol area and was definitely something that someone like Edna Gibson would say in 1911.

Variations of, 'A gentleman is someone who can play the [objectionable instrument] but won't,' first appeared in print in 1917. In the original version it was the cornet. Over the years it has been the banjo, the bagpipes, the ukulele, the saxophone, and the accordion. It has been attributed to Mark Twain, Oscar Wilde, and G. K. Chesterton, among others, but I am informed by the website quoteinvestigator.com that it was first printed in *The Atchison Weekly Globe* in Atchison, Kansas, where it is credited to a local man by the name of Frank Feist. Armed with the knowledge that it wasn't the work of some celebrated witty wordsmith but of an ordinary chap not unlike Harry Featherstonhaugh, I'm comfortable with the idea that Harry might have come up with it independently some years before (or overheard it in the bar at his club).

A male African elephant stands roughly 3.2 metres (10'6") tall. All the heights have been accurately converted into standardized elephants.

The description of the Bristol Aviation Dunnock is inspired by the 1911 Rumpler Taube (*die Taube* is German for pigeon). It was a German plane developed from an original 1904 Austrian design and it appealed to me both because of its bird-like appearance and because it was, unusually for the time, a monoplane. Naming the aircraft proved more difficult than I had foreseen, though. It turns out that almost every creature that has ever flown has been used as the name for an aeroplane. In desperation, I tried dunnock (*Prunella modularis*), a common European and Asian bird about the size of a sparrow (and regular visitor to my own garden), and it turned out no one had used it. So that was a relief.

'Babber' is a Bristolian word for baby or child, often also used as a generic term of endearment. 'All right, my babber? 'Ow bist?' ('Hello, how are you?')

The Eurasian badger (*Meles meles*) is a much more easy-going and fondly regarded creature than the unrelated North American animal of the same name (*Taxidea taxus*). You'd still be unwise to anger one, but they're less inclined than their snarling North American namesakes to have a pop at you down the pub just for looking at them funny.

The summer bank holiday in England and Wales was originally intended to allow bank clerks to attend cricket matches. It fell on the first Monday of August from 1871 until the mid-1960s, when it was experimentally moved to the end of the month. The Banking and Financial Dealings Act 1971 fixed it as the last Monday in August. The holiday still falls on the first Monday of August in Scotland.

Battenberg cake (which used to go by a variety of names including 'chapel window cake') is now made commercially with just four alternating squares of pink and yellow sponge, with the whole thing wrapped in marzipan. The original recipe, though, had nine squares. Tradition has it that the cake was invented (and named) for the wedding in 1884 of Prince Louis of Battenberg and Queen

Victoria's granddaughter, Princess Victoria. There's some doubt about whether that's actually true, though, and the first published version of the recipe (with nine squares) didn't appear until 1898.

Harry refers to Germany 'backing down' over Morocco. In 1911 there was a revolt in Morocco which confined the Sultan to his palace. In April, France sent a large number of troops in support of the Sultan. On 1 July, Germany sent a gunboat to the Moroccan port of Agadir as a protest against France's military presence in the country. Great Britain, meanwhile, pledged to back France and it was feared that war could break out at any moment. A financial crisis in Germany – which resulted in a 30 per cent drop in the value of shares on the German stock market – threatened the government with financial ruin and they were forced to bring the gunboat home and attempt to seek a peaceful solution. Harry wasn't kidding – Europe was already veering towards war.

The first patent for a method for synchronizing the firing of a machine gun with the rotation of the propeller was filed in 1913 by the Swiss engineer Franz Schneider and subsequently published in a German flying magazine, *Flugsport*, in 1914. Once again it amused me to have Emily casually solve the problem two years early.

By 1911, the British army was becoming more interested in the possible tactical uses of aeroplanes. In April the Balloon Section of the Royal Engineers was reorganized as the Air Battalion, split into two companies: No. 1 (Airship) Company based at South Farnborough in Hampshire and No. 2 (Aeroplane) Company based at Larkhill in Wiltshire. The figures Harry quotes for their strength are broadly correct. The commanding officer was Major Sir Alexander Bannerman who had fourteen officers, twenty-three non-commissioned officers, one hundred and fifty-three men, two buglers, four riding horses, thirty-two draught-horses, five aeroplanes and an assortment of kites, balloons and airships.

In May the Air Battalion took delivery of a Bristol Boxkite. It was an endearingly flimsy biplane built by the British and Colonial Aeroplane Company at Filton, and a replica (made for the 1965 film *Those Magnificent Men in their Flying Machines*) hangs from the ceiling of the Bristol Museum and Art Gallery. By the time of our story in August 1911 the battalion had a Royal Aircraft Factory FE2 biplane, which was designed and flown by Captain Geoffrey de Havilland. After WWI he founded the de Havilland Aircraft Company. Actors Olivia de Havilland and Joan Fontaine were his cousins.

I've always been quite relaxed about naming the main road that takes Lady Hardcastle and Flo from the fictional village of Littleton Cotterell to the very real city of Bristol. The modern road, the A38, has many names along its 292-mile length from Bodmin in Cornwall to Mansfield in Nottinghamshire, and the roads it was made from, or replaced, had many names, too. As it leaves Bristol on its northward journey it's known as the Gloucester Road and, for simplicity, that's how I've always referred to it.

For once, real life was on my side and the moon was indeed full on the night after Flo's break-in on 10 August. It was also in the right part of the sky to illuminate the imagined orientation of the fictional factory. Sometimes things do work out.

I was once challenged on the fact that Emily wears a wristwatch. 'People didn't wear wristwatches until officers started strapping their pocket watches to their wrists in WWI,' they said. While that's arguably true for men (though some sources suggest it started earlier), women had been wearing watches on their wrists since Patek Philippe made one for Countess Koscowicz of Hungary in 1868. They became an essential fashion item, often worn on decorative bracelets. Emily, whose livelihood – and sometimes life – often depends on knowing what time it is, wears a less flamboyant but no less accurate Swiss timepiece on her wrist.

As well as a cavalier approach to the naming of roads, I've also always taken a relaxed attitude to the organization of the Bristol police force at the turn of the twentieth century. Obviously Inspector Sunderland, based at the Bridewell and assigned to A Division, would have had no business tackling cases fifteen miles away in a little Gloucestershire village. But I needed a policeman with city contacts as a regular character, so Oliver Sunderland always somehow manages to get involved in cases that aren't really any of his business.

Various people on the Internet will try to tell you that you can't crack a combination safe using a stethoscope. But you can also find a video of someone actually doing it. I prefer to believe that you can or, more importantly, that Flo can. She can do anything.

Horfield Common is a real place and does offer a pleasing view across the city. The spot where the meeting bench once stood has been built on and is now a row of houses. Indeed, the whole stretch of the common traversed by our ladies during their observation of the bench was developed for housing in the 1930s. Lady Hardcastle would be pleased to know that there are tennis courts on the common now, though, as well as a children's playground.

I was a member of the Bristol University Hot Air Ballooning Society while at university and accompanied the balloon on many trips. On one occasion we were taking our ease after a particularly pleasant flight in the countryside while we waited for the van and the rest of the crew to arrive. Packing up could wait. Our pilot had been careful to avoid landing in a field of cows, but the cows were not so keen to avoid us. They came in from the next field to investigate and did, indeed, end up licking the balloon to see what it was all about. It didn't seem at all unreasonable to me that the cows would lick the stricken Dunnock.

The first citation in the Oxford English Dictionary of the word 'saboteur' is from 1921. 'Sabotage' appears in 1910. Both are much older French words derived from the wooden clogs (*sabots*) worn by workers and are thought to come from the noisy protests made by clog-wearing labourers stamping on the floor. Or something. (And not from chucking clogs into machines – someone made that up.) Anyway, because neither word was well known in 1911 when our story is set (and certainly not with the same general meaning we have now), I couldn't, in all conscience, have the characters use them. Which is a shame – there are no elegant English alternatives.

About the Author

T E Kinsey grew up in London and read history at Bristol University. He worked for a number of years as a magazine features writer before falling into the glamorous world of the Internet, where he edited content for a very famous entertainment website for quite a few years more. After helping to raise three children, learning to scuba dive and to play the drums and mandolin (though never, disappointingly, all at the same time), he decided the time was right to get back to writing. *The Fatal Flying Affair* is the seventh story in the Lady Hardcastle Mystery series. His website is at tekinsey.uk and you can follow him on Twitter @tekinsey as well as on Facebook: www.facebook.com/tekinsey.